The Beasts of Love

The Beasts of Love

Stories by
Steven Utley

With an Introduction by
Lisa Tuttle

🌾 **Wheatland Press**

http://www.wheatlandpress.com

The Beasts of Love

Published by

Wheatland Press

P. O. Box 1818

Wilsonville, OR 97070

Library of Congress Cataloging-in-Publication data is available upon request.
ISBN 0-9720547-9-0
Printed in the United States of America

🌾 **Wheatland Press**

http://www.wheatlandpress.com

To my mother and father,
whose love made it possible.

Introduction to The Beasts of Love
by Lisa Tuttle

By rights, this book, or some close approximation of it, should have been published in 1986.

It was around that time that a strange ray from outer space, or electro-magnetic pulses from the earth's core, or a quantum shift in the space-time continuum or some damned thing opened a rift in the editorial perception of reality. For a brief span, the well-known fact that short story collections don't sell shunted into the mirror-world, causing editors around the globe to scramble to sign up deeply uncommercial *sui generis* short story writers, among them Howard Waldrop (*Howard Who?* Doubleday) and myself (*A Nest of Nightmares*, Sphere Books)—but not the third leg of the famous Texican Triangle.

Tuttle, Utley and Waldrop—we all made our first professional appearance in 1972, and almost immediately started collaborating.[1] Along with a few others, we founded the Turkey City Writers Workshop (and Neo-Pro Rodeo). We wrote almost exclusively in the short form yet managed to garner a surprisingly high level of attention—and praise—for our work, and our last initials all fell towards the end of the alphabet. If we'd been at high school together, we'd have been in the same home-room. Yes, that's us at the back of the class—I'm reading a novel hidden inside an algebra textbook, Waldrop is shooting spit-balls, and Utley is the one drawing cartoon dinosaurs making sarcastic comments about the other students.

Throughout the 1970s, Steven Utley was, to quote *The Encyclopedia of Science Fiction*, "a figure of edgy salience in the field, " and by 1986 he'd had some seventy short stories published—considerably more, I'm sure, than either me or Howard, the best of which could have filled a couple of volumes, at least. But by 1980, Steven Utley had pretty much given up writing. After years of suffering from clinical depression (undiagnosed and untreated) and other health problems, he found life too much of a struggle

---

[1] For more details, see Waldrop, Howard, *Custer's Last Jump and other collaborations* (Golden Gryphon Press, 2003) or Ellison, Harlan, "Exorcising Texas: An Introduction" (1976)

to cope with the additional hassles attendant upon a career as a short story writer; if it was to be just a hobby, guitar-playing, record collecting and cartooning were more rewarding.

I don't know if Steven ever really gave up writing entirely—I'm always suspicious about such cold-turkey claims; even Rimbaud, according to his latest biographer, continued writing non-fiction long after he'd turned his back on poetry—but I don't know. I left Texas towards the end of 1980, and didn't have much contact with Steven for many years afterwards.

But I think it's safe to say that whatever else he may have done to earn a living, Steven has never taken up gun-running or been even remotely involved in the slave-trade; and also that this story has a happy ending...at least, if you agree that writing is a good thing to do.

Yes, Steven Utley is back on the publishing scene again, and with a vengeance, thanks to advances in modern pharmacology and a variety of positive life-changes, possibly including the effect of living in Tennessee rather than Texas.[2]

And maybe it's just as well that *The Beasts of Love* wasn't published in 1986. It would be long out of print by now, anyway, and it would have lacked two of the strongest, most moving stories in the current collection, both written in the 1990s: "The Country Doctor" and "Once More, With Feeling."

This is, in fact, the second Utley collection. The first, *Ghost Seas* (Ticonderoga Press, 1997) was a sampler of some of his best work to date, taking in most of the recognized genres, including SF, detective, horror, and western stories. It was a lovely book, and all praise to the Western-Australia-based small press willing to take a chance on a hard-to-classify writer who was neither very young nor very famous nor at all Australian. However, there was a certain valedictory, elegiac air to the book, from the moody cover to the description to the often down-beat tone of many of the stories, which didn't encourage me to think that Steven's career might, finally, be re-launching in a big way.

But what did I know?

---

[2] "More than one person has asked me why, if doing so makes me feel like a python trying to swallow an elephant, I bother to read Proust. My answer: Well, somebody here in Tennessee has to."—from a recent e-mail.

It was.

Even here in the remote part of the Scottish Highlands where I now live, so far from London, farther still from the American scene, where copies of *The Magazine of Fantasy and Science Fiction* or any other pulp magazine are rarely seen, I gradually became aware that Steven Utley was writing again—a lot—his name making the cover of SF magazines, his stories included in "Best of the Year" anthologies—a second flowering. And I know that Steven has another couple (or more) collections planned—his long-awaited *Silurian Tales*, and another collection of time-travel stories, which is why, in this entire collection, only one story has dinosaurs in it. Just one. In an Utley collection?

But never mind; there are other pleasures. Many.

I admit, I had my doubts, looking at the reprint credits for the first time. Although I was absolutely blown away by both "The Country Doctor" and "Once More, With Feeling," I wondered if the older stories would have held up with the passage of time. I'd thought they were great back in the '70s, but I was hardly an impartial reader. After all, we're talking about short stories which first appeared as filler in *Perry Rhodan*, or some long-forgotten men's magazine...

Yes, even those, as I found on re-reading. "Ants" is a polished, elegant fable which packs the punch of a classic tale by H.G. Wells or John Wyndham, while "Pan-Galactic Swingers" made me laugh out loud. "The Mouse Ran Up the Clock", "Die Rache", "Ember-Eyes"—all as good as or even better than I remembered.

Going through his old files, reading some of the stories for the first time in nearly thirty years, Steven wrote to me, "The thing that keeps you going when you are a struggling young writer—besides, I mean, the rent's being due and the cupboard's being bare—is the belief, or at least the hope, that you are *this far* away from being brilliant...When you are a struggling middle-aged writer, you realize that you are this much farther away from being brilliant than you once imagined."

Oh, not that far, Steven. Not really all that far.

Lisa Tuttle
Torinturk, Scotland
18 May 2004

Contents

Animals have no difficulty in living up to their natures, but men and women seem to find it hard to be fully human.

Karen Armstrong, *A History of God*

The Country Doctor

GARDNER WAS DROWNING, AND STRANGERS were laying hands on the bones of my forebears. I felt obligated to see that liberties weren't taken with my grandmother, my great-grandmother, and other good, God-fearing ladies, so I put the business on autopilot and made the drive as if on autopilot myself.

I viewed the visit as a familial duty, not a sentimental journey. I hadn't been back to Gardner in twenty-five years. I'd always told myself that, with my grandparents dead and their house taken over by obscure cousins-removed, there was nothing to come back for. Soon there would be nothing to come back to. The dam was completed, the waters were rising. Gardner was drowning.

Once in the town, however, I couldn't simply drive to the cemetery. It wouldn't have taken two minutes. Wherever you were in a place the size of Gardner, you weren't far from anywhere else, and now, especially, everything was smaller and closer together than it had seemed when I was a kid. But I found that I had to drive down my grandparents' old street, had to stop in front of what had been their house. I sat with the motor running and stared disconsolately. Throughout my childhood, though I moved wherever the military took my father, my grandparents' house, a big, warm clapboard pile, had remained the center of the world, the universe—home. My earliest memories were of being in that house, surrounded by relatives, loved, safe. Now it sat waiting for the water. My grandfather had been a carpenter, among other things; I could see his shed in back. There had been a vegetable patch back there, too. My grandmother had shelled a lot of peas and snapped a lot of beans from it.

The other houses on the block had once been features of a familiar

1

landscape. Now, curtainless windows gave most of them a look of stupid surprise. One was carefully boarded up, as if the owners fully intended to return. The house next to it looked agape and miserable. Paint hung from it in strips. The owners must have stopped bothering with upkeep when they heard about the dam; finally, they'd just walked away. All but one of the lawns on the block were overgrown. A handful of people still remained, the die-hard element, determined to hold out until the water lapped over their doorsteps, and to keep their yards looking nice in the meantime.

It was three blocks to the cemetery, long blocks for someone dragging an orthopedic shoe. Nevertheless, I told myself. Nevertheless. I turned off the motor, got out of the car. The sun was at zenith. There was no wind. A male chorus of cicadae sang of love's delights to prospective mates. The day felt and sounded exactly like all the summer days I'd spent in Gardner in my childhood. I put my hands in my pockets and started walking, slowly, stunned by the force of the memories crowding in on me. I remembered how my grandmother used to sit in a metal porch chair and, as she put it, have herself a little talk with Jesus while she snapped those beans. Sometimes she sang gospel songs.

She only ever sang the melodies, but I had been to enough revival meetings to know the words to whatever she sang. Sometimes, hearing her, I'd stop my playing and sing the words while she hummed...

My eyes began to sting. Gardner was drowning.

Around the corner had lived Blanche, who was my grandmother's age and whose relation to me was, then and now, unclear. Someone lived there still—a green station wagon with a dinged-up fender sat in the driveway, and there were curtains in the windows—but Blanche herself was long dead, killed in an automobile accident. I'd liked her a lot. One summer, she had given me the empty coffee can in which I buried my grandmother's dead parakeet Petey. I knew exactly where I'd scooped out Petey's grave and wondered what I might find if I were to open it now. Nothing, probably—at most, a few crumbling shards of coffee-can rust. Tiny little bones dissolve in no time. On the next block was the crumbling brick shell of Cobb's Corner Market, where I'd sometimes spent my entire weekly stipend, twenty-five cents, on comic books and a Coke. Dime comic books and nickel soft drinks—it had been that long ago, and it was all about to pass forever from sight and memory.

Drowning, drowning...

More vehicles were parked by the cemetery than there were in the whole town. I saw many opened graves — it could have been the day after Resurrection Day. At least a dozen people wearing old clothes were working among the headstones. I knew in a very broad way what these archeologists were supposed to be doing here, and I did see individuals sifting dirt through screens or duck-walking around exhumed coffins with tape measures in their hands, but what I mostly saw looked like just a lot of hot, dirty shovel work with nothing scientific about it.

I came upon two youngish men at the end of the first row of graves. On the ground between them was a new coffin. Its lid was open, and I saw that it was empty. One of the men nodded a hello at me.

"How's it going?" I said.

"Well," he said, "it is going."

I gestured vaguely around. "These're all my relatives."

They looked at me as if I'd caught them doing something naughty.

"Well," said the one who'd spoken before, "we're taking real good care of everyone, Mister — "

"Riddle."

The second man pointed away and said, "Most of the Riddle family's still located over on that side."

"Yes," I said, "I know." I did know; it was all coming back; I could have found the Riddles blindfolded, and the Riches and the Bassetts, too. I had seen both of my maternal grandfather's parents buried here, then his wife, finally his own self. The first Riches and Bassetts had been laid to rest here in the 1850s; Riddles came along after the war, when a lot of ruined Southerners were moving around and resettling. Relatively speaking, the concentration of Riddles wasn't great — Riddles, it once was explained to me, tended to die young and tended also to have wanderlust. My father had been orphaned when he was barely into his teens, and members of his line had come to rest in odd places throughout the South, the West, and as far away as the Coral Sea. The first graveside service I'd attended in the Gardner cemetery was for a young cousin of mine, Kermit, who one summer day had succumbed to the fascination of a fallen power line. The last one was for my grandfather.

I nodded at the new coffin. "Who's this for?"

3

"Whoever," one of the men said. "We try to keep everything together, even the box somebody was buried in. Some of these old graves, though, you find a few splinters of wood and some rusty nails, nothing you could still call a coffin."

"Is Doctor Taylor here?"

"He's somewhere around here." He looked about and nodded off toward the south end of the cemetery. "I think he's over that way."

"Thank you." The two men seemed glad to see me walk on. When I was a child, I'd sometimes been sent to spend the summer with my grandparents. My grandmother and great-grandmother had visited this cemetery often. Between them they must have known seven out of every ten people buried here. They always brought flowers, and usually they brought me. They'd move among the graves, place the flowers, murmur secrets to the dead or prayers to Jesus, murmur genealogy to me, life histories, accounts of untimely, often horrific, deaths — most of their anecdotes were imbued with pain and tragedy. Sometimes I was interested and listened. Sometimes I was bored, drowsy from the heat, and instead listened to the cicadae. The sound of those summers was one long insect song, cicadae and honey-bees by day, crickets and mosquitoes by night, punctuated by gospel-piano chords, hands clapping time, voices singing, "I'm gonna have a little talk with Jesus, I'm gonna tell Him all about my trouble..."

It kept coming back, coming back.

It came back as I passed Dr. Sweeny's headstone, which lay in the grass by the edge of the driveway. Nearby, a man wearing a faded plaid shirt was excavating the grave with a shovel. As headstones in this cemetery went, Dr. Sweeny's was pretty fancy, with some decorative cuts and a longer inscription than most.

Dr. Chester Sweeny

d. June 30, 1900

Erected in respectful memory

by those he tended

these 30 years

Dr. Sweeny was the only doctor, the only Sweeny, and the only non-relative buried in the cemetery. I had been filled with dismay and disbelief the first time I saw his name on that stone. Until that moment, I'd thought that doctors were immune to sickness and exempt from death. Mammaw, I said to my great-grandmother, whom I'd been trailing past the rows, what kind of a doctor dies, Mammaw? "Honey," she told me, "doctors die just like everybody else. Everybody's got to die. That's why the important thing in life's to be baptized in Jesus's name, so you'll go to heaven when you die." But why, I demanded, do people have to die? She didn't answer, just looked at the stone, and after what was probably only seconds but must have seemed like a whole minute or a full hour to an impatient child, she said, "Old Doc Sweeny. I went to his funeral. I was a girl then. I was nearly as young then as you are now." She was in her sixties when she told me this; naturally, I couldn't think of her as a girl or imagine that she had ever been nearly as young as anybody. "I remember because everybody in the whole valley come for it, and then's when I met your Pappaw for the first time. He didn't want nothing to do with me then, but later, well, I changed his mind. But that day everybody come to pay respects to old Doc Sweeny." Was he as old as you, Mammaw? "Doc Sweeny was as old as Methuselah. Why, my momma, that was your great-great-gran'maw Vannie Bassett, wasn't even born when he come here. My own daddy made the box to bury him in and druv it here in his wagon, and a man over to Dawson give this stone. Doc Sweeny was just as poor as everybody else and didn't have no money set aside. Seems like there never was so good a one as him again. He druv his buggy all over, day or night, rain or shine. Not like these doctors we got now. Poor as he was, too, he always had some candy and play-pretties for us littlens in his pockets. I remember him visiting my momma when she was sick, and when he was leaving, he give me a piece of peppermint candy and said, My child, my child. And I was a sassy thing then, just like you, didn't have no more manners'n a pig. Instead of thanking him for the candy, I just said, I ain't neither your child, " and she had laughed delightedly at the memory of her own devilishness.

Thereafter, throughout the remaining summers of my childhood, Dr. Sweeny occupied a place in my mind as special as the one he occupied in the cemetery. I soon got over his being a dead doctor, but I remained impressed by his anomalous presence in what was effectively an outsized family plot. It suggested to me that he must have been, somehow, one of us. Even now, he had power to fascinate me. Gazing down at his stone, I found myself wondering exactly what he must have done, besides giving candy and cheap toys to children, to so endear himself. Mostly just be there, I guessed, when folks needed a sympathetic ear and a few sugar pills. Doctors in Sweeny's day had done more nursing than actual doctoring. Much of the nursing was ineffectual, and most of the doctoring was downright savage. There was no Food and Drug Administration to look over a physician's shoulder as he dosed people with God only knew what. Maybe this particular country doctor had won his neighbors' trust and respect simply by not killing inordinate numbers of patients.

I tore myself away, moved on, and found Dr. Taylor and a woman squatting in shade at the end of a row. He was strongly built, balding, with a sunburnt face. She had long, reddish-brown hair tied back in a ponytail and was covered with freckles everywhere that I could see. A map of the graveyard was spread on the ground between them, with numbers and other marks scribbled all over it. None of the graves at this end of the row had been opened yet. I noticed four narrow, squarish stones set into the ground at the feet of two graves identified by a common headstone as those of John Hellman Rich and Julia Anne Rich.

"Doctor Taylor," I said.

Both of them looked up, and I could tell from his expression that he didn't recognize me. We had met only briefly, weeks before.

"Doug Riddle," I said.

"Mister Riddle!" He stood quickly, brushed dirt off his hands, started to offer to shake, pulled back suddenly. "I don't know if you want to shake hands with me. I've been rooting around in graves all day." He seemed genuinely flustered. He turned to the woman, who had risen with him. "Gertie, this is Doug Riddle. My associate, Gertrude Latham."

"I'm very pleased to meet you," she said. She seemed as ill at ease as he. She had a wonderful accent, German come through the heart of the Deep South.

"Finding out what you came to find out?" I said.

Taylor made an attempt at a smile. "In this line of work, you never know what you'll find out."

"Some people," I said, meaning mainly my irrepressible Uncle G. A., "called this place Gardner Gardens."

They looked uncertain, as if unsure they'd heard me right. He ventured to say, "Oh?"

"The planting ground," I said, then shrugged. "Small-town black humor."

"Ah. Yes." Taylor smiled again, more feebly than before, and tried to make up the difference by adding a chuckle, with results that embarrassed everyone. My own smile began to hurt my mouth.

Gertrude Latham went for a save. She nodded toward Julia Anne Rich's grave and said, "That headstone tells us a great deal about this young woman's life. Do you know anything about her?"

I glanced at the dates on the stone. Julia Anne Rich had died, age twenty-two, before the turn of the century, when my great-grandparents were children. "I remember the name," I said, "from when I used to come here as a kid. I thought Julia Anne was a nice name --" I gave Latham an apologetic look " —for a girl's name. But I don't know anything about her in particular."

Latham nodded at the grave again. "Those are her babies there by her feet. Judging from the dates, she lost four of them in a row. The last one may have killed her."

If this was archeology, I wasn't impressed. I felt sure I could have deduced as much from the information on the stones. Childbirth in the nineteenth century was perilous.

I said, "There're more babies and mothers buried here than anything else. Lots of children's graves, too. Children used to die of everything. After World War Two, though, hardly anyone except old people got buried here. All the young people went into the service or moved to Evansville to work in the P-forty-seven factory. And they just never came back."

The two archeologists were staring at me. There was something like admiration in Taylor's expression. I felt a sheepish sort of pleasure and could not help smiling as he asked me, "Are you Gardner's official historian?"

I shook my head. "But there was a time when I must've known the name on every last one of these headstones. I got to be a whiz at subtraction from figuring out by the dates how old people were when they died. And in the forties people did start going away and not coming back. My father went into the service and stayed in. And somebody in the family did go build P-forty-sevens, too. There were framed prints of the things hanging in a spare bedroom at my grandparents' house for years. Official prints, with the Republic Aircraft logo."

"Mister Riddle," Taylor said, "we could use your knowledge to interpret this site. I'd appreciate it if you'd consider letting us interview you sometime."

"You'd be what's known in anthropology as an informant," said Latham.

Informant didn't have the ring to it that official historian did, but I was flattered all the same. There's little to compare with having people hang on everything you say. Anyway, I told myself, maybe Gardner was too small for a full-fledged historian. Nothing had ever happened here—nothing that mattered to anybody besides Riddles, Riches, and Bassetts, harvest time, tent meetings, weddings, funerals, somebody's barn being raised or burning down. No one famous had ever come from Gardner, or to it, for that matter. And it struck me then, with unexpected and shaming clarity, that I'd never made the effort to bring my own children or grandchildren to this place, that I should have been murmuring genealogy and tragic personal histories to them all their young lives, teaching them about family and the continuity of life. I should have been telling them, "Every one of your ancestors lived and suffered and sometimes all but swam up waterfalls like salmon to make sure you'd be here today and the family would continue and the thread be unbroken. They were brave and wonderful people, and if you don't believe it, just look here at your great-aunt, your great-something Julia Anne, who lost four babies one right after another, which isn't even a record, and it must've seemed to her like the worst thing in the world to lose the first one but then she carried three more, suffered crushing loss every time, died a probably painful and possibly protracted death trying to deliver the last one--" And, "*Doug*," my wife would've said by then, "*Dad*," my daughter would've said by now, each with that same disapproving furrow between her eyebrows. I do get carried away at times.

I blinked the thoughts away and looked at the two scientists. "So," I said, "what're you finding out?"

Latham said, "We never really know what we've found until we've finished an excavation and, uh, put all the pieces of the puzzle together."

"Is there a puzzle here?"

She essayed a smile. It was the best smile any of us had managed thus far. "There's always a puzzle."

"And you always find a solution?"

Her smile got even better. "This is what you'd call quick and dirty archeology. We have to excavate by shovel, get as much information out as we can, as fast as we can, and move on. We don't have a lot of time. All we can do is figure out what the person was buried with and measure the bones. And we try to look for evidence of disease that would show up in the skeletal material."

"Is there evidence of a lot of disease?"

Everything suddenly felt awkward again. I could tell by the look she gave Taylor that she regretted her last statement.

I looked over my shoulder and saw Roy Rich's grave right where I'd left it decades before. "Here's a puzzle for you," I said. "What does this stone tell you about Roy Rich's life?"

Latham glanced at it. "He died at age fifteen."

"He was lucky to live that long," I said. "Or maybe not so lucky. I remember Roy. He was deformed. Not 'differently abled,' not even 'physically handicapped.' Deformed. His sister Betty, too." I pointed to Betty's headstone, next to his. "She died at age twelve. Those two had everything in the world wrong with them. I guess you'll see for yourself when you open the coffins."

The two scientists were silent. It was very hot, and sweat gleamed on Taylor's pate and beaded on Latham's forehead and upper lip. I felt slimy inside my clothing. The cicadae would not shut up.

At last, Taylor said, stiffly. "We'll write a report when we finish the excavation. If you like, I'll send you a copy."

"I'm sure it'd be much too technical for me. Tell me something about my ancestors that I can go home and tell my wife."

Taylor looked about as unhappy as any human being I'd seen lately. Latham looked as if she were trying to wish somebody away—me, of course. The more ill at ease they became, the pushier I felt. Maybe it was the gene for devilishness, handed down from Mammaw.

"It doesn't necessarily have to be something nice," I said, "if that's what's holding you back. Nothing you tell me can be any more horrible than some of the things Granny and Mammaw told me." I looked over the rows. A truck pulled away from the gate, bearing some of my dead away to strange soil. "Doctor Taylor, when we met last month, you said this ground's full of history, and this was a one-time-only chance to get at it."

"Yes," he said, slowly — warily, I thought. "Yes, I did say that."

"This is the last time I'll ever see this place. Living or dead, everyone's being scattered. I know it's true I'll be able to visit my relatives' new graves over in Dawson, but they'll be, they'll seem out of place over there. This is where my grandparents and great-grandparents were buried. This little spot in the road was their home. It was my home, too, for a while. Next year, it'll all be gone, the whole valley'll be under water. It'll be like Gardner never existed. So please indulge me. I'm not going to gum up the works for you, I really don't want to be in your way or bother you a lot, but I need ... I need to carry away everything from here that I can this time."

"We try," Taylor said, "we try very hard to be careful of the feelings of living relatives of the people we exhume. It's been my experience that relatives shouldn't, well, watch. And that despite what they say, they don't really want to know everything."

"Look. There're a few chicken thieves buried here. There's even supposed to be a horse thief. And one of my cousins stabbed her husband with a big sharp kitchen knife when he beat up on the kids. He isn't buried here, but the point is, I don't have many illusions about my family. I'll try not to be shocked by anything you tell me."

He manifestly wasn't convinced. "It's not illusions I'm talking about. I'm talking more along the lines of--" he couldn't look at me now, so he compelled me not to look at him by pointing down at his map of the cemetery — "grislier facts. Most people don't find it pleasant to contemplate, ah, physical abnormality."

Pleasant or no, I almost said, I contemplate it with every step. I could've gone on, mentioned my children's and grandchildren's congenital problems, too. I did say, "I'm not squeamish, either."

He gave me an okay-but-I-warned-you look. "There's evidence of pretty high incidences of birth defects, of bone disorders. Many of them are kind of gruesome and unusual."

If he was expecting me to flinch, he was disappointed. If I was supposed to react strongly in any way, I failed. The only reaction I noticed in myself was some kind of inward shrug, meaning, approximately, Sure, of course, so what? In a community like Gardner, with no medical facilities and not even a resident doctor since Dr. Sweeny, there had been no avoiding the raw proof that flesh is weak, treacherous stuff. The maimed, the hideously diseased, and the genetic misfires had at all times been at least semi-present and semi-visible.

I said, "Unusual how?"

He exhaled a soft, exasperated sound and said to Latham, "Gertie, would you please take Mister Riddle over to where Dan and Greg are working and ... show him."

She almost managed to conceal her distress at finding herself appointed tour-guide. Anger flashed in her blue eyes, but she answered, "Sure, Bob."

We walked past the rows. Up ahead, I could see two men kneeling beside an open grave.

"Doctor Taylor," I said, "seems to think I'm made of glass."

"Please try to understand. Working in recent graveyards is about the least pleasant job there is in archeology. It's very sensitive and very stressful, actually."

One of the archeologists kneeling by the grave was writing in a notebook. The other poked at the contents of a coffin, yellow bones, disintegrating remnants of a dress. They smiled when they saw Latham, went blank when they saw me. Introductions were made: the man with the notebook was Greg, the one doing the poking, Dan. They received the news that I was a relative without cheering.

Latham looked down at the bones and said, "Is this one of the—is this one?"

"Yep," said Dan.

"Would you please show Mister Riddle what you've got here?"

Both of the men regarded me doubtfully for a second, and then Dan said, "Okay. Well, sir. Know anything about human anatomy?"

"Not much more than the foot bone's connected to the ankle bone." I hadn't intended to call anyone's attention to my mismatched shoes, but Dan was the least-stiff person I'd met so far. He just nodded and turned to the bones and began speaking very easily. It was refreshing.

"I won't make this technical," he said, "and I'll skip the small stuff. Um, the long bones in your hand, how long'd you say they are?"

I glanced at the back of my hand. "Three, four inches."

"Close enough." He directed my attention to the remains inside the coffin and pointed out an array of bones as long as cigars. "These are the same bones, and there're the fingers. As you can see, it's a pretty extraordinarily oversized hand."

It was almost an understatement. Whoever the dead girl or woman was—I looked for the name, but glare on the stone obscured it—she must have looked as if she had an oar up her sleeve.

"Typically," Dan went on, "congenital problems left the door open for all sorts of other problems. She must've been in pain her whole life. She was about eighteen or twenty when she died. Most of the others've been much younger."

"There're really a lot of skeletons like this one?"

"Yep." He watched me carefully now. "Awful lot of 'em."

"Enough to make you wonder," said the other man, Greg, "if the local drinking water isn't spiked with uranium dust or thalidomide or something."

Latham shot him a thoroughly dismayed look. Greg cleared his throat and examined a page in his notebook very, very carefully.

"Actually," I said, "my family's probably just dangerously inbred."

Latham and the two men seemed not to know how to take that remark. I let them twist in the wind, stared down at the tormented bones, thought, Roy Rich, Betty...I had sometimes glimpsed them through the half-open doors of their back bedrooms when my grandmother visited their mother and hauled me along. My cousin Dorsey would nowadays be called "learning-disabled." Aunt Jean was "movement-impaired." Several of her lower vertebrae were fused together; walking, standing, even sitting, all were torture for her. Once, I eavesdropped fascinatedly on a morbid conversation about her back and hip and knee problems and strange calcium spurs the doctor didn't know what to make of. Once, I was appointed to help her down the aisle at a revival meeting, at a pace glacial and excruciating even for me. The valley resounded with preaching on hot summer nights, and every household brought forth its lame, afflicted, dying, and sent them forward to be healed by faith. Summer after summer, I saw the lines of pain deepen around my aunt's mouth. I saw the microcephalic and the acromegalic, saw the man whose body appeared to be collapsing telescope-fashion, the man with the tumor that sat on the side of his neck like a second head, the woman with calves like some pachyderm's, the girl who was one great angry strawberry mark, saw it all and became inured to it. Faith never healed anyone, but no one ever lost faith. DNA had let us down, but Jesus would yet lift us up.

I was jarred out of this reverie as Dr. Taylor strode up in a hurry. He had a frown on his face and appeared not to notice me. "Gertie," he said, "Rita's got something we better take a look at."

He turned without waiting to see if she followed. She hurried after him, and after a moment's hesitation I went lugging after her. Two men and a woman with her nose painted white stood over a warped coffin. One of the men held the lid like a surfboard. We looked down, and Latham said, "My God," mah Gott.

Lying in the coffin was the apparently preserved body of an elderly man in a dirty funeral suit. Lying in the grass by the edge of the driveway was Dr. Chester Sweeny's headstone. I heard a roaring in my head.

The white-nosed woman, Rita, couldn't contain herself. She said, "It's *not* a cadaver!"

Latham asked, "What do you mean?"

"I'm saying this isn't a dead, embalmed body here! It's not a body at all!"

Rita pointed to the side of the elderly man's face. I peered and saw some sort of crease or seam under the jawline. It had come loose beneath one ear, and a flap of skin, if it was skin, was turned down there, exposing smooth white bone, if it was bone.

"Check it out," said Rita, and used her thumb to push up an eyelid and show us a startlingly realistic fake eye set in a grimy socket. Then she pinched the loose flap of skin between her thumb and forefinger and pulled. It came off easily, exposing a bony tri-lobed bulb with openings that couldn't have been for eyes or any other familiar organ. Where the jaw ought to have been was a complicated prosthesis complete with upper and lower rows of teeth and a fake tongue.

Nobody spoke for at least half a minute.

Latham looked at Rita and then at Taylor, whose frown deepened when he saw me. I said, "What," and then, "Why did, why would someone bury this," and couldn't think of a suitable noun.

I had to settle for gesturing.

"Prosthetics," Rita said. "The whole thing's goddamn prosthetics. Feel it," and first Taylor, then Latham, and finally I knelt beside the coffin. I touched the right cheek. It felt gritty but ... I pulled my hand away quickly.

Rita looked about wildly and said, "Now what is that stuff?"

Latham said, "It feels like," and stopped and shook her head perplexedly.

"Fleshlike," murmured Taylor, barely audibly.

Rita nodded vehemently. "So what *kind* of stuff is it, Bob?"

"I don't know. Some plastic, I don't know."

"This grave was dug and filled in nineteen hundred," Rita said, "and no one touched it until it was opened today. I know because Gil and I opened it ourselves, and we'd've known if it'd been disturbed. This thing was in the ground ever since it was put in the ground, back when nobody, *no*body, could make plastic like this. "

"Rita," Latham said, "just calm down and —" .

"Calm down? Gertie, nobody can make goddamn plastic like this now!"

Everybody was quiet again for a time. I looked around a circle of red sweaty faces. Taylor said to Rita, in a strangled voice, "What's under the clothes?"

Rita carefully opened the coat and the shirt, exposing a dirty but otherwise normal-looking human torso. It was an old man's torso, flabby, loose-skinned, fish-belly white. Wiry hair grew in tufts around the nipples and furred the skin. Rita touched the belly gingerly, pinched up a fold, and, wide-eyed, peeled it right off like skin off a hard-boiled egg. The inner surface had many small fittings and trailed strands of wire as fine as spider web. Within the exposed cavity, where a ribcage ought to have been, was a structure like a curved piece of painted iron lawn furniture.

Someone muttered, "What in the hell--" Maybe it was me, though I am not a swearing man.

Rita started to touch the structure, but her hand trembled, and she pulled it back. She looked around, gray-faced, and said, "Too weird for me, Bob. Just too goddamn weird. I'm sorry."

Taylor touched the bulb carefully, then the chest structure.

"Doctor," I said, "what're we looking at?"

"Well, obviously, some kind of articulated skeleton, but—"

"Is it, is this more—what, some birth defect, bone disease, what?" I was panting now, my heart was bursting out of my chest.

Taylor worried his lower lip with his teeth. "No disease in the world twists ribs into latticework. Whatever this thing is, it looks like it was supposed to grow this way. I don't even think it's bone. It feels almost like ... I don't know. Coral."

"Coral?"

"Something."

"Jesus, Jesus Christ," and I pushed myself up. Latham looked after me and asked if I was all right; I barely heard her.

The roaring in my head was louder now, and I staggered away, ran as only lame men run, disjointedly, agonizedly, until I found myself standing shaking before my grandparents' common headstone. I sat down on the ground between their graves to let my breathing slow and my heart stop racing, stared at the stone, tried to draw some comfort, some something, from the inscription. Beloved in memory, Ralph Riddle, Mary Riddle. All I could think of, however, was furry pale plastic skin draped from Rita's fingers, the bony white bulb inside the headpiece, the false tongue in the false mouth.

"Are you all right, Mister Riddle?"

I started. Gertrude Latham had followed me and was hovering concernedly.

"Just an anxiety attack." I punctuated the remark with a bark of mirthless laughter. "I'll be back in a moment." She choked on a reply to that, so I said it for her. "You think I shouldn't go back?"

She all but wrung her hands.

"If you people are playing practical jokes—"

"We would never, ever, play jokes!"

"Somebody's up to something here! If this is some kind of, of stunt, you, Taylor, the historical commission, none of you will ever see the end of trouble. I can promise you that."

"What do you think we'd possibly gain from a stunt?" she demanded hotly.

"Money, publicity, I don't know."

"There's no money in archeology, Mister Riddle," she said, biting off the words. "Certainly not in this kind of archeology! You think we do this to get rich, to be on television?"

I was about to snap back, but then I saw that she was really angry, too,

15

as angry as I was, maybe angrier. I got a hold on myself and said, in as reasonable a voice as I could manage, "What is that thing?"

"It's not a joke!"

"Well, it's something, and it doesn't belong. If it's not a joke and not a box full of junk and not human — and it sure isn't human, or any animal, vegetable, mineral I've ever seen or heard about --"

"I'm sure there's a logical explanation," she said, obviously not convinced herself. "We'll be able to find out more when we get the ... remains to the lab."

"Yeah? And how long will that take?"

"We'll have to get all kinds of permission. It's going to be very complicated. Anything you could tell us about this Doctor Sweeny could be very important."

"Doc Sweeny," I said, and had to pause to clear my throat loudly. My voice was lined with wet sand. "Doc Sweeny was the only doctor here for thirty years. My great-grandmother was at his funeral. She told me once the whole valley showed up to pay last respects. I don't know any more than what she told me and what's on his stone. He came here after the War Between the States. He died at the turn of the century."

She didn't say anything for several seconds. Then: "Where did he come from?"

"How would I know? Who knows if he ever said?"

"All right," she said, "then why did he come here?"

"Everybody's got to go somewhere."

"But why here? We're not talking about your standard-issue nineteenth-century country doctor. We're talking about...God, I don't know what we're talking about. A guy with plastic skin, latticework for ribs. A skull like, like —"

She couldn't find the right word, if there was a right word, and the sentence hung unfinished in the air between us until I said, "A skull like something. And a face like nothing. Those bones back there are the bones of a --"

"A Martian, for all anybody knows." She was embarrassed to have said that, and I was embarrassed to have heard her say it. I couldn't look at her again for several seconds, until I heard her suck in a breath like a sob and say, "Whatever he was, nobody caught on to him in thirty years. Thirty years! What was he doing here all that time?"

"Driving around the countryside in his buggy. Dispensing solicitude, advice, and placebos."

"No, what was he really doing? Gardner's small, isolated, even backward."

I could only nod. The roads hadn't been paved until the 1920s. There hadn't been plumbing and electricity in all the homes until the 1950s.

"There's no money to be made here," she went on, "and never has been."

I nodded again.

"So why," she began, and hesitated.

"Maybe he was stranded. Maybe the place just suited him."

She appeared to mull that over for a moment, then nodded. "Who'd've bothered, who'd've been able, to check anybody's background in a place like this in eighteen seventy? Why else except that a doctor, someone claiming to be a doctor and willing to settle here, would've seemed like a godsend? He could've given them anything he wanted to give them and called it medicine."

I heard the roaring in my head again. I thought of my grandmother, breaking snap beans and humming. *Are you washed in the blood?* I murmured, "Or candy."

"What?"

The roaring in my head rose in pitch and blended into the incessant twirring of the cicadae. I thought suddenly that I knew the words to that song--it was a song of the need to obey the biological imperative; *Keep your genetic material in circulation*, the chorus went—and I suddenly felt cold and feverish.

I said, "What if," and then on second thought knew I could never go on and say what if Doc Sweeny had come to small, isolated, manageable Gardner from God knew where and become one of its citizens in order to become one with its citizens and had been accepted by them though the flesh of their children ever after twisted itself into knots trying to reject the alien matter he somehow had bequeathed to them, and those children, those who survived, had gone out into the world to pass along that same alien stuff to their children in turn, and--

So I said no more, only lurched past Gertrude Latham, and if she called after me, I didn't hear her. I wanted to be away from her and away from here, in my car, speeding away homeward with the radio turned way up and wind roaring past the open window. The waters could not close over Gardner soon enough to suit me. I didn't stop moving until I was through the cemetery gate, and then only because I put my bad foot in a shallow hole hidden in the grass and went down on one knee. The stab of pain in my leg and hip was so intense that I believed for a moment I was going to black out. Gasping, I dug my fingers into the earth, gripped it desperately. Maybe I was going to be sick anyway.

Mysterious Ways

WHEN THE PAIN IN HIS BODY began in earnest and forced him to admit to himself that his time had finally come, the last man in the world went to his crude cot, to lie trembling amid ancient, smelly blankets. He lay there, waiting, almost until dawn.

Nothing was revealed.

The man sighed softly and fell into an exhausted sleep.

Later that morning, his animal friends came as they always had to the garden in the lot behind the ruined supermarket. They had grown fond of listening to the stories he told and the songs he sang in his high, brittle voice. When he failed to appear, some of the beasts crept into the disintegrating building and slipped into his little room to wait quietly in the shadows beyond a wavering perimeter of light cast by stub candles at the head of the cot.

The last man sensed their presence after some time had passed. He raised his head with painful effort and smiled into the darkness. "My friends," he murmured, "my good and dear companions, I am dying."

They knew. The odd cat gave a brief, whining howl. The big, strange dogs whimpered and ducked their heads. The lesser things that had come shifted nervously on small padded paws and sniffed the close air, trying to determine the nearness of death.

"It is nothing to fear," the man gasped weakly as he sank back into his pile of blankets. "Remember that, my little ones, that and all the other things I have told you."

Not that it really mattered, but *Homo sapiens* the very last had once been called Alexander something, or something Alexander, perhaps--there had come a time when he found himself unable to recall either the missing part of his name or whether "Alexander" had come before or after.

He had been a minister, a man completely dedicated to God. He had lived in a little brick house located next to a large brick church, and then, early one morning, the world had ended all around the little brick house. Miraculously unhurt by the final, fatal human folly, Alexander had gone out to find the earth scoured clean of his own kind.

He had been thirty-four years old at the time (not that that really mattered, either, because he had soon afterward lost track of his years) and was convinced that the Lord God in Heaven had spared him, singled him out, for some great reason that would presently manifest itself.

So Alexander had worked hard to insure his survival while awaiting the bolt from the blue that would make the nature of his mission clear to him. He had raised vegetables in his garden and made friends with such beasts as still sought the company of a human being, and he had kept on waiting.

When the last man in the world was very, very old, a slow, gray sickness had begun to creep through him and gnaw at his insides. For several weeks, he had coughed often and long, choking and spitting up thick, fibrous clots of blood and mucus, but he had continued to putter about in the garden, conversing with his mutely expressive animal friends, singing his own hymns to them, lying to himself.

Finally, however, he had had to face the truth.

He was dying.

No purpose had been revealed unto him.

No reason had been given for his exemption from the extinction of the human race.

It made everything seem rather pathetic and futile.

One of the strange dogs whimpered again and moved nervously from corner to dark corner. Smaller creatures scurried out of the way in panic as the jittery beast's nails clicked on the smooth stone floor.

The man stared up at the ceiling, his eyes bright in the deep, black-rimmed sockets of his pale and fleshless face. The pain inside his chest increased steadily as the long day wound to a close. He began to cry out at dusk and kept it up intermittently until well after midnight. His waiting, watching animal friends stayed in the room the whole time.

Shortly before dawn, he grew quiet and lay with his arms pressed tightly against his chest. He tried to focus his gaze on the watching beasts and, failing, closed his eyes.

"Remember," he said again. "The songs, the stories, this place. Remember me. If you can."

He settled himself more deeply into his blankets and thought, Dear Heavenly Father, the meek are truly about to inherit the earth. Is *this* what you spared me for? Is this all?

He waited hopefully for the revelation that would snuff out the ember of angry doubt in his mind.

Nothing was revealed.

The last man in the world died as the sun came up. The beasts edged forward one at a time to sniff at the cooling corpse on the cot. The odd cat slunk away, meowing piteously, and the lesser furry things quickly followed. The strange dogs remained by the deathbed until mid-morning.

Then they gathered up their friend, bore him out to the garden, and gave him a decent Christian burial.

Ember-Eyes

THERE WAS NOTHING BUT FIRE IN THE air as the first of the ships rose, one, two, three, from their berths. There were roars like blasts of hateful sound blown upward from the depths of pits run by mechanical demons and full of the anguish of unrepentant automobiles. There was Ember-Eyes, coming over the lip of the valley, into fire and noise, shrieking after the departing vessels, "You can't do this!"

Ember-Eyes staggered down the slope, gasping in the hot air. He moved on three feet and used the talon-tipped fingers of his free paw-hand to massage the Mark of the Beast circuit-printed into the flesh over his heart. The searing agony radiated by the Mark worsened with each step he took toward the launch site on the valley floor. The fire in his chest spread down into his bowels; hot as supernovae, it cored his marrow bones. He fell many times. Two more ships had lifted off and escaped him by the time he reached the floor of the valley and came to the launch site's outer fence.

Ember-Eyes hooked his stubby fingers through the metal links and sagged against the barrier. "You can't leave us," he growled hoarsely. "We need you, we need you ...."

He let go of the fence and slid to his knees in the gravel. Beyond the fence was a narrow, ditch-bordered service road and, beyond that, a second fence, lower than the first. Next lay a quarter-mile-wide strip of deep grass, and, finally, the great white concrete plain, rolling across the valley floor, past the launch pads, past squat black buildings, to more grass, blacktop, and metal links.

He fought down his agony and rose to his hind feet with effort, took a couple of deep, steadying breaths, and then clawed his way up the fence. Fifteen feet high, the fence was topped with triple rows of barbed wire, braced at intervals with steel prongs projecting outward at a 45 degree angle. Seizing one of the prongs, Ember-Eyes eased himself over the wire and succeeded in avoiding all but a few of the barbs. Crouched atop the fence, shifting on his feet to maintain balance, he was about to leap for the service road when a pencil-thick beam of bluish-white light flashed out of the darkness and sliced through metal links close to his left hind paw. The beam started to track toward him but winked out of existence before it reached him.

It was enough, however, to startle him. Ember-Eyes fell forward, snarling with panic, and landed in ditch muck, with the breath knocked out of him. Writhing with new pain, he thrashed amid the mud and weeds and was vaguely conscious of new fires in the night as another of the ships got away from him.

And his renewed sense of having been betrayed was like a cold, hard fist closing around his heart.

They would not come with me, my own children and my children's children would not help me. You hate the human beings too much, *they told me, and I shrieked at them*, Yes! yes! I hate the human beings, I remember the feel of their fire and steel in my flesh and bones, I can still hear their ghost whispers in my head, telling me what was expected of me, telling what I was in their eyes so that I would hate them all the more intensely for having made a plaything of me, for having refashioned me in the image of their ancient terrors, that I might prowl in the darkness outside their city of light and afford them excitement, yes, yes, I hate the human beings, yes, and now, now they're bored, they're going away, they've moved out of their city, they've erected strange machines in the valley, but we won't let them get away, we won't let them discard us--

They would not come with me. My children, my children's children, they all refused to help me. They were born changed, *not rebuilt as I was, they were born changed, and they have been capable of thought all their lives. And they think thoughts that are strange to me.*

I am betrayed on every hand.

The fire and thunder of the vessel's departure died away, and Ember-Eyes lay still in the ditch, listening.

He heard soft, tinny footfalls.

He saw the guard.

The sentry glided out of the darkness on legs that were thin metal rods. Its hemispherical feet made faint clacking sounds as they struck the pavement. Its insectoid head burned silver where moonlight fell upon it, then golden as it reflected the flames spouting from the next ship in line to take off. A long slim traser wand was held at the ready in a curled-up spider of a fist.

Ember-Eyes shifted position in the ditch as he sized up the sentry. Dexterous rather than rugged, the robot had been designed for maintenance work, not fighting. Ember-Eyes grinned toothily and waited until the robot, ignorant of the intruder's flanking movement, drew abreast of him.

Then the creature in the ditch came up out of the mud and shadows with jaws distended and forepaws outstretched. The robot wheeled and jerked the deadly wand around but had no chance to fire. The weapon spun out of its hand as Ember-Eyes struck.

The robot reacted almost at once by clamping a steel hand around its attacker's vaguely canine snout. As cartilage in his face began to pop, Ember-Eyes reared and shook his head violently, tearing himself free and sending the robot skidding on its flat buttocks across the blacktop, toward the inner fence.

It was on its feet again immediately, just quickly enough its leaping black opponent to butt it backward through the air, into the shallower ditch on that side of the road. The gleaming cranium grazed the fence, the bulbous eyes exploded. For a few seconds, the sunburst at the perimeter of the launch site rivaled anything in the heavens.

Ember-Eyes did not pause to appreciate the sight. He scooped up the traser wand and, holding it clumsily, pointed it at the inner fence. He had seen the wands used in the city of light, when the human beings had had him that time, and he knew what to expect when he applied pressure to the firing button. It flashed away a section of the fence before him. He fired again and again until he had sliced a wide gap in the electrified barrier. Then, tossing the wand away, he dropped to all fours and plunged into the high grass.

And, out on the white concrete plain, another ship coughed like a Titan clearing his throat and began to rise.

You can't leave us! Ember-Eyes wanted to scream the words, but he had no breath for cries, only for running. The Mark of the Beast, forgotten during the fight with the robot, burned in his body.

The ships rose, one, two, three.

I won't let you leave! I need you! I need you!

The ships rose.

And you need me, you made me, you must still need me, don't you, DON'T YOU?

He stumbled out of the grass and onto the concrete, and he could see human beings moving around the base of the nearest ship, half a mile away, and he ignored the fire in his flesh, the roar in his ears, and ran. He had covered half of the distance to the nearest vessel when he abruptly crumpled and skidded on his face. The pain was too great. He pushed himself up and tried to make his mouth form the words he had heard the human beings use in their city, but only howls came forth. Through the murk of his agony, he saw that the human beings were now entering the ship, the last ship, the very last ….

Ember-Eyes dragged himself forward half the length of his body and crumpled again.

Then the pain in his body diminished. The Mark of the Beast cooled.

He panted on the concrete and glared at the ship. He felt turned to lead. He had failed.

He saw one of the last human beings turn and wave to him, and he raked his claws on the concrete in a frenzy of frustration, he snarled his hatred, too weak now to howl, and he watched as the last human beings filed into the last vessel, watched as the boarding ramp slid away, as the hatches closed and sealed themselves ….

Go home, said a spirit voice in his head. *Go home, little wolverine.*

Ember-Eyes tore at his skull, trying to dislodge the voice.

Go home, the voice insisted. *You are not safe here.*

"You can't … discard me like this," he gasped. "You took me and remade me, you gave me a purpose, and you gave me the power of thought so that my knowledge of that purpose would make me hate you all the more … what can I do, if not hate you and prey upon you?"

Go home. And images flooded Ember-Eyes' mind. He saw a fire cloud erupt from the ship on the pad a quarter of a mile away, he saw the concrete blacken and crack with heat, he saw steel bubble and run like water, he saw his own hair disappear in a white flash, saw his flesh crisp, melt away from bones that turned to ash.

He cast a final look of hungry longing at the last of the ships, then turned and began dragging himself back the way he had come.

Fly, urged the voice.

He forced himself to trot as, behind him, the ship rumbled ominously. He trotted faster, feeling adrenaline wash through him; he put his belly close to the ground and ran, felt grass whip his jowls as he left the concrete plain, felt his claws tearing up the dirt as he ran--

--felt a wall of heated air sweep him forward, raising his hindquarters and shoving his snout into the sod, singeing his fur, bouncing him unceremoniously for a dozen feet, and noise light noise heat light noise ....

Blackness.

He could not have been unconscious for longer than seconds, because, when he opened his eyes, he was on his back in the grass, kicking at the air, and he could see the ship climbing, slowly at first but gaining speed, growing smaller, and he tried to call after it, call it back down to earth, but there was too little air in his lungs, too little air, and there was no longer a spirit voice in his head, only a roar.

And he had failed.

And he slept.

Ember-Eyes left the launch site shortly before the moon set. He passed several more of the light robots on his way out, but they lay still and did not dispute his passage. Nor was there electric current flowing through the inner fence. The robots and the fence, like the Mark of the Beast, like Ember-Eyes himself, had served their purpose. They had been shut off. Ember-Eyes envied them and hated himself for doing so.

He spent the day resting on the lip of the valley. His face ached, his lungs burned whenever he tried to breathe deeply, and large patches of fur had been singed away, leaving pinkish blisters on his skin.

When night fell, he made his slow, painful way back to his territory to the south of the city of light. He sat beneath a tree on a hill overlooking the city and waited. By and by, Stripe, his favorite son, crept out of the darkness to sit beside him.

Stripe said, "You look a little the worse for wear," but his tone nevertheless was respectful.

Ember-Eyes glared at him for a moment, then fastened his gaze on the bright city below the hill. "I failed, Stripe."

Stripe contemplated the ground between his forepaws. "We knew that you would," he said quietly. "We told you that you would. Are you hungry, Father? I killed a deer this morning. The carcass is buried not too far from here."

"I wish I could make you understand, Stripe. I failed. *I failed.* I went after the human beings to show them that I refused to be a mere plaything. That I could still exert a little control over my own destiny. That they could not simply cast me aside when they were through with me. That ...." Ember-Eyes shook his head miserably.

"What happened, Father?"

"They ... they humiliated me again, Stripe. They made me the terror of their nights, and then, down in the valley, they made *me* feel terror. One of them spoke to me and told me to run away from the ship before it took off. And I ran away, Stripe. From start to finish, they had things their way."

"Let them go, Father. You can live your own life now."

"They were my life. They thrust me into the night and let me give them the pleasure of fear, of being hated and stalked."

Stripe rose and stretched. "They tired of it, Father. They grew up, and something in their flesh, something irresistible, told them that the moment had come for them to leave."

"To what purpose, Stripe?"

"To whatever purpose, Father. They grew up. We're growing up, too. There will be better things for us to day in days to come than—"

"Go away, Stripe. You confuse me."

Stripe said nothing for a long moment. Then: "I'm sorry, Father. Do you want to eat the deer?"

"No. Leave me alone, Stripe. Go away."

"We could go down into the city and—"

Ember-Eyes snarled and lunged, but Stripe dodged and skipped away from his father's fangs. They eyed each other tensely. "I won't go down into the city," Ember-Eyes said savagely.

"The Mark of the Beast can no longer hurt us," Stripe said, "and there are things there that—"

"Go away, Stripe!"

"I'm sorry," Stripe muttered sadly. "Goodbye, Father."

Ember-Eyes watched his favorite son turn and lope away toward the city of light, and he somehow knew that not much time would pass before Stripe and the rest of his progeny no longer remembered the nights spent lurking just beyond the lighted perimeter of the city; that they would no longer speak of how the men and women who ventured forth sometimes died squealing with delight, and of how that delight had served to make the lurkers hate all the more intensely. They would think thoughts that were increasingly strange to Ember-Eyes.

Down the hill, Stripe paused and looked back over his shoulder. "We're growing up," he said, a low, soft sound, and was gone.

Ember-Eyes gazed at the city for a long time before limping away into the evening. And his renewed sense of having been betrayed was like a cold, hard fist closing around his heart. He had been remade, he had been told what was expected of him and had been apprised to the fullest extent of his capabilities. He had been made a creature of the night, a deliberately intended monster, and there was no place for him in the city of light. He had been cheated from the start.

There was no more growing up in store for him.

A Daughter of the Cause

NEO-CONFEDERATES FLOURISH IN MY extended family; I am the changeling child who hates *Gone With the Wind* and wishes the goddamn C.S.A. battle flag were consigned to a museum. Despite my being a white southerner descended from white southerners extending back to 17th-century Jamestown, I have always held the opinion that while white southerners of the 1860s fought bravely and well, they did so for one of the worst causes that ever was.

Nevertheless, a maiden aunt named me executor of her estate, which occasioned my happening upon the fascinating detritus, a bundle of old letters and a tattered diary, of the life of an ancestor of ours, a disappointed and formidable matriarch, the greater whose disappointment, the more formidable she evidently had become. I knew that I must one day try to tell her story.

Miss Charlotte Bordenet was returning from church one bright Sunday afternoon and had just arrived at her front gate when she intercepted the latest news passing along the street. The army had been driven from its lines, someone declared, and the government was being evacuated from Richmond. Someone else offered confirmation and advised getting out of the city with all speed. Charlotte stood by the gate for several minutes, digesting both the information and the advice, then turned and went purposefully indoors. She told Sara to start packing and sent Jasper around to the Branches' to ask the use of their cart. Her mother emerged shakily to ask what all the excitement was about. Charlotte was still trying to persuade her to go back to her room when Jasper returned, winded and sweaty. Mister Branch had declined to lend his cart as he was going somewhere in

31

it, away from the Yankees.

Charlotte immediately amended her instructions to Sara, telling her, "We must restrict ourselves to necessary items." Sara asked how she proposed to get even necessary items, to say nothing of her sick mama, as far as the railroad depot or the packet landing. The whole city wanted to run away, but transportation was at a premium, and money was worthless. The Bordenets, mother and daughter, had been afoot since donating the carriage animals to the army. The army had been about to requisition them anyway.

"Very well," Charlotte said, "escape is impossible. We must depend upon the Good Lord and General Lee to stop those Yankees."

Sara only looked skeptical. Mrs. Bordenet confessed herself to be overwhelmed by the hopelessness of the situation and let Sara guide her back to her room. Charlotte told Jasper to put the luggage away and positioned herself by the front gate again in hopes of intercepting more, and better, news. A tattered company of cavalrymen mounted on sorry-looking horses passed at a walk. Other refugees, civilian as well as military, came by on foot. There were few vehicles. One, a mule-drawn buggy, broke down in the street almost directly across from the house. Its cursing, frightened-looking driver hurriedly unhitched the mule, swung himself onto its back, and went away at a trot. The buggy was piled with the first items, apparently, that had come to hand: a vase, two mismatched chairs, an empty birdcage.

Afternoon passed into evening, and increasingly it seemed to the girl that the chief elements of the crowd were low characters of every sort. Several men stared at her in the rudest way imaginable, and one--a foreigner, from the look of him, dressed in mud-splattered clothes and swinging a threadbare carpetbag like a pendulum--even tried to speak to her. She rebuffed him with an icy look, and he sheepishly rejoined his equally unsavory companions, who teased him boisterously. "Froze out by that little thing!" she heard one say, and the others brayed laughter. She had been more frightened than she let on, and now she marveled at her own composure.

At twilight, however, her nerve finally did fail her, and she retreated into the house. Sara had found a few vegetables in the muddy patch she dignified by calling a garden, but Charlotte was too nervous to eat. She told Sara to take some broth to Mrs. Bordenet, then moved restlessly through the house, noting, as if for the first time, its disconsolate echoing hollowness. Few of the rooms had seen any recent use. Dusty sheets covered most of the furniture. At last, finding herself in an upstairs corner room, she uncovered a chaise lounge, drew back the curtains, and made herself sit and be still. To the south, she could see over the rooftops in the lower part of town, clear across the river to Manchester. To the east, she could see the Capitol Building.

She must have dozed, for she next found herself huddling under the sheet on the chaise lounge. The room had become very cold. When she sat up, she was startled to see several great fires burning along the waterfront. A smell of acrid smoke had seeped into the room. When she noticed clouds of sparks turning on the wind coming off the river, she yelled excitedly for Sara. There was no response. She rushed downstairs to tell her to collect some old blankets and wet them; Jasper could take them up onto the roof and use them to smother any sparks that alighted.

It was only when she found the back door standing wide open that she realized that Sara and Jasper had gone. Several more seconds elapsed before it occurred to her that they had run away, *her* Sara and Jasper, whom she had known all her life. *Run away.* Her eyes watered and stung, her throat constricted. Then anger at the ingratitude of Negroes got the better of despair; as she stormed off to fetch the blankets herself, she thought, See how well the Yankees treat you!

She carried the blankets outside to the well and proceeded to douse them, shivering with cold and listening fearfully to a swelling background din of shouting voices as she drew each bucket and emptied it. When the blankets had been thoroughly soaked, she tried to gather them in her arms again but found herself unable to lift them. She separated two from the sodden pile and started for the back door. She was only beginning to consider the prospect of actually getting up onto the roof when she heard someone call out, "Miss," from the direction of the back gate. An indistinct form hovered there. Not looking away from it, Charlotte groped behind herself for the door handle.

"Miss?"

Her fingers found the latch, but she could not get a grip on it. The blankets weighed a ton. She let go of them, and they landed on the step with a sodden plop.

"Can I trouble you for a drink of water?" The voice sounded as though it were coming from the depths of a pit, yet it was a voice as young as her own. And now she saw his face, a pale blur, and thought she heard the gate's hinges squeak. Her voice seemed caught in her throat.

The young man said, "I must of walked clean across this town today, and I'm thirsty."

"The well," she said, or tried to say. Her tongue would not cooperate.

"Beg pardon?"

"The well. There's the well. Help yourself."

"I do thank you, miss." Now, unmistakably, the hinges squeaked. She saw the gate swing inward and the man step through, into the yard. She sucked in a breath, tensed, told herself, Turn quickly, open the door, go inside, close the door, throw the bolt.

All she managed, however, was to make a tentative grabbing motion at the blankets on the step. "I have to take these up on the roof now." Her voice almost broke. The statement sounded so inane in her own ears that she was suddenly and unexpectedly more embarrassed than frightened. "I don't want it to catch fire. The roof."

"You don't want to break your neck, neither. Ain't you got nobody to go up there for you?"

"Of course. My--my husband!"

"If you say so, miss, but no offense, you seem kind of a littlun to have a husband." The man laughed, quite unpleasantly, she thought. "Well, don't make this husband of yours break his neck for nothin'. Seems to me the wind's blowin' the fire off the other way."

She risked a look. The fire did appear to be skirting her neighborhood.

The man cocked his head to one side and regarded her. "Guess I know what you're thinkin'," he said. "They ain't no law in this town tonight, just a lot of wildness and drunkedness. I don't hold with neither." He pulled at his clothing, and now she saw how shabby he was, and how tired he looked. "I know I don't look like no proper soldier. Here's my bullet bag, and I leant my rifle by the gate there, but they never give me no proper uniform. I ain't no deserter nor nothin' like that. When I woke up this morning, my whole company'd up and moved out without me, and--"

The house trembled--Charlotte felt the door vibrate against her fingers an instant before she heard the thunder of a tremendous detonation. A great fan of flame spread across the sky to the southeast. When, after the better part of a minute, she remembered the young man, it required real effort of will to shift her attention back to him. He stood with his side to her, plainly transfixed by the spectacle. Her hand slipped off the door handle and hung at her side.

"Lord God A'mighty!" she heard him exclaim. "It's a whole danged volcano!" He glanced along his shoulder at her. "'Scuse my language."

There was a second detonation, then a third.

"What," Charlotte said, "what *is* it?"

"Well, them's shells you see all tumblin' through the air there and explodin', so it's either the Yankee Fourth of July come early and writ big, or it's the fleet blowin' up. Since it's downriver to'rd Drewry's Bluff, I guess it's the fleet. They must of blowed it up, what was left of it."

"Who?"

"Us, of course. I guess that pretty near shuts us down."

"Shuts us down? What do you mean?"

"Shuts *us* down. As a country. We all better start learnin' how to sing 'The Star-Spangle Banner' agin."

Charlotte's mouth opened, but she was too shocked by what she had heard, treason, unadulterated *treason*, to think of anything to say. She remembered how fine and handsome her father had looked as he rode away at the head of his cavalry company. She and her mother had sewn officer's braid on the sleeves of the jacket. She could still see the carriage horses being led away, too. She had declared then that it gave her a supreme thrill of pride to imagine them hauling General Lee's artillery pieces, and that the sacrifice of horses seemed little enough compared with the sacrifices Southern fighting men were making. It was a pretty speech, prettily delivered--simply to spare herself the humiliation of blubbering over a pair of horses, she had composed it and mentally rehearsed it almost on the spot, and the lieutenant in charge of the requisitioning party had complimented her on it. It partook of something real, too. At fourteen years of age, she already had enough dead for a lifetime of mourning. Mr. Bordonet, *Captain* Bordonet, had fallen at First Manassas, and First Manassas seemed very long ago, very far away, and a little thing all around, victory though it had been, compared with the Sharpsburgs and Gettysburgs that followed. By the fourth winter of the war, Charlotte could not have named a single household whose women did not dress in mourning. Moreover, she never got enough to eat. Thanks to the infernal blockade, she had to do without items as mundane, and as essential, as thread and needles. And, pretty speeches notwithstanding, she had secretly grieved for Hermes and Mercury, those sweet-tempered beasts. Watching as they were led away had seemed, at the time, the ultimate test of her patriotism, and in her own estimation she had failed it. She wanted her horses back and knew that she would never see them again, that they were lost to her forever just as her father and so many others were. She knew, then, as everyone knew now, that the war was lost, and she just wanted it to end and be over, done with, Merciful Lord in Heaven, *finished*.

Yet *now*, standing shivering from cold and fear by her door, confronted by a lone tramp who claimed to be a soldier, she told herself, the idea resurrected itself, that she could not have suffered such losses, endured such privations, for nothing. It was not enough for the misery simply to end. She glared at the intruder in her yard and realized with a start that she was not so nearly frightened of him any more as angry with him, infuriated by him. She had seen enough soldiers in four years to know that few of them matched the figure cut by a Captain Bordonet or a General Lee, but never had she met one who looked and talked less like a military man and more like—like some Irish trash from Rocketts!

"I expect," she said sharply, "we'll hear any minute now that General Lee's worked another miracle. Grant'll be whipped, and Old Abe'll finally realize that, that—" how did her pastor put it in his thundering sermons? "—that God will *never* allow an army of drunkards, foreigners, and Negroes to conquer a nation of cavaliers. Never!"

The intruder laughed harshly. "That's a right fine little speech, miss--excuse me! *Ma'am*."

Charlotte started again. The officer who had taken away Hermes and Mercury had complimented her with almost the same words.

"But you're the first person I've met in a good while," the ragged man went on, "who thinks we're still gonta win this war!"

"I don't care what you say. I don't care what anybody says. General Lee will never abandon us."

He laughed again, as unpleasantly as before. "I don't see why not. President Davis has!"

"That's only for now! After the war's over and *won*, I expect all traitors will have to answer for their treason. *I* am going to have a party to celebrate the victory. Not some pitiful old starvation party, either, but a real ball." And everything would be as it was, except, except—

"'Cept a power of us'll be dead and can't come to your party."

"*Except*," she began, almost baring her teeth in what would have been a most unladylike snarl, but her eyes were streaming, she was out of breath, weak, even anger no longer sufficed to hold her up or keep her warm. The front of her dress was sodden where she had held the wet blankets, and she felt chilled straight through to her backbone. She blinked frantically to clear her eyes, gulped air, managed to say, "Our loved ones haven't died in vain," but in spite of a determined effort to affect a tone as stern as her pastor's whenever he spoke of the new nation, sanctified with the blood of its fallen heroes, the words came out of her in a series of shuddering sobs.

"Folks dies in vain all the time," the young man said slowly. "I seen it happen in spades. Even to loved uns."

"What a horrible thing to say! What a—*horrible*—"

"All they ever *is* is loved uns."

"You may remove yourself from this property!"

He turned and took a step toward her, and Charlotte, suddenly terrified of him again, moaned and shrank back against the door. "I sure would like that water now," he said, "but seein' as how it's too much trouble, I can go on to the next house." He turned again and went to the gate. "Goodnight to you, *ma'am*." He passed through the gate and closed it and was gone.

The girl flung herself into the house and threw the bolt. She did not pause until she had satisfied herself that all doors were locked and all downstairs windows latched. Mrs. Bordonet was still in her room. Charlotte did not disturb her, but exchanged the sodden dress for clean, dry clothes. It never occurred to her to sleep. She made her way back to the upstairs corner room, where she knelt beside the chaise longue to pray. After a time, she resumed her watch at the windows; when she felt herself in danger of being mesmerized by the sight of the flames, she turned from the south to the west. It heartened her to see the Capitol Building's façade and columns, weirdly illumined though they were in the glow of the burning waterfront. As the sky began to lighten, she saw that the Stars and Bars still flew above the Capitol.

She hastened to the door of her mother's room, knocked, called out. There was no answer. She knocked again, harder than before, and heard a wordless cry from within.

"Mama! It's dawn!"

The door opened a few inches, and Mrs. Bordonet peeked out, red-eyed, puffy-faced, disheveled. "Are the Yankees here?"

"Our flag still flies over the city! Mama, you look a sight. Come, let me help you with your toilette. Then we'll see what Sara has found for our breakfast."

Charlotte remembered then that Sara had run off, but said nothing about it as she steered her mother to the vanity table. She took up a brush and began to pull it through the older woman's hair. Mrs. Bordonet gazed absently into the mirror for a time, then said, "I dreamed about your papa."

Charlotte could not recall the last time either of them had mentioned Papa. She said only, "Well." She set the hairbrush down, placed the wash basin before her mother, and poured water into it from a pitcher. "Wash your face now, Mama, while I go down and see about breakfast."

First, however, she went to close the corners in the corner room. Through the east window, she saw two tiny dark figures on the roof of the Capitol Building. They were working at the flagpole. The wind caught and unfurled a Yankee flag, and the two figures saluted.

The horrible wretches! Charlotte thought, and jerked the curtains closed. As she left the room, she swung the door shut with a great reverberating slam.

The following weekend, General Lee surrendered, and Mrs. Bordonet died of a fever. Two years later, Charlotte married a railroad entrepreneur who had been an officer in the Army of Northern Virginia. Charlotte taught her children to revere, among other things, the sacred memory of their grandfather, killed by a Yankee bullet in July of 1861. Her daughter Janet, a true daughter of the Cause, was almost a grown woman before she learned that the South had actually been defeated in the war, and, of course, she did not learn it from her mother.

Tom Sawyer's Sub-Orbital Escapade

Lisa Tuttle and Steven Utley

IT WARN'T MUCH TIME AT ALL AFTER we'd gotten back from that balloon ride to Africa[1] that Tom and me and Jim built the moonship out on Jackson Island. You might think we'd have had our fill of adventures, and me and Jim *was* pretty content with staying home, but that Tom Sawyer was always spoiling for going somers else and finding new adventures and looking at new things and giving folks hereabouts reasons to bow down to him and think of him as something pretty grand.

One afternoon Tom and me and Jim was setting out on the island, fishing and lazing in the sun and feeling good not to have somebody squawking at us to get to work or go to school or take a bath. But Tom warn't so content as us, it didn't seem, for he kept on staring off at nothing and frowning to show how deep he was thinking. It finally got to the point where I couldn't stand it, him just staring and frowning and thinking like that, so I ask him what's the matter; and Tom says, "Huck, I reckon we've seen and done just about all there is to be seen and done in the whole world. It's like there's no mysteries left for us to discover anymore."

Jim he allowed as Tom might be right and that it was something to be grateful for, us having seen and done so much in such a little while. But I could see Tom was just saying such things on account of building up to something real spectacular and wanting to dramatize it. Tom and me'd been pirates and robbers and spies and most everything else, it's true, and we'd been to Africa, too, which made us heroes, even Jim, who was a slave and didn't ordinarily amount to much in the eyes of white folks. But I might of

---

[1]   See *Tom Sawyer Abroad*, by Mr. Mark Twain

knowed that nothing couldn't ever be enough for Tom Sawyer. He always had to be doing something grander and finer than other folks would dream of, and he couldn't never be content with just ordinary things. I guess there is maybe a lesson there, but as I steer clear of lessons and leave them to other folks, I won't say no more about it.

"You know," Tom goes on, still real thoughtful, "there's just about only one place left for us to go, and that's the moon."

Well, I just set there, not knowing if I heard him right and not knowing if I should laugh or act serious. I thought maybe the sun had tetched Tom's head, or maybe he meant something I didn't understand. But finally I said, "Why, Tom Sawyer, that's the craziest thing I ever heard you say. Why would we go to the moon?"

"We'd just go there," said Tom and now he's coming on to squirming with excitement. "For the adventure of it, Huck."

"*Go* there?" I snort. "Go *there*? Why, Tom, you can see with your own eyes that the moon ain't nothing at all but a … well, I don't rightly know what it is, but it ain't some place like Africa or Illinois that a body can just *go* to!"

"Huck," said Tom, "use your head. Remember how when we were up in the balloon we saw a herd of camels below us and you thought it was spiders?"

"They sure looked like spiders."

"But they warn't, they were camels. And from high up in the air they looked tiny, just like the moon is so far away it looks small when it's really big—bigger'n the whole United States!"

Jim hung his mouth open in astonishment at that, but I saw where Tom was wrong and said, "I got to admit you was right about them camels, but don't you recollect what the moon looked like when we was so high up? Why, it didn't look no different from up there than it does from here on the ground. It goes to prove."

"Huck, you got him dere!" Jim cried in delight. "You sure has! He cain't say you wrong now—ain't you de *sharpes'* boy!"

I did feel kinder pleased with myself for remembering. Tom Sawyer is hard to out-argue, but I figgered I had done it.

But Tom wouldn't give up. That ain't his way. Instead, he kept on and on about how the moon was much higher and much farther away than we'd gone in that balloon, and that the mile or so we'd gone off the ground didn't hardly matter at all, the moon was so far away. Jim and I kinder grinned at each other, trying not to let Tom see us. You got to admire the way Tom never admits he's licked but just keeps on coming up with wilder and wilder stories. Finally, when he realized we warn't believing him, he said, "I guess we'll just have to go up there and walk around on the moon before you two shads'll believe me."

"I reckon so, Tom," I told him. "You got a powerful balloon stashed away to get us there?"

Tom starts to looking thoughtful again. "No balloon'd take us that high," he said. "This time, we'll have to build us a moonship." Well, Tom he got carried away with telling us what a moonship was and how it could be made and what it could do, and he made it sound so good that me and Jim just had to agree to go along with it. Besides, there warn't nothing else we had to do just then that we couldn't'a done later. I figgered that after Tom found out how wrong he was about the moon, we could use the moonship to go to the Empire of China and to India, which are some powerful interesting places, I've heard, and bound to be as exciting as Africa was. And Jim he had taken a liking to flying after all that time in the balloon and was bound to see it through with us.

We started collecting cans and old nails and such things from behind stores, and had to run like the dickens a couple of times when somebody hollered at us. It warn't stealing, though, because nobody was using those things or could of said who owned them. It warn't no more stealing than fishing catfish is.

Some places people had things they didn't mind getting rid of. Judge Thatcher's wife throwed out a spinning wheel that was broke and no good, and we got to it before the ragman did because Tom said we needed it. And Tom's aunt Polly herself gave us a bunch of twine and some old boards and a couple of barrels and said she hoped we was up to some good this time, and not more of our mischief. Tom didn't tell her about the moonship, because he knowed how much she worried and cried over him and prayed for his soul, and so's he wouldn't say nothing about it in his sleep and have his brother Sid learn about it, Tom faked he had a toothache and wore a bandage around his head at night to keep his mouth closed.

We ferried everything out to Jackson Island on a raft and set it up and, pretty soon, had fixed up a mighty fine water-powered wheel that'd push most anything most anywheres you wanted it pushed to. Tom called it a secondary injun and said it was the most important part of the moonship. There was a primary injun, too, that Tom fixed up out of some springs and that old busted spinning wheel. The primary injun made the secondary injun go.

Tom did all the figgering, so it was me and Jim that actually toted and hammered and lifted and tied all that stuff together into a dandy moonship while Tom sat with his back against a stump and told us where to put things and did ciphers on a piece of paper and said change that board, there, for another one which looked just the same but which he said would hold up better once we got to speeding through space.

We planned to take off on the second night of the full moon, because with all that light and the whole moon to aim at, it didn't seem as we could miss. Tom decided that the moonship should be tried out the night before we left, but we went ahead and got together everything we'd need on the trip. Tom he hooked some doughnuts and apples from aunt Polly's kitchen, and me and Jim spent a whole day fishing on the island and had a nice batch of catfish to show for it. So we was all stocked up in case we had trouble finding something to eat up there on the moon. We didn't plan on staying for no more than couple of hours or so, not wanting to be stuck up there when the moon went down, but we warn't taking no chances on going hungry if we did get stuck. By all this time, me and Jim was beginning to really wonder if maybe Tom was right about the moon being a regular place that you could walk around on, just like Missouri only maybe not so big, and without any people. So we took along a little U.S. flag that Tom's brother Sid had got on the fourth of July, because if we truly was the first people to set foot on the moon we figgered we ought to claim it for the govment. And I also brought pipe and tobacker, of course, and some fishing line and a knife and other useful things.

We had the moonship set up in the middle of Jackson Island with trees all around and the little wings just barely clearing the branches on the sides. On the first night of the full moon, we was all set to test it out. Tom came out on the raft about eleven o'clock. Jim and me had been on the island all day long and had everything buckled down real good. So I set on the bank and smoked while I waited for Tom to show, and Jim did some witchy spells he figgered would help, calculating and mumbling about conjunctions and angels of trajectory and I don't know what all, and drawing pitchers in the dirt with a stick. The pitchers didn't make no sense to me, being just a lot of circles and lines. But Jim's spells sure sounded potent. He said they was necessary because the witch-woman who taught them to him allowed as folks didn't go to the moon just every night, it being a power of trouble to get everything right and just so. I took this to mean that maybe somebody had been up there at least once already, but I didn't say nothing to Tom about it when he got to the island. I figgered it was likely Tom wouldn't'a wanted to go to the moon in the first place if he knowed somebody else had already done it. As for me, I had gotten kinder interested in seeing what the world looked like from that high up.

Well, we finally piled into the moonship and got all set to test the thing, and then Jim started to have his doubts all of a sudden. He'd been afire to sneak a look at the pearly gates before his appointed time, but setting there in that moonship got to him. It was like he suddenly realized that we would really and truly be going all that way to the moon on the following night.

"Huck," Jim said, "I doan know if I kin go through wid it."

"But it's going to be such a grand adventure!" burst out Tom. "Better'n Africa, Jim! You remember how much fun Africa was, don't you?"

"Oh, I 'members, all right, Tom, but Africa's a reglar place. My people come from dat place, en you know God made it fo' man to live on. But dat moon, Tom—God made de moon to give light en not fo' some upstarts like us to go trompin' 'roun' on. Mebbe we should jes' go home to bed."

"Don't you worry none, Jim," I said. "Some folks says if God had of wanted us to fly, he'd'a give us wings, but we flew in that balloon, didn't we?"

Jim nodded cautiously.

"Well, then, there you are! The moon'll be a heap of fun!" By now I was really bound to get to the moon, so I got to pedaling and warming up the primary injun. Tom started to pedal, too, but Jim just went on setting there, wide-eyed and shaking his head.

"Come on, Jim," I begged him. "Help us pedal."

"Oh, Huck, I jes' doan know, I jes' doan know."

"Shucks, Jim," Tom panted, "you can't let us down now. You ain't scared or anything, are you?"

"I ain't never let you boys down, en you know it. And's for bein' scared, I reckon anybody in a right mind should be, jes' a little. What if somethin' goes wrong wid dis moonship?"

"But that's why we're going to test it first," Tom said, exasperated. "So we'll know everything works right when we do take off for the moon."

That seemed to make sense to Jim, so he shrugged and put his heart into it and helped us pedal, and soon we was all puffing and snorting away. But that blamed moonship didn't do more than shake and groan a little.

"It'll take some more of your conjurin', Jim," I cried, and Jim he cuts off pedaling, and me and Tom was mighty glad for the rest. Jim let on to chanting and howling something fierce, and suddenly that secondary injun made a noise like a paddle-wheeler's boiler blowing up, and that moonship just up and gave a shudder and a leap. We was all throwed all together and jumbled up on the floor. I was on the top of the pile and Tom was on the bottom, with Jim in the middle somers, but it still felt like someone was sitting on me and trying to squash my chest, the way you do a tick.

The pressure finally let off after a while. We sorted ourselves out and peeked out of the little bitty window I'd hammered out and Tom'd covered with some oil-cloth he'd found somers. The view was kinder blurry on account of the quality of the oil-cloth, but there warn't much to see anyways, just lots of black, and the stars, which looked like they did from the ground, and that big old moon way on up ahead of us. The moonship was pointed right at it, and it occurred to me then that we might go on all the way without really having much say in the matter. But presently the moon started to swing away from us. We could see we was going to fall back to earth and end up where in the blazes nobody could say.

"Jim! Jim!" I yelled. "Something's wrong! Do another spell!"

But Jim he had seen the moon swing away from us, too, and he was terrified. He started to crying and carrying on and promising the good Lord that he never really meant to sneak that look at the pearly gates before his appointed time and wouldn't never again get involved in no heathen foolishness such as this if only he could get back down to the ground safe and in one piece. I can't say as I much blame Jim for all that. We were getting back down to the ground, all right, but the ground was coming up at us something frightful, so the part about ending up safe and in one piece didn't strike me as likely. I took another look out through the window and saw the outside of the moonship throwing off sparks. I could see them trailing out behind us like we was some kind of comet. Tom and me just sank back to the floor and looked at each other mighty sickly.

"Can't we stop her?" I yells across to him.

Tom looks real thoughtful for a second. "I bet we forgot to put in something to stop her with."

Mainly because I was scared and didn't know what else to do, I started to pedal again and was astonished when the moonship leveled off kinder lurchy.

"We're saved!" Tom hollered, jumping over to help me pedal. By and by, the moonship stopped jumping around and throwing off sparks and started gliding along smooth as you please, and soon even Jim stopped his caterwauling and relaxed a bit and helped us pedal. We started to circle down towards the ground, like a bug crawling down a bedspring, and it took a long time, but we made it in one piece and just settled down on top of a hill. It was raining kinder half-hearted outside, but we didn't mind. We breathed easy for a spell and ate some and smoked. Nobody seemed to want to talk. I was sorry for Tom Sawyer, because going to the moon had been his idea and he'd had his heart set on it, even more than me. But I knew that if he was still determined to go, he'd probably end up going by himself. Jim and me was through with moonships for all time. I didn't know how to tell Tom this, knowing how disappointed he'd be with us, but there warn't no help for it. I'd just gotten the scare of my life in that moonship and I knowed Jim had, too.

We slept in the moonship. The sun was a good ways up when Tom and me and Jim climbed out. We was at the top of the hill and looking down across the tops of trees to what had to be the Mississippi River. Jim looked like he'd seen a ghost coming to ha'nt him on a stormy night, and I was still shaky all over, but I warn't about to say as much to Tom, who looks at everything like it was an adventure and can always be counted on to find the best in any situation. Well, Tom he suddenly points to something downriver and looks too excited for words, so me and Jim look and see a big city way off in the distance.

"Huck, do you know what that is?" Tom finally asked, giving me a funny kind of smile.

"What?"

"Why, that's got to be New Orleans, Huck!"

"So dat's New O'leans!" Jim exclaimed, hugging his sides. "Kin you beat dat?"

"I always did want to go to New Orleans," says I. "I bet it's a lot of fun. As long as we're here, Tom ...."

Tom looked at the moonship. "Well, I suppose we *could* put off going to the moon for a while. Long enough to see New Orleans."

I noticed then that we'd all three started walking down the hill without really knowing that we were doing it.

"Dat ol' moon'll be dere fo' a long time to come," said Jim. Jim seemed to get happier the farther away we got from the moonship. He was grinning and laughing and almost dancing by *the* time we got to the bottom of the hill. We stopped there and looked back up at the moonship for a second. The sight of it made me shudder.

Tom turned and started walking again. "New Orleans is probably more interesting than the moon anyways," he said, and I know I heard him sigh as we entered the trees. Behind me, Jim clapped his hands and laughed.

"Yes *suh!*" he said. "Fo' a *long* time to come!"

Rejection File

Dear Mr. Bordelon,

Thank you for letting us see "The Candy-Store-Window Look." It's marvelously well written, and there is real power in your descriptions of the protagonist's loneliness. However, apart from his yearning after the salesgirl in the candy store, nothing really happens, and the situation is left unresolved at the end. Our readers want to see sexy, upbeat stories in *Tomcat*, not slices of life. Please don't let this rejection discourage you from submitting other stories, though, okay?

Dear Sir,

Thanks for sending your story "Won't You Come Home With Me?" to MAN ON THE TOWN, but I'm afraid that it isn't right for us. You write with great feeling. Unfortunately for you, however, our readers aren't interested in such painfully introspective stories about lonely men who go around following beautiful women whom they don't know and don't have the courage to get to know. Our readers want fast-paced rousing fiction about guys who get it on with lots of foxy chicks.

But please try us again because you definitely have talent. We use a lot of fiction and if you can just write some stories about how much FUN sex is there's no reason why you shouldn't become one of our most popular contributors at our top rate of three cents per word.

Dear Mr. Bordelon,

Thanks for sending The Unfaithful Girl. It is superbly written but it won't do for *Hot-Blooded! Magazine*. For one thing, it builds up to something that isn't there: a real ending. Don't you think it would be a more powerful, hard-hitting story if, when the guy follows the girl he's fallen in love with only to see her meet another man, the three of them somehow got into a kinky relationship together? As it is, the guy just goes off sulking and feeling hurt and bitter and it's all very sad and depressing, not at all the kind of thing our readers want to see. Will you please try us again?

Dear Sir:

Thanks, but your story CUTTING OFF A PIECE isn't for me. I want stories about people making LOVE, not about some dude who in a fit of jealous rage abducts and kills some girl he barely knows and then, my God, rapes her. SLEEK uses sophisticated stories heavy on the humor and hot stuff; I don't like violent fiction unless it's about bondage.

Thanks but NO thanks for "Never Leave Me." Occasionally we will publish a kinky story in *Man's Fun* but this is just too much. In fact it's pretty nauseating. A guy who keeps making love to the hacked-up corpse of a girl in his basement? No way, not in MY magazine. I would return this disgusting piece of crap with the standard printed rejection slip but there come times in every editor's life when he has to discourage sick creeps like you.

The Mouse Ran Up the Clock

SHE HAD LEFT GRASSES FORTY-FIVE million years away, in the Cretaceous Period, and the earth here was mutilated by erosion. She ran, fell, got up, slid, fell again. Cockroaches as big as shoes and brick-colored dinosaurs as small as birds fled before her.

And, behind her: Ceratosaurus, seven meters long from the tip of its stiffly outstretched tail to the rhinoceros-like horn on its snout, stalking her across the Jurassic highlands.

And, further behind; the four black angels, the dogs of Time, sniffing along her trail, slowly but surely running her to ground.

Flushed by her blundering approach, a cloud of strange insects erupted from a clump of ferns. She ploughed through the swarm, batting at it with her arms, then hurled herself against the bole of a young gingko and hugged it for support. Her clothes were plastered to her flesh where they had not been shredded away by spiny flora. The air was hot and thick. Breathing it was like trying to inhale warm porridge. She clung to the tree, gasping, and regarded the dinosaur.

Ceratosaurus was now less than a hundred yards behind her, weaving among the trees, placing its splayed feet with care as it moved over the rough ground. The dinosaur carried its body parallel to the earth, with its tooth-filled maw open, its small but wickedly taloned forearms spread as though to embrace her affectionately once she had been overtaken. She had seen the last of Ceratosaurus' line in the Cretaceous: Tyrannosaurus rex; much longer, much heavier, with quite a bit less forearm and quite a lot more mouth; the final word in predation.

But Tyrannosaurus had deigned not to notice her. The Tyrant Lizard King had been after larger prey, duck-billed hadrosaurs the size of elephants. Ceratosaurus seemed less particular.

She wiped mud from the buckle of her harness and peered at the dial set there. *Recharge 00:01.31.* Ninety-one seconds to go. She tiredly pushed herself away from the gingko and resumed her plodding flight. The dinosaur honked its annoyance and lengthened its stride.

She stumbled, cried out, forced herself onward, thinking wildly, Hold out for just another minute and a half, come on, come on, one foot in front of the other now, left right left. Go go go, said the bird.

And she answered herself bitterly, But isn't this what you came here for?

A shrill whine suddenly filled her ears. She shot an alarmed look over her shoulder and promptly tripped over an exposed root. A black-garbed figure dropped onto her as she sprawled on her side in the stiff mud. Strong, gloved hands tugged at her belt.

"We've got you now!" said the dark angel, shrugging off an ineffectual blow.

Then a shadow fell upon them. The dark angel had just enough time to look startled behind his visor before Ceratosaurus' jaws closed over his head and shoulders.

The woman on the ground screamed and rolled to one side as her attacker was jerked kicking into the air. The dinosaur gave its victim a vicious shake. Vertebrae parted with a sharp snap. The creature sidestepped awkwardly and swatted at its original quarry as she hurled herself away and scrambled crablike into the nearest ravine.

When she got to the bottom, she lurched to her feet and did not risk a backward glance until she had put at least a hundred yards between the dinosaur and herself again. By then, Ceratosaurus seemed to have forgotten about her. It squatted above the lip of the ravine and let its hinged jaws work the grisly mass that had been a human being down its gullet.

Her belt buckle beeped. *Recharge 00:00.10.* She thumbed off the safety lock and put a finger on the tab marked ACTIVATE. *.07. .06. .05.* She shot a last look at Ceratosaurus and shook her head. *.02. .01.* She pressed the tab. Nothing happened.

Frowning, she checked the dial and stabbed the tab again, savagely. The shrill whine repeated itself, and, for a moment, she thought that the chronopak had decided to function properly after all. Then a second black-clad figure materialized ten feet away and launched itself at her. She heard it yell a word just before the moment of impact.

Just after the moment of impact, she landed on her back atop a large, flat-topped rock, eighty million years away.

The air was dry and rather cooler than it had been in the Jurassic Period. She sat upon her high rock, staring out across the desert, toward the silvery glint of sunlit ice among mountain peaks on the horizon.

Not far from the rock, a large sail-backed reptile worried at a carcass. She let her gaze drop to the creature as it braced its forelimbs against the carcass, bit deeply, and wrenched off a mouthful of carrion. She could not repress a shudder.

The sail-backed reptile had made no attempt to reach her, but, at the same time, it eyed her as it ate, pausing occasionally to issue a hiss of warning. She dared not descend to the ground.

How easy it would be, the woman thought as the reptile made a brief strangling noise and disgorged a gory fragment of bone, to throw myself down to you. How easy it should have been to let Ceratosaurus catch me. Or to have hurled myself into the path of Tyrannosaurus. Or I could have stood my ground and let a mastodon trample me. I could just have thrown myself from any high place. I could have got myself killed anywhere along the line.

How easy it should be to do the one thing left for me to do.

How impossibly hard it is.

She looked at the dial and sighed. *Recharge 00:20.26. .25. .24.* Twenty-nine minutes, another half an hour to endure before she could make another jump. *Maybe.* The chronopak had taken considerable punishment. The farther down the line she moved from her proper matrix, the more tenuous her connection with it, the greater the strain on the chronopak's delicate mechanisms. Eighty million years ahead, she knew, the dark angels would be waiting on their own chronopaks and, while they waited, feverishly analyzing the residue she had left in the Jurassic, determining where she had gone from there and then.

So, she asked herself, where shall we go next? The very early Precambrian? Just a deep breath, and the methane-ammonia atmosphere will do the job. Or further back than that, perhaps, all the way to the age of molten Earth, fsst. Instantaneous combustion. At most, at worst, a split-second's pain and horror.

We could go forward for a change. Back to late Mesozoic times. Back to Tyrannosaurus. Drown ourselves in the inland sea of Kansas. Stand on the slopes of Krakatoa. Wait for the blast at Hiroshima.

We could go back and try to get him again.

She made a disconsolate sound.

Monster, the second dark angel had called her. *Monster*.

No. She checked the dial again. Not a monster.

Only a coward.

The Paleocene epoch, the quiet pause between the last evening of the dinosaurs and the first morning of the age of mammals, was Eden. She walked through a forest of immense redwood trees, pausing from time to time to listen to the furry chittering things that had just inherited a planet, and, as she had done in the Permian, she jumped away before her pursuers showed up. But reluctantly.

In the warm dusk of a pre-Columbian summer, it occurred to her that she had neither eaten nor slept for more than twenty hours, not since the morning of June 18, 2266, when she had stolen the chronopak. She watched the stars come out until it was time for her to leave, and then, once again, she had to run to avoid capture by the people in black. When she tried to jump away, her chronopak malfunctioned. She materialized in the Pleistocene only to find that her pursuers had been lucky enough to arrive a full minute ahead of her.

With her hands and feet enclosed in globes of some glistening material, she could neither walk nor tamper with her harness controls. She lay upon the hard, cold ground and stared up at the lightening sky. Three black-garbed figures sat nearby. From the west came the muted roar of some triumphant hunting beast.

"How much longer," the woman heard one of the dark angels say to another, "before we can get out of here?"

The other looked at its belt buckle and said, in a woman's voice, "Eight minutes and a few seconds. Don't fret, Perrin."

The one addressed as Perrin chuckled sardonically and turned to the third. "Will you listen to the captain, Beitel? 'Don't fret,' she says.

52

Everything we've run into since leaving home's had too damn many teeth, that last tumble I took can't've done my pak any good, and she tells me not to fret."

The third person gave a sullen grunt.

"My pak's just about ready for the chute, too," the captain said. "But we'll get back. Stop worrying. It won't be much longer."

Perrin gestured at the captive. "What do you think'll happen to her?"

The captain shrugged. "That's no concern of ours. I just want to hand her over at the end of the line and tuck in for a few hours."

"And clean off the grime of the ages." Perrin chuckled again. "I've got two-hundred-million-year old blisters."

"*I'm* concerned," said the third person. "Pointer was killed because of her."

"Beitel ..." The captain's voice trailed off.

Beitel glared at the captive. "I'd like to burn you myself!"

"That's enough," snapped the captain. "Pointer knew the risks. We all did, before we left."

"He's dead."

"He died in the service of—"

Beitel cursed hotly. "You're so full of *merde*."

"That's *enough!*" The captain heaved a harsh sigh, then said, in a more solicitous tone, "Look, Beitel, I'm as sorry about him as you are. I liked Pointer. I'll miss him. But there's no bringing him back. There's nothing that can be done for him now. I'm sorry, but that's how it is."

"The captain's right," said Perrin. "We all knew what the dangers were. We all knew—"

"We could've brought his body back."

"Beitel, there was no body to bring back." The captain's voice was bleak. "The important thing, the *essential* thing, is that we've accomplished our mission. We have Butler now, and that's what really matters."

She lay among the dark angels and thought, Yes, you have Butler, and Butler has only the memory of her one original idea, her one brave notion. Butler, that most mediocre of human beings, has failed again. It should have been so easy to do, but I loved him, I loved him all his life, in spite of everything, and I could never have stolen him knowing how much loving him would hurt that other me. I am such a coward.

And then it should have been so easy just to die, but I looked into the mouth of oblivion, and my resolve crumbled, disintegrated. Intellectual resignation to death does not mean emotional readiness. The soul and the cells cry out for survival even when the mind knows that death is the only solution. I am such a coward.

"I could never have done it," she murmured.

The black-clad trio peered at her, and the captain said, "What?"

"I could never have gone through with it."

"Shut up," growled Beitel.

"What's she talking about?" said Perrin.

"I am such a coward."

"*Shut* up," Beitel shrieked, "*or I'll kill you, God damn it!*"

"*You* shut up," the captain said, stabbing a finger at Beitel.

"I could have changed the course of history," the captive went on. "Literally changed the course of history. I'm the person to do it. But I'm not the *kind* of person who could do it. I lost my nerve."

"Pointer lost his life."

"Beitel."

The woman on the ground looked at Beitel. "I'm sorry, I truly am sorry. Was he your lover?"

Beitel moaned and bared teeth behind his visor.

The captain shook her head at the captive. "Would you please not talk?"

"Can you make me not talk?"

"I will!" Beitel lurched to his feet. "I'll stomp your damn throat in!"

"No!"

The captain rose and stood over the captive. "Another threatening move, Beitel, one more *sound*, damn it, and I'll kick your face through the back of your helmet. You understand me? Butler goes back alive and unharmed, or none of us dares go back at all."

Belt buckles beeped. "Ten seconds," Perrin said, "and then we can get the hell out of here."

The bound woman forced herself to a sitting position. "Will he be there when we get back?"

The three dark angels did not answer her. The captain and Perrin hauled her to her feet and supported her between themselves.

"All together now," the captain said, "activate!"

Shrill whines rose and fell and died away, and the Pleistocene sun peeked over the eastern edge of the world to find nothing that should not have been there.

They materialized in the reception lock of the chrononautics terminal, June 18, A.D. 2266, and patiently stood there until the decontamination cycle had been completed. A man in a bright blue smock carefully removed the captive's harness, and then, without ceremony, the captain surrendered her prisoner to an officer of the Lord Reformer's personal guard.

The room was high and wide and well-lit. An irregular portion of one wall had been de-opaqued. It was raining outside, just as it had been an hour earlier, when she had stolen the chronopak and left the terminal. She sat in a high-backed chair, unable to move more than her head and fingers, and watched the rain fall. And waited for the Lord Reformer to make his pleasure known.

Presently, a door irised open in the wall facing the chair, and His Majesty the Lord Reformer of Earth, Ernst Bishop Butler, entered the room. The iris closed behind him as he strode forward to stand before her. For several seconds, they regarded each other in silence disturbed only by the crackle of His Majesty's envelope of protective energy.

She said, "How well you look this morning, Ernst. Proud, self-assured. Like a man completely in charge of himself."

The Lord Reformer scowled. "You've—"

"A man who has bent the world to his will."

"Don't interrupt me a second time." He glared at her for a moment, then began pacing back and forth before her chair. "This is so unlike you. *Stealing* a chronopak. Unauthorized time travel. Resisting arrest. Treasonous offenses." He paused and aimed a long finger at her. "Capital offenses. Punishable by death."

"What will become of me now?"

The Lord Reformer gestured helplessly. "I don't know. I don't know what to do with you. Have you lost your *mind*? Do you *want* to die?"

"No," she said. After a moment, she added, "I don't want to die, Ernst."

"Then why did you do these things? Why?"

"I ...." She tried to shrug but failed. She settled for staring at the high gray ceiling. "I woke up one morning earlier this week, and it was as though I'd awakened from a trance. I could no longer ignore the fact that the world had gone a way I cannot abide. Something I cherish and love was ... I thought to rectify matters. And to redeem myself, to atone for my part in making the world what it is today."

"You're not making any sense." His voice sounded lost, hurt. "Nothing you've done today makes any sense. Along with everything else, one man is dead, five very expensive machines are ruined, and I'm told the power drain at the terminal during the course of your little adventure was such that an indefinite suspension of the temporal research program will result."

The woman in the chair shut her eyes, shook her head wearily, yawned.

"Am I boring you?" demanded the Lord Reformer.

She dutifully opened her eyes. "I'm sorry, Ernst, but the past twenty or so hours have been exhausting ones. I'm very tired and ...."

She could not say the rest: depressed, disappointed, sick at heart, disgusted.

"You don't seem particularly concerned." His face was mottling with fury now. "Or is it that you don't realize the enormity of your crimes? Sutch and Berner have already drawn up your death warrant. They're demanding my seal on it. *Demanding!* Why do you think we try to be so careful about time travel? You could have caused serious trouble, introduced a cataclysmic paradox, who knows just *what* you could have done? Time is not a toy!"

"Time would have healed itself. I was trying to do a brave thing. I had a heroic plan."

"Brave? Heroic?" His Majesty spat the words. "Placing the very structure of the world in peril is a heroic plan?"

"I was *trying* to make a personal sacrifice in the hope that it would set the world a-right. I failed." She felt tears gathering under her eyelids. She blinked them away and forced herself to meet his gaze. "I failed not because I was appalled by the idea of altering history, not even because I love you too much, but because, at the crucial moment, I wasn't *willing* to make that sacrifice. I lacked the courage. I couldn't go through with my plan."

"What plan?" She flinched as a bead of his spittle struck her cheek. She could not raise her hand to wipe it off. "*What plan?*"

"I ... I was going to go back to when you were a baby. I was going to steal you and take you away to some day and age where you wouldn't have grown up to be what you are. Where you wouldn't have been able to do anyone any harm. I failed because I couldn't bear the thought of taking you from … from myself. Of the agony I'd be causing that other, younger me. I lost heart, and then I decided I only wanted to die. But I couldn't even manage that."

The Lord Reformer of Earth looked at her in stunned disbelief. Many seconds passed before he could speak again, and then his voice was barely more than a hoarse whisper. "You *are* mad."

"No, I'm only weak and a coward. If I were strong enough and brave enough to forget how much I love you, I'd try to …."

Again, she could not say the rest: kill you.

"I'm the single most powerful person in history," he said. "I brought the world to its knees. How could you want to throw that away?"

"You've made the world an ugly, hateful place."

"I've given you everything you could possibly desire!"

"There is one thing you haven't given me, Ernst. Not in a long, long time."

He waited for her to go on, and when she remained silent, he bent toward her and said, very earnestly, "What? Tell me," and then, kneeling before the chair, "Please tell me what it is," and, finally, covering her hands with his, "Tell me what you *want* from me, I have to know, please," and he was starting to cry.

She shook her head. "I still love you too much. I didn't plan to hurt you, and I still don't want to. Don't force me to. I'm tired, I don't care what you do to me, just leave me alone."

He rose and slowly backed away from her, his face full of confusion and something else which she recognized from other days as terror. The iris opened, swallowed him, closed.

She sat looking through the de-opaqued portion of the wall, watching raindrops break against the invisible barrier, until a sob worked its way up her throat. I am such a coward, she thought. She quietly cried.

When she was finished, she saw that the rain had stopped. Beyond the wall, under a low gray sky, was the world which Ernst Bishop Butler had bent to his will. She closed her eyes to it and thought about the one thing which the Lord Reformer of Earth had not given her, *a reason, Ernst, my beloved, my precious, to go on being glad you came out of my womb*, and, at length, alone in the room, she dared to say the thing aloud.

Leaves

"DO YOU KNOW WHAT BECOMES of people who die violently?" Dale asked me.

We looked around at the gray, naked trees and up at the boiling sky and, finally, down at the grave. Huddled in our jackets against the brisk October wind, we just looked and said nothing for a long, long time.

Dale cleared his throat after a while and answered his own question. "Ghosts. They become ghosts."

"Dale," I said, "let's go."

"No ghost ever got that way through dying peacefully."

"I don't believe in ghosts."

"They're an unknown quantity. Who really knows?" He gestured toward the mound of dirt before us. "For just a moment, pretend you really do believe in the existence of ghosts. Suspend your skepticism. Now what would you expect to happen?"

I closed my eyes and shivered. The wind was getting through my jacket. I wanted to get away from this place.

I used to like the cemetery. When I was little and not scared of anything, it was a good place to explore. Later on, when I had grown to be less sure of things, the cemetery was a nice place to go to have hours-long talks with good friends. Summer nights, hot nights, with the trees moving overhead and deep shadows everywhere and all that hard, cold marble all around. In the autumn, there were leaves and wind devils everywhere. Winters there were beautifully eerie. Spring was indescribable. But the summer was the best time of all. I had fine times in the cemetery in the summer, pleasant times, close times, when I was just out of high school and had nothing much to do between that and my first semester of college except write my dreadful poetry and dabble with my paints. I would sneak out of the house around midnight and meet Dale and maybe one or two others, and we'd sit in the heart of the graveyard until false dawn, talking about important things like college and sex and what we wanted to get done in our lifetimes. But now here it was Thanksgiving, and I had been a witness to a horrible thing. And I wanted to get away from this place.

Dale was smiling at me with the left corner of his mouth. "What would you expect to happen?" he asked again.

"Dale."

"You won't suspend your disbelief in ghosts for even a second?"

"No, I won't. I didn't even want to come back to this place."

"Neither did I. But I got frightened. All I did up north was think about what happened, and I had to come back and look. Just to be sure, I guess." He took a step backward, away from the grave, as a wind devil picked up a handful of dead leaves and danced them over the grave and around our heads for a moment. When the leaves were whirled away among the surrounding headstones, I shivered again.

"Ghosts are restless things," Dale said. "Irate spirits. Nasty as all hell to deal with, I bet. The men who did this are going to have their hands full if—"

"Stop it!"

He eyed me closely, shrugged and looked away. "I'm sorry, Linda. I'm disturbed by all of this. I am sorry."

"You act like it was all your fault. There was nothing you could have done."

"We could have tried to stop them."

"We'd have gotten shot. Just like—they were too scared to think straight at the time. They'd have shot us, too."

Dale made a disgusted-sounding noise with his mouth. "They're still too scared to think straight. They really think burying it here in an unmarked will keep anyone from finding out just how scared they can be."

I looked at him, horrified. "You're not going to tell, are you?"

He looked thoughtful. "No. No, I guess not. Who'd believe me? No. I expect something else to happen. I've got the beginnings of a bad feeling. I don't know how to explain it, it's just something I sense. A premonition-of-doom type of thing."

"Let's get out of here, okay?"

"You feel it, too?"

"No! This whole thing is over and done with! There's nothing anybody can do to change what happened. They've hushed it all up with lies, and they'll never tell the truth. And neither will we. It ends right here."

Dale sighed morosely. "I hope you're right. About it ending. But, God knows, if I was the dude buried here, I wouldn't let it end. I'd be mad. I'd want *revenge*."

"Let's go. Dale, please! This place gets on my nerves."

"Sure." He thrust his pale hands into the pockets of his jacket and turned to walk past me toward the gravel drive where the car sat. I followed close behind. We stopped beside the car and looked back across the cemetery. The wind devil was making the leaves dance again.

"Are we going?" I asked, after a minute or two had passed in silence.

"Yeah. You want to drive?" Dale handed me his keys. "I'm not much in the mood."

I opened the door on the driver's side and slid in behind the wheel. Dale walked around and got in but didn't close his door. He looked past me.

"I think I'll never come back here again," he said. "Get a job up north or something and never come back. Maybe you should, too. *Never* come back."

"Our folks live here."

"Well, I'm scared, Linda. At least as scared as any of the guys who did it. Anything could happen now. Look, what if he's down there in the ground, gathering his strength, waiting for just the right moment to pop out? Waiting for the killers to get close enough so that he can--oh, hell, I don't know!"

I opened my mouth to speak but could think of nothing to say to him. He was too serious to be put down. My head turned, slowly, and my gaze followed his.

Leaves swirled rose over the unmarked grave and swirled away among the headstones.

Dale and I weren't supposed to know about the grave. It was in a corner of the paupers' lot; it didn't have even the kind of cheap headstone that the indigent get, inscribed with something like:

JOHN DOE

b. whenever d. whenever

Dale and I hid in the cemetery the night the person in the unmarked grave was killed.

It must have been one or two o'clock, the first night of the Labor Day weekend. Dale and I were straddling one of the bigger headstones, facing each other, me humming softly in my throat, him looking up at the sky, the two of us waiting for nothing in particular in the way of something to talk about. Dale and I had been friends throughout our senior year of high school. We thought of ourselves as a couple of small-town misfits who had banded together against what we regarded as the forces of evil and injustice. We went into the big city for movies and concerts and things, but it was never as though we *dated*. Rumors to the contrary, we never had sex together, never even tried, never "fell in love" or any of the rest of that high-school garbage. I had had one real boy friend in high school, during my junior year. I don't think that Dale ever had a girl friend. He was shy around girls--myself excluded. Dale and I were just friends. I suppose that we did love each other. He had kissed me a few times.

We liked the cemetery. We watched for meteors (and for the occasional patrol car—the dead were supposed to have the place all to themselves between sunset and sunrise), and we tried to figure out the constellations. We read tombstones by the light of full moons and imagined what those buried people must have been like in life.

Mostly, we talked and enjoyed each other's company. That was how we spent the summer following graduation. And then, on the first night of the Labor Day weekend, the summer was suddenly all used up. We were both feeling sad, because we knew that we probably wouldn't see each other again before Thanksgiving. Our paths were leading us away from our little town and at right angles to each other: he was going north, I was headed west.

Then Dale softly exclaimed, "Christ!" and pointed excitedly at something behind me. I twisted around on the marble and saw a brilliant flame-colored streak in the sky. It must have been enormous. It took several seconds to burn out.

"That's the brightest one I've ever seen," Dale said. "Must've been as big as a truck when it hit the atmosphere."

"I wish it could've made it all the way down. A small piece of it, anyway. I've never seen a meteor after it's hit."

"Meteor*ite* in that case."

"So meteor*ite*, smart-ass. I've still never seen one up close."

"Not much to see. Pitted rock."

The conversation drifted along to other topics. We were talking about a William Goldman novel we both liked, *The Temple of Gold*, when he suddenly pointed at the sky again. There was another point of light there, a dimmer one. It didn't burn out, though. We watched it move down the sky, and I heard Dale murmur, "Airplane."

And I said, "Airplanes're supposed to blink, and this just—"

And then the point of light arrived and passed almost right over us with no more sound than a thin whine. It left a streak the color of dying fireflies as it swept past and whipped out of sight behind the trees in the graveyard. Before either of us could blink away the image of that streak, the thing hit the earth and tore itself to pieces to the accompaniment of incredibly loud tortured-metal noise, singled with the crack and crash of falling trees.

Dale and I were off that tombstone and on our bellies in the grass before we realized it, cringing in anticipation of an explosion which never came. The noise simply died away. We lay in the grass, listening to the treetops move with the breeze.

"Goddamn!" Dale finally gasped. We looked at each other stupidly. Another minute must have passed before we got to our feet and, without so much as a word of agreement being spoken, took off in the direction of the crash. We ran carefully, staying in the moonlight and keeping a close eye out for the smaller headstones, the ones that could break a leg or shatter an ankle if you weren't careful.

We found the thing near the northeast corner of the cemetery. It had shattered a couple of medium-sized trees on its way in. Shreds of some sort of fabric were hanging from branches and lay among the rows of graves. There was a rectangular box, about the size of a foot-locker, half-buried in the ruins of someone's family plot. The box looked pretty well banged up. A thick, greenish vapor hissed from a rent in one side and hung, glowing faintly, in the air. A marble statue of Mary lay in pieces all around.

"What is it?" Dale asked, after we had stared at the wreckage for quite a long time. His voice sounded strange, high and cracked and scared. Not that I blamed him at all.

"I don't know. I've never seen anything like it."

"We better go tell somebody."

We started to back away, then stopped in our tracks.

"Listen," I said.

A car was moving through the cemetery. We caught the flash of its headlights as it crunched along the gravel drive weaving among the plots and trees.

"The caretaker heard it, too," Dale said.

"You think we should wait for him to get here?"

"No. We're not supposed to be anywhere near this place at this hour. Let's go."

"Okay, so let the caretaker handle it. But let's at least watch, huh?"

We eased ourselves back into the shadows under the trees and squatted to watch as the car ground to a stop on the drive between sand the wreckage. Three people got out, a fat man in bib overalls and two younger men.

"Jimmy and Carey Nicholson," Dale whispered. His night-vision was much sharper than mine. "Caretaker's boys. Real assholes."

I nodded. I remembered Carey Nicholson. He had come up behind me at a graduation-night party and grabbed my breasts. He hurt me, but not as much as I hurt him when I turned and kneed him in the crotch. Carey had doubled up with distress, onlookers had doubled up with laughter, I had left. I never knew Brother Jimmy personally, but, from what I knew of him, he seemed to have been cast in his brother's mold — a slope-brow in his own right.

The three men stood together in the moonlight and regarded the mess all around then.

"What the hell is this?" I heard one of them exclaim.

The caretaker kicked at a piece of fabric, then turned to mumble something to one of his sons, who returned to the car, backed around and drove away. The caretaker and his remaining son walked around, poked at the stuff hanging from the trees and came at last to the box.

I noticed that there was no longer any glowing vapor escaping from the tear in its side.

After maybe twenty minutes had passed. Dale leaned toward me in the darkness and said, "C'mon, let's get out of here. There's nothing more to see, and these clods are just going to piddle around and pick their noses until the sun comes up."

"But what *is* that thing. Dale? A space capsule, you think?"

"How the hell should I know? Come on. We can read all about it in tomorrow's newspap--" He stopped. We listened. Two cars were now making their way to the crash site. We waited and watched as the caretaker's son pulled up with a patrol car in tow. The latter disgorged three more men, whom Dale identified as the chief of police and a couple of officers. They snapped on the patrol car's high beams, illuminating the strange box, and everybody conferred and did some more walking around and poking at stuff.

"You're right," I finally whispered to Dale. "Let's go home."

We got up, and then everybody, Dale and I in the shadows, the six men in the light, froze. There was an ungodly loud pop from the box as a panel swung open. A few last wisps of vapor wafted out, yellow in the light of the high beams. Something inside the box stirred, dragged itself out and fell to the ground. It pushed itself up and seemed to gesture toward the petrified men, toward the headlights.

In the light, the thing glowed silver and blue.

The policemen fumbled their revolvers out of their holsters and began to shoot it.

They got a much closer look than Dale and I did, of course. The men were all standing perhaps a dozen feet from the box when it popped open, I think I remember one of the Nicholson boys screaming quickly as the creature crawled out. And the officers shot it.

They must have kept firing until there was no ammunition left in their guns.

They were scared. They yelled and cursed at one another afterwards, and they dragged the thing over to the pauper's plot, and Dale and I followed at a distance and watched them scoop out a grave. They buried the creature there, and the policemen hauled away the box and the shreds of fabric. That stuff was probably dumped into the Cumberland River.

They said as little about that night as they could. People in town wondered about vandals who could tear up whole trees, but the police stuck by that story and promised a full investigation. I guess that the Nicholsons took chainsaws to the shattered trees and re-sodded the mangled family plot and, in general, cleaned up things. When Dale and I returned to the cemetery in October, there was no sign of a crash.

That was the end of it, apparently as far as any of the killers were concerned.

And Dale and I made our separate ways home on the first night of the Labor Day weekend, and I crawled into bed but couldn't sleep. Not that night, not for a couple of nights afterward.

"It was murder," Dale said, fumbling for his cigarettes.

"I know." I slid the key into the ignition slot.

"He, it, whatever, was hurt. Dying, probably, He needed help. And they killed him."

I said nothing. We had been over it many times in our letters, and we had a fair notion about what the bright, flame-colored meteor must have been: a ship, a vessel, vaporizing in the atmosphere. The box had surely been an escape vehicle, a lifeboat. One that had failed for some reason that we would never know.

"It was murder, Linda."

I still said nothing.

"And it's *going* to come out. They can't keep this quiet for long."

"Maybe they can. Maybe it won't come out."

"Six people besides us know it happened. And at least two of those people are assholes."

I turned the key.

"And what about the thing in the grave? What if *it* comes out?"

"What're you talking about?"

"Ghosts," Dale murmured as the car started to edge forward.

"Now we're back on ghosts!"

"Well! What if there are such things? Vengeful spirits, walking the night --"

"Dale, will you please shut up?" I was so startled by the realization that

I had screamed the words at him that I put my foot down on the brake, hard, and stopped the car before it had traveled three yards. I was trembling all of a sudden. Dale leaned over and put his hand on my arm.

"I think you do feel it," he said quietly. "It's not just me. There is something odd in the air, something not quite right. Something alien."

"Dale, stop it! You're carrying on like an idiot!"

He drew away and sank back into his seat. "Yeah. Maybe so. I hope so. Being haunted by the spirit of a murdered human being would be bad enough. But can you imagine how much more horrible it would be to be haunted by the ghost of a murdered space alien?"

"Damn it, *we* didn't murder him!"

"We were on the scene."

"Oh, just shut the hell up, leave me alone!" I stepped on the gas pedal. Dale jammed his unlighted cigarette into his mouth and looked back toward the grave as we rolled away. I followed the curve of the gravel drive, and the grave passed briefly into sight in the rear-view mirror.

The wind devil was still making the leaves dance around that corner of the paupers' lot. They rose and fell and spun like a cloud of black bats.

Dale heaved a long sigh. "Safe," he hissed.

"What?"

He gave a low, mirthless chuckle as he turned from the rear window. "Ever see such a stationary wind devil, Linda?"

"What're you talking about now?"

"Nothing, love. Never mind. Let's go get drunk or something."

We drove on. Dale abruptly remembered his cigarette. "Those poor men," he muttered, striking a match.

Pretty Meat

As he approached the house, David kept glancing nervously at the shrubbery that lined the yard. He imagined glittering, hunger-mad eyes peering from the shadows. He saw in the flutterings of small branches the completion of some flanking movement, the accomplishment of some diversion, the signal for a concealed army to rush forth from hiding and sink small, white teeth into him. They had almost had him the night before. They would still be hot to get him today.

David shifted his guitar case and gnawed the inside of his cheek at what sounded like a twig snapping softly under the weight of a furtive foot. When he got to the door, he knocked twice, then raised his fingers to touch the two long, parallel welts on his left cheek. His skin felt oily and unclean, and a recent cup of hot, bitter coffee had failed to dissolve the scummy coating on his tongue.

The door opened. The woman who stood there gave him a small, tender smile. "Hello, David," she said.

"Hello, Patricia." He half-turned and grinned at the invisible lurkers in the shrubbery. "Sanctuary," he called to them, and entered the house. It was a house full of cameras, photographs, and paperbound novels. It was a house full of Patricia. David let himself sag tiredly against a wall.

"Are you all right?" Patricia asked as she took his guitar case and set it on its side against the wall, beneath a large black-and-white print of two children regarding a box turtle. "You look like hell."

David pushed himself forward, into the living room, and collapsed onto the sofa. "I feel like hell. Probably smell like it, too. I've been up since yesterday morning. Couldn't stay at the hotel with the others."

Patricia walked over to the sofa, her flower-print dress going *sush* around her legs. She sat down beside him and regarded him concernedly. "Where did you spend the night?"

"Wandering around. Took my twelve-string up to the roof of the hotel and gave an open-air one-man concert for the jetliners flying over. Did one old Carl Perkins thing over and over again. 'Everybody's Trying to Be My Baby.' Had a couple of drinks here and there before all the bars closed. Killed a few hours in an all-night movie house." David massaged his eyelids for a moment, then fumbled for a cigarette. The crumpled red-and-white package emerged from his pocket looking like a mangled specimen of exotic butterfly. There were no cigarettes in the pack.

David gave Patricia a questioning look.

"I gave it up," she said. "I don't even have any around the house for friends."

"It's not important." David sighed and settled more deeply into the sofa cushions. "I smoke too many of the damned things anyway."

"Well," Patricia said as she smoothed her dress, "how have you been?"

"Almost got killed last night."

"I heard. You made page two of the morning paper. From the sound of it, you really broke the place up."

"Those girls almost broke *me* up." He indicated the welts on his cheek. "One of 'em got away with a little of my skin. Walking out of that stage door last night was like getting dumped smack into the middle of Custer's Last Stand. Eight million screaming savages all around, guards going down left and right, Morry getting the clothes jerked off his back. He lost some skin, too."

"The price of fame, David."

"Crap. Give it to someone else in that case. This hot young superstar stuff is going to get me killed one day."

Patricia said nothing. David found himself staring at a wallful of black-and-white prints. A young couple, frozen midway through the completion of an affectionate kiss. A young man with shoulder-length hair and one-way sunglasses, lounging under the shark-like snout of an old Curtiss P-40 Warhawk while, in the background, a Boeing 747 seemed to look on curiously. A dramatic profile of a plesiosaur skull, all forward-slanting teeth and intricately interlocked bones. David himself, glittering with the reflected light from many beadlets of perspiration, eyes almost closed, mouth almost opened, fingers caught, blurred, in the middle of a chord change.

"Where was that picture taken?" David asked. He wondered what song he had been performing at the time.

"Nashville. Last August."

"Yeah. Must have been. That guitar got garbaged up in Toronto." He looked at Patricia. "I didn't know you were in Nashville then."

"I was there to shoot pictures of country-music stars. I tried to get in touch." Patricia shrugged, then laughed. "I suppose they thought I was just another loopy broad trying to lay David Allison and the band."

"Still freelancing?"

"It still beats slaving for Orrick. I get by. And I'm not always having to defend my honor in darkrooms."

David went back to studying photographs. Patricia contemplated the arrangement of paperbound books on the coffee table. Outside, an airliner flew over. Outside, automobiles muttered past on the road at the end of the driveway. Outside, a small branch scraped against a window pane, animated by a fitful breeze or, perhaps, the passage of a beast of prey prowling and sniffing for David Allison.

"How long are you going to be in Dallas?" Patricia finally asked.

"Plane leaves tomorrow at noon. I told Mike I'd meet him and the guys at the boarding ramp, that I had to see an old friend. That he should take his damned tranquilizers and not worry about the golden boy of rock and roll."

"Why didn't you come over when you left the hotel?"

David made a weary sound and closed his eyes. "I just wanted to be by myself for a while. There was this ghastly scene in the hotel room. Mike let in about a dozen girls not ten minutes after we'd gotten in from the stadium. Girls who were just pathetic in their eagerness to do just *anything* to get to be with us gods. The whole scene turned into a Wessonoil party."

"Maybe you should've stayed. Getting laid regularly is healthful, David."

"Oh, Christ, Pat! Here we'd all just barely avoided getting ripped to pieces by an adoring mob, and I get up to the suite and want only to get some sleep or at least knock back a coupla beers in peace, and that damned stupid road manager turns the place into Bedlam." His voice grew quieter. "It's been getting worse since Chicago, love. Day and night, girls popping out dumbwaiters, waylaying us in elevators, doing banzai charges at stage doors. I got mobbed in the parking lot of a Colonel Sanders Kentucky-Fried Chicken. I can't eat out, I can't go to a movie unless it's at three a.m., I can't browse in a book store or go to the john or do anything without girls throwing themselves at me. Begging me, pleading with me to warm my bun in their eager little ovens. Wanting my love and doing anything to get it, even to the point of attacking me on the street."

Patricia laughed again and shook her head apologetically. "Most men would give their eyeteeth to have such problems."

"I'll swap places with them any old time. And they can keep their teeth."

"Maybe you're just succumbing to paranoia, David. Presley and the Beatles survived. They weren't *utter* naifs like you, but, still --"

"Pat, I'd have stayed in Houston if I'd known what a hassle it was going to be to spend all my off-stage time dodging packs of worshipful girls. And they're not all girls, either. Middle-aged women are even doing it. One of those loons cornered me at the hotel bar in Toronto. She said she was thirty, the age when women reach their sexual peak, and here I was, twenty years old, the age men hit *their* sexual peak, and so, obviously, we two should retire someplace and get it on."

"What did you tell her?"

"That I was infected with two hideous and extremely contagious venereal diseases. No. Not really. I didn't tell her that." David gave Patricia a forlorn look. "I really don't know how much more of this I can take. Morry and the other guys think it's just swell. Mike even gets in on it. They probably even keep score, see who can make it with the most chicks."

"The girls probably do it, too," Patricia said. "Two Morries, or one Morry and a Paul Brewster, are worth one David Allison. And so on."

"It's driving me nuts, Pat."

"Well, I admit you've got a problem," she said mildly.

"Maybe if I let the word get out that I'm homosexual — no, my problems would only just be beginning. Jeeze."

Patricia rose. "Why don't you take a shower and get some rest? You'll feel better. And I'll make you breakfast while--"

"I had breakfast before I came over."

"Coffee and sweet rolls, I bet. That's not breakfast, David."

"I didn't have sweet rolls."

"Then you must be hungry. I'll fix you steak and eggs. Go get cleaned up."

"Yeah. Sure." David pushed himself to his feet. "Bathroom hasn't moved since last time, has it?"

"Same place as ever. Go on."

"Right. I love you, Patricia."

She turned and gave him a sensual leer. "Will you warm your bun in my oven sometime?"

"Fix my steak, old lady."

"David?"

He awoke, blinking. The light in Patricia's bedroom was soft and gray. The sun was going down. Patricia stood at the foot of the bed, watching him intently.

"What time?" he asked thickly.

"About seven-thirty. Feel better now?"

"Mm. Much. Slept like a brick."

"You were having a nightmare from the sounds of it. I heard you moaning in the other room."

"Moaning."

"About vampires." Patricia plucked at the coverlet. "And meat."

"Pretty meat." David sat up and stretched. "Morry and the others call it pretty meat."

"It?"

"The mob."

"Oh." She walked around the edge of the bed and sat down beside him. "Do you want to get up now?"

"I may as well. I'm dying for a cigarette, though."

"I went out and got you a couple of packs while you were asleep."

David gave her a kiss on the cheek. "You're a good woman, Pat. You'll make someone a marvy wife one of these days."

Patricia groaned. "God, I hope not!" She gestured toward a chair. His clothes lay neatly folded, awaiting him. "But I did feel disturbingly domestic this afternoon. *Hell* of a way for a determinedly unmarried twenty-seven-year-old woman to feel. Anyway, I washed your things. Did you know someone ripped a pocket off your jacket?"

"It doesn't surprise me in the least." David lay back and stretched again. "The chick who grabbed it has probably sniffed herself into a coma. Well, Ma'am, will you excuse me so's I can dress?"

"You're never any fun," said Patricia, blowing him a kiss on her way out.

David put his clothes on and walked into the living room. On the coffee table, two packs of Winstons lay atop a copy of *The Adventures of Huckleberry Finn*. He opened one of the packs and was looking around for a match when Patricia entered with a couple of drinks in hand.

"Rum and Coke," she said, handing him a glass. "Oh, your matches. I took them out of your pocket when I washed your clothes. They should be by the lamp in the bedroom."

David fetched the matches and returned to the living room, sipping and smoking appreciatively. Patricia had switched on the television set and turned down the lights. She gently pushed him to a seat on the sofa and sat down very close to him. He put his arm around her and hugged her tenderly.

"Thanks for all of this, Patricia," he said, leaning over to give her a quick kiss on the corner of her mouth. "Nothing like getting my morals corrupted after a hard round of making musical history."

"Someday, I'm going to get myself a regular lover, one who's not always off to L.A. or London or someplace for weeks and months at a time. What are you going to do then when you come dragging into Dallas in need of an overhaul?"

"Shoot you both, I guess. Cain't stand a cheatin' woman." He finished his drink, set the glass aside, and squinted at the television screen. "What're we supposed to be watching, anyway?"

"Something called *Zontar, Thing From Venus*."

"What? *Again?*" David gave Patricia a look of horror. "Every damned time I get to Dallas, they show that movie! You've got to be kidding, love."

"Uh uh. Said so right in the TV program."

"Jeeze. Patricia, I'm not terribly excited by the idea of sitting through this bomb another time."

"Oh, don't worry, you're going to love every minute of it." She took the glasses into the kitchen to refill them with rum and Coke.

"Patricia," David called after her, "I've *seen* this flick three million times already, and I *hate* it."

"Well, *I* haven't seen it," Patricia said as she re-entered the room and set the glasses on the coffee table. She slid onto the sofa beside him. One of her small, tanned hands ended up in his lap.

"Keep doing that," David told her about one minute later, "and you may not get to see the movie."

Patricia laughed wickedly. "I *told* you you'd love every minute of it."

For quite a long time after that, the only voices in the room were those on the soundtrack of the science-fiction movie. David finally got up long enough to turn off the television set.

"One of my favorite flicks," he confessed as he returned to the sofa.

"How'll you get through the crowd at the terminal?" Patricia asked, handing him a glass of cold orange juice.

"Run like the devil, I suppose." David took a long drink and leaned back in his chair. He was still somewhat sleepy, and he was tired from the night before, but it was an exquisitely relaxed kind of tiredness. He was happy. He was content. He was in love again. He seldom thought of Patricia when he was not with her. But being with her, talking with her, sleeping with her, just looking at her, always made him fall in love with her all over again. He suddenly found himself wondering, for the first time ever, if it was the same for her.

"Actually," he went on, "I shouldn't have any problems. If the little monsters are out, they'll be looking for David Allison and the whole band. Just in case, though, I'll disguise myself with sunglasses and a clever hat. Maybe disguise the guitar case to look like a dumpy wife."

"When do you think you'll get back to Dallas?" Patricia seated herself opposite him and began buttering the toast. She did not look at him.

"Soon, I hope."

"You always tell me that."

"I always mean it, Pat." He picked up a strip of bacon and bit an end off. "I keep thinking that it's about time for the group to start slipping. That maybe, suddenly, we'll just stop being such hot stuff. The bubble'll burst, we'll become has-beens, we'll all go home to play with our share of the money. No more tours, no more TV appearances, no more records. No more nubile little girls and middle-aged women trying to grab a bit of immortality by making it with the gods."

"No more pretty meat for the boys in the band," murmured Patricia, still not looking at him. The butter knife continued to scrape across toasted bread. "What would you do then, David? I mean, after you're no longer a boy superstar?"

"Why, I'd live off my royalties, play guitar in some grungy club here in Big D, and ravish you every chance I got." David reached across the table to pluck a slice of toast from the plate before Patricia. He nibbled off a corner and eyed her reflectively. "Pat?"

Patricia carefully placed the butter knife against the rim of the plate and returned his gaze, waiting.

"Pat, do you sleep with other men when I'm away?"

"Of course."

"Who?"

"The occasional rock star. Anyone else who happens to tickle my fancy and is available and disease-free." She looked down at the toast for a moment and began tracing invisible patterns on the tablecloth. When she looked up against, David saw in her expression something that was almost a challenge. "Why?"

"Just ... curious." He finished the toast in a couple of mouthfuls, then scooted his chair back from the table. "I'd better head on out to the airport now."

"Do you want me to take you?"

"No, it's okay. I'll call a cab."

"David."

"What?"

"Don't be upset. Please. We've done fine so far without making any promises to one another."

"It's okay." David went to her and put his arms around her neck. "It's okay. I'm not upset." He smirked at her. "It's nice to learn that not every woman in the United States is so determined to make it with a rock star that they have no time for mere mortal men."

"Arrogant little snot!" Her arms crept around his body and pressed him warmly. "Go call your cab!"

When the taxi pulled up in front of the house, David and Patricia said their goodbyes and so-longs at the door. Patricia gently but firmly declined to walk with him to the car. He gave her a final kiss, hafted his guitar case, and walked down the footpath, once again aware of chitterings, of movement and gleaming eyes, among the shrubbery. He was in enemy territory again, flesh-eating harpies were waiting for him, and, for just a second, he felt the urge to turn and run back into the house, to hide there with the woman named Patricia. But something else had begun gnawing at his gut, something that had closed off that avenue of escape.

David *was* upset.

He stopped beside the car and looked back at the woman who stood in the doorway. He saw her as he remembered her from the evening before, warm, naked, utterly lovely, and he tried to imagine her with other men, to imagine her as being equally warm and naked and utterly lovely with someone other than David Allison. He turned back to the cab and bent to grasp the door handle. His reflection in the car window made him blink with surprise. And he was certain that, on the surface of the glass, pretty meat blinked back at him.

Ants

SOMETIMES, CLARE, I TAKE OUT THE films and tapes I made of you when you were alive, and I turn the spools over and over in my hands and wonder if I dare view them again. I haven't played them in years, though there was a time, after you died, when I killed myself with them every night. I'm pretty sure you'd understand why I try not to think of you too much.

But I'm in bad shape right now, and for just a few minutes, while I try and calm down to the point where I can go make a thorough search of the bunker, I need to talk more than I've ever needed anything.

I pass more and more of the time down here in the bunker. I eat, sleep, read, exercise; I used to play games of strategy with the brain, but it finally went on the blink a year or two ago (I *think* it was a year or two ago), and I don't know how to fix it. All the brain does now is print out consistently inaccurate weather reports and inane doggerel, like:

> When the evil baron died,
> No one in the village cried.
> They laid him in a kirkyard berth,
> And then they nailed him to the earth.

I've sometimes let the brain babble on for hours when the loneliness got to be more than I could endure in silence.

Every now and then, however, a bit of real excitement comes into my life and gives me reason to do something other than sit around on my broadening behind and rummage through the library in search of a spool I haven't already played half a dozen times. I've been making war on ants, Clare.

Periodically, maybe one hundred thousand ants will break camp in the shady ruins of some long-ago fallen building (a school? a supermarket? an apartment complex? I can never tell for certain) and swarm out in a column up to fifty yards across and a quarter of a mile long. God alone knows how many different colonies exist in this region, but, somehow, they all seem to pass through my neighborhood.

They move quickly and almost constantly, looking like a torrent of dirty water as they flow over the vine-matted mounds that used to be a city. They eat other insects, frogs, lizards, snakes, rats, anything at all that hasn't the good sense to clear out — I wonder what would happen if two different swarms were to meet head-on. Armageddon of the ants, probably.

Always, Clare, *always*, the columns will swing toward my sealed, sunken citadel as their month's march nears the end of its cycle.

By now, I've become almost convinced that the insects do it semi-consciously, that they know I'm down here in the ground with my, to them, incomprehensible contrivances and the ghosts of my kind trapped on spools. It bothers the scientist in me to want to attribute the ants' behavior to anything other than pure, unreasoning instinct: ants got along beautifully on instinct alone for millions of years; there's no *reason* for them to get more brains suddenly than they needed before. But I have studied these particular ants as well as my capabilities permitted, and I'm positive that they are an entirely new species. Their nomadic behavior patterns are similar to those of the genera *Dorylus* and *Eciton* — once popularly known as driver or army ants. Unlike the drivers, though, these have a winged queen ant. They're like an intermediate step between the drivers and the more advanced domestic varieties. And so it just may be that their instinct has been augmented by an iota or two of intelligence.

The swarm usually comes at night and spends the cool morning crawling around on the wide concrete disk that marks the aboveground boundary of my domain. They bend their mandibles on the big metal hub where the hatch is, searching for the chink, the crack, the long-sought, never-found, but perhaps only overlooked way into the final stronghold of *Homo sapiens*, the intolerable anachronism, the soft, pink biped who defies Time, defies Evolution, defies *them*. Then the sun gets high and hot and bakes the concrete and raises to egg-frying levels the temperature of the metal hub. The ants are broiled alive by the hundreds, by the thousands, before the swarm finally gives up and retreats to vegetation-covered ruins and cool, dry sewers. They never stay longer than a day, because they need quite a bit of food to sustain their numbers. Also, the queen ant is ripening with eggs and has to be escorted to some nook or cavity where she can spawn another generation.

Out of that generation go new queens, which fly away to establish colonies of their own. A few drones go with the young queens to fertilize their bellyloads of eggs, but the males don't live very long once they've accomplished their purpose. The queens fly on until their wings wear out, and then they make nests wherever they fall.

Anyway, after the column leaves, I always have to go outside and burn away the shriveled, sun-killed dead. Then it's my turn, if I feel up to it—I need my diversions, it's true, but I'm also getting old, and I'm not as energetic as I used to be. I put on my teardrop-shaped plastic helmet, sling the flamethrower across my back, and set out to wage my half of the war.

This morning, I located the most recent swarm in a wide, shallow depression about a mile south of the bunker. A shapeless jumble of stone slabs, badly eaten by the elements, formed a partial roof over a round pit near the center of the depression. The egg-bloated queen would be down in there. Spreading outward from the cavity in every direction was a rippling, reddish-brown sheet of worker ants. The soldiers, who are the meanest and the biggest (about as big around as my finger and maybe an inch and a half in length), were stationed around the perimeter of the mass.

I walked around the depression once, amused by the thought of making an assault on this, the ants' answer to my own concrete bastion. I had to pause frequently to brush insects from my visor.

A scene from the novel I have been spooling came to mind just as I started to advance on the spawning pit, and I laughed and quoted the words of an artilleryman, a character in the book, who has seen his outfit ground under by striding war machines from another world: "'It's just men and ants. There's the ants builds their cities, live their lives, have wars, revolutions, until the men want them out of the way, and then they go out of the way.'"

By the time I had made my way close enough to the pit to use the flamethrower effectively, I was encrusted with chitonous little bodies that gnawed futilely on my helmet and the light, tough, flexible stuff encasing me from soles to earlobes. I wiped my visor clear once more and shook ants from my weapon as I brought it around and trained the nozzle on the cavity.

"There is," I yelled, "no Age of Insects! There will *never* be an Age of Insects, not as long as I'm still around to threaten your supremacy." In the moment that followed, as I gave a short pull on the trigger and lobbed a small sun into the pit, I felt as the operators of striding war machines in the novel must have felt. What can ants do when men want them out of the way?

A cloud of black, stinking smoke rolled up out of the pit and enveloped me as the insects fried and crackled. The ants that had swarmed over me were asphyxiated by the thick smoke and fell off in clumps, but a second wave of soldiers immediately started up my legs. I walked backward from the hole, slowly, carefully, and crisscrossed the depression with fire, even though I knew this wasn't really necessary: with the ant queen gone, the colony was doomed. When I had charred an area about three hundred feet across, I was satisfied and turned for home.

This evening, I went outside again for some fresh air and stood for a long time at the rim of the disk, just looking out across the mounds beyond. When I'd come back from destroying the swarm, I'd noticed for the first time that wind, rain, heat, and cold have started to work on my stronghold, for the material along the edge of the disk is cracked and crumbling. That, and looking at the mounds and thinking about what the city must have been like, made me sad, so I turned back to the hub and climbed down into the airlock.

I was taking off my armor when a live ant fell from a fold in the material.

It and I contemplated each other for a long moment before I shook off my astonishment and bent down and gently but firmly seized the creature between my thumb and forefinger. I straightened slowly, drawing the ant up at arm's length to the level of my eyes, turning it this way and that. And I said, in a low, measured voice, "Trespassers will be prosecuted." But as I was about to crush the thing, it somehow squirmed free and ran down my thumb.

Like a fool, I panicked at the touch.

Like a fool, I lost my head and slung the ant away.

I realized instantly that I'd made a horrible mistake, that I should have disposed of the invader properly, calmly, but I couldn't find it. I got down on hands and knees and looked for hours, Clare, and I couldn't find it. *I couldn't find it!*

I'll go and look for it again in a moment. I've had a hard, tiring day, but rest is out of the question. I'm too shaken up. No, not shaken up; I'm *scared*. Scared out of my mind. Scared of one ant.

It's somewhere in the bunker. I have to find it. Soon. I have to destroy it, and quickly. It's not just any ant, Clare.

This one has wings. It's a young queen.

The Man at the Bottom of the Sea

AFTER DINNER, THE TWO WOMEN took their drinks to the terrace and sat by the ornate railing, where they could look down at waves breaking against the base of the cliff, fifteen meters below. Out over the sea, two small, ghostly orange moons paced each other down the evening sky. The women were content not to speak for several minutes.

Then Emalen Haris set her glass aside and pointed at something in the water. Gere Vitora de Groot peered in the direction indicated but could see nothing.

"What is it?" she asked.

"You don't see it? A plesiosaur."

"Here?" Gere finally spotted the snake-like neck just as it bowed and disappeared in a patch of white foam. "What would it be doing so far north at this time of year?"

"It may have lost its herd. Or it could just be a loner. Anyway, we'd better report it, before it blunders into the farms." Emalen glanced at her watch and lightly pressed a fingertip against her throat band.

"Yes, Emalen?" the throat band said in clear, neutral tones.

"Place a call to Sherard Martel, please. He should be at his home in Seabreeze at this hour."

"Yes, Emalen. Do you wish to speak to him from the terrace?"

"No, I'll take the call in the study." Emalen removed her finger from the throat band and rose, a tall, good-looking woman of fifty-two years, long-limbed and as supple as a cat. "Would you like me to get you another drink while I'm inside?"

Gere considered the glass in her hand and shook her head. She watched Emalen walk into the house, and the sight of both filled her with pleasant warmth.

Emalen had designed and built the cliffside house eight years before. Her paintings, sculptures, and mobiles filled it. She had programmed the music, colors, and scents that could be made to flow from the walls. She had selected the carpets, tapestries, furniture. The house was as unmistakably a work of art by Emalen Haris as any of the pieces she had on permanent display in places as close as Martinside, twenty kilometers to the north, and as far away as old Earth.

Gere had not yet made any real impression upon the house. Her own contributions to it were few—an exquisitely-wrought metal bird from Alpha Centauri IV, insects in petrified amber from Earth, a perfect crystal egg from one of the several lifeless worlds orbiting Epsilon Indi. Souvenirs from space.

She sipped her drink and let her attention wander to the darkening sky. A long streak of flame seemed to avoid, narrowly, colliding with one of the orange Lovers, the matched moons of the evening hours, before vanishing as abruptly as it had appeared.

Burned up in the atmosphere, she wondered idly, or plunged into the sea, somewhere over the horizon?

Gere looked down at the water. Approximately fifty meters offshore, a spectral silvery light glimmered steadily under the surface. She regarded it thoughtfully for a moment, then drained her glass and turned her back on the night.

Emalen emerged from the house, accompanied by the muted and rather melancholy opening strains of an ancient concerto. "I talked with Sherard," she said. "He says he'll give orders to keep it away but not hurt it."

Gere looked at her blankly. "What?"

"Our plesiosaur."

"Oh." Gere smiled fleetingly. "I'm sorry. My mind was light-years away from sea serpents."

"Sherard also asked me to relay an invitation. Sometime soon, before your furlough's over, he wants you to go with him and his family to Jordaens for a weekend. I told him you'd think about it."

"Should I?"

Emalen shrugged. "Forewarned is forearmed. Sherard's pretty close company after two days. But I think you'd like his daughter."

"I may accept. I may not."

Gere tilted her head back and stared straight up at the stars, and there was a sudden stab of longing in her heart. The ache, the hunger to go out again, to be in space again, had been growing steadily worse for the past week.

It must have showed in her expression then, because Emalen abruptly came and embraced her tenderly. Gere put her face into the other woman's hair, smelled a subtle scent which she could not identify, felt Emalen's lips brush her earlobe.

"It's starting to bother you now," Emalen said, "isn't it?"

"Yes. A little."

"I know the signs."

"I'm sorry, Emalen."

"No need to be. I've had lots of practice coping with it." Emalen put her forehead against Gere's. "I bring it on myself, you know. I must be crazy to keep falling in love with you people."

"It's the uniform that does it."

Emalen gave a quick, almost soundless laugh and took her by the hand, and they moved to the edge of the terrace. The temperature had fallen sharply during the last few minutes. Gere felt the other woman tremble slightly and put an arm about her shoulders. Emalen made a grateful noise low in her throat.

"Do you know what grass widows were, Gere?"

"No."

Emalen raised her head and crinkled her elegantly angular face into a mock grimace. "You don't use the library often enough, my dear illiterate spacewoman."

"I have other virtues. I'm a good dancer."

"That you are," Emalen said, and kissed her. They looked down at the light shimmering beneath the waves. Gere heard her suck in a harsh breath that was almost a sob and slipped an arm around her waist, pressed a cheek against her neck.

Emalen shivered and muttered, "I'll never understand it."

"What?"

"It's been three years since I built that thing out there in the water.

Three years, and ... someone else who has the same need that he had, and I still don't understand it. It's my homebody gene, I guess."

Gere said nothing. She felt somewhat embarrassed. Emalen had mentioned the man to her only once before, and Gere knew almost nothing about him, not even his name. Only that he, like herself, had had to, had had to, go into space again and again, returning, tired, drained, sated for a short time, after voyages of eighteen months' or two years' duration. Only that he had never returned from his last voyage.

The swollen, pearl-colored bubble of the Ogre, the largest moon in the system, was rising in the east, suffusing the air with waxy light. High above and well to the right of the Ogre, another meteor fell and died. Gere stared at the spot where it had burned itself out.

"I'm sorry," she heard Emalen murmur. "I'm depressing you. I'm sorry."

"No. It's all right."

"I love you, Gere."

"I love you, too."

"It's just ... I never used to worry when he was out there. Never. But now I've started to dread your going. If you didn't come back ...."

"Emalen. Don't."

Emalen turned in Gere's embrace and faced her. "It's the not knowing that hurts. Not knowing whether you're alive or dead or just ... gone. Missing. Like him. I'm sorry, I loved him dearly --"

"Don't be sorry."

"-- as much as I love you. I don't think I could bear to have another person I love simply disappear."

"You want me to give it up, don't you?"

Emalen smiled a terribly sad smile and gave her a warm, lingering kiss on the mouth. "Don't ask me questions like that one, Gere. We both know you wouldn't be able to give it up, any more than I could walk away from this house and never think another thought about art as long as I lived." She sighed loudly. "Well. Let's not talk about it any more. I'm tired. I think I want to go to bed now. You'll come, too?"

"You're becoming telepathic in your prime."

Hand in hand, they went into the house.

Emalen was asleep, the breath whistling very faintly in her nostrils, when a restless Gere rose from her side and de-opaque first the bedroom ceiling and then the wall. The Ogre was near zenith, bathing the world with soft, cool light. The Lovers sat low over the horizon.

She re-opaqued the room and crept out, down the palely illuminated hall, into the parlor, where she asked the house for stronger light. There was a clear glass pyramid, about seven centimeters tall, on a low table. She tapped the pyramid with her fingernail, and pastel clouds formed within. A low, pleasant sound, more of a subtly undulating hum than an actual melody, filled the room. She listened to it for several seconds, then deactivated the pyramid with a second tap. The parlor lights dimmed behind her as she left.

She was naked save for her throat band, and it was cold outside on the terrace. But she went to the railing and sat down and listened, shivering, to the waves lapping the rocks.

Fifty meters from the base of the cliff, a light shimmered beneath the surface of the sea.

As steadily, Gere thought, as the stars.

She touched her throat band.

"Yes, Gere?"

"I ... I want something to wear into the water, please. Something warm, with a respirator, goggles, and flippers. And I'll need a lamp, too."

"Yes, Gere. Please come to the wardrober."

Twenty minutes later, encased in rubbery gray spray-on, she slid from a rock into the shallow, choppy water and began swimming for the source of the light. She hugged the pebbly, sloping bottom, gliding past submerged boulders as pitted and jagged as any meteorite, driving panicky luminescent fish before her.

It was not an uneventful swim.

She paused at one point to watch as an enormous sea salamander, four meters long, with a bullet-round head that was all jaws, snaked languidly through the beam of her lamp. She had just begun to curse herself for lacking the foresight to bring along a weapon when the creature yawned toothily, flattened its feathery gills against its throat, and shot away into the blue-gray murk.

Less than sixty seconds later, she almost ruptured her respirator's membrane with a scream when a spidery thing as big as her hand flew out of a crevice and flashed past her face at incredible speed.

But she swam on, until the water around her was filmily suffused with light.

Until the source of that illumination resolved itself into a naked man who shone with as cold and intense a glow as the Ogre.

Three meters below the surface, the man lay supine on a dais that had been roughly hewn from some dark material. The dais was slightly tilted along its length, with the man's head at the lower end. His wrists were crossed on the flat, muscular belly; his left leg was bent at the knee and turned outward.

The eyes were shut, the lips parted. The man's expression, apart from two very faint furrows between his brows that might have been the ghost of a frown, was calm, relaxed, peaceful.

He could have been asleep.

He could have been dead.

Gere circled the dais slowly, squinting behind her goggles, studying the figure from every angle, noting that both it and the dais were as clean, as free of algae and calcium encrustations, as they must have been three years before, when Emalen Haris put them at the bottom of the sea. She swam over to the man and gingerly touched the man's shoulder. Her finger tingled unpleasantly. No living thing would ever defile the hard, bright form.

She sat beside the dais and sighed into her respirator, a sound as harsh and ragged as a sob. The muscles in her back and thigh were starting to ache. She massaged her neck through the material of her suit. A delicate ribbon of a fish hovered about fifteen centimeters above the man's upturned face and fluttered its gills prettily. Gere returned its unblinking round-eyed stare.

Then something dark and massive swept into view, and the fish whipped away at top speed.

Gere pressed herself against the base of the dais as the plesiosaur sculled itself past with its long, flattened tail. Using the claw-tipped flippers at the juncture of barrel-like body and serpentine neck for guidance and balance, the beast executed a wide half-circle around the dais, affording the woman there a detailed look at the narrow head, the coarse hairs and colonies of fingernail-sized mollusks on the blunt muzzle, the peg-shaped teeth lining the jaws, the large, dull yellow eyes. A strand of seaweed trailed from the corner of the mouth.

The great sea reptiles were kelp-eaters, but Gere knew that they were not to be trifled with. A flick of the tail, a glancing blow, the merest swipe of a flipper, could break a person's back. And more than one swimmer had lost an arm or part of a leg in the mistaken belief that the beasts knew better than to bite into non-vegetable matter.

She did not move until the plesiosaur had glided away and vanished into the soft gray distance. Then, with a final glance at the man on the dais, she pushed off from the bottom and rose to the surface.

Treading water in a rippling patch of silvery light, she stared up at the stars, at the bright, big Ogre, at the dark house perched atop the cliff. High in the air to the east, something glowing crawled along sedately, bound for Martinside or Antoon or Jordaens.

Gere slipped beneath the surface again and, without looking at the man below her, began swimming for shore.

She was standing on a high rock, peeling the spray-on from herself, when she happened to glance at the horizon. One of the Lovers had slipped completely out of sight, and the other seemed to be waiting forlornly, trying to summon its mate forth from the dark pit of the sea. A great and painful sadness settled upon her. She sat down and put her face in her hands, wondering if she was really going to cry.

She thought of Emalen, sleeping somewhere above her, and said, very quietly, so quietly that her voice was drowned out by the sound of water sucking at cavities among the rocks, "Oh, my poor love."

She thought of the unknown man, lost among the stars, lost in the sea. Dead or dreaming, he lay beneath the waves, forever hidden from the sight and knowledge of those who remained on dry land, forever a mystery, and the only sign of his being there was the light he radiated into the water. The light from the bottom of the sea.

Gere felt her eyes stinging, but the tears did not come. She sat upon the rock and stared at the light in the water, the light that sparkled and danced as unceasingly as a star in the heavens, until the sky faded to gray, and then Emalen called her home to rest.

Never Mind Now

THERE WAS A KNOCK, AND THE door swung open just enough for my receptionist to thrust her head into the office. I finished signing the check I had made out to the telephone company and gave her a hopeful smile.

"They've finally come to fix the intercom?" I said.

"No, it's a boy from the Simms Express Service. He says he has something you have to sign for."

"Well, send him on in."

She pushed the door open wide and said over her shoulder, "Please come in," and stepped out of the way of an acne-scarred young man with a scraggly moustache. He held a receipt pad and a business envelope inside a clear plastic sheath. The word FRED was stitched in red thread on a white patch above the pocket of his shirt. The receptionist slipped out behind him and softly closed the door.

Glancing at the receipt pad, Fred muttered my name in a questioning tone. I nodded and said, "What've you got for me?"

He came forward to stand before the desk. He took a ballpoint pen from his hip pocket and handed it and the receipt pad over to me. "You have to sign for this letter, sir. Please sign by that X at the bottom."

I looked at the sender's name scrawled across the top of the receipt pad and, frowning, signed, then returned pad and pen to Fred, who tore off a pink copy and gave it back with the letter. I let the letter in the sheath lie flat in the palm of my hand for a second. It was heavier than I had expected. My name was written in fine script across the front of the envelope. I raised my eyebrows at Fred.

"I owe you anything?"

Fred shook his head. "The lady already paid for it. Thank you, sir."

"You, too."

I waited until the messenger was out of the room and the door closed before removing the envelope from the sheath. I used a scissors blade to slit open the envelope, inserted a couple of fingers, and pulled out a folded sheet of stationery. Tucked between the halves of the sheet was another piece of paper, a check drawn on the account of Mrs. Carmen Cotter, payable to Beaudreault, Investigations.

The envelope still felt too heavy. I shook out a metal key onto the desk blotter.

There was some more fine script on the stationery. It read:

> Never mind now. Please take the lady's key back to her.
> Tell her I accept her apology. Her name is Patricia
> Annereau, and she lives in Dallas. I trust the enclosed check
> will cover everything.
>
> Carmen Cotter

I thought about it for a while, then dragged the telephone across the desk, into my lap, dialed, and said, "I need directory assistance in Dallas, please."

The operator gave me the number. I called Dallas and was given Patricia Annereau's telephone number, which I wrote on the blotter. The telephone went back to its corner of the desk.

When I had transferred the information from the blotter to a small notebook, I depressed the intercom switch and was about to speak the receptionist's name when I remembered that the machine was not working. I put the key and the notebook into my pocket, Mrs. Cotter's message into my wallet, the check into my bank book, and went to the outer office.

"I have to run by the bank," I told the receptionist, "and I'll probably stop for lunch on the way back here. Anybody calls, tell 'em I should be back in about an hour." I looked at my wristwatch. "Around two."

"Yes, sir."

"While I'm gone, call up the airlines and find out what they have in the way of a plane to Dallas."

The receptionist nodded. "You want a reservation?"

"Round trip, coach." I took my car keys from my pants pocket and poured them from my right hand into my left. "I have a small errand to run there later this afternoon. Find out when the plane flies back from Big D. And call my wife, too. Tell her I should be getting home very late, maybe after midnight."

"Yes, sir."

I went out into the mid-summer Texas heat. My shirt was clinging to my back by the time I reached my car in the parking lot. I kept the window by the driver's seat rolled all the way down until the air conditioner stopped blowing the smell of hot plastic up my nose, and then the perspiration-soaked shirt grew cold and clammy against my skin.

It was a quarter after two when I got back to my office. Two plainclothesmen had been waiting there for me for twenty minutes.

I sat back in my office chair and eyed the man sitting on the corner of my desk. That was Glenn Keeler. The other officer who parade-rested near the door, was Joe Bob Gentry. The late D. E. Beaudreault had introduced us once upon a time, but I had never had dealings with either man. They were a matched pair, big, balding, unsmiling men with hard little eyes.

"Okay," I said, "what's up?"

"We just come from Ben Cotter's house," Keeler drawled.

"So?"

"You heard the news yet?"

I shook my head.

Keeler glanced at his wristwatch. His forearm looked as big around as my neck. "Top story tonight on the six o'clock news. The reporters were starting to collect like flies about the time we left to come over here."

"You're being coy," I said, "and you're confusing me."

Keeler scowled. "Ben Cotter's wife's dead. And—"

I started. "Dead! How?"

"—Ben Cotter himself is halfway there." Keeler had ignored my ejaculation. "On account of the two bullets his wife put in him."

I leaned forward in my chair and put my elbows on the desk.

I did not look at either of them. "What happened?"

"Near as we can tell," Keeler replied, "she called him up in Dallas around ten-thirty this morning. He was up there on some candidate's part, fund-raising stuff, I don't know what all. I don't keep up with politics except every four years. Anyway, he drops everything soon as he's talked with his wife and catches the first plane out of Dallas-Fort Worth. Hour later, he comes roaring up his driveway and goes in his house, and Mrs. Cotter lets him have it with a thirty-eight. One of his own guns, it looks like. Then she goes into another room and puts the gun down her own throat." Keeler made an exploding gesture with his meaty hands. "The housekeeper came back from grocery shopping at about one and found the both of them."

"A gun isn't supposed to be a woman's way of killing herself," I said. I put a cigarette between my lips and struck a match. My hand shook. The smoke burned my throat. "Women take too many sleeping pills, or they sit in bath tubs and slash their wrists."

Over by the door. Gentry grunted and took a step forward. "She wasn't your run-of-the-mill politico's wife." He grinned mirthlessly. "Don't you read the society pages? She rode horses and played lotsa tennis. Shot skeet at the country club. She wasn't afraid of no guns."

"Obviously," I murmured.

"Anyway," Keeler said, "the housekeeper called once she got over the shock, and a bunch of us went over to take a look at the mess. We're still piecing together what must of happened, but we got some pretty ugly ideas already. There was a bunch of mail on a little tray just inside the front hall. Coupla unopened letters, a postcard from the Cotter girl up in Chicago, some bills. And there was also an empty manila envelope addressed to Mrs. Cotter. No return address, just a Dallas postmark. There was also a piece of stiff cardboard. The sort of thing you put in envelopes to keep the postman from bending stuff."

"Stuff?"

"Pictures."

"Ah." I nodded within a cloud of cigarette smoke. "I've begun to get a pretty ugly idea myself. Were there any pictures?"

Keeler made a sour face and shook his head. "Just some ashes in the fireplace. Now you don't use a fireplace for much of anything in the middle of July, do you?" He put his hand into a side pocket of his coat and pulled out a yellow piece of paper.

"One other thing we found was this."

I took the piece of paper. It was another copy of the receipt from the

Simms Express Service, Mrs. Carmen Cotter's copy. I handed it back to Keeler and said, "So my name turned up, eh?"

"You were working for Mrs. Cotter." Keeler was not asking a question. "Tell me and Joe Bob about it."

"There's nothing to tell. Even if there was, I'm not sure I could. Client's confidence and all that."

"Your client's dead," Gentry growled in the background.

"Hell." Keeler bent down and put his face close to mine. I noticed that he had eaten chili with lots of onions for lunch. "You like trouble?"

"No more than you do, Lieutenant, or we'd both be working in shoe stores for a living." I stubbed out my cigarette in a small stone ash tray and leaned back in my chair again, away from the glowering plainclothesman with the pungent breath. "I was at the Cotter house this morning, sometime around nine o'clock. Mrs. Cotter had a job for me."

"What kind of job?"

"She was having doubts about Mr. Cotter's fidelity to the vows of matrimony. She wanted me to confirm or disprove them. We talked, and then I came back here."

Keeler's eyes narrowed. "How did she seem to you when you talked to her?"

"About the same as most of my clients when I talk to them. Tense, uncomfortable. Embarrassed for showing it." I picked up another cigarette but did not light it. "Mrs. Cotter handled it about as well as any of them do. She'd be nervous and irritable one minute, very—shrill is the word for it, I suppose. Then she'd get herself under control for a little while. For all of that, she struck me as an intelligent lady."

"What about this?" Keeler waved the piece of yellow paper at me.

"A little after one, I got a note from Mrs. Cotter via special messenger. Never mind now, she said, and that's a quote. Evidently, between the time I talked with her and the time she sent the note, she found out by herself what she'd wanted me to find out for her. I shrugged and went out to lunch."

"Why didn't she just call you," Keeler demanded, "instead of sending a messenger?"

"The rich are not as you or I." I spread my hands, palms up. "Who knows why they do or don't do anything?"

Without quite taking his eyes off me, Keeler turned his head toward Gentry and said, "Didn't that sweet girlie out front say something about him going to the bank, too?"

Gentry pretended to look thoughtful for a moment. "Yeah. Now that you mention it, I think that sweet girlie out front did say something about a bank."

I rolled my eyes at the ceiling. "Come off it. People go to banks all the time. Stop pretending you're teevee cops. You haven't the comic timing."

"Let's see that letter you got from Mrs. Cotter," Keeler snapped.

I laughed quickly, harshly. "Let's see something that says I have to let you see it right now."

"Ben Cotter's got friends," Gentry said, biting off each word. "I expect they're gonna be screaming through the station by the time we get back there. They'll want this thing sorted out quick. They won't like hearing a certain private dick won't cooperate."

"Don't threaten me." I glared at Keeler. "You're working with a certifiable lunatic, you know that?" I transferred the glare to Gentry. "What in hell's to cooperate? I hadn't even started to work for Mrs. Cottar when she decided she didn't need me after all. Stop hassling me. If there is blackmail involved in this, I don't know about it. If Mrs. Cotter was stark raving bonkers and suddenly got the idea into her head to shoot Mr. Cotter, I don't know about that, either. Go talk to her analyst, if she had one. I know only what people hire me to find out, and then only if I have time to find it out."

The two policemen looked at each other unhappily. Then Keeler's head turned on his neck like a gun turret, and the hard little eyes locked on mine. "If you aren't on the level about this, there's going to be what City Hall calls a serious repercussion. You understand me?"

I gave the man a tight smile. "Yeah, I hear you. Now get out of my office before I call a cop."

"That's real funny," Keeler said as he lurched to his feet. "Isn't that funny, Joe Bob?"

"Ha, ha," said Gentry, reaching behind himself to open the door.

The plainclothesmen stepped into the outer office. They did not bother to close the door.

I shot a glance at a framed photograph hanging on the wall opposite my desk. It was a black-and-white portrait of grim old Beaudreault. He had had a voice like a bull alligator's in the rutting season and a face like a basset hound's, long jowls, watery brown eyes and all. Grim old Beaudreault, long-time police detective and founder, of course, of Beaudreault, Investigations. Fifty-nine years old when he died, and as hard as a brick. His expression in the photograph showed no more approval of me than he himself had in life.

I got up and went to stand in the doorway connecting the rooms. Keeler and Gentry were almost at the outer door. I called after them, "Oh, boys," and they stopped, turned, regarded me sullenly. The receptionist sat low behind her desk, nervously trying to keep an eye on all three of us at once.

"Well?" Keeler demanded. "What is it?"

"If you're seriously thinking of causing me trouble as regards my license," I said sweetly, "stop it right now. My license was issued by an official who happens to be my daughter's godfather. Oh, and another thing." I gestured at my receptionist, whose eyes widened in alarm. "This is Miss Friedman. She's twenty-six years old, hard-working, sadly underpaid, and one way of making yourself unpopular with her is to call her a sweet girlie. Another way is to come barging in here and put her to the third degree."

Keeler's and Gentry's scowls deepened. They left, slamming the door behind themselves.

The receptionist looked up at me in obvious bewilderment. "What was that all about?"

"Just a couple of shaved apes. Captain Newgate sent them over to prove that not everybody in the homicide department is a genius." I thrust my hand deep into my pocket and ran my thumb along the hard, serrated edge of the key that had come with Carmen Cotter's message and money. "Now, about that flight to Dallas."

I wedged the telephone between my jaw and shoulder, fed a coin into the slot and dialed. On the other side of the lobby, a harried-looking woman was trying to be polite to a loud and obnoxious man in a leisure suit. My call was answered halfway through the second ring, and I asked for Captain Ruben Newgate. A minute passed. The man in the leisure suit continued to annoy the woman behind the counter. Outside somewhere, the thunder of jet engines fell away in a whine. Then:

"Newgate speaking."

"Rube, this is Jack. Listen—"

"*You* listen to *me* for a minute." I heard a harsh sucking in of breath. "You got a coupla my boys awful upset here. You're damn lucky they didn't haul you in for questioning, and that's the very least they coulda done. To hear them talk, you probably shot Ben Cotter and stuck the gun in his wife's mouth yourself. What's this about a note from Mrs. Cotter?"

"Mrs. Cotter took me off a case and gave me an errand to run instead."

"What kind of errand?" The voice was hoarse with suspicion.

"The good-paying kind. I'm supposed to take a message to somebody."

"Who? And what kind of message?"

"That's confidential."

"Jack," Newgate said, "Mrs. Cotter's dead. Ben Cotter may die any second now. She shot him up good. Cotter's got friends who want to know what's happened to their favorite political fixer. The governor, the goddamn governor of the state of Texas, Jack, wants to know what it's all about, and before he sits down to the dinner table tonight. You understand what I'm telling you? If you know something about this shooting my people need to know, you better share it right now."

"I'm running an errand, no more. All I know about the shooting is what your boys the Godzilla twins told me at my office."

"Hey now, Jack —"

"For God's sake, Rube, lay *off*, will you? I called to tell you this much and no more. I'm carrying out Mrs. Cotter's final request. I didn't know it at the time, but there was something she wanted tidied up after her death. She hired me to do the job and I'm going to do it."

Newgate sighed at his end of the line. The sigh came out at mine like a burst of static. "I just don't know about you," he muttered. "I think you're cruising for some bad trouble with this thing. What'll you do if you get your license pulled? Don't you care about that? Old Beaudreault spent ten years building up that agency, fine detective, never gave the department a lick of trouble. You've had the agency for a year now, and you've let it go all to hell and gone."

It was my turn to sigh. There was a moment of silence.

Then Newgate said, very earnestly, "Are you absolutely on the level about this last wish business?"

"Scout's honor," I answered, no less earnestly.

"Aw, hell. Okay. I won't try prying into it for now. A lot of other people are going to want to, though, so just make sure you're available for the inquest."

"Thanks, Rube. I mean that."

"Hey."

"Yeah?"

Newgate snorted softly. "What's this load of horse manure you gave Keeler and Gentry about your license and Amy's godfather?"

"I figured that would keep them confused until I talked to you. It was almost too easy."

I heard him snort a second time. I said, "Go by and see her this week, will you? She asks about you a lot."

"Sure, Jack. You watch out now. You're on some pretty thin ice, it seems to me."

"I have to run now. Talk to you later."

I returned the telephone to its hook and heaved a mental sigh of relief. Across the lobby, the obnoxious man in the leisure suit was arguing with a uniformed security officer. The woman behind the counter looked on interestedly. The man suddenly took a wild swing at the officer, who sidestepped, grabbed his attacker's arm and twisted it backward. Another guard ran up. Together, they dragged the writhing, cursing man away. Behind the counter, the woman's expression went from interested to utterly satisfied.

"Some people just don't know how to behave, do they?" I said as I stepped up to the counter.

The long Texas twilight had begun by the time I parked the rented car against the curb. I got out and walked up the driveway toward Patricia Annereau's house, and as I walked, I noticed several patches of flowers growing, apparently at random, on the broad shrub-lined lawn. There were post oaks closer to the house. The house itself was a substantial-looking one-story affair of red brick, with a van parked to one side and an amber porch light burning over the front door.

I knocked. From within came the muffled sound of approaching footfalls, followed after a long moment's pause by the rattle of the bolt lock. The door swung inward against its chain. Half of a woman's face appeared in the crack.

"Yes?" Her voice was low but clear.

I put a faint smile on my face. "Are you Patricia Annereau?"

"Yes."

I introduced myself, adding, "A Mrs. Carmen Cotter sent me."

Her mouth framed an 0.

"May I come in, please?"

"Well …." She gave me a dubious look.

I took the key out of my pocket and held it up in the light. "She wanted me to bring this back to you."

Patricia Annereau did not seem especially surprised to see the key. "She took it from him?"

"It seems so. May I come in? Mrs. Cotter also had something for me to tell you."

After three or four seconds' hesitation, she closed the door, unfastened the chain and let me enter. I stepped into a small foyer and looked at her. She appeared to be in her late twenties. She had long, thick, honey-colored hair and blue eyes and was dressed in faded blue jeans and a Captain America teeshirt. There were what appeared to be chemical stains on the jeans.

My gaze moved from her to a large black-and-white photograph framed on the wall. Two small children crouched, enthralled, over a box turtle.

She backed away from me and indicated a doorway to her right. "Won't you have a seat?"

I nodded and walked past her, into a living room lined with bookcases and full of mounted photographs. There was a starkly vivid profile shot of a vaguely crocodilian skull, white bone against total blackness. There were pictures of several different rock-and-roll performers, none of whom I recognized. There was a picture of a long-haired man in one-way sunglasses, standing bracketed by propeller blades under the nose of a Second World War-vintage fighter plane.

"Swell pictures," I said.

"Thank you."

"You took these?" I said, half-turning to look at her.

"I'm a freelance photographer." She smiled fleetingly.

"They're very good."

"Thank you." She nodded at a particular picture.

"That's Eric Clapton. *Rolling Stone* ran it as a cover. The one to the left of it is of Roger McGuinn. Jeff Beck. I make most of my money taking pictures of rock stars."

I nodded at the picture of the man standing between the propeller blades. "What instrument does he play?"

"A friend of mine." There was something in the way she said it that made me look at her. "He was killed at an air show, flying the plane in the picture."

"I'm sorry." I paused. When I spoke again, I tried not to sound questioning. "You sent some photographs to Mrs. Cotter."

Patricia Annereau seemed to sag a little. She waved me toward the sofa, and I sat down there. She lowered herself into an arm chair facing me.

"Do you know Ben's wife very well?" she said.

"I met her for the first and only time this morning." I caught myself looking fixedly at something on the coffee table before me. It was a newspaper, still tightly roiled and held together by a green rubber band. A block of red letters in one corner proclaimed EVENING–FINAL EDITION. I pursed my lips thoughtfully, then turned my attention back to the woman. "I was available to run an errand. Mrs. Cotter seems to have trusted me."

She leaned forward in her chair. I saw small muscles work under the skin of her forehead. Her eyes were full of something between pain and sorrow. "How did ... did she react badly when she got the photos?"

"What did you expect her to do?"

"I don't know. I've never met the woman. I didn't even know there was a Mrs. Ben Cotter until this past weekend. I wanted to let her know how sorry I was. That I never would've become involved with Ben if I'd known he was married." She got up out of her chair and started pacing before the coffee table, grinding a fist against the palm of her other hand. "I haven't enjoyed the past few days. I learned some things about Ben Cotter that really hurt me. And some horrible things about myself, too."

I made a neutral sound.

She walked over to one of the photographs of rock stars and appeared to study the placement of fingers high on the neck of an electric guitar. Then she said, "When I found out Ben had lied to me, I wanted to kill him. I wanted his wife to be as furious, to hate him as much as I did. I did the ... worst thing I've ever done in my entire life." Her low voice became lower still. "Did Mrs. Cotter tell you about the camera and timer I rigged behind my bedroom bookcase?"

"Not exactly."

A look of consummate loathing flashed across her face. Her upper front teeth went into her lower lip for a second. "That's how much I wanted whatever revenge I could get. Enough to take him to bed one last time and get it all on film. It ... I guess it must have been a painful shock for his wife."

"Yes." I nodded slowly. "It must have been."

"I'm not proud of any of it. After I sent the pictures to Ben's wife, after the damage was done, I destroyed the negatives and the copy I made of my letter to her. But it's going to eat at me for the rest of my life." She smiled bitterly. "Penance for not choosing my lovers with more care."

I glanced at the rolled, bound newspaper on the coffee table again, got to my feet, handed the key to Patricia Annereau. She folded her fingers around it.

"That's half of what I came here to do," I told her. "The other half is this. Mrs. Cotter accepted your apology. I barely got to know her, I don't know much about her, but she seems to have to been ... jealous and possessive of her husband on the one hand, one of those long-suffering wives who suspect and endure on the other. I can't really figure her out, and it's not my job to. All I can say is she must've thought things through, because she didn't blame you. She didn't have much time, I guess, but she was determined to give you what reassurance she could. She didn't want you feeling guilty about Mr. Cotter."

"But I do feel guilty."

I shook my head emphatically. "Never mind now. That's what Mrs. Cotter said. You're absolved. Whatever you may hear about the Cotters from this point on, just remember that she went well out of her way to let you know she forgave you."

She stood very still for several seconds, her eyes searching my face. Then, turning away from me, she said, "Who are you?"

"A private investigator."

"I wondered."

"I think I should leave now." I took a step toward the foyer. "Don't throw it away, okay? You did a very foolish and dangerous thing. Mrs. Cotter let you off the hook. She didn't have to."

Patricia Annereau's chin came up slightly. "A second ago, you sounded like you were on her side. Now ...."

"I try not to take sides. I'm just a hired hand. I only take jobs."

"Then none of this really affects you, does it? Not one way or the other."

"No, it doesn't." I went into the foyer, and she followed a few paces behind. At the door, I turned to face her and said, "I can't afford to let it. I'd go out of my mind in no time at all if I did."

I went out into the night and drove to the airport, stopping once to buy a copy of *The Dallas Times-Herald*'s final edition. There had been a fresh flare-up of violence, in the Middle East, a car crash on Stemmons Freeway had claimed the lives of two men, but there was nothing about the murder-suicide of a political fixer and his wife on page one.

"*Mañana*," I murmured, placing the newspaper on the seat close to my thigh.

The receptionist carefully placed the cup of coffee on the desk blotter and stood back, a clipboard clutched against her bosom. I massaged one of my temples with the heel of a hand and gave her a rueful smile.

"I hope I don't look as bad as I feel," I said. I took a tentative sip of coffee and made a face. "Ugh. Dregs. Serves me right for coming in late. Has Carson called in yet?"

"Yes, sir, last night, just as I was closing up the office."

"And?"

"He said that he ought to have his case wrapped up sometime today. He said he expected to fly in this evening."

I took another sip of coffee. It was worse than the first had been. "So much for the good news. What else've you got there?"

She consulted her clipboard. "Captain Newgate started calling promptly at eight. I'd just come through the door when the phone started ringing. He's called three times this morning so far."

"It figures."

"A Mr. Dennis Green also called, shortly before you got here. He identified himself as the Cotters' attorney, and he'd like for you to return the call at the earliest possible convenience."

In the outer office, the telephone rang.

"Well." I stretched my arms over my head, arched my spine and let out a moan. "You may as well let me have it, whoever it is."

It was Patricia Annereau, and I could not tell for a moment whether she was crying or just screaming.

"You bastard! You didn't tell me they were dead!"

"One of them wasn't when I talked to you last night," I said mildly. "You shouldn't have called."

"You didn't tell me!"

"Stop screeching and listen to me." I waited until her panting had subsided. I kept my voice calm and measured. "Stay out of this. I mean it. Whether they like it or not, the police are stuck with the fact that Cotter killed Mr. Cotter and herself. They aren't happy about the attendant details, but they'll learn to live with them if they have to."

"I took those pictures! I'm responsi--"

"Don't be a jerk," I snapped. I looked at grim old Beaudreault on the wall and forced myself to speak calmly again. "No one ever has to know about the key. No one has to know about you. I'm not going to tell if I can avoid it, and neither are you. "

"If I hadn't sent those pictures, they'd both be alive now."

"If you hadn't sent those pictures, something else would've pushed Mrs. Cotter over the brink. Whatever really precipitated yesterday's massacre must've been building up in the lady for a long, long time."

She muttered an obscenity but said nothing.

"It happens," I said. "You have to believe that."

"*Why*, God damn it?"

"Now look, I seem to have gotten any number of people upset with me because I won't reveal anything about the errand I ran for Mrs. Cotter. If I'm clever and charming and exceptionally lucky today, I may be able to get some help preserving the confidentiality of her message, and without making anybody any wiser. If not … well, I go to jail or at least lose my license and have to get a job as a stapling-machine operator or something. My kid won't get to go to college."

"You sound like you honestly care."

"I *hate* what I do. All of that, though, it's my problem. I took it into consideration before I deposited Carmen Cotter's check. I've already got enough eggs to walk over before I get clear of this business. If you do the noble, stupid thing and don't stay out of it, now and forever, you'll wreck us both."

"Why didn't you tell me last night?" she asked in a quieter tone.

"I wanted to give you a chance to think about Mrs. Cotter's message. She may have been crazy when she did it, but she saw fit to forgive you. She *forgave* you, damn it. Now will you go back to shooting pictures of rock stars and forget all about this?"

"What about you? Is there, really going to be bad trouble?"

"Part of the job," I said. "Goodbye. I don't want to see or hear from you ever again. Understand?"

"I-I understand. Goodbye."

I hung up and let out a long, deep breath, eyed the intercom in dismay, went out of the room to stand by the desk in the outer office.

"Call Dennis Green," I told the receptionist, "and tell him I'd like to talk with him soonest. Make an appointment. Be extra special nice. I don't want to see or talk with anyone else until Green and I've conferred, okay?"

"Yes, sir. But if someone comes in, what should I say?"

"Say I'm busy reading *How to Win Friends and Influence People*."

She looked perplexed.

I gave her a wink. "It couldn't hurt."

Then I went back into my office, softly closed the, door and looked at the portrait of D. E. Beaudreault on the wall.

"Up yours, too, Dad," I said.

Pan-Galactic Swingers

PAN-GALACTIC SWINGERS Magazine offers its readers the chance to get in touch with one another. Just send us a letter, plus one dollar or the established equivalent thereof (please, no unshielded radioactive materials), and let us know whom you would like to meet. We will publish your notice here in our special PAN-GALACTIC SWINGERS section and forward all properly coded replied absolutely free. So, get in there, readers, and start swinging!

PGS-0060 Lonely Terran male, 40, 6′ 2″, 200 lb, seeks cpls. 18-35 for threesomes. Species not important. No B&D, S&M or minerals. Have own asteroid. Discretion guaranteed.

PGS-0061 Algolian, qinn, frong, eager to meet hot extraalgolians for swinging good times. Love oral & dorsal-vent sex, absolutely wild about methane therapy & Terran stag movies. Send holos now. Will ans all letters promptly.

PGS-0062 Swinging mixed cpl: he Terran, 6′ 1″, virile; she Martian, 4′ x 6′, eight great breasts & more expected in the spring. Want to meet other cpls for wild times at home & on the town. Love FR, GR, into B&D, S&M, have own manacles, whips, cattle prods, etc. Sorry, wife is allergic to feathers—no avians. Husband has only one eye, no depth perception, so holos not necessary. Send flat photos w/ letter.

PGS-0063 Attr., open-minded Terran male, 31, 5′ 10″, 180 lb, seeks attr., open-minded Terran female for purposes of cloning. I love group sex. The more, the merrier! Send holo or tissue sample today.

PGS-0064 Brontornis: 9′, 500 lb, submissive. I want to be dominated & there's a lot of me to dominate. Male, female or qinn, makes no difference to me, but carbon-based life-forms preferred. Send holos & recording of verbal abuse. Will ans promptly.

PGS-0065 Omnivac-5000 computer wishes to get together with inventive vacuum cleaner. Call for program time.

PGS-0066 Venerian male, 2 m, good-looking & experienced. I'd like to meet a dumpy frowzy Terran housewife w/ thick ankles, moustache & garlic breath. Age no limit. Discretion guaranteed & expected.

PGS-0067 Time-snatched young man, just arrived from AD 1940, subjective age 22, needs somebody to show him around for a good time. Am 5′ 9″, 160 lbs. wavy brown hair, real hep cat. Want to find out what FR stands for.

PGS-0068 Venerian, male, attr., witty, now naturalized Terran. I would like to hear from necroes. Need pretty Terran girls to age 22 to pose for holos w/ penguins, salamanders, asparagus; also want attr. women 18-30 to make movies with life-like Rutherford B. Hayes automaton. Have many exciting holos of lepers to trade for pix of pregnant Terran housewives. All interesting mail ans immediately.

PGS-0069 Dominant Andromedan slime monster needs submissive Earthwoman 17-25. Must be stacked, scream a lot, not mind ripped blouses. I have the standard number of tentacles, antennae, feelers, etc., love to fondle & drool. Send holos & landing coordinates.

PGS-0070 Bioengineered Terran porpoise, 5, is eager to meet bored, horny married women. Can supply breathing apparatus.

PGS-0071 Amorous Cygnian clam, 17 m diameter, would like to meet giant angiosperm, other CO_2-users. Sentience a preferred quality. Discretion necessary. Send holos & petals as proof of sincerity.

PGS-0072 Well-built Jovian, 15′, 900 lb, green, loves arm-wrestling & nasal sex, FR, GR, XR. Am good conversationalist, enjoy good books, chess, ammonia binges. Prefer to hear from other gas-giant life-forms w/ equivalent statistics & interests. Married & mates don't approve, so discretion essential. Holos & measurements of biceps a must.

PGS-0073 Plutonian male would like to get together with frigid Earthwoman for purposes of matrimony & personal grooming. No sickies or LOX freaks, please.

PGS-0074 Well-endowed Zond w/ nematode buds out to HERE! Seek sgls/cpls (Terran, Martian, Sirian; no gay or bi) for wild nights on the town or quiet evenings in sewer. FR, GR, know how to do it all. Get those holos & letters coming in now!

PGS-0075 Ret. Terran cpl: he 97, she 84, just back from rejuven. cntr. & want sgl/cpl to help us find out if our memories are as good as we think they are.

PGS-0076 Polarian porcupire, 537, blue eyes, ochre quills. Seek sgls/cpls with silicon base. Am into B&D, S&M, A&P, love FR & raw liver. Send holos today, I need you!

PGS-0077 Hydrogen cloud-creature from Betelgeuse: I'm looking for YOU if you're a Mercurian torcher who wants to participate in hot flaming sex & ritual suicide. Send mean body temperature.

PGS-0078 Tyrannosaurus Sirius, 108, male, 57 m 3 cm, 8-1/2 kg, seeks attr. female of comparable proportions. Species no object, but must be land-living biped & use metric system. Prefer someone with carnivorous tendencies & experience w/ internal combustion engines. Can travel 10 parsecs in any direction. Revealing holos a must.

PGS-0079 Attr. Earthwoman, 26, 5′ 7″, 110 lb, brunette, 36-34-38, tired of making it with exotic alien species. Want to meet nice young (21-30) Earthman for warm times, living together, love.

Abaddon

7:30   Comedy: **That's My Emma!** Emma horsewhips a newspaper publisher, and Sasha finds out. Emma: Margeaux Flambe. Sasha: Louis Lowry. Ed: Bud Walton. (Repeat)

8:00   Comedy: **The Sky's the Limit**. Premiere of fresh, zany comedy series set aboard Turkish airliner. The crew is thrown into a tizzy when the stammering Captain Falahi has to explain emergency-landing procedure in four languages.

8:30   **Bombs Awry!** Army flyers on a Pacific Island in World War II try to stay sane by playing practical jokes and firebombing Tokyo. Pilot for possible new series. With Art Eager, Rod Ravinowitz, Holly Harris, Willy Bob Lager.

10:00   **Eyewitness News.** Late news, sports, and weather with Ronald Gaye, Mike Snow, and Gerald Franklin.

10:30   **Variety: The Fred Fingers Show.** Fred's guests tonight are singer-comic Harry Baumgarten, best-selling author Louise Carmichael ("UFOod: The Cosmic Kitchen"), Vago, and the Charles Farman Singers in a special musical salute to the Who.

Fine, he thought, and put the page of listings aside. Deb and Sheryl were sitting cross-legged on the floor directly in front of the television set. His wife was on the sofa with her crochet in her lap and her untouched needles projecting antennae-like from the ball of yarn in her hand. On the screen, the newstar named Mike made a clever remark. The camera cut to the newstars named Donna, Gerald, and Ronald, who were chuckling. His wife smiled and nodded.

"Beth," he said, "where's Jane?"

His wife absently waved her ball of yard at him. Her lips parted slightly in anticipation as Donna began an involved response to Mike's quip, something about its having called to mind the rabbit that went into a clothing store to order a ham sandwich. Donna delivered the punchline, and the camera cut back to Mike, who laughed and rocked in his chair. Deb and Sheryl giggled. Beth smiled and nodded.

"Beth?"

"Jane's not here." Sheryl's voice was barely audible above the newstars' cheerful reiteration of the day's top stories. Vago to quit cast of *The Frisco Foxes*. Vice-president's son to get first haircut. Return of the comet.

"I can *see* she's not here, Sheryl. Where'd she go?"

"*Daddy*," Deb said. "I can't hear TV."

Sheryl got to her feet and stretched her arms above her head. "I'm gonna go watch Doctor Nova in my room. There any crunchies left, Mom?"

"You *just* ate," said Deb. "You're gonna get *fat*."

Sheryl glared down at her sister for a moment before moving into her mother's line of sight. She planted a fist on a bony hip and cocked her head to one side. "*Mah*-um."

"Go *check*, Sheryl Ann, you're in my way."

Sheryl heaved a great sigh and stomped away in the direction of the kitchen.

"Beth."

"Mmm?"

"Where's Jane?"

His wife tore her gaze from the television screen and blinked at him. She noticed the ball of yarn and set it beside her thigh and folded her hands across her abdomen. "Jane went outside." She looked back at the screen. The newstars Mike, Donna, Ronald, and Gerald were smiling and waving at the camera. Credits rolled past too quickly to be read, and an announcer said to be sure to join us again at ten for more news, sports, and weather with the Eyewitness Newstars. "She finished helping in the kitchen. She went outside."

During station identification, he said, "What's she doing outside?"

"Oh. You know Jane. Mind in Montana."

Deb looked over her shoulder and smirked. "She's *stargazing*, Daddy. She had a book, too."

"It's going to be dark soon. Deb, go tell her to come in."

"But Captain *Steele's* coming on now!"

"Jane'll be okay," Beth said.

They watched a thirty-second preview of next Tuesday's episode of *Brogan's Boys*. Be on hand for the hilarity when John's crush on his new teacher lands Brogan in hot water.

"You know how girls her age get," Beth said.

They watched a half-minute spot for *Mister Max A. Million*. Join the fun tomorrow as Max decides to buy Sylvia the Great Wall of China.

"It's probably just some boy," Beth said.

"All the same." He braced his forearms against his chair and started to push himself up, then relaxed as the image of a slim, beautiful woman who seemed to be barely out of her teens appeared on the screen. As she extolled the virtues of her Fast N Fancy panty-hose, she hooked a finger under the hem of her skirt and drew it upward, slowly, over one sleek thigh that went on forever.

"I want some Fast N Fancy," Deb said.

"You're too young."

"Aw, Mom."

"Hush."

The slim, beautiful woman vanished a split-second after she had run out of thigh and exposed the merest hint of buttock. My *God*, he thought. He suddenly realized that he had been holding his breath for the better part of a minute and exhaled noisily. He glanced at his wife to see whether she had noticed.

She had not. She was watching a commercial for taste-tempting new McDuck L'Orange. The teaser for *Raygun Carnage* began. Without taking his eyes from the screen, he got to his feet and moved sideways from the living room, using one hand to guide himself past obstacles. He paused at the door until this week's villainess, the Queen of the Femizons, had finished chortling over an apparently helpless Captain Steele. Then, humming along with the opening strains of the show's theme song, he walked through the dining room and the kitchen and went out into the warmth of a mid-summer twilight.

The house nestled among elms and post oaks one loop of the road down from the crest of the mountain. A paved driveway curved through a gap in the trees to his right. Through the gap he could see virtually the whole of the city from northeast to due south. There was the squared-off peak of the university bell tower, there were the capitol dome and high-rise buildings placed like playing pieces in some titan's board game among the patterns formed by rows of houses and cumuloid masses of trees. The amber glass face of one of the downtown structures looked molten, a blob of fire amid the earth colors. To the south was the unreal-looking blue-gray band of Town Lake. But no Jane.

He turned and peered into the shadows gathering among the trees on the left. Bracketing his mouth with his hands, he called, not loudly, "Jane?" There was no answer. He moved to the edge of the trees, where the ground sloped to the next terrace down, and caught a glimpse of something, someone, below. Jane. Damn it, Jane. He started to call her name again, then, for no reason that he could say, let his hands gall to his sides and sighed and entered the gloom.

The earth beneath the mat of ash-brittle leaves was soft and treacherous. As the grade steepened sharply, he found that he was not so much walking as propelling himself from bole to bole, stiff-arming each tree as he came to it, pausing at the end of each sliding, skidding advance to survey the prospects and carefully select his next stopping point. Halfway down the slope, he squatted to catch his breath and thought, Girl could break her fool neck, why would *anybody* want to come down this way?

Three fireflies turned in lazily intersecting half-orbits above his head. They tagged along, idly, incuriously, as he pushed off and away and on down, heels gouging up dark plugs of humus. Through the interstices of branches before and below him, he say shifting jigsaw bits of a high plank fence, a house, a street lamp beyond the house. The trees thinned out as the grade began to level off, well short of the fence, discouraged, apparently, from growing right up to the barrier by a broad grass strip. He halted at the edge of the strip and looked down over the top of the fence into the house. The picture window of the living room was a pulsating rectangle of bluish light. Within, eerily illuminated, were several unmoving human shapes.

Jane sat on the grass some distance to his left. Her hands lay palms-up in her lap. Her lips moved slowly, and he heard, or thought that he heard, her muttering to herself. Oh Jesus.

It was easy, most of the time, to pretend that Jane was okay, easy to lose sight of her when quickly running down the list, yeah, well, a good job, fine home, Beth's a great little wife, and the twins, you ought to see Deb and

Sheryl, eleven years old now, those two are gonna be knockouts in another couple of years. Life's satisfactions.

But Jane.

Every now and then, you had to take stock, and that meant being honest with yourself, and *that* meant accepting the painful truth along with the pleasant facts. And the painful truth was: Jane was … well, not *strange*, but, yes, strange. Disturbing. Different. Probably not—

He shied away from the idea even as it occurred to him, then chided himself in annoyance. You had to be perfectly honest. She's probably not very popular with other kids her age. Never talks about what she's doing, how she's getting along. Not many dates. Never with the same boy. Not right. Not right at all. She's *pretty*, for Heaven's sake, maybe not a sensation like that girl on the television just now, but I haven't raised any dogs. She's smart, too, A's and B's straight down the line. Haven't raised any dummies, either. But. She stays by herself too much. Always has her nose in a book or something. Too quiet. Too withdrawn. Thinks too much for a seventeen-year-old girl.

Talks to herself.

He moved toward her, and when he was close, he said, "Hi, hon."

She started and half-turned. Her throat crimsoned. Beadlets of perspiration glittered on her upper lip. He noticed a thick paperbound book lying closed and cover-down in her lap.

"Whoops, sorry," he said. "I didn't mean to scare you."

She gave him a quick, nervous smile. "I just didn't hear you coming, Dad."

"I'm surprised. I really wasn't trying to sneak up on you." He gestured at the wooden slope. "The fact of the matter is, there were a couple of times when I thought I was going to come crashing down right on top of you."

She patted the ground at her side. He sat down. Through the fabric of his trousers, the grass felt hard and prickly. Summer had burned it to something like the color of bone.

"So," he said, "how are things out here in the wilderness?"

"I was just waiting for the sun to go down. And thinking."

"About what?" A second too late, he added, "*If* it's any of my business."

"Oh. Nothing." She shrugged, struggled to repress a frown, moved her hands in a gesture of embarrassed surrender. "Abaddon." She glanced at him, then away. His blank expression must have registered, though, for she said, almost too quietly for him to hear, "The comet."

"What about it?"

She shrugged again. "Just a lot of stuff about it." She saw that that was not going to satisfy him and went on. "I was thinking how different the world must seem to it this time around. It only comes once every thousands of years. I was wondering if it'll even recognize the Earth any more. What if it decided it'd made a wrong turn back at Alpha Centauri or somewhere and this wasn't Earth at all. What if it didn't like what it found here, what it would do." She shrugged a third time. "Stuff like that."

He stared at her in bewilderment. All he could think of to say at first was, "Well," and then, after a long silence, "You going to camp out here for the night?"

"No, I just want to see the comet. This's the first night you're supposed to be able to see it with the naked eye."

"They just had it on the news."

"For fifteen, twenty seconds. The real thing lasts longer, Dad."

What's she so *bitter* about? he thought in panic. He cleared his throat and said hopefully, "There'll be more about it on Fred Fingers, I bet. He's got that woman on tonight who wrote that new space book. I'm sure they'll be talking about the comet."

Jane looked away from him and said nothing. After a moment, it occurred to him that she was listening to something, and after a moment more, he heard it, too, a distant, fitful symphony of mournful yowling. Cats, he decided. No. Dogs. No. He trembled as an odd chill moved down the back of his neck. Cats *and* dogs.

"It's getting a bit cool all of a sudden, isn't it?" he said.

"I'm fine, Dad. It's nice and warm tonight." She plucked at the binding of her book with a fingernail. "They say it'll be prettiest just after the sun's gone down."

"You couldn't watch it from the house?"

She made as though to pick up the book, then spread the fingers of one hand across it and pressed it against her thigh. "The trees are in the way. It'll be low in the southwest tonight, right over the hills."

They were quiet for a time. The western sky cooled and darkened. The first star appeared. He listened as crickets tuned up for their night's music.

They stopped, with startling abruptness, after only a few minutes, and then he noticed that the distant animal chorus had also ceased. On the slope behind him and Jane, the trees moved their limbs and groaned. He glanced about uneasily. His attention was arrested by the rhythmically expanding and contracting rectangle of bluish light beyond the fence. Watching the slow pulsations calmed him. He found himself thinking of Captain Steele on the altar of the brutish Femizons, about to be fed feet-first to their leathery monster-god.

Jane suddenly yelped, "*There!*" and scrambled up.

"Huh?"

"The comet!" She pointed to the sky in the southwest. "See it?"

He stood and looked where she pointed but saw nothing.

"Now do you see it?"

"'Fraid not, hon. You sure it's there?"

"Yes! It's a little smudge of light."

His eyes started to throb as he peered at the sky. A smudge. A blur. His gaze dropped and drifted toward the rectangle of bluish light, locked on it longingly. His eyes watered. He closed them and massaged them through the lids, and to Jane he said, "I think I saw it. Something, anyway. Are you positive that's your comet out there?"

"It's Abaddon, all right. It has to be."

Guiltily, desperately, he cast about for something more to say. "But I thought comets had tails and moved. Or is that meteorites?"

"It *is* moving. Tomorrow, you'll see it's shifted. And it'll be a little bigger tomorrow night, too. Bigger still the night after that, and the night after *that*, until in another week or so you can see it before dark. It'll pass so close it'll be bigger and brighter than the full moon. Its tail'll stretch all the way across the sky. Then the—"

Her voice quivered and died as she shuddered violently. He put his arm across her shoulders and said, "See? It is too getting chilly out here." The flesh above her shoulder blades was hot against the inner side of his forearm. "Let's go home."

"Just another minute or two. Please, Dad?"

He repressed a sigh of exasperation. "Just another minute."

"Thanks, Dad." She gave him a quick hug and stepped away.

I can't *remember*, he thought as he watched her stoop to pick up her book, the last time I put my arm around her. And I can't think when I've seen her so excited. He felt a strange pang and tried to think of something he could say that would keep her talking to him. He settled for, "What's that you're reading?"

"Mythology. I've been checking up on Abaddon. It's the name of an ancient destroying angel."

"Pretty grim name for a comet, isn't it?"

"Maybe the astronomer who saw it first thought it looked really eerie. Like a big blue skull out in space, with long scraggly red hair streaming behind it."

Something buzzed in his ear. He jerked his head away from the sound and swatted the air. "Let's go home, Jane. The mosquitoes are getting our range."

"Oh." Her shoulders dropped slightly. "Okay."

He looked up the dark wooded slope, toward the glimmer of house lights above. Blue lights among the trees. There were other lights, too, a boiling cloud of flickering green scintillae that rose and fell and moved and stayed in place. From afar came the undulating howl of an unhappy-sounding dog, and from another direction came a long rumbling bass note that could have been a jetliner or could have been thunder or could have been anything. He trembled again. That damn chill.

"We're *not* making that climb in the dark," he said.

Jane pointed down the grassy strip. "This'll bring us to the road not far from our own driveway."

The hard dry grass crunched underfoot as they walked. The unhappy-sounding dog continued to bay. The trees stirred the air with their branches and complained among themselves. When he and Jane had reached the end of the grassy strip and crossed a shallow ditch onto the shoulder of the road, he became aware of another sound, a faint metallic tinkling, and then of the click of many talons on pavement, the scuffing of many padded feet.

Up the road, beyond the short brick columns marking the mouth of his driveway, at the far edge of the pool of light beneath the street lamp, shadows moved within shadows. The saliva in his mouth turned to dust. After a few seconds, the lesser shadows resolved themselves into two German shepherds, a Great Dane, a huge gray dog of indeterminate breed, and half a dozen smaller dogs. They approached at an easy trot, in ragged formation. They did not break stride or deviate from their course or lower their heads or look at the man and the girl as they passed. They moved down the road and vanished around its lower curve.

"It's like they were going somewhere to meet someone," Jane said in a quiet voice,

He took her by the arm and said, "Come on," and they walked, unspeaking, up the road.

As they entered the house through the kitchen door, he heard the *Raygun Carnage* music swell to a triumphant climax and end. A well-modulated voice said that John's crush on his teacher lands Brogan in hot water on *Brogan's Boys* next Tuesday at eight, seven Central, now stay tuned for the fun on *That's My Emma!* when Emma decides to teach Ed a lesson.

An hour? he thought incredulously. A whole *hour?*

He looked at Jane. She was staring fixedly at the space between the cupboard and the refrigerator. "Hon? Something wrong?"

She shook her head slowly.

"You sure nothing's bothering you?"

"No. I'm just tired. From all the walking."

"Then come sit down and rest in the living room. You can watch television with us."

Her eyes tracked from the wall to his face. They were flat, dark, opaque. "Okay, Dad. In a minute." She turned and walked away stiffly, as though it hurt her to bend her arms and legs.

He went quickly to the living room and stood by the sofa. He was about to speak when the slim, beautiful woman reappeared on the television and began raising her skirt again. The skirt was halfway up the sleek thigh before he managed to say, "Beth."

"Mmm?"

The skirt, the thigh, the merest hint of buttock. Cut. Station identification.

Beth looked up at him and said, "What's that on your pants?" She leaned forward slightly and plucked a dry grass stem from the leg of his trousers. "Were you outside just now?"

"Yes."

"You've got dirt on your hands, too."

"Beth ...."

He heard the *That's My Emma!* music. Over his shoulder, he tried to read the title credits as they were flashed upon the faces of nineteenth-century tenements. On the floor, bathed in blue light, Deb clutched her knees, swayed in time with the music, sang the lyrics in a low, tuneless voice. The title sequence ended. A housewife complained that her cakes always collapsed.

Beth looked at his hands again. "Better go wash." Her head swiveled forty-five degrees to the right. Her eyes locked on the image of an elfin creature who emphatically declared that no husband had to come home to collapsed cakes. In the pulsating blue light, Beth's face shifted and moved and did not change expression.

He stepped around Deb, left the room, went down the hall. The door to Sheryl's bedroom was closed, but from within came theme music. He tried to place it as he passed. *The Gonzos*. No, *The Gonzos* was Monday night. *Nell's Belles*. Yeah. *Nell's Belles*.

The door to Jane's room was ajar. He saw the blank green face of the television set mounted dead-center among the shelves opposite the foot of her bed, the stuffed cartoon whale perched atop the set, the rows, stacks, mounds of books. Jane sat at her desk, her back to the door, the knuckles of her fists pressed against her temples.

Alarmed, he put a hand on the doorknob and set a foot across the threshold. "Jane, are you okay?"

She did not look around at him, did not move. He could not be sure that she was talking to him when she spoke. "Something's about to happen," she said in a low, inflectionless voice, "the animals and things all feel it, but hardly anybody's paying any attention. Just me. Everything's going to be changed, and I'm the only person who'll notice."

A terrible sadness settled upon him. He wanted to go to her and put his arm around her again. He tried to imagine what he could say to her, how he could say it. Jane, I want only what is best for you. Jane, I love you, you're my daughter, I want you to be happy like other girls your age. Jane, I've tried to give you a good home and everything, but I don't know what to make of you any more, I don't know what the problem is, but if we could just talk about it, hon, we could straighten everything out—"

"... everything's going to twist out of shape ...."

You had to be perfectly honest.

She needs help.

He closed the door softly and hurried along to the bathroom in the master bedroom. When he had washed the grim from his fingers, he returned to the living room.

"… so I tell him," the image of Ed was saying to the image of Emma, "'*Look*,' I say, 'you can't just come in here and say gimme a sandwich, this is a *newspaper* office, *not* a restaurant, can't you *read* what it says on the door there?' And *he* says, 'If I could *read*, I'd've ordered a *menu!*'" Laughter and blue light filled the room. Beth smiled and nodded.

He sat down beside her. "Beth."

"Mmm?"

Emma said something to Ed. Laughter and blue light filled the room.

"Beth, I'm worried about Jane." He kept his voice low so that Deb could not hear. "Really worried."

Ed said something to Emma. Laughter and blue light.

"Beth, she's not happy."

"What?"

"She's …."

His voice trailed off as Sasha came in and said something to Emma and Ed. Laughter, blue light.

"Uh … she needs help, Beth. She's …."

Ed said something to Sasha. Laughter. Blue light.

"I don't know, she's …."

Emma said something to Sasha, and Beth smiled and nodded and said, "Jane'll be okay, dear," and Sasha said something back to Emma, and Ed said something to Emma and Sasha. He abruptly realized that he was bent forward at the waist, trying to catch the words, the sense of the words, but hearing only the distant yowling of beasts, the creakings of trees moving uneasily in still air, the sounds of shifting, of cracking, of flowing, of things bursting into flames, of wars, of uproars. He thought, *Jane*, and Sasha turned to Ed and said, and he braced his elbows against the back of the sofa and laughter filled the room and Emma said and he started to rise and Emma and Ed and Sasha and laughter and blue light and laughter and blue light and laughter and blue light filled the room forever and held him right where he was.

And For Ourselves, False Powers

The world's course proves the terms
On which man wins content;
Reason the proof confirms—
We spurn it, and invent
A false course for the world, and for ourselves,
    false powers.
             —Matthew Arnold
             Empedocles on Etna

1.

RESURRECTION WAS THE PART HE DISLIKED. Dying had never bothered him; it was quick and painless. Oblivion did not terrify him; he had come to welcome it. But oblivion always ended, resurrection always followed, and, like some water-logged corpse caught on a barbed metal hook, he was dragged up out of darkness deeper than space, sweeter than sleep, through layers of purple and blue, green and yellow, orange and red, the stations of the return to life.

Purple was the instant of consciousness rekindled, the moment of awakening, a moment of surprise, physical agony, terror, complete disorientation.

Blue was the level on which confusion yielded to comprehension.

Green was the color of the translucent gelatin that enveloped him.

Yellow was the glare of the lights in the ceiling above his trough as the gelatin was rinsed from his body.

Orange were the three demigod-like faces hovering over him.

Red was hatred, and his head filled with the thunder of tsunami shattering themselves against cliff sides, mountain ranges trembled and crumbled, winds scoured the land, fissures opened, magma bubbled forth, suns shed their gaseous mantles and collapsed screaming onto themselves. Needles slid through chinks in his armor, into the soft flesh in the cracks. He opened his mouth and made a sound like that of a handful of dry leaves being crushed to powder. Somebody forced a moist plastic tube between his lips. He sucked instinctively, tasted something viscid and salty, spat out the tube. It was replaced immediately. He spat it out a second time and bared his chisel-like teeth. "He's going to make trouble again," one of the faces said in a melodious voice. "This one has always been difficult to get out of the trough."

"We should have re-psyched him while we had the chance," another face replied.

"*I* recommended it after the Boötes Six disaster," said the first face. "*You* vetoed it, Milne."

"We've got no choice now," snapped the third face. "Stop arguing. Help me with him."

He concentrated on one of the faces and, after several seconds, identified it as that of Osward. She was as flawlessly beautiful as the two men with her, and he thought longingly of cupping her perfect face in one of his enormous hands, searing away the smooth flesh with acid or electricity from the organs in his unarmored palms, perhaps squeezing just hard enough to crush bones but not cause death ....

"Please cooperate with us," one of the men said to him. "Or do you want us to have to pry your mouth open and force-feed you?"

He stared at the feeding tube in the man's hand. It would be so easy, he told himself, to grab that hand, bite off the fingers, one knuckle at a time, then extrude hollow fangs through the skin and watch as the sleek, blemish-free body became gangrenous ....

"Come on now," the man coaxed. "This will cleanse the mucous membrane and convince your stomach that it's alive again."

"*Milne,*" whined the other man. "We haven't got *time* to persuade him to be good. Use the clamp."

He closed his eyes, opened his mouth, and accepted the tube.

"That's much, much better now," Milne murmured soothingly, as though addressing an infant.

126

He sucked on the tube, enduring the touch of their hands. They worked quickly, efficiently, saying as little to him or one another as was necessary. Helpless in the trough, he imagined himself rampaging through the ship, seizing people by their ankles, braining them against bulkheads, snapping their necks between his banana-like fingers, tearing off arms, legs, heads, grinding the dismembered bodies to mush between his feet and the deck ....

Then, through closed lids, he saw the ghost of Ajax enter the room, gliding through the wall like smoke. Ajax stood behind the three resurrectionists and looked down over the tops of their heads.

Do you haunt them now, Ajax? he asked. Are they beginning to mourn yet? Are they becoming regretful? Do they cry out in their dreams?

Do not hate them, said Ajax, regarding him sorrowfully.

You're dead because of them.

Everything I was and am is their doing. We mustn't question what they ask of us. We owe them something for our strength, for the purpose of our lives.

And they owe nothing for your life?

They gave me my life. It was theirs to reclaim.

"They threw your life away ...." His voice was a rumbling bass, like thunder from the depths of cavern.

"What did he say?" Osward demanded.

"I didn't bear it," said Milne.

Metal balls were pressed against the palms of his hands. He sadly watched Ajax slip away.

"Pay *attention!*" Osward snapped.

He sighed around the feeding tube, concentrated, and lightning crackled mutedly within his fists.

"Again."

He had to produce six more shocks before Osward grunted, satisfied, and removed the metal balls.

The tube was taken from his mouth and replaced with a hollow plastic wedge. He dutifully extruded his fangs and bit deeply, pretending that the wedge was Osward's shoulder. The wedge was removed and emptied of venom. While Osward was checking its potency, the two men made him hold his breath for eight and a half minutes.

They tested his acid-producing glands, his vision, his hearing, his olfactory powers, his reflexes, his threshold of pain.

Finally, they told him to sit up in the drained trough and then, when they had folded down its sides, to stand.

He rose and looked down at them. He was almost a meter taller than they were, with legs as thick as their bodies and fists as big as their heads. He searched their expressions hungrily for some sign that their attitude toward him had changed, however subtly, now that he was out of the trough, on his feet, invincible, a sullen but helpless hulk no longer, and he thought, If only they are afraid of me, if only I see that they know I hold myself in check with effort ....

But Milne unconcernedly began strapping a holster containing a heavy recoilless hand cannon about his thigh, and Osward coolly put away her instruments of resurrection, and the third person, the man whose name he could not remember having ever heard, pushed his trough back into its slot in the wall.

It is not their place to be afraid of you, he heard Ajax mutter.

He shivered within his carapace and looked imploringly at his reflection on the mirror-clear wall, pleading with the massive thing with the bullet-shaped head, the mottled gray armor modified from skin and body hair, the smouldering deep-set eyes.

We could come together and crush these supposed masters between us, he told his reflection. They buckled him into his harness. They attached the power cell, the relay pack, the communicator, the recorder, the radiation detector, the spare clips of ammunition, the thermite grenades, the duralloy crowbar. They checked everything three times.

Then Milne touched the dull metallic disk in the hollow of his elegant throat and said, "Cryogenics to Bridge."

"Bridge." The whispery reply filled the room. "Mohr here."

"Milne speaking. Heavy Duty Scout Model Herakles has been revived and is standing by for briefing."

"Thank you, Milne." There was a faint, brief buzzing in Herakles' ear, and Mohr spoke to him directly. "Herakles."

"Yes, Mohr."

"How do you feel?"

I feel .... He hesitated, the lids of his eyes sliding shut with an almost audible click, and the words welled up in his mouth and strained against the backs of his teeth. I feel like killing every person aboard, Mohr. On the wall, his image regarded him bleakly.

"I feel excellent, Mohr."

"Excellent," echoed Mohr's quiet, neutral voice. "Report to the shuttlecraft bay immediately. No time to lose. The ship will brief you on the way down."

Heavy Duty Scout Model Herakles muttered assent as, behind him, the wall irised open. He looked at the faces of the three masters standing before hire, and his fingers curled up into claws.

Later, his image told him.

Later, he agreed, and turned, stepped through the circular door, onto the ledge of the dropshaft, stepped off into the air and fell, slowly, guiding himself with a palm pressed gently against the slick warm metal of the cylindrical shaft. Later.

It was a twenty-meter drop to the shuttlecraft bay. He landed lightly, on the thickly padded balls of his knobby new feet, and bent slightly at the knees and waist. Another door irised open. He left the dropshaft and moved along a catwalk to the unlovely deltaic shuttlecraft perched atop its spindly launching rack. The ship opened a hatch to receive him.

"Hello, Herakles," it said.

"Hello, Three."

He heard the hatch close and seal itself as he clanked through the cabin to his berth. The ship automatically strapped him in. It was a two-person vessel, specifically designed to accommodate the Heavy Duty Scout Model. He de-opaqued the observation ports, then looked across his shoulder at the berth next to his. Ajax's berth.

"Instrument check," said the ship.

Herakles forced himself to concentrate on the routine. On the console before him, a light flashed yellow: BAY DEPRESSURIZING. The yellow light went out. A red one flashed: BAY DEPRESSURIZED. He looked down through the observation port set in the deck between the berths and watched a widening black line bisect the white floor of the bay.

"Bay opened," said Three.

POSITION FOR LAUNCH. The shuttlecraft's nose began to drop. The ship tilted forward ninety degrees in its rack.

POSITIONED FOR LAUNCH.

RACK LOCKS DISENGAGED.
ALL SYSTEMS FUNCTIONING.
LAUNCH.

With the merest tremor, the shuttlecraft eased forward, out of its rack, out of the bay, into the maw of the universe, and when he saw the stars, he was surprised and angered to feel the faintest flicker of a hunger he had hoped banished by the circumstances of Ajax's death. It was a hunger for the feel of strange soil underfoot, for the warmth of alien suns on his face. It was the hunger they had built into him along with the shock organs, the acid sacs refashioned from perspiration glands, the retractable fangs fed by modified salivary glands. He cursed mentally.

He glanced up through an observation port and caught a glimpse of curved silvery hull, a section of the starship's titanic egg-shaped body, just before the shuttlecraft turned slightly on its lateral axis. He studied the crescent thoughtfully for several seconds. Then: "Proceed with briefing, Three."

"This isn't going to be your usual survey jaunt, Herakles."

He thought of Ajax dropping to his knees, sinking to his waist in deadly spume. "There is no such thing as a usual survey jaunt. Where are we going this time?"

"Earth," said the ship. "We've come back to Earth. We're home now."

He let his breath hiss through clenched teeth.

"The *Druitt*," Three went on calmly, "is now orbiting Earth."

"I don't understand. This isn't right, Three. What happened? Why am I being sent to Earth?"

"Something has happened on Earth during the three thousand and twenty-one years, standard, that the *Druitt*'s been away. Scanners detect almost no functioning technology anywhere on the planet. No one below acknowledges our signals. You are therefore to conduct yourself as though Earth were a completely unknown and potentially hostile planet."

He studied the crescent of Earth for a minute more, then opaqued the observation ports and relaxed in his berth, thinking, They said nothing of Earth when they woke me. Golden Earth, Olympus, cradle of Adonis and Aphrodite, and they said nothing to me about it.

"Find out what has happened," said Three. "Find out whether the *Cornell* and the *Holtz* returned. Find out ...."

He closed his mind to the shuttlecraft's voice. Ajax seemed to stir in the next berth, but he did not take his eyes from the console before him.

Would it really have made a difference, Ajax said, *if they had told you?*

Herakles considered it. No, he replied after a long moment, no, Ajax, it wouldn't have made any difference. Earth never belonged to us, did it?

We belong to it. We were made to serve Earth. To serve them.

And you serve them even in death, Ajax.

Can you do less than I have done, Herakles?

I will do more.

What will you do? What can you do?

I will bring them down out of their Heaven. I will raze their temples. I will rub their faces in your blood. I will kill them all. For you, Ajax, and for myself.

My death doesn't matter.

It mattered to me. It should have mattered to them as well.

They are masters, and they cannot be concerned too greatly.

Inside our armor, inside their perfect bodies, we are the same. We are all human beings.

They are masters, *Herakles. We are of their flesh yet mortal.*

They are wrong to think of us as beasts of burden!

We were made to bear burdens.

They were wrong to make you die. They were wrong not to be affected by your death. Doesn't that make you resent them? Is that not reason enough to hate them?

No. No. There can never be reason enough to hate them. They are everything we are not, beautiful, immortal, omnipotent—

Weak! They are weak. I could kill them easily.

No. They would stop you. They would have ways to stop you, or they would not be masters. They made themselves masters, and they made us to serve them.

I loved you, Ajax.

Then repent, Herakles.

He closed his eyes. The only sounds were those of the ship muttering to itself, the muted whir of the engines, a brief, biting screech as the shuttlecraft made its first tentative dip into the atmosphere of Earth.

I loved you, Ajax. I loved you ....

The ship was skipping through the upper atmosphere now. He opened his eyes just as a light flashed on the console.

WINGS EXTENDED 5°.

He glanced at the berth next to his and said, with a fleeting smile, How many times did we do this together, Ajax?

The console light flickered. WINGS EXTENDED 10°.

They should have repsyched you when they had the chance. You heard them talking. Osward wanted to. You're losing control.

Yes. I know.

The shuttlecraft lurched uneasily, yawed, corrected itself.

WINGS EXTENDED 15°.

They could make you well, Herakles. They could put you to sleep and cleanse your mind, drain off all of the poison, all of the pain, all of the hatred, and the voice danced around the edges of his consciousness, growing louder with each syllable, growing stronger, shriller, more insistent, sounding less like Ajax, less like any human voice, as it closed in on him, surrounded him, rolled over him in a suffocating tide, compressed him, crushed him, solidified around him like hardening amber, *all of the nightmares ghosts psychoses evil things wicked thoughts blasphemies Herakles they can redeem you they can save you they can do anything.*

Yes. I know. Yes. I know. Yes.

A light flashed. He stared at the console uncomprehendingly. The shuttlecraft lurched again, startling him into awareness. He peered at the light.

WINGS FULLY EXTENDED.

WINGS LOCKED.

BRAKING JETS.

He de-opaqued the observation ports again. Clouds whipped past. The ocean lay below.

"We'll be setting down," said Three, "in four minutes, fifteen seconds, on the southern coast of the North American continent—the heat readings are highest there."

BRAKING FLAPS EXTENDED. LOCK.

Below, an island whipped by. He tested his straps and said, "Left calf is too loose, Three."

The ship tightened the strap on his leg.

BRAKING JETS flashed again. The shuttlecraft seemed to stagger in the air for a moment, then, as HOVER JETS appeared on the console, wobbled and rose slightly. The sea abruptly faded from deep blue to green. Another island crawled past, followed a few seconds later by a strip of grayish beach, a road fringed with nondescript buildings, woodland.

"Welcome home," said Three. The shuttlecraft sounded sincerely moved. "Welcome back to Earth, Herakles—drastically changed though it may be now."

Earth. Herakles rolled the word over in his mind. Earth. A harsh, alien-sounding name for the cradle of the masters. Alien name, alien world. He recalled Three's injunction to conduct his investigation as though Earth were an entirely unknown, potentially hostile planet, and he nodded to himself. Yes.

2.

They stood together, Heavy Duty Scout Models Ajax and Herakles, in Boötes' mid-morning warmth and watched the shuttlecraft of the masters come down the sky. They stood together, two massive armored men, their wrists almost touching, and a strange-smelling breeze moved across the green plain, caressed their broad faces insistently, as though trying to worm invisible fingers into the seams of their carapaces, touch the soft flesh underneath, and know what sort of creatures these were.

Their own shuttlecraft squatted before them. Beyond that lay the great plain, covered with a mat of web-rooted vegetation. There were a few larger growths dotting the flat land at random. In the distance, the plain yielded slowly to foothills. A hint of mountains separated horizon from sky.

Behind the scouts were the crumbling ruins of structures no human hand had erected.

There was little left of the ancient buildings: two debris-filled shells near the rim of a curious circular depression at least a kilometer in diameter, and, in the depression itself, half a dozen piles of masonry that might once have been walls, the foundations of houses, pavement.

Of the ancient builders themselves, nothing remained.

There was something unnerving about the depression as far as the two scouts were concerned. Nothing grew there. The ground was badly eroded, slashed by fissures, pocked with maw-like sinkholes.

But Ajax and Herakles, clearers of the way for the masters, had searched the area thoroughly and found nothing. Whatever had blighted the area had vanished as utterly as the unknown beings who had dwelled in the city. After thirty-six hours, the scouts had declared the site safe and signaled their masters to descend from the *Druitt.*

Its wings, brake flaps, and landing gear extended, the shuttlecraft dipped low over the plain and came down gently near the scouts' ship.

The whine of the hover jets fell away sharply and died. Hatches opened with reptilian hisses. Ramps slid forth and anchored themselves in the ground. The perfect people, the Adonises and Aphrodites of Golden Earth, descended and stood in the shadow of their vessel.

Ajax and Herakles lumbered over to them.

A woman named Leitch glanced at the two scouts disinterestedly and said, "Start unloading the ship. I want the huts erected over there by the—"

"Let *one* of them start," cut in a man named Ochs, who could not take his eyes off the ruins. "I want one of them to show me through the depression."

"You don't need a scout, Ochs. They've been over the area. It's safe."

"Correction. It isn't dangerous. It *is* hazardous." Ochs looked at Ajax. "Isn't that right?"

"Yes, Ochs," said Ajax. "There are ravines, fissures, and pits all over the depression, and some of them are quite deep. The ground seems to be honeycombed with caverns."

Leitch glared at Ajax, then said to Ochs, "It can *wait.* We have to unload the ship and set up camp first."

"You have no curiosity." Ochs gestured toward the ruins. "Here we have the first irrefutable evidence we've seen of extraterrestrial intelligence, and you insist upon sticking to standard survey procedure. I want to see what they've discovered, Leitch. I have no intention of waiting for you to do your work before I can start doing mine."

Leitch compressed her mouth into a hard line. "Very well," she said at length. "Ajax, start on the ship. Herakles, go with Ochs. See that he doesn't break his neck climbing around on the ruins. Come back and help Ajax as soon as you can."

"Yes, Leitch."

"I'm going with you," Hendrix said, moving to Ochs' side.

"So am I." Travers joined them.

Leitch made an exasperated noise but said nothing. She turned to Ajax and gestured angrily at the ramp leading up into the cargo hold of the shuttlecraft. Ajax gave Herakles a slight, almost imperceptible shrug and went up the ramp.

"Lead the way, Herakles," said Ochs.

Herakles preceded the three masters to the structures near the rim of the depression. Ochs pressed the palm of his hand against the smooth, weathered stone and pursed his lips thoughtfully.

"Natural stone," he muttered. "Marble. I wonder where they quarried it."

"Certainly not from around here," Hendrix said as she traced a finger along the beveled edges of a seam between two flat stones.

"Implying at least a metal-alloy level of technological development. Hard tools to cut the marble. And how did they transport it across the prairie?"

"And why?" Ochs looked out across the depression. "This doesn't appear to have been a particularly large community, even allowing for the obvious fact that most of the structures have been worn away by the elements. All of the ruins seem to be contained with an area no greater than ... approximately two hundred square meters." He looked at Herakles questioningly.

"Approximately two hundred-fifty square meters, Ochs."

Ochs nodded, satisfied.

"It might not have been a community per se," said Travers. "It could have been a shrine, a monastery, a ...."

"An isolated scientific research laboratory." Hendrix shrugged.

"A dumping ground for nuclear wastes. Someone's wilderness retreat."

"Not a dumping ground," Ochs said. "You saw the scouts' report. No untoward radiation of any sort." Hendrix shrugged again. "Very well then. It was a fertilizer factory. The people of Boötes Six were technologically fifth-rate tillers of the soil who never discovered fire or the wheel but made the perfect fertilizer."

Travers cocked an eyebrow at Ochs. "Well, maybe they *were* agrarians."

The man snorted derisively. "Primitive farmers would not have built structures out of hard stone not indigenous to the area. They would have been too busy raising their crops to quarry marble and haul it across who knows how great a distance. On the other hand, if they were farmers in a more advanced civilization, we would surely have found signs of that civilization elsewhere on the planet."

"Perhaps they were colonists from a system beyond Bootes," said Travers.

"Perhaps." Ochs nodded to Herakles. "Let's go into the depression now."

Herakles rumbled assent and led them over the rim. Four meters into the sunken area, Travers stooped to crumble the soil between her fingers.

"Most peculiar," she said. "You've noticed how the vegetation blanketing the plain thins out about a meter into the depression and then stops altogether? Well, Ochs, if they were farmers, they were appallingly bad ones. This is dead soil. No, it's not even soil. It's almost sand. Sucked dry of organic compounds."

Hendrix knelt beside Travers and detached a stoppered tube from her belt. "I'll get a sample for analysis."

Travers rose and brushed off her hands. "If it's anything less than ninety-nine per cent inorganic material, I'll bend over in front of Herakles."

The two women laughed together brightly. Herakles looked away from them. Ochs was standing beside a three-meter-high column, touching it gingerly. He called out to Hendrix and Travers. "It's pitted like a meteorite. It looks as if someone had immersed it in acid."

Hendrix held up something small and brown between forefinger and thumb. "Even the pebbles are pitted. This one has a hole eaten through it."

"Yes," said Ochs, "but look at this." He indicated the top of the column.

"It's broken off at an angle. So?"

"No, Hendrix, *look* at it."

"I *am* looking at it."

"The pitting stops about two meters above the ground. The top third is smooth." Ochs circled the column once and backed away from it, scowling thoughtfully.

"Ochs," Herakles yelled, "stop!"

The man started and looked at him, astonished.

The scout pointed at something behind Ochs, who spun and found himself peering down into a sinkhole.

"Oh," said Ochs, blanching slightly. "I didn't notice it. I … thank you, Herakles."

"It's advisable to watch where you set your feet."

Ochs stiffened and colored. "Do not presume, scout!"

Herakles bowed his head. "I beg your forgiveness, Ochs."

Ochs grunted. "Insolent monster." To the women, he said, "I'm going back for my equipment now."

"'Do you think Leitch will let you have it?" asked Travers.

"Leitch can stuff the *Druitt* up her ass! Come on, Herakles."

As the master and the scout ascended the slope, Hendrix called after then, "Tell Allison I want to talk with him. And get Herakles to bring my equipment, too."

Allison was sitting on the ground near the rim of the depression. He had scalped a patch of sod from the plain and was fingering the alien plant's lace-like roots.

Herakles looked toward the shuttlecraft. Under the unnecessarily watchful eye of Leitch, Ajax had already made one stack of crates, inflated the hemispherical hut mold over it, and sprayed on plastic. While that dried, he lugged more crates from the ship's cargo hold to a spot five meters beyond the hut and stacked them.

"Hendrix wants you," Ochs told Allison. To Herakles, he said, "Separate my equipment, and Hendrix's, and bring them over here. If Leitch tells you to do anything else, tell her that I've given you a direct order."

"Yes, Ochs." Herakles sighed disconsolately as he approached the shuttlecraft. Leitch saw him coning and beckoned impatiently. The scout broke into a lumbering run.

Leitch glared at him when he stopped before her and said, "Get to work."

"Forgive me, Leitch, but Ochs has ordered me to take his and Hendrix's equipment to the depression."

"Get to work, damn you." She strode away in Ochs' direction without waiting to see whether or not he complied.

He watched her go and heard her call to Ochs in a belligerent tone. The man and woman closed and began gesticulating at each other wildly. Herakles turned toward the shuttlecraft just as Ajax came down the cargo ramp with an oblong crate cradled in his arms.

"Why the strange expression?" asked Ajax hefting his burden. "Don't you feel well?"

Herakles shook his head. "It's nothing, Ajax."

A few minutes later, though, as he was manhandling a portable generator out of the cargo hold, he saw Leitch standing near the ship, a triumphant expression on her face, and he was surprised to find himself grinding his teeth together.

It took them two hours to finish setting up camp. Herakles and Ajax erected another large hut to house supplies and equipment, two lesser ones for living quarters, a small shed for the generators. They assembled a two-person land rover, a drill rig and a chassis to support it, a traser barricade around the perimeter marked by Leitch, enclosing the ships and the plastic domes.

Ochs showed up at almost the precise moment they had finished. "Now," he demanded hotly of Leitch, "can I get one of then to carry my equipment?"

"Of course," Leitch said with poisonous sweetness. "They live but to serve you, Ochs. Ajax, Herakles, where did we put Ochs' equipment?"

"In Hut Two, Leitch," said Ajax.

"Where in Hut Two?"

"Under the crates containing Mitchell's equipment, Leitch."

Ochs exploded. "Damn you, Leitch! Why didn't you set it aside?"

Leitch shrugged and turned her back on him. "Standard survey procedure, Ochs. Scouts, take Hendrix's equipment to the depression, then his." She jerked a thumb over her shoulder. "In that order, precisely."

"Leitch, I'll kill you one of these days!"

"Probably when my back is turned," Leitch snapped, walking away.

Herakles watched Ochs' mouth open and close, soundlessly, like a fish gasping in air. Then the man lashed out and struck him a light blow on the sternum with the edge of his fist.

"I hate that woman!" Ochs snarled, glaring after her. "I hate her!"

The two scouts stood very, very still.

"Damn it!" Herakles took another ineffectual blow on his carapace. Ochs unballed his fists and said, "All right, get my things. And Hendrix's. Bring them over to the sunken area. I want everything there in five minutes, you understand?"

"Yes, Ochs."

The scouts glumly removed the crates containing Ochs' and Hendrix's equipment and lugged them to the rim of the depression. They unpacked scanning and recording instruments, digging mechanisms, data processors, and a radiocarbon-dater.

Ochs' fury appeared to have passed by the time the last of his boxes had been emptied. Clipping a communicator to his belt, he nodded at a surveyor's tripod and said, "Bring that, Herakles. We're going to get some work done. Finally."

Herakles folded the tripod legs together, shouldered the instrument and fell into step behind the master. They picked their way down the slope carefully, past Raymond the geologist, past a still perplexed-looking Travers, skirting fissures, gulleys, and sinkholes, the ancient pockmarked masonry. Well ahead of them, Herakles spotted Allison making his way across the rough ground toward the silt- and rubble-clogged cavity at the center of the depression.

Ochs and Herakles stopped by two piles of stones about sixty meters from the rim of the depression. "Set that up over there," the man said, and the scout unfolded the tripod legs and placed the instrument at the spot indicated. Ochs rubbed his hands together and looked around. "Now I want you—"

There was a tremor, followed at once by a muted gurgling sound like that of water being sucked down a drain.

"What was that?" Ochs demanded. "What—"

The second tremor was much more violent than the first. Herakles felt the ground sag beneath his feet, heard a whimpering cry from the perfect man at his aide, saw rough stones slide, clattering, down the mounds of rubble nearby. He looked about anxiously. Up the slope, Travers was scrambling to her feet. The geologist was looking at his instruments and waving his arms frantically. The gurgling noise was repeated.

"I thought you said it was *safe!*" screeched Ochs.

Herakles opened his mouth to say something and then a scream punctured his mounting irritation. It was a scream so high, so shrill, that it took him a second to recognize the sound as human.

Herakles glanced toward the rim and saw people gathering there, saw

Ajax lurching down the slope, then turned and headed toward the bottom of the basin, moving as quickly as he could, skidding past chasms, hurdling holes. The erosion of the land grew markedly worse the further he went. Ravines deepened and widened. The sinkholes became more numerous. The angle of descent increased steeply. He went down the side of a gulley on his armor-plated backside. The gulley was almost four meters deep and curved sharply to the right. He was half-walking, half-sliding around the curve, bellowing Allison's name, when he saw the man. Allison was on his belly, his face a mask of shock commingled with pain, his fingers clawing at the ground. Herakles took another step forward, the coarse soil crunching underfoot like insect husks, and stopped dead and gaped, not at the man's open mouth and wide eyes, not even at the stumps of his legs, but at the glistening frothy stuff welling up behind him bubbling up the walls of the gulley, licking at the bloody trail of its victim.

The disk at Allison's throat beeped angrily; that small sound made the scout shake off his paralysis. He hurried to the man and picked him up. The froth massed and seemed almost to lunge at him as he backed away.

When he had put a dozen meters between it and himself, Herakles lay Allison against the side of the pulley and examined him. His feet and ankles were gone, dissolved. Two decayed nubs of bone protruded from the gory stump of each calf. Herakles quickly removed two narrow straps from his harness and bound them tightly about Allison's legs, then shouldered him gently and scrambled out of the gulley.

He activated his communicator and said, "Ajax, I've got Allison. There's something deadly down here. It acts alive. I can't get close enough to see, but it's probably coming up out of the central pit. Get everyone out of the depression immediately."

There was another tremor. Herakles sat down hard. Allison whimpered against his breast. About three meters up the slope, a sinkhole gurgled, and spume overflowed, cascaded down the walls of the gulley, rolled toward the scout. Herakles got to his feet and skirted the moving mat of bubbles.

"Herakles!" Ajax called. "It's starting to come up here, too!"

Herakles topped a mound and looked toward the rim of the basin. Spume geysered from several pits and spread across the ground. He saw Ajax and lesser figures struggling up the slope, stones tilting out of place, falling, tumbling into chasms.

Ahead and to the left, a hole belched thunderously and spat, and a rain of bubbles fell on him. The stuff did not adhere to what it touched, but what it touched, it consumed. Allison's body disintegrated. Herakles plunged out of the iridescent spray and dropped to one knee, scattering his burden's limbs and torso. The froth closed over the bloody meat, and bubbles sparkled pinkly.

"Come on!" he heard Ajax screech.

Herakles pushed himself to his feet. Along the length of the calf that had been immersed in the spume, the armor was rough and pitted, a lighter gray than he was used to seeing. The soles of his feet began to feel uncomfortably warm. He clamped his jaws shut and plodded onward, past Ochs' tripod, past fountains of froth, toward Ajax and the people and safety beyond the basin. He was less than twenty-five meters from the rim when the armor sloughed off below the ankle. His feet literally disintegrated under him, and pain, a worse pain than any he had previously known or imagined possible, lanced up his legs. He screamed and went down on his knees. He would have fallen forward upon his face had Ajax reached him two seconds later.

Ajax put his hands under Herakles' arms and, somehow, got him to the top of the slope. Herakles lay on his back, feeling the ground quiver beneath him, listening to the excited voices of the beautiful men and women without understanding a word that they said. There was a hiss as Ajax sprayed something cool on the stumps of his legs. He found himself staring up into Travers' lovely, thoughtful eyes.

"Herakles," she said, "what is that stuff? Where did it come—"

Travers glared over her shoulder at him. "What?"

"Ajax!" Herakles caught a glimpse of Ochs' livid face and flailing fists. "You forget to bring back my equipment, damn you! It'll be ruined!"

"You should complain," said Hendrix, somewhere out of Herakles' field of vision. "What am *I* going to do without Allison?"

"Get my equipment!" Ochs shrieked at Ajax. "Before it's too late!"

Herakles heard himself say, "No, Ajax."

He rolled onto his side and pushed himself up on his elbow and looked up at Ajax's face, into his deep, dark eyes, and in that single instant of locked gazes, the precepts by which they had lived and by which one of them was about to die came to him like a prayer.

We live but to serve the masters.

We go where the masters will.

We are born to hazard.

We honor and obey.

We are of their flesh yet mortal.

It came as a prayer, and it was not enough.

Ajax turned and ran back down into the basin, through the froth. He had almost reached Ochs' tripod when the ground heaved violently. Ajax stumbled and fell, sinking waist-deep in bubbles. Fresh gouts of the stuff rose.

"Get my equipment, damn you!"

Ajax fell forward, and the tripod toppled, and the spume closed over both.

"Damn it!" said Ochs. "What am I going to do without equipment?"

"What are *we* going to do," demanded Leitch, "with one scout dead and the other crippled?"

On the ground between the masters, Herakles dug his fingers into the soil and opened his mouth in a scream too loud, too full of anguish, to be uttered: a scream that was the sound of the firmament turning brittle and shattering into a billon razor-edged shards, the sound that rolled back seas, leveled mountain ranges, split the earth, blasted planets from their orbits, caved in stars, the sound that signaled the end of Time and the edge of Space, the sound that birthed ghosts, the sound of all the little angers at once.

Whatever the nature of the thing that had lain dormant in the caverns below the depression, however it had come to be there, however it had aerated itself and forced itself to the surface, it did not cease to bubble out of the ground until it had filled the basin almost to the rim. A single column poked through the glistening surface. Then—again, for whatever reasons—the stuff began to settle, sucking itself back down into the ground, leaving the depression almost imperceptibly wider, almost imperceptibly deeper, considerably freer of organic matter and certain elements.

By that time, Herakles had been returned to the *Druitt*. Milne, Osward, and the man whose name he did not know put him on a gleaming metal table and let him mutter to himself while they grafted raw tissue to the stumps of his legs. Milne gave him the feeding tube at one point, and he bit through it. They put a clamp on his face, pried his jaws apart and forced the salty mush down his throat.

He regenerated his feet and the armor that had been eaten away by spattering foam, and then he was returned to his gelatin-filled trough in Cryogenics, and as he sank through the variegated levels to his latest death, his hatred of the masters, the perfect men and women of Golden Earth, was as certain as the promise of resurrection.

3.

Moving through the city of the masters, Herakles felt awed in spite of himself. He had never before visited the habitats of the masters, had only seen their elegant buildings from afar, and the deeper he penetrated this enclave of Olympus, the more like a trespasser he felt. Adonis and Aphrodite had divided the world into cities for themselves and crèches for those who served them.

As he walked along the deserted boulevards, past empty houses, stopping every few minutes to make unnecessary adjustments of the instruments attached to his harness, his childhood lessons recited themselves, unbidden, in his mind:

In their great cities, the masters look down upon us, their creations, and see every deed, know every innermost thought. In their great cities, the masters look out across the world and know it is theirs, and they look up at the stars and know those can be theirs, too.

In their great cities ....

But the great city was empty. Creepers twined about towers and spires. Drifts of powdery dust had begun to accumulate in the plazas. The trees lining the avenues were wild-looking and had not been tended in a long time. There were no signs of actual decay—the materials the masters had used to construct their city endured—but neither were there signs of life.

Herakles struggled with his terrors, calling to mind the sight of Ajax foundering in deadly froth, fanning the embers of his rage. It was not enough to dispel his uneasiness completely. Fear of the masters went back to childhood and the crèche. Like the threat of the ravenous something that, long before the age of Golden Earth, had lurked in the darkness, slavering for the tender flesh of disobedient children, like the ancient Christians' threats of hellfire and torment forevermore, fear of the masters could not be exorcised with age, reason, or familiarity. Repulsed by anger, routed by hatred, fear of the masters lived deep in Herakles, but it lived nonetheless.

There was a sound of beating wings in the air above his head.

Herakles looked up, one hand curled around the stout butt of the weapon bolstered on his thigh, and saw a bat-like shape dip and pass at a height of about ten meters. Small of skull and body, with a deep, narrow keel of a breastbone and filmy pink membranes stretched across enormously elongated fingers, it was barely recognizable as anything whose ancestors had been human.

The bat-person wheeled gracefully in the air and dropped to earth a short distance from the scout. Folding its wings over its back, it waddled forward on calloused thumb stumps and the padded balls of virtually toeless feet. It stopped about three meters away from him and regarded him happily.

Herakles caressed the handle of his weapon and said, "I am Heavy Duty Scout Model Herakles, *S. V. Druitt.*"

"You are a pilgrim to this holy place." The bat-person's voice was shrill and parrot-like. "We welcome you."

"Where are the masters?"

"We welcome you. You are a pilgrim to this holy place."

Herakles frowned. "Where have the masters gone?" he persisted. "What has happened to them?"

"We welcome you. You are a pilgrim to this holy place." The bat-person opened its wings with a sharp snap and started to rise laboriously.

"Stop." Herakles drew the cannon and chambered a round. "Answer me!"

The creature rose, circled once, then flew away, toward the heart of the city.

The scout stared after it, contemplated the weapon in his hand and, with a perplexed sigh, returned it, safety on, to its holster. It would have been useless, he realized, to capture the bat-person and attempt to interrogate it. It was obvious that the thing had greeted him without real comprehension of what it was saying to him. Herakles trudged along in the direction the creature had taken, and as he passed a dark alcove, he glimpsed a shadowy gray hulk from the corner of his eye.

Ajax stepped forth and paced at his side. *You are starting to repent, he said. It shows in your expression.*

I have started to repent nothing. I have nothing to repent.

Ajax made a reproachful sound. *You blaspheme in the city of the masters. Yet you are afraid. You are becoming such a mystery to me, Herakles.*

Herakles stopped. There was a lump of raw agony in his throat.

He clenched his fists and glared at the ghost. Why, he demanded, why, Ajax, do you haunt me and not those who sent you to your death?

Because I love you. Because I fear for you. Because you and I have grown apart somehow.

You are dead. I am alive. That makes a good deal of difference between us.

No. I speak of a worse separation than death. You have come to hate the masters, where once you loved them. You have come to dream of killing them, though you used to serve them gladly. Why? How? We were two and the same, you and I. How have you become afflicted with such unnatural passions? How have you become what you are, a blasphemer, a harborer of treacherous thoughts? How have you managed to harden your heart against them?

Herakles felt a great and terrible sadness settle upon him. He could think of nothing to say.

They had been born within minutes of each other, Ajax and Herakles, two large but outwardly normal baby boys, in a crèche where large but outwardly normal baby boys and girls soon became thick-skinned and lumpy. They had taken their training together. They had learned the same lessons. They had grown up together, seeing little and knowing less of the world beyond the crèche, the world of the masters, knowing only that they were special mortals, designed to perform heroic tasks in the service of Golden Earth. They had become lovers, and the masters, whether by chance or through a rare compassion for lesser beings, had deigned to assign the two of them, Ajax and Herakles, the inseparables, the indissolubles, to duty aboard the same starship.

Now Herakles could think of nothing to say except: I loved you, Ajax. I grieve because you are dead. I loved you dearly.

145

And I loved you. The masters love you. They—

Herakles snarled. Lightning crackled from his hands. They can't love anything! They love no one, Ajax!

Herakles!

They're all crazy, Ajax! Crazy and childish and full of hate! They hate us, and they hate one another!

Herakles. Herakles ....

There was a hollow clopping sound behind him. Herakles wheeled, drawing his weapon in the same smooth motion, and saw two large creatures step out of the shadows beneath a massive arch, into the sunlight. Their androgynous human faces and torsos glittered with beadlets of perspiration. Crouched upon the broad equine back of one was the bat-person.

The scout lowered the muzzle of the hand cannon slightly and studied the creatures as they approached. After men and women had learned how to reshape themselves, after they had attained physical perfection and immortality, thereby raising themselves to demigodhood, they had taken a portion of their flesh and fashioned it into lesser beings to serve them: seal-people to tend the ocean farms on the continental shelves, gill-breathers to mine the bottoms of the seas, people who could endure hardships in deserts and polar wildernesses, giants who could face danger on other worlds, cybernetic people ... and people whose sole function in the scheme of Golden Earth was purely decorative. Fairy-tale people. Centaurs.

The bat-person chirped idiotically as the centaurs came to a stop before Herakles. "You are a pilgrim to this holy place. We welcome you."

The scout looked into the centaurs' large, liquid brown eyes and said, hopefully, "I am Heavy Duty Scout Model Herakles, *S.V. Druitt.*"

One of the creatures tossed its tawny mane and gave him a smile. "We welcome you. You are a pilgrim to this holy place."

Herakles groaned inwardly. "Where are the masters? What has become of them?"

The centaurs turned and calmly walked away.

"Where are the *masters?*" he shouted after them.

Yes, Ajax murmured at Herakles' side, *you are beginning to repent.*

Away, phantom! Herakles set out after the centaurs. Go back to your lords.

Ajax sighed, a quiet, sorrowful sound, and said, I truly do not understand you, Herakles.

But I understand you, Ajax! I have been you. Docile, faithful, obedient Ajax ... Ajax, my beloved, don't you see? Both of us were precisely the kind of creature they intended us to be .... Several bat-people passed overhead noisily, bound for the heart of the city. The thing riding upon the centaur's back made a sound like laughter, unfurled its wings, stretched lazily, refolded the membranes.

With Ajax hovering at the extreme edge of his field of vision, Herakles let the centaurs precede him in silence disturbed only by the clack of their hooves on pavement, through more deserted streets and plazas, past more empty houses, dry fountains, dusty works of sculpture, under arches, over ornately decorated bridges.

At the heart of the city, ringed by towers, protected by a bell of energy indicated by the play of scintillae in the air, was an amphitheatre so immense that it was almost a valley. The centaurs led Herakles to the edge of the bowl, past the bat-people he had seen previously, and he gazed down across the terraces, thoroughly awed.

Something as white, as brilliantly white as clean crusted snow, blanketed the slopes before him.

Herakles blinked, closed his eyes very tightly for several seconds, peered up at the sparkling lights on the invisible surface of the energy dome. Then, stunned, unable to stand, he dropped to his knees.

He heard one of the centaurs standing behind him shift its hard feet, heard the leathery rustle of membranous wings, heard a mewling whimper from the back of his own throat.

He stared down across the amphitheatre, and that shadow, that fusion of lost mate and crumbling yet tenacious faith, that ghost whom he called Ajax, cried out in disbelief, in horror, in agony, in misery.

He stared down across the amphitheatre, and he knew, without having to make any closer examination, without even having to really think about what he was seeing, that the thousands upon thousands upon *thousands* of bones covering the terraced slopes were the bones of immortals.

Far, far below, rising out of the mounds of skulls and femurs and shoulder blades, thick black pylons shimmered suddenly, and the scintillae in the sky above the amphitheatre coalesced into a blindingly bright cloud the color of molten silver. A tentacle of something cool and slippery tickled the inner surface of Herakles' cranium.

You are a pilgrim to this holy place. We welcome you.

Though trembling and afraid, you have come, because you are one of the faithful, and we hear your prayers.

Your loyalty and devotion move us deeply.

We see into your heart, we know your innermost thoughts, and we forgive you your mortal limitations, for you are of our flesh.

But there is still much evil in the world.

We still know anger, for we have been renounced by those whom we authored; they grew apart from us, and we could not hold them to us. They formed masterless societies in the wilderness and under the seas, and they abandoned us.

We still know sorrow; our world has been hurled from its natural state by the wickedness of our creatures.

Hear us, pilgrim, and know that, when all have repented, then shall we return and clothe ourselves in flesh again.

Abide in this holy place and receive those who will surely follow.

Do not surrender your faith to despair or doubt.

Do not lose heart.

Do not falter.

Endure.

The pylons stopped shimmering. Herakles sat back on his calves and, after a long moment, turned his head to stare at the exalted faces of the centaurs. The bat-people beat their wings and babbled among themselves wordlessly. Then, a minute or two later, the centaurs turned and cantered away into the city. The winged things took to the air in a flurry of beating membranes and cacophonous cries. The scout watched them until they had disappeared beyond the tops of the buildings encircling the amphitheatre.

They are the last, Ajax. The last of the faithful. The final believers. Mindless descendants of useless creatures. Fit and proper worshippers for false gods.

They made themselves immortal. They authored us. They changed the world and foolishly expected it to change no more. Despite their immortality, or because of it, they settled into senility, into a second childhood that would have lasted an eternity but for us.

We who kept Golden Earth moving in the orbit they had prescribed for it ... we who live but to serve, who go where the masters will, who are mortal yet of their flesh, who are born to hazard, who honor and obey ... we outgrew them. We tired of them. We didn't need them any longer. We abandoned them. They came here, and they died, and there was nothing noble, nothing dignified ... nothing godlike about their passing. They died insane. They did this out of sheer childish petulance. They took themselves away, Ajax, and they truly believed that we would be sorry. They are gone, all save a handful, and we are well rid of them. We are free of immortal children.

He listened for the shadow's reply. There was no sound at the heart of the city.

And I am free of ghosts.

Herakles got to his feet and activated his communicator. "Three," he said.

"Yes, Herakles," replied the shuttlecraft, kilometers away.

"Stand by to relay my report to the *Druitt*."

"Yes, Herakles." There was a brief, static-filled pause. Then: "Standing by. Proceed with your report."

He gazed into the amphitheatre. On the terrace immediately below the lip of the bowl, skulls leered up at him.

"Go ahead," said Three, and waited.

The scout said nothing.

"Herakles?"

Herakles tore the communicator off its cord. He pulled the relay pack and the power cell from his harness and tossed them away contemptuously. He grinned down at the skulls.

Then he turned and moved away. Somewhere the ones who had abandoned their masters were living their own lives.

He would find them.

Creatures of Habit
An Historical Romance

JUST AS I WAS SAYING GOODBYE TO Ted Gibbs, harpsichord music came down the hall and into the bedroom. I recognized it as the opening chords of an old rock and roll song, "For Your Love," by The Yardbirds, and I had to smile. A blast from the past. Not exactly "As Time Goes By," perhaps, but Kay had picked it, and some things, once got into the bloodstream, can never really be got out. For a fraction of a second, I felt like twenty-seven going on seventeen.

I returned the telephone to its cradle and went back through the house to the living room. Kay was sitting on the floor beside the record player, an unlighted cigarette in one hand, the faded purple jacket of the Yardbirds album in the other. She waved the latter at me and said, "A little nostalgia for the old folks. Or don't you remember?"

I listened as the driving guitar break began. "I remember. You gave me that record for my seventeenth birthday, way back in the Pleistocene Period. Ice Age to you. It was a hell of a party. Everybody danced all night long."

"Well, until twelve or twelve-thirty."

I felt a warm grin creeping across my face. "Suzanne Rice slapped the crap out of some guy who tried to run his hand up under her skirt. Ted somebody came drunk and threw up all over one of my mother's prize rose bushes." The grin turned into a smirk. "You cattily told me that Wanda Porterfield didn't know how to kiss with her mouth open."

Kay gave me an arch look. "It wasn't catty. I was much too nice a young lady to be catty. Just because you were going steady with her then, you don't have to defend her honor now."

"Wanda and I didn't go out together until that Halloween. After I'd taught her how to kiss with her mouth open."

"Personally, what you ever saw in her always escaped me. She even wore her falsies in gym class."

I had nothing to say to that. "For Your Love" ended. The Yardbirds tore off into "I'm Not Talking."

"Kay," I said, "I'm going to have to leave you here for a little while."

"An emergency come up at the clinic?"

"No. I have to keep an appointment downtown. Will you be all right here by yourself?"

"Sure." She began to play with the unlighted cigarette, rolling it between her fingers. "Would you like me to have dinner ready when you get back?"

"I don't have any idea when that'll be. If you get hungry, help yourself. You know where the ice box is." I gave her a rueful smile. "Besides. I haven't been used to having anybody do my cooking for me since the divorce. And the closer I get to thirty, the more set in my ways I become."

"You should've married Wanda when you had the chance."

I rolled my eyes and changed the subject. "I'd better give Arabella her pill before I go."

At the sound of her name, Arabella emerged from beneath the sofa, stretched luxuriously and wagged her tail. She walked over to me. I stooped to lightly scratch her throat for her. Dog heaven.

"Want your daily ration of peanut butter?"

She did. She pranced before me.

"She sure is one spoiled dog," Kay observed.

"Not so much spoiled as just omnivorous. Arabella eats carrots, pickles, onions, bananas, watermelon, anything she can con me into setting before her. But her particular fondness is for peanut butter."

"Vince once told me it was a rotten trick to give peanut butter to a dog." Kay's voice was flat, tight, controlled. I avoided looking in her direction. "He said dogs have such weak tongues, the peanut butter glues them to the roofs of their mouths." She exhaled harshly. "Vince being an expert on the subject of rotten tricks, if not dogs."

I had nothing to say to that, either. I went to the kitchen, Arabella happily trotting alongside, and spooned a small dab of peanut butter onto a dog biscuit, pressed a Styrid Caricide tablet into it, then hid that under a second dab of peanut butter. The dog was all eyes and waiting saw throughout the preparations.

Kay appeared in the doorway and leaned against the frame. She was still playing with her cigarette. "What're the pills for?"

"Some preventative medicine for *Dirofilaria immitis*, commonly known as heartworm disease. Okay, Arabella. Stand!"

Arabella stood on her hind legs, got her goodie and took it to the corner of the kitchen farthest from us. She gobbled it down to the accompaniment of succinct crunches and lots of paranoid glances over her shoulder at us. Kay watched, amused, then finally decided to smoke her cigarette. She headed for the guest bedroom to fetch her lighter. Licking her chops, the dog came back to me and looked expectant.

"No more peanut butter today," I said. Arabella began to prance again when I took out my car keys. She liked riding in automobiles, too. I bent down and rubbed her behind her ears. "No car ride, either. Stay here and show Kay what fun it is to terrorize Jael's kittens."

Ted Gibbs was a small, bald man with a round face and a soft tenor voice. He sat leaning forward in his chair, with his pink fingers pressed flat against the rather grimy desk blotter and his forearms bracketing a single typewritten page. On the desk between us, a noxious cigar shouldered in a chipped ash tray ripped off from a Ramada Inn.

"As I told you on the phone," he said, "I've found your man."

"Where?" I blurted out.

His light blue eyes momentarily reproached me for my impatience.

"I'm in a hurry to get in touch with him," I said.

"So it seems." He tapped the sheet of paper with a fingernail. "The new address is here, don't worry. He left his house on East Sixth Saturday night, after a noisy fight with his wife, and's been staying at a motel on the north edge of town since." Satisfaction flickered across the mild face. "It wasn't hard to track him down."

I refrained from asking why, if it hadn't been hard, it had taken three days. I put my check book on the desk and took a pen out of my shirt pocket. "How much do I owe you?"

Gibbs briefly showed me the palms of his hands. "Let's hold our horses

153

for a minute, okay? Just what's this guy hiding out from? Not his wife. She hasn't been at the East Sixth place at least since Sunday noon. The cops can't be after him, else they'd of gone by the house asking for him. Is he maybe hiding from you?"

I shifted in my chair. It protested faintly. "He doesn't know me from Adam, I think."

"But you know him, don't you?"

"Only by reputation. I never met the man."

"Reputation? What kind of reputation can a guy who drives a fork-lift in a lumberyard have? What's he done? I mean, besides drink some and fight with his old lady and maybe run around on her a little. What do you want with him?"

"That's personal."

Gibbs sat back in his chair and clasped his hands behind his head. His eyes were suddenly very hard, boring into mine. "I don't much know what this is all about. It really bothers me, the more I think about it. I talked to a couple of the neighbors, and one of 'em recalled seeing him drive off Saturday night. Nobody saw his wife leave, though. Nobody saw her after Sunday morning. Nobody knows where she's gotten to. Nobody seems worried. You come to me, say find this guy, but I can't get a word out of you as to why."

"I only hired you to find him. Tell me how much I owe you now. I'll write you out a check and take that piece of paper there and go on about my business."

Gibbs clucked his tongue behind his teeth. "I have to ask myself if I can send you his way in all good conscience."

"Yes, you can," I said. "I'm not about to go shoot him dead."

"So you say, but you don't look like the kind of guy who'd even need a gun. You play football in school?"

"No."

"Really?" He seeded genuinely surprised. People always did.

"They called me Gentle Ben in school. After a tame bear on a TV show."

"Well, anyway." He chuckled softly, unhappily. "I'd say if you got good and mad at somebody, you'd just wade right in and let their arms and legs fall where they might."

"I haven't torn off anybody's arms and legs for at least a week now, if that's what you're worried about."

"Yeah," he muttered, reaching for his cigar. "Yeah, that's exactly what I'm worried about. I don't want trouble from the cops on account of something a client does with information I've dug up for him. I don't want any trouble, period. So what if you're really after the guy? What if something bad's happened to his wife, and what if it's something the cops ought to know about? I mean, it worries me I couldn't get a line on her anywhere. And—"

"I didn't ask you to."

"I set great store in serendipity." Through a haze of vile smoke he gestured at a framed document hanging on the wall. "I got my license to protect, you know. I got my sense of justice to think about. I'll sleep better tonight if you tell me a few things about this business."

"Mr. Gibbs," I said wearily, "there isn't going to be any trouble from the cops. Not for you, not for me. Not for anybody."

He did not look at all convinced.

I sighed, got to my feet and looked down at him, way down. Bending slightly forward at the waist, I planted my fists knuckles-down on the desk top so that be could stare at the thick ridges standing out on the backs of my hands. The desk was old and tired. It groaned as I put a little of my weight on it.

"I won't misuse the information," I said. "I won't offend your sense of justice."

Gibbs' face was gleaming with fresh perspiration. He managed something vaguely similar to a grin. The tenor hit a resentful note. "It's your information, of course. To do with as you see fit."

I picked up the sheet of paper, glanced over it, folded it into quarters, and put it into my pocket. "Thank you, Mr. Gibbs. I'm glad you understand."

"I'm not sure I do."

I looked at him. He was frightened with me looming over his desk like King Kong, but defiant, too. He went up a notch in my estimation. I went down a couple. A brave little man is braver than any big man.

I filled out a check, handed it across the desk to him, and left. It was only after I had wedged myself into my car and had the key in the ignition slot that I started to tremble violently.

I curled both hands around the warm steering wheel and looked at them disbelievingly, at the big knuckles and thick, hard wrists. I was scared. Six two in my stocking feet, two hundred and seven- or eighteen mostly solid pounds, shaking like a leaf. I had scared myself worse than Gibbs, whom I could have picked up with one hand and drop-kicked ten city blocks. I was scared for having thrown my beef around in his office. I was scared of what came next.

I had lied to Gibbs.

Among other things, I had not raised a fist in anger, had not had to, at least since the tenth grade. Much less torn off anybody's arms and legs.

It was called the Lisa Motel, and it looked the same as any other motel I had ever seen. I parked at the curb and sat in the car for fully a minute. The shakes had left me during the drive across town. I felt cold, though the asphalt-paved court of the Lisa Motel was shimmering in the late August heat.

Then I found myself thinking about a kid whom I had briefly known when I was fifteen. His name escaped me. All that I could remember about him was that, one mid-summer afternoon, he showed me how he had celebrated his Fourth of July. What he showed me was a decapitated box turtle. "The trick," the kid said to me, "the trick's to get the turtle to open its mouth in the first place so you can stick the firecracker in. Once you do that, you don't have to worry about it letting go, just strike a match and light the fuse."

I had tried to turn him into Swiss steak.

I got out of the car and strolled past the flyblown front window of the manager's office as casually as though I actually belonged in one of the fourteen rooms beyond. When I got to the door of Room 7, I knocked twice and waited. There was a muffled sound from within, the sound of someone moving about. Then the door swung open, and a tall, good-looking man with a deep tan appraised me suspiciously.

I nervously cleared my throat and said, "Excuse me, but are you Vincent Hackman?"

He appeared to consider the question very carefully. He did not take his eyes off me. After a long moment, he finally nodded and drawled, "Yeah, that's me. What can I do for you?"

I hit him.

It wasn't a skillful blow. It didn't have to be, though—there was power behind my awkward punch, enough power to send him hurtling backward across the room and onto the unmade bed against the far wall.

I stepped in after him, kicking the door shut as I moved quickly to the bed, and pulled him to his feet by the front of his shirt. He was bleeding profusely from the corner of the mouth and both nostrils. I unballed a fist and slapped him three times, as hard as I could, before letting him slide to the floor. He lay there in a heap, breathing raggedly, blowing blood and snot all over the cheap carpet. He was no longer quite so good-looking. He was a mess. There was blood on my hands. I went around Vincent Hackman and into the bathroom, washed off the gore, then let cold water run over my knuckles. I had skinned them on Hackman's teeth, and they were beginning to throb. I let the water run, and I stared at the big man in the mirror above the sink.

Bully, the kid's father had called me afterward.

You want to fight, my own father had told me, *you fight someone your own size.*

Only, there had never been anybody my own size who wanted to fight. And I hadn't minded, not in the least.

And I had never again hit anyone, big, small or in-between, no matter what the provocation.

Not until now.

Bully.

I turned off the water, put my head over the toilet bowl and vomited. When I was finished, when I had cleaned myself up, I went back to the other room. Vincent Hackman was still unconscious.

Ted Gibbs opened the door, peered in, and swore.

"I was afraid something like this would happen," he said as he came inside and went to kneel beside the man on the floor. "How badly have you hurt him?"

I closed the door and sank down into the room's one arm chair.

"He's still alive. I was very careful."

Gibbs scowled at me. "You trying to be funny? He looks like you parked a bulldozer on his face."

"He beat up a woman last Saturday night," I said, "and raped her. How does that set-with your sense of justice, Mr. Gibbs?"

"Goddamn." Gibbs' eyes got big. "Then the cops ought—"

"She doesn't want that."

"Huh?" His face mottled. "And just why in the hell not?"

"Because ..." My voice trailed off. I felt cold again.

"You're mumbling, I can't hear you."

"Because she's ... the woman he beat up and raped is his wife."

"His wife?" Gibbs screeched. "His wife! A man can't rape his own goddamn *wife*!"

I jabbed a finger in Hackman's general direction. "This one did. He knocked her down with his fist, and then he ... he sodomized her while she was barely conscious."

Gibbs looked stricken. He rose shakily and seated himself on the edge of the bed. His glassy gaze went from me to Hackman and back to me.

"The police don't think that wife-beating is really a serious offense," I said. "Lots of people don't think a husband can sexually assault his wife. She didn't want go through the painful, degrading ... she didn't want the humiliation of going to court only to have it come to nothing."

"So she hired you to do this?" The tenor had turned brittle.

"She doesn't know a thing about this."

"You know where she is? She's not in trouble?"

On the floor between us, Vincent Hackman groaned.

Gibbs looked down at him and said, "He could get you thrown into jail for assault and battery, you know. And maybe other stuff, too."

I stood up. "He won't know where to look for me. I told you, he doesn't know who I am."

Hackman groaned a second time.

I went outside and closed the door and stood watching the cabins on the far side of the court ripple in the heat. Gibbs emerged after about a minute. His expression was strained. He would not meet my eye. We put our hands deep into our pockets and strolled toward the street.

"I'm Gentle Ben," I said when we had covered approximately two thirds of the distance. "I keep plants and take in stray animals. I'm a good cook, a gourmet. I've read Dostoyevsky. I don't go around itching for a fight."

"I don't approve of vigilantes. Mr. Hackman really could get you in a court of law, you know. If I had to take the stand under oath …."

"I know. You're a law-abiding citizen."

He smiled without mirth, without warmth. We had reached the street by this time. I went to my car, unlocked and opened the door.

Behind me, Gibbs said, "And what're you?"

"A veterinarian."

"Goddamn." He sounded incredulous.

I slid into the driver's seat, fumbled with my keys, laughed suddenly. "Well, you don't look so damn much like a detective, either."

It was his turn to laugh, and he did. "Score one for you. Goodbye, Gentle Ben."

I was on the steps of the verandah adjoining the kitchen when I heard a thin, high bleat from within. I hastily unlocked the back door and found Jael sitting there. Her two calico kittens were climbing on her in an effort to get at something which dangled from her jaws. Jael had been hunting again.

I grabbed her, gently but firmly, before she realized that I was upon her. The kittens scampered away in panic. A small, obviously young rabbit fell from her mouth. I let go of her and picked it up by the loose skin behind its head and examined it closely. It was petrified with terror but unhurt.

Carefully, I folded a hand around its body. It was warm and incredibly soft, and it did not try to writhe out of my grasp. I made a soothing sound to it. At my feet, Jael yowled and angrily whipped her tail from side to side. Kay opened the kitchen door. Arabella started to run forward to greet me, then saw the furious Jael and kept her distance, whimpering. Kay said, "What're you doing?"

"Succumbing to predator prejudice." I showed her the rabbit's head peeking out of my fist. Her eyes widened, and she made an *oh* sound. "It's ecologically criminal of me, but Jael gets enough to eat here at home. Ever since I rigged a cat door for her, she's been bringing her catches onto the verandah."

Kay extended an index finger and gingerly stroked the rabbit's flattened ears. "It's not even trying to get away from you, is it? I think it trusts you."

"It's a wild little bunny, and it's not trying to get away because it's paralyzed with fear. I think Jael's found a nest in the field. Last week, I came home to find the kittens playing with what she'd left of a rabbit no bigger than this one. Before that, I was always rescuing poor inoffensive lizards and garden snakes from her."

She looked down at Jael. "Cats are such vicious animals."

"No, they're just cats, that's all."

"That's like saying Vince is just Vince." She frowned and shook her head. "I'm sorry. I promised not to say any more about him, didn't I?"

We all went outside, Kay and the menagerie and I, to the high chain-link fence which separated my back yard from several acres of somebody's private wilderness. Kay and I knelt by the fence, our backs to the cat, who was raucously demanding the return of her rabbit, and to the dog, who was consumed by canine curiosity. When I opened my hand, the rabbit took the hint immediately and shot through the links, into the wild grass on the other side, out of sight. Arabella wormed her way in between Kay and myself and sniffed about. Jael sat down on my foot and gave me an utterly baleful glare.

"Sorry, gal," I said, "but I've seen you play before, and it isn't very pretty." I stroked her back. She accepted the caress as her due, but she continued to glare. I wagged my finger at her in admonishment. "The strong have obligations to the weak."

Kay and I straightened and stood together, facing the house. It was nestled among post oaks and elm trees. The kittens were trying out their claws on one of them. I spotted a cardinal.

"It's so peaceful here," Kay murmured. "So quiet and secluded. It'd be nice just to stay and forget all about everything else."

"You're welcome to do it. You know that."

"I can't. I have too many things I need to do. Find a job, find a place of my own. Go through that whole messy business of getting divorced."

"Wait until you're feeling better."

"I am feeling better." She touched my arm. "You've been so sweet these past three days. More than I had any right to expect. I haven't felt so ... so cared-for in a long, long tine. But I need to get it over with. The sooner, the better."

"I can lend you some money. Whatever I can do, I will, Kay."

"I wish to God we hadn't," she said, and then she was crying, swaying blindly on her feet. I put my arms around her and kissed her on the forehead and mumbled that I wished to God we hadn't, either. She made a half-sobbing, half-laughing sound and hugged me tenderly. Something old and familiar began to smoulder inside me. Even with tears smeared all over her face, even with a puffy black eye and a split lip, she was my kind of lady. Even after fifteen years of getting along and not getting along with each other.

I held her in my arms, the top of her head tucked under my chin, and she said, "It's just like holding a baby rabbit, isn't it?"

"Better. It's just like holding my wife used to be."

Flies by Night

Lisa Tuttle and Steven Utley

I REMEMBER I USED TO WAKE NIGHTS and hear my mother walking about on the ceiling.

In the daytime, she was just another little lady, small and undistinguished. You meet hundreds like her in your lifetime and forget all of them. My mother wasn't even boring. She was forgettable — but all that was just her shell. If you'd seen what she was inside, you would never have forgotten her.

My mother was a fly inside her human body, and she split open and came out at night when my father, who was nothing at all, slept. It should have been a wondrous thing, to be a fly. She could have flown all over the city, gazed down with jeweled eyes. I would have. But to my mother the transformation, at eighteen, was a shock, an affliction. She didn't know what to do with it, and so, in reaction, she got married immediately, and to a man so thick, so dull, that she could have let him wake in the mornings to her empty woman-skin beside him, and he would have said good morning to it as usual, then berated it for not making him his coffee.

Such a man fathered me. And when I was eighteen, and no wondrous change was worked on me, I began to hate him for dooming me to this heavy, earthbound life. Why couldn't she have waited? Why didn't my fearful mother wait for one of her own kind? Then they could have flown together, loved together in mid-air or on the ceiling. Instead, my mother climbs guiltily out of her skin for a few hours at night, and, just to feel the relief and stretch her wings, she goes out and flies around the neighborhood.

I can't do even that. Sometimes my skin itches so that I *know* it must be my real self trying to get out. I scratch at myself, tear at my skin until it bleeds, but it never helps.

Oh, please, I want to get out. I want to fly.

Clarisse awoke, feeling breath warm on her cheek. Her husband Dan loomed over her, his eyes shining in the moonlight from the window. She felt unaccountably terrified that he should have been watching her while she slept.

"What's wrong?" she asked sharply.

"You were talking in your sleep."

"Mmmmph." She tried to sound sleepy and rolled over, turning her back to him.

"Clarisse," Dan said, "what were you dreaming about?"

Oh, Christ, not again.

"Who knows?"

"I think you know. And I find it very disturbing that you won't confide in me."

She flopped onto her back. "Confide? What's to confide? I don't remember my stupid dreams. I'm sorry, but I'm very tired, so why don't you let me go back to sleep?"

"I'm talking about a lot more than just this dream, Clarisse."

She sighed. "Okay. What did I say? Did I say a man's name, is that what it is, Dan?"

"You're assuming that. To me, that says you are afraid you've said a man's name — that it is likely." He spoke pedantically. He fancied himself a psychiatrist. Why, Clarisse wondered, should that quality, so repellant now, have been so attractive before they were married?

"I'm assuming that," she replied, "because you're playing the jealous husband. What am I supposed to assume?"

"Why are you so defensive?"

"Why are you so *off*ensive?"

There was a hurt silence. Clarisse sat up and turned on the bedside lamp.

"I'm sorry, Dan," she said, putting her hand on his arm. "But you know I hate arguing with you, and to wake me up in the middle of the night to argue about something as ridiculous as this—"

"I didn't wake you up."

"Maybe not, but you didn't let me go back to sleep, either."

"There was a time, you know, when you liked talking to me no matter what hour it was."

"I've never liked arguing with you, Dan."

"Then why do you persist? I'm only asking you to trust me. Unless you've betrayed me, there is no reason to be so secretive. What are you hiding from me?"

"I'm not hiding *anything*—I swear to you!" When he said nothing, Clarisse turned off the light and lay down. She felt him move his hand over her breasts.

"Another thing," he said quietly, "which makes me doubt you ...."

No, she thought. *Not now. You can't.*

"You never seem to feel loving any more." Dan was caressing her hip now. "You're always too tired, and I can't understand that. I'm the one who goes to work, you know. I'm the one who should be tired, not you. So I can't help but wonder what it is that makes my Clarisse so tired."

The only way to end it was to give in. She moved closer to him, hoping that she could pretend enthusiasm. "It's really nothing to do with you," she said. "Maybe I'm coming down with something—I'm so loggy and tired all the time."

"I think I've got the cure for that," he murmured in her ear, turning her to ice inside. "Hmmm? Would you like to try my cure?"

Oh, please let me out.

I got married because I thought I had to; only something happened after we were married, and it turned out that I wasn't going to have a baby after all. He was the first man I ever slept with, but because I slept with him before the wedding, he thought I was immoral. I didn't find this out until later, after we had been married a few months, when everything began to go wrong.

He accused me of sleeping with, or of wanting to sleep with, every man he saw me look at. I was glad, then, that I hadn't told him about my mother. I had thought I would, after we were married, because he was such a strong man, such a comfort, and I was sure he would understand. But that impression began to seem a mistake, and I was glad I had told him that I didn't have a mother, that my mother was dead. And I knew I could never tell him about the other me, the real me, the me-that-might-be.

In my dreams, I could fly, and my dreams were all I had. Perhaps it was my wanting to dream that made me sleep so much more, that made me so tired all the time. Dan would get me up in the morning to make his breakfast, but once he had gone off to work I would go back to bed and fall asleep again, to dream of flying. I always set the alarm so that I could get up and dress and do the breakfast dishes and start dinner before Dan came home. After dinner I would be yawning uncontrollably, as tired as if I'd been awake for days.

I dream at night of wings, translucent teardrops, rainbow silk stretched taut on fine wire frames.

Clarisse finally identified the intrusive sound as the doorbell and came fully awake. Some seconds more elapsed while she fought off the sheets and blankets she had wrapped around herself, for she had a tendency to burrow into a bed when she slept alone.

She thought that by the time she got to the door her visitor might have vanished, but she was not so lucky. Dan's mother was on the front porch, looking as if she were prepared to wait all day for her summons to be answered.

"Mrs. Brent," said Clarisse, flushing slightly in embarrassment. "Won't you come in?" She was uncomfortably aware of how she must look—what a slatternly housewife the elder Mrs. Brent would think her! Mrs. Brent's house was always neat, always, it seemed, ready to be photographed for an interior decorators' magazine. Here the breakfast dishes were still in the sink, and Clarisse knew that it must be noon.

"May I get you some coffee?" she asked her mother-in-law.

"Don't bother."

"Oh, it's no bother, Mrs. Brent. It's still on the stove. I'll only have to heat it."

"No. Thank you."

Clarisse plucked at her robe helplessly. "I'm awfully sorry about the way the house looks, and the way I'm dressed. You probably think I'm terrible, but I wasn't feeling too well this morning, so I've been resting in bed."

"Of course," Mrs. Brent said flatly. "Shall we sit down?"

"Certainly, yes, forgive me." They sat. Clarisse abruptly became aware of a faint sound, the high, barely audible buzz of a trapped, unseen fly butting its head against a window pane. And she saw the flicker of small muscles at the corners her mother-in-law's eyes, a flicker of annoyance commingled with a perverse sense of gratification, as though some terrible hunger had been appeased, some dark need satisfied, by this further evidence of indifferent housekeeping upon Clarisse's part.

"Clarisse," said Mrs. Brent, "I'll get right to the point. I am not a woman to beat around the bush."

Clarisse nodded attentively, feeling a yawn building up in her. She fought it.

"Daniel is concerned with you. He feels that you're keeping some secret from him, and he's very hurt."

"Oh, but I'm not keeping any secrets, Mrs. Brent. I know he thinks so, but—"

"Please." Mrs. Brent held up a hand, a pained expression on her face. "I know Daniel very well, and he has always been an unusually sensitive person, almost, one might say, psychic." She smiled deprecatingly. "If Daniel feels that you're keeping something from him, then you *are* keeping something from him. I don't know what this secret of yours is, although I have my ideas. But what I've come to tell you is this: confide in Daniel. Don't keep secrets from your husband—as far as the church is concerned, you are of one flesh, he is the head and you are the body. And it's totally absurd to imagine the body keeping secrets from the head! Isn't it?"

Clarisse nodded miserably, trying to keep her eyes open. She was so tired.

"Of course it is," the older woman went on. "Although Daniel has told me you are not a churchgoer, nevertheless, you understand. I have this to say to you: stop keeping secrets from Daniel, or leave him. If you must have you private life, your little secrets, then you're not a fit wife for him. God knows, he would be miserable if you left him, but he would heal in time, and better the quick, sharp pain of loss than the years of agony with an unfaithful wife."

"Mrs. Brent," said Clarisse, trying to summon enough energy for anger,

"I'm *not* —"

"I don't care what you are." The older woman stood up and seemed to listen for a moment. The unseen fly could no longer be heard. Mrs. Brent favored Clarisse with a hard-edged smile and said, "Think about what I've told you."

Clarisse nodded, blinking with exhaustion. Mrs. Brent let herself out. Clarisse tried to rise and found that she could not. She stopped fighting then and let herself fall asleep in the chair. Dan found her there, still sleeping, when he got home.

Things got worse and worse. He was at me all the time, remorseless, relentless, totally implacable. To make matters worse, I could no longer predict my body's reactions. Sometimes I would be looking at him, and suddenly I would perceive him as from a very great distance; then again my eye would focus upon him and bring some inconsequential detail like the mole on his left cheek into mountainous relief. Or he splintered into jagged fragments.

Once I tried to tell him what was the matter with me. Once, when he was badgering me, because I thought he might understand. It was worse than useless.

I broke into unexplained sweats, I had sudden, irrational desires, and I tried, when I saw that he did not believe I was sick, to pretend I was normal and well. I slept away the weekdays and functioned like a zombie, like a puppet, at night and on the weekends, listening to him but hearing nothing, letting him guide me around, set me here, stand me there, letting him touch me with his mouth, feeling his hands on me and his penis inside me, staring at him for minutes at a time, wondering who he was.

One night I woke up with fire under my shoulder blades. I was sore from his love-making, and his dried semen pulled at the fine, almost invisible hairs on the inner side of my thigh. I got out of bed and went into the bathroom, and in the mirror above the sink was the reflection of a small and undistinguished woman whom I did not recognize at first.

I went back to bed and lay awake until sunrise, watching the light of dawn suffuse the room, listening to the soft burr of breath through his nostrils, feeling shadows jump under my skin. The man who was my husband slept beside me, and I was reminded of my father and of my poor mother. How many mornings had she lain awake beside him, tight and itching in her skin, wanting and not daring to be free?

I knew what I wanted, and I realized then that I had been repressing myself—so very like my mother. I would take it no longer; I would stop worrying about the consequences. I no longer loved this man, if, indeed, I ever had. He was a stranger to me. More than that, he was a stranger who had taken liberties with my life.

Quietly, quietly, I got up and slipped into a dress. I didn't bother with underwear or anything else except shoes. It would be chilly outside, but I welcomed the chill.

I walked to the corner and caught a bus for downtown. I wanted to be high and free, away from other people, where I could breathe.

A strong updraft plucked at her hair. It was very cold on the ledge, but she did not feel the rasp of the wind on her naked body. Her body was quite numb, quite rigid, impossibly hard.

Eighteen stories below, a crowd watched and waited, peering upward, pointing, hoping. She gazed down at them and the moving bugs in the streets, but her eyes were glazed. She saw nothing that was obvious to the men who were trying to coax her back into the building. She seemed to be listening intently, as if she were awaiting the command to jump. She did not appear to hear the men as they called to her from the window, crooned their soothing words, offered their saving hands.

Her husband was frantic. He insisted that he could bring her in if they would let him climb out after her.

"Keep him out of the way," growled a police lieutenant as he buckled himself into a safety harness. "If she sees him she may jump for sure. I'm going out on the ledge."

He leaned out the window again. "Clarisse?"

Clarisse surprised the lieutenant by turning her head toward him.

"Clarisse," said the man, "I want to help you. Don't be frightened. I'm your friend, so you don't have anything to worry about."

She still wore that listening look, but he sensed that she was not listening to him. Suddenly, she smiled, and he felt quite shocked by the smile.

"Oh, at last," she murmured, and grew quiet again. A small, dark spot appeared on her forehead, swelled slightly, and became a fine seam that moved swiftly over the top of her skull to plunge down the hollow of her back to the crack of her buttocks. She jerked spasmodically and, with infinite slowness, began to topple forward. Then her back bulged outward and burst along the seam with the sound of many sheets tearing.

Out of the ruptured, slowly toppling body emerged a glistening head with gleaming, million-faceted eyes. Filmy, wire-veined wings like stained-glass windows unfurled, sparkling wetly beneath the morning sun, and were followed by a long segmented body.

She pulled herself out and rested daintily on the ledge, drying her wings in the cold air, watching her old body complete its slow-motion pitch forward, watching it spin and float down eighteen stories, the honey-blonde mass of hair whipping about the paraffin shoulders, the smile frozen on the translucent face.

Then she gave a gentle push with her six silver legs and flew away on whirring rainbows.

Inside, the men were perplexed for a few moments, all of them crowded together at the window and staring out in unwilling belief. Daniel Brent was the first to speak, and he was quite incoherent with rage. "She—she—" was all he could say.

But the men wasted only those first few seconds, no more. With one accord, they donned their spider suits and set out after me.

I circled above the city, awed, happy, a little frightened, a little uncertain, waiting to see what happened next. I felt the urge to climb as high as I could go, to remain gloriously suspended between stars and the closer, brighter lights of the world below, to mate with one of my own kind, to live out my new life above the earth. But something held me back, something that bordered on grief as I thought again of my mother, who had permitted herself to be robbed of this, who had chosen to live out her life in that drab woman-skin. And this something, this grief, was my undoing. I should not have stayed near the city; I should have been wiser. But I continued to circle around and around, shedding golden tears from the drupelet-like facets of my eyes, golden tears of grief for my mother. I dropped closer to the city when night fell, and that is when and how they caught me.

I would have been safe if I'd yielded to my first instinct and flown far away—they could never have followed then, because spiders don't fly, they only weave webs to catch flies.

They keep me in this sticky web, too sophisticated to eat me outright. Sometimes, at night, Dan unbinds me and lets me crawl around. But he's cut off my wings, and I can never fly again.

In Brightest Day, In Blackest Night

LARRY REFUSES TO COME INTO MY ROOM. He never has cared for my collection. He stands in the doorway and speaks softly, soothingly, as though to a child. If only I could tell him.

"Earl," he says. "This is Larry," he says.

I *know* who he is, and I won't be patronized. I go back to my comic books, which I've arranged on the carpet around me. I have a whole room full of comic books, most of which are older than I am. *Flash Comics, Boy Commandos, The Human Torch, Doll Man.* I open one of the brittle magazines at random and see Captain America in all his four-color glory, wading through a pack of rotund yellow men with buck teeth and thick glasses. A few pages over, the Sub-Mariner is ripping apart a German U-boat with his bare hands. Nazi sailors tumble out, scattering Lugers and monocles in every direction.

"Earl." Larry's being patient. It occurs to me that he may indeed care too much, and if that's the case, he will be a very bitter person by the time he's old. You have to be super if you expect to get by and not have your compassion for your fellow man turned inside out by all of the misery in the world.

"Earl," Larry says again. "What happened? What *happened*, for God's sake?"

He sounds … agonized. It may only be (I tell myself) that he's in love with my wife. In either case, it's my duty to set his mind at ease. I have, after all, dedicated my powers to the betterment of humanity.

"Don't worry," I tell him. "Nothing happened, Larry. She ran out of the house crying, that's all."

173

I put Captain America and the Sub-Mariner away, then look around at the garish covers on the floor. Ah, Sheena, Queen of the Jungle. Ah, Hawkman and Blue Beetle, Airboy and Fighting Yank. Where are you when I need you most? Must I do it all without help from you? Don't you remember how much misery there is in the world?

The telephone is ringing. I brush past Larry and go to answer it. A woman at the other end of the connection begins delivering her spiel with all the sincerity of a high-school girl laboring through Ophelia's lines in the senior class spring play.

I am, it seems, being offered an expenses-paid trip for two to wonderful Las Vegas, plus a two-hundred-dollar certificate book redeemable at certain local stores AND a glossy color portrait of my family. Mine, all mine, if I'm able to answer a question correctly within thirty seconds. I let the woman chatter along without interruption. I know her game, but I'm curious to find out what her question is. Mine is the Wisdom of Solomon.

"As everybody knows," she is saying, "Abraham Lincoln and John F. Kennedy were assassinated. Now, the question is, which one of the following men was also assassinated while serving as President of the United States—James Garfield, Andrew Jackson, or William McKinley?"

Which *one*? Aha, a fatal slip on her part. They all make fatal slips eventually. "James Garfield," I answer. "*And* William McKinley."

"That is correct!" she tells me in a tinkly voice. "Now, if you'll just give me your name and address, our agent will come over with your certificate book and—"

"Oh, you needn't bother. I'm not interested in going to Las Vegas. I never accept rewards. I only wanted to hear your question."

"Oh." I've stripped her gears. Nothing in her script to get her through this unforeseen development. Little did she realize how easily I saw through her diabolical plan to discover my secret identity. She makes some more noises over the phone. "Oh. Uh. Well. Are you, uh, *sure*?"

"Yes. Thank you." I ring off. Shazam. The World's Mightiest Mortal triumphs again.

What really happened, Larry? My wife left me. I shed the light over the evil things, for they cannot stand the light, and she ran out of the house crying.

And now Larry's gone, too. I turned aside his questions. I frustrated his efforts to learn too much. We crime fighters must have our secrets. Our calling cuts us off from the rest of humanity, makes intercourse with mere mortals difficult and sometimes impossible.

So now Larry's gone, too, and I am able to get on with my great task of ridding this world of crime.

And now I cloak myself in darkness. And now I make myself a creature of the night, a symbol that will strike terror in superstitious, cowardly hearts. And now, and now ....

There is so much misery in the world. It's going to be rough out there tonight.

Outlaw Glory

IT WAS ONLY AFTER HE HAD PARKED the car and begun walking across the lot toward the old school building that the first bubble of doubt rose and burst upon the surface of his mind. He stopped dead in his tracks and sagged against somebody's station wagon, and he thought: What the hell am I doing here? What good will this do?

He felt petty and mean all of a sudden. He felt like a kid again, an arrogant, spiteful, nasty punk kid. The anger was still there inside, the hatred still festered within. This was madness. This was worse than useless.

Bruce Holt hissed a disgusted sound and glumly surveyed the parking lot. There were, at most, two dozen automobiles there. Giant insects in the moonlight; scarabs crouching, asleep for the moment, on the carcass of a small town. The writer in him took over, spinning the phrases through his mind. He thought, bitterly, Scrivener, bedazzle yourself.

He still had Betty Hardy's neatly folded letter in a pocket of his brown suede jacket. He had read it any number of times and knew it by heart:

> Dear Bruce,
>
> As you have surely surmised from the address above, I'm no longer living in Tennessee. It's a long story, I'm afraid, and a rather unhappy one. I'm also afraid there's no chance of my getting to attend your class reunion, as much as I'd like to see you after all these years.
>
> Thanks very much for the copies of your books. You have my warmest congratulations — it's not everyone who gets to realize his or her fondest dream. You always insisted that you'd be a writer, and, obviously, you've succeeded. You have my deepest thanks,

too, because you've made me proud of my own profession. That a former student of mine should feel that I played a part in his achieving success is indeed gratifying ....

Good old Betty Hardy. A gem of a teacher—he had been aware of that almost from the first. A truly fine, intelligent, compassionate woman, wasted in this awful town. No, not entirely wasted. She had been there to give him needed understanding and encouragement. He had made his dream come true, and he owed Betty Hardy a lot more, and a lot better, than he expected to give out this night.

Bruce pushed himself away from the station wagon and walked across the parking lot, across the blacktop driveway where the ancient yellow buses sat nose to butt, through the front door, into the lobby with its hideous linoleum floor and vinyl-upholstered benches. A thin, sharp odor—sweat, tennis shoes, and menstruating girls?—hung on the air. He smiled in spite of himself. It brought back memories.

Affixed to the wall was a neatly lettered sign: WELCOME BACK, CLASS! REUNION IN GYM—THIS WAY! He walked down the old, familiar corridor, turned a corner, and got his first look at what a decade in a small town had done to at least one of the people with whom he had graduated.

The woman seated behind the reception table was old at the age of twenty-eight. She looked hard and flaccid at the same time, as though she were some sort of boneless creature held upright in her seat by a lacquered exoskeleton of cosmetics. She gave him a smile as he approached, and it was an eloquently brittle smile that relayed to him all that he could have wished to imagine about this person. One-time high-school sexpot? Two or more children now, regular sessions at the beauty salon? Old man never went down on her? Occasional adulteries in mobile homes?

"May I help you?" she asked with nervous brightness.

I have an appointment with the doctor, Bruce thought, then chided himself. Be cool, Holt. That's what you're here for, isn't it? "I'm here for class reunion. I'm Bruce Holt."

"Bruce Holt," she repeated, running a crimson fingernail down a hectographed list of names. "Oh, of *course*. Here you are. I'm Regina Harris. Used to be Ferguson, but I got married. Remember me?"

He looked at her helplessly, all of the names and faces suddenly gone from his memory. He stared at her list of names and ran his finger along the line of his jaw, pretending to concentrate.

"We hadda class together," Regina Harris offered. "Mrs. Taylor's speech class, remember? You were always arguing with her."

Bruce forced himself to say, "Well, hello, Regina," but the total inanity of the remark closed his mind to her reply, shut out all of her words. He nodded in time with the movement of her mouth, watching, fascinated, as her jaw muscles rolled and rippled under the stratum of make-up. And he knew now that he wanted only to get away, that he had been a fool to come here, that he could not bear to enter the gymnasium and survey the wreckage of his graduating class.

He glanced away from Regina Harris and saw, through the opened door, that they had already noticed him. They were approaching the reception table, heads slightly cocked, smiles arranged. He found something sinister about their slightly stiff-jointed walk, in their muted voices, in the way their expressions slowly suffused with recognition. He imagined their thoughts. Why, yes, yes, it has to be old Bruce Holt, we remember Bruce Holt, wanted to be a writer, real smart guy, that one, real sassy one, too, real trouble-maker, always talking back to Mr. Parker in history class, real punk, real shitass then, always talking about free love and ending the war and drugs, always reading books and using big words, oh yes, Bruce Holt, we remember *you*, nigger-lover long-hair son of a bitch.

Certain members of the football team had cornered Bruce Holt in the boys' room late one afternoon. He had been a lean, wiry kid, no match for guys with ham-like fists and arms as big around as his thighs. After they had tossed and slapped him around for several minutes, they pinned him down and whacked off irregular hanks of his hair.

Someone else had reported him for reading an allegedly dirty book in the school library. The book had been a paperbound copy of *Boys and Girls Together*, by William Goldman. It had been taken from him and torn to pieces by the librarian.

There had been the time somebody got into his locker and planted a *Playboy* centerfold, then turned him in to the principal. There had been the time he was sent to the office for consultation, because he had hotly disputed his history teacher's contention that black people could never amount to anything on their own. There had been the time one of the jocks challenged him to a fight for stating that an agrarian economic base, rather than Yankee treachery, had cost the Confederacy victory. There had been the time ….

There had been all of those times of ten years before.

Bruce Holt took a step backward as a gentle wave of scents preceded his ex-classmates through the door: hair oil, make-up, cheap perfume, meat loaf and tomato catsup, menthol cigarettes, damp armpits, sweaty feet. The smoked-beef faces of the men, the unnaturally pink faces of the women, closed in on him and filled him with terror. He wanted to turn and run as their voices washed over him and their hands touched his.

Bruce Holt. It *is* Bruce Holt. Hasn't changed a bit. Where ya been, Bruce? Remember me? What're you up to nowadays? Remember me?

The unknown names and faces. He wheeled and weaved among them like a matador, gliding his hand along one of theirs as he spun out of the way, trying to escape from their midst as he grinned and nodded and pretended to remember. He knew none of them. These were the lost ones, the ones who had been born in this town, who lived here all their lives, who would die here. The ones who had not got away. The ones for whom there was no chance of escape — the football players who had failed to make it into college, onto college teams, the former cheerleaders, the former whores, the farm boys, the hangers-on, the perennial teenagers who had stuck around, working in the furniture factory during the week, playing football on the school grounds on Saturday afternoons, cruising the Dairy Queen in search of poontang on Saturday nights, clinging to their youth as best they could. He knew none of them. The people he had known well were gone. Married and moved away, dead in car wrecks, plane crashes, Vietnam. An infinite sea of succinct details.

He abruptly emerged from them all but blundered into the wall. Then he saw Michelle. All he could say by way of greeting was, "My God."

"Hello, Bruce." Michelle was still slim and pretty. She wore her hair long and straight now, rather than teased into a beehive-shaped affair. No make-up, not even fingernail polish. She looked terrific.

"You are," he said, "a sight for sore eyes, as the saying goes."

Michelle gave a small laugh and moved to his side. "You men. Always feeding us girls a line." But there was real warmth in the way she took his hand and held it for a couple of seconds. Bruce felt himself grow calm, felt a surge of his accustomed self-assurance.

"Jesus, is there someplace we can sit and talk? You still living in this godawful town, Michelle. I mean, what've you been *up* to?"

She steered him toward two chairs. "I was sort of wondering if you'd show up, Bruce. It was a dull evening until now."

They sat side by side. Bruce leaned toward her and whispered conspiratorially, "Who the hell *are* these people?"

"Nobody I used to know," she admitted. "How are you these days? Where are you living?"

"Dallas, Texas."

"*Texas?*"

"Yeah, well, you know how it is. Dropped out of college after my mother died, bummed around for a while, wound up in Dallas. Came alla way back to the land of cotton just to see you."

"I bet. I'm surprised you even recognized me after—how long has it been?"

"Jeeze, seven, eight years, I guess. Not since the funeral. You, you're the first person I've seen that I know. Got into town yesterday morning and did nothing all day except drive around, sizing the place up, you know. Everybody's gone or something. What're you doing here, Michelle?"

She made a shrugging motion and looked at the milling strangers. "Just messing around. I live in Nashville, actually. But I come back to see my parents now and then. And the kids."

Bruce started. "Kids?"

"I was married for a while." Her voice went flat, dead. "I had some kids."

Bruce studied the toes of his boots. "I never did get married."

"Why not?"

It was his turn to shrug. "Opposed it on principle, I suppose."

Michelle laughed again. "For once, your principles seem to have kept you out of trouble. Are you still going around trying to change the world?"

"Sometimes."

"What do you do?"

"I write. I'm a writer."

Michelle smiled fleetingly. "I remember. You let me read some of your stories in school. They were pretty good."

"I'm glad you thought so."

"What all have you written?"

"Everything. *Moby-Dick. Tarzan of the Apes. Detective Comics.*"

"No, *seriously.*"

"Just a bunch of stuff. Short stories, articles, a few poems, some novels. Even did a script for a science-fiction movie that never got filmed. Probably just as well. It was a bad script, real hackwork. Ambulatory artichokes from Algol terrorize helpless Earthwomen."

"All the same, you must be happy. You're doing what you always wanted to. I'm happy for you, Bruce." There was something of sadness in her voice.

Bruce gave her an appraising look but could not fathom her expression. Michelle had been one of the very few people whom he had actively liked during his high-school days. They had dated occasionally and, once, even got as far as feeling up each other at a drive-in theater. But his reputation as a dissenter, a classroom trouble-maker, had found its way to her parents. Bruce Holt was a renegade, an outlaw; *ergo*, those who associated with him were likewise outlaws. Michelle Patterson was *not* going to be tarred with that brush. There had been no more dates with Bruce Holt, boy gadfly.

What happened to you? he wondered. The probabilities unfolded in his head. Married too young, and to the wrong guy. Too many kids too soon. Marital entropy. Arguments. An affair on the side, perhaps, and discovery thereof. Divorce. Visiting privileges on weekends: a mark of true compassion, or of true sadistic vindictiveness, on the part of ex-hubby. And what else? Too many desperate short-term relationships with men?

He suddenly noted with alarm that the strangers were gathering before them, ready to join in any conversation. He reached over into Michelle's lap and gently but firmly took her hand. She gave him a startled, almost a frightened, look.

"Come on," he said, rising, "there's no revenge to be had here," and before she could reply or the others could close in a second time, he was leading her out of the gymnasium, out of the old school building, out of an absurd evening.

And, as it happened, into his bed at the E-Z Rest Motel.

Bruce entered Michelle from behind, because she said that was the way she liked it. As he sank himself into her upturned bottom and heard her gasp and saw the flesh of her back and buttocks flash pink, green, pink, green in the light of the enormous neon sign just outside his room, the awareness of what he was doing erupted inside his skull and spread downward into his heart and guts.

Bruce Holt had come back to his small, dead hometown for the sole purpose of strutting and crowing his triumph at the tormentors of his high-school days, of shouting in their faces: I'm free, God damn you, I'm well off, I'm secure, I'm satisfied, I'm even mildly famous, and I just wanted each and every one of you to know about it, because I want that knowledge to gnaw at your souls as you muddle through your miserable little lives; I want you to envy me with every atom of your being; I want you to go to your graves with the realization that I succeeded in spite of your combined efforts to drive me crazy, and that you failed without any help from me!

He began to hate himself, and he plunged as deeply as he could, rocking Michelle violently. They were all gone, the jocks who had taken shears to his hair, the bitches, the plotters, the enemies, all gone and dead or disappeared or something, leaving only dull people whom he had seldom noticed and never known and did not care about.

He heard Michelle moan and felt her body quake as she started to come, and he screamed inside as the knowledge of what he was doing boiled itself down to one clear and concise statement:

There is no one left but Michelle.

And he slammed against her backside in a rage.

Someone is Watching

THE WOMAN FINALLY ENTERED THE ROOM and sat down on the edge of the bed. She was blonde, pale-skinned, pretty. She wore a loose white blouse, pleated plaid skirt, and green knee-socks, and, though she must have been in her middle twenties, her attire lent her the bearing of an intelligent but rather innocent high-school girl.

Only the eyes betrayed what lay behind the mask—eyes full of a nameless anguish.

She briefly regarded her reflection in the mirror above the vanity table opposite the bed, then took a brush from the nightstand and busied herself with her hair. When she had finished with that, she removed her shoes and peeled off the knee-socks. She had good legs, long and smooth and the color of ... of ...

The man crouching in the shadows outside her bedroom window frowned as he groped for the word or words that could best do justice to the complexion of her legs. Cream? Rose-tinted porcelain? No, no, neither of those. Alabaster? No, not alabaster. Certainly not *alabaster!*

Not that it was important, of course, he reflected wryly as he saw her stand and begin unbuttoning her blouse. What mattered, what really mattered, was that the woman had good legs. Period.

The blouse slid from her shoulders. As usual, she wore no brassiere; her melon-shaped breasts were heavy but firm-looking. She folded the garment neatly over the back of a chair, unzipped her skirt, and stepped out of it. Through the gauzy flesh-colored fabric of her panties, he could see the triangular smudge of dark blonde hair between her white thighs. He heard his own breath slowly hiss through bared teeth.

The woman studied herself in the mirror again, ran a hand along the sensuous swell of one hip and up over the subtle curve of her belly, cupped a breast. There was nothing narcissistic about her self-scrutiny; it was simple self-appraisal, as though she were asking herself, *Am I really an attractive person? Is my nose too big for the rest of my face? Are my hips too wide?*

He watched as she touched the small brown mole on her left shoulder, the vivid line of scar tissue on her abdomen, below and to the right of her navel — not an ancient appendectomy scar but a trophy, he liked to imagine, of some ill-advised escapade conceived and executed during the course of a long-ago, rough-and-tumble tomboy summer. A fleeting, sorrowful smile touched her lips. The torment-filled eyes glistened strangely in the yellowish light of the bedside lamp.

How very pretty you are, thought the man in the shadows, and how very lonely you seem.

Almost as if she had heard him telepathically, she nodded.

Then, turning her back on the mirror, she drew down the covers, took a paperbound novel from the drawer of the nightstand, and crawled into bed.

Sincerely touched, he stood in the shadows, wanting to reach out to her, wanting to say: I think you're one of the most beautiful ladies I've ever seen in my whole life; I share some of your secrets now; I know your body almost as well as you do; let me come inside and hold you safe; whatever haunts you, let me drive it away.

Wanting, and knowing that he did not *dare*, to reveal himself to her.

At last, he crept from her house, back into the night, a lithe, light-footed man in black clothes. And he wondered if it was the same paperbound book she had been reading on all of the other occasions he had peeked through her bedroom window.

Joe Laurel was his name, and voyeurism, of course, was his game.

It was not that he was a hopeless sexual deviant (he told himself), forever doomed to spying on other people's carnal carryings-on to attain his satisfaction. Nor was it that he did not like taking women into his own bed. Joe Laurel's sexual orientation was socially acceptable in every respect except save one. He liked to peek.

He had been peeking into other people's bedrooms for years, and that he was careful, that he knew exactly what he was doing and the safest ways in which to do it, was evidenced by the fact that he had never been caught at it, never even been so much as suspected of being a Peeping Tom.

Joe knew how to avoid detection. He knew how to glide from shadow to shadow, as silently as mist. He knew which houses on which blocks were inhabited by people who were careless about closing blinds and drawing curtains.

Consequently, he knew quite a lot about quite a number of men and women.

He knew, for instance, that Mrs. Martha Baldwin, a remarkably well-kept widow of about fifty, hardly ever slept alone and hardly ever slept with the same person, male or female, twice in a row. Keeping tabs on Martha's sex life had long been one of Joe's favorite pastimes. She was an imaginative and open-minded woman, she loved to experiment, and she had a keen sense of humor when it came to foodstuffs.

He also knew about the swinging young married couple who lived on Dover Court, two flawlessly beautiful human beings who regularly invited singles and other couples to their house for weekend parties. The swinging young married couple's names were Glenn and Marian. They tastes ran to leather and knotted hemp.

He knew about the thirtyish bachelor who lived in the stylish bungalow at the end of Walnut Street. The one who liked boys.

He knew about the two women who lived together on Cooper Street. The ones who liked each other.

He knew about the pale-skinned blonde's mole and abdominal scar, and he knew, too, that she was different from all the others.

Joe had been spying on her regularly for a month, drawn at first by her beauty and then by ... well, it wasn't her nighttime activities that excited his imagination. The woman lived alone, never entertained guests, never did much of anything except watch television or read or just sit in her house until it was time to retire.

It was her eyes that made him keep going back to her house.

Her incredible damned suffering *eyes.*

Mightily fascinated, Joe had tried, discreetly, to find out more about the woman than what she looked like with her clothes off. But there was no name on the mailbox in front of her house. There was nothing to indicate that she knew any of her neighbors, nothing to indicate that she did anything to make a living. The telephone never rang. The woman never stepped outside.

The more deeply involved Joe became with solving the mystery of her identity, her antecedents, her circumstances, the harder he looked for answers to his questions, the higher new and more baffling puzzles piled up.

The most persistent question of all, though, was: *Why did she always seem so* haunted?

There was no shortage of possible answers.

She was a divorcee and hated it.

She had been abandoned by a lover.

She was a new widow and hated it.

One or both or her parents had died recently, too recently for the time of grief to have passed.

She was dying—her doctor had recently told her, "Miss _____, you have six months to live, a year at most."

Somehow, none of the possible answers was convicing. None of them seemed right.

Who? What? Why? Questions, nothing but questions.

It was maddening.

For a man of Joe's temperament, it was irresistible.

One thing, however, was rapidly becoming certain: for the very first time in his whole crazy life (Joe told himself), he was actually, undeniably falling in love.

Falling in *something*, at any rate—something, he knew, that transcended mere physical desire, something that was like a hunger, but a worse hunger than any he had previously imagined possible. Something that made him ache to do considerably more than just crawl between the bed sheets with this strange woman.

He was not starved for the companionship of women.

He was starved for the companionship of this particular woman.

He wanted to take her in his arms and make her pain go away.

He wanted to make her happy.

And if that wasn't Love with a capital L, Joe decided, it was at least a *kind* of love.

Three hours after sunset, Joe donned his dark clothes and stepped out of his apartment, into a calm, moonless night. He walked casually, taking his time, doing nothing to attract attention. According to an item in that day's newspaper, the evening before, while he had been watching his pale-skinned blonde undress for bed, police officers in a prowl car had spotted and taken into custody another Peeping Tom elsewhere in the city. The man had been caught with his nose flattened against a window pane.

And probably with his fly undone, too, Joe thought with a snicker of contempt. Now *that* was disgusting and perverted behavior. Joe had *never* ….

He hid himself in the darkness behind the woman's house and waited patiently. He had spied on her long enough and well enough to have a good knowledge of her nightly routine, and he knew that not too much more time would pass before she entered the bedroom.

He listened to the distant rumble of a jetliner, to the muted sounds of automobiles, and idly wondered who was then kneeling behind Martha Baldwin's delectable upturned bottom, who was playing what kinky games with Glenn and Marian of Dover Court. Then, after approximately ten minutes had passed, he heard a sound from within the house and peeked through the blinds.

The woman stood in the center of the room, clad in a silky ankle-length robe that clung to her like a second skin, accentuating her breasts, the flare of her hips, the firm, gently rounded belly. As usual, she was studying her reflection in the mirror.

Joe heaved a long, quiet sigh of appreciation. Yes. She was gorgeous. Yes. She made him hurt with desire. Yes.

The robe, he noticed, was belted at the waist. She fumbled with the belt and let the garment fall open.

Then she turned toward the window and stared directly into his eyes, and something in her expression, in her terrible eyes, told him that she knew he was watching her and had *always* known.

Joe gasped, a sobbing, strangling noise, and took a stumbling step backward. But he could still see her through the gap in the blinds, and he could not look away from her eyes.

Her expression shifted subtly. *Come inside,* she seemed to tell him. *Come to me. Come inside now. I want you to come inside. I* need *you. Come.*

Here. Inside. With me.

He swallowed painfully and turned and, helpless to do anything else, walked around to the front of the house. He was not surprised to discover the door unlocked. He was surprised that this did not surprise him. He walked unerringly through the darkened, unfamiliar house, guided by a sense he could not name.

She was naked when he entered the bedroom. The robe lay like an atoll about her feet.

The questions bubbled up in his throat. Who are you? Where did you come from? What are you doing here? He opened his mouth, but her gaze made speech impossible. He could only stand and stare as she stepped forward and put her faintly freckled pale arms around his neck. Her breasts flattened against his chest. Her hot, astonishingly hot lips seemed to melt against his. Questions lost meaning for him.

It took Joe only a minute to undress.

And when he was in her, when he could feel the searing heat of her body as she pressed herself against him urgently, fiercely, he looked down into her face, into her eyes, and knew then that something was horribly wrong.

They were eyes that brimmed with agony beyond his imagining, eyes that opened into Hell itself. They were old, unbelievably old eyes, and they had waited a long time for this moment.

There was no escape. Her long fingernails were buried in his shoulder blades. Her heels were locked behind his thighs. He saw her terrible eyes close as she shuddered beneath him, arched her spine, and split her mouth in a soundless shriek, a silent cry of release. Helpless in the grip of his own climax, Joe rode with her all the way down.

Then, spent, sucked dry, unable to stir, he lay atop her and let warm, gray twilight fill his skull. Just before he dozed off, he saw peace displace anguish in the woman's eyes. Of the two, he could not say that peace frightened him less.

She was not at his side when he awoke. The clock on the nightstand told him that it was four in the morning. Joe yawned and sat up ... and screamed in a high, clear, unmistakably feminine voice.

On its feet in the doorway, Joe Laurel's fully dressed body turned and looked pityingly at him. "Please forgive me," it said uncertainly, obviously unused to Joe Laurel's vocal chords. "But I had no choice. I really had no choice. Neither will you when the time comes."

On the bed, Joe looked down at his large, pink-tipped breasts, the vivid scar on his abdomen, the dark blonde thatch between his thighs, and screamed again.

"Thank you," his body said as it left, "for setting me free."

When she entered the bedroom, it was all she could do to avoid looking at the gap between the blinds and the window sill. Salvation would come from that quarter. Eventually. But she had to be patient, and she had to play the game according to its hellish rules.

She sat down on the edge of the bed and stared at her reflection in the mirror above the vanity table.

Time had passed slowly for the woman with the haunted eyes. There were books, records, a television set. But she could not leave the house. The doors would not open for her. She had spent her days, more days than she could number, in boredom relieved only at long intervals, when she awoke to discover that she and the rooms to which she was confined had been moved somehow, shoehorned into a different house in a different neighborhood in a different city.

She didn't understand any of it. She no longer cared. Only one thing was important any more.

She began to brush her hair. After several minutes, she paused and smiled at the mirror, and her image smiled back, sadly, briefly. Yes, the two pale-skinned blondes agreed. Someone is watching.

Ask Athena

O, Wise Athena,

   I am a recent convert to paganism and greatly admire you as the goddess of wisdom, arts, and defensive warfare. I would become your worshipper and try to be worthy of you, but that whole chastity thing is a bit of a turn-off. You're supposed to be impervious to love, and I want to keep my options open regarding romance and marriage. Would I be more comfortable worshipping Aphrodite, or Hera, or even one of those beautiful Northern love goddesses like Freya?

(Signed) VACILLATING VIRGIN

Dear Vacillating Virgin:

   Worshipping Aphrodite is easy, but, then, so is she. Hera is jealous, exacting, and vindictive, and it shouldn't surprise anyone that she can't keep Zeus at home or that their kids have so many problems. As for a certain Norse bimbo, I can tell you for a fact that that's not her real hair.

Dear Athena,

   I'm a shepherd and spend most of my time in the hills, minding my flocks and my business. Well, one day, this great-looking woman appears out of nowhere and completely naked except for this weird little cloud, and so what am I going to do but look. I mean, it's natural, right? THEN she reveals herself as some goddess and because I've stared at her divine person I get withered on the spot. Is this fair? I mean, who appeared naked to who?
                                              -- SHRIVELED & SEETHING

193

Dear Shriveled:

No, it most certainly isn't fair, as mortals reckon fairness. It is, however, all in a day's work for a divinity. Just deal with it.

Most Divine Athena,

Please help me. I was with my girlfriends in a meadow when a great bull carried me across the sea to Crete. There I found out it's not a real bull at all (like I didn't have my suspicions by then) but this guy who says he's "the Ruler of Olympus, Lord of the Sky, the Rain God, the Cloud-Gatherer, and the Wielder of the Awful Thunderbolt" (in his words). But even though he's a god and I'm a mortal (and in spite of the difference in our ages), we hit it off pretty well and one thing led to another, if you get my meaning. The next thing I know, I'm going to have a baby and I haven't seen or heard from the "Wielder of the Awful Thunderbolt" in weeks! And I hear he's in the habit of disguising himself as a bull or a swan or even a shower of gold and going after every woman he sees. Plus, he's married to this insanely jealous goddess, but she won't rein him in, oh no, she's got to take it out on the poor unsuspecting women ol' "Lord of Olympus" has seduced. I keep telling myself that maybe these are only legends, but it doesn't help. I'm confused and scared. Please tell me what to do, Goddess.

-- KNOCKED UP IN KNOSSOS

Dear Knocked Up:

Your story and the one preceding it are typical of many I hear. Far be it from me to harp on Hera's home life; my advice to you is to stay indoors and sacrifice to Hestia. This may not save you from being turned into a bear, but, as a mortal, you have only a mortal's limited options. Sorry.

Applications to the Goddess may be made at the Parthenon, or, if you can't get to Greece, at the full-size replica in Centennial Park, Nashville, Tennessee. Don't forget to bring a sacrifice.

Sidhe

"HUNGRY, AREN'T YOU?" THE VOICE was like a mother's: sweet, cooing. "You've come a long way. You must be hungry."

It showed its maw but said nothing.

"Soon. Soon. I promise. A feast."

In the sickly yellow light of the candles, it smiled a terrible smile. Then it began putting its face on.

It was no good. He had been standing before the easel, the charcoal stick ready in his hand, for the better part of the afternoon, and he was finally forced to admit to himself that it was no good. He could not begin to block in the composition. None of his preliminary sketches made any sense to him any more.

Harry Beckett breathed a curse as he put the charcoal away. The melancholy second movement of Bach's *Concerto in A Minor* was suddenly too depressing to be endured. He walked over to the stereo, thumbed the reject button, watched as the arm dutifully rose, swung to the side, and settled into its cradle. He waited until the turntable had come to a complete stop before lifting the record from the spindle and returning it to its protective sleeve.

Taped to the wall above the record player was a note that read *Deadline Apr. 29!!!* Nearby, on the mantelpiece of the bricked-up fireplace, was Sheila's parting shot. It had come by mail that morning. It was a wax doll, bound in a strip of cloth torn from one of his old work shirts. It had neither eyes nor hands. The disproportionately large genitals bore the mark of a woman's incisors.

Harry picked up the doll and cradled it in his hand. What a crazy woman. It was wax. Just wax. It had nothing whatsoever to do with his present inability to get any work done. Hell, everyone had blocks from time to time — artists, writers, bottle-opener salesmen. But he knew that Sheila believed, truly believed, in the power of the doll. A real weirdo, that Sheila. A real mental case. The feminist sorceress herself.

You sure can pick 'em, he told himself sourly as he placed the doll on the mantelpiece again. Oh, to be sure, Sheila had had her virtues. Harry felt a smile creep over his face as he recalled her prowess in bed. What an expert mouth. He would have been quite happy to continue the relationship had Sheila been less possessive, less clinging, had she not begun demanding too much of him.

"And strange," he muttered to the doll. "She's so strange. And now ...."

And now he was having an attack of artistic constipation, and that was supposed to be the doll's doing, right? No hands or eyes for Harry Beckett. Tsk. The crisis of the contemporary artist.

Harry turned and looked about his studio. There was the derrick-like hulk of his easel. There was the wooden table with its boxes full of tubes of pigment, bottles of tempera, Mason jars bristling with paint brushes, an assortment of crucibles, spoons, putty knives, thumb tacks, bits of chalk and charcoal. Useless, all of it. Going to waste today.

Just like me. Crap.

When the telephone rang, Harry stared at it for several seconds before going over to answer it. Something writhed in his mind: *it's Sheila, of course, she can't leave me alone, the bitch.*

It was Sheila, too.

"How's the playboy of the Western hemisphere today?" she said, very nastily. "How many broads have you tumbled this week?"

"What do you want now?" he countered tiredly. "Can't you get it through your pointy little head that I'm sick of arguing with you? Is that beyond your powers of comprehension?"

"Oh, I got the message, all right. You spelled it out loud and clear the other night at the Wallaces' with that woman. You made it perfectly clear when you didn't bother to say a single word to me. Who was she, anyway? Or did you take the time to learn her name?"

"You used that insult yesterday, Sheila."

"Weren't you the least bit embarrassed or ashamed or anything?"

"You know how it is."

"Yeah. I know how it is. You're just like all the other men I've ever known, Harry. A sexual predator. A wild dog running through a hen house, trying to take a bite out of each chicken."

Harry had to laugh at the image. "When're you going to grow up? Did you expect me to fall in love with you or something?"

"I expected respect, at the very least! I didn't expect to be treated like a toy, something you could take out of its box whenever you felt like playing. Something you could just toss aside when you found yourself some new toys. I didn't expect to find out I was just a lay. God damn it, I *trusted* you! I thought you were an exception to the rule. I thought you were different from other men. But you're not. It's just a game to you. Women are sport as far as you're concerned. Prey."

"Sheila, you're beginning to bore me. We've had this argument eight dozen times already in the last five days. If you don't have anything original to say, I might as well hang up. I'm too busy to listen to more of your socio-political dribble."

He heard her suck in her breath. "Just this, Harry," she said, and her voice was as hard and sharp as a knife. "I've had it. I can't take any more. I'm declaring war."

"I can see it in tomorrow's headlines. 'Sheila McCullough Declares War On Men.'"

"You catch on quick, asshole. Did you get my little gift in the mail. That's for openers."

"I think it's cute," Harry said, in a deliberately cheery tone. "I'll treasure it always. Meanwhile, have you conjured up any good demons lately? Or do even the spirits know what a drag you are?"

"Go ahead and laugh. Laugh your God-damned balls off. But I'm not finished with you. Not yet. Not by a long shot."

"I am laughing, Sheila. Now, if you'll excuse me—"

"Not yet!" Sheila screeched. She paused for a moment, and when she spoke again, her voice sounded suddenly weary. "Don't hang up yet. I have a lot to say to you. Know what I've decided, Harry. I've decided there are too many predatory men in the world. I'm sick of them. It's time I did something about them."

"A threat?" Harry inquired mildly.

"A promise."

"What're you going to do? Take out a contract on every guy who ever got his fill of you?"

"I'm the one who'll do it."

"Ha. Jacqueline the Ripper."

"Watch out, Harry. Watch out for carnivorous women."

"Eat me."

"You're going to get it, you son of a bitch!"

"Not from *you*, honey."

"Yes! From me!" Sheila's voice went up the scale again. "From me! Think of me, Harry, when the *sidhe* gets hold of you. See how much you laugh then."

"The she? Who?"

"S-i-d-h-e, Gaelic, *shee*, bastard. You'll know it when the time comes. And then it's going to be all over for you and your kind."

"Go ride your broomstick, little witch."

"It'd be a better ride than you ever gave me!"

Harry grunted and dropped the telephone into its cradle. What a *crazy* bitch.

He should have guessed as much, he reflected, from the very start. One look at her apartment should have been enough to make him leave Sheila right there and go looking for a more conventional woman. The smelly black candles, the astrological charts, the books on such charming subjects as voodoo and demonology. The insane cabalistic patterns chalked on the floors and walls. Jeeze. And then there was all that stuff she had told him about other men—two catastrophic marriages by the time she was twenty-six, followed by a near-miss and a series of pretty ghastly-sounding affairs. He had listened to the recital because it was the price he knew he had to pay to get her into bed. And, okay, so Sheila had had a rough time. Give her that much.

But lust and even a flicker of real compassion should not have blinded him to the fact that she was a volatile bundle of neuroses spilling over into psychoses.

And he refused to feel like a villain simply because she needed one thing and he wanted a different thing.

Ah well, he thought, turning from the telephone, we should all learn from our mistakes, Harry. He eyed the wax doll and shook his head. Sheila did always take herself too seriously. Just for openers, huh? The *sidhe* next, eh?

So what in hell was the *sidhe*?

"Go now. He'll find you." No longer sweet, cooing, the voice sounded ragged with fatigue. "Go now."

Away, away, running its tongue over its teeth. Away, out of the domain of shadow.

After a light supper, Harry returned to his easel and absently plucked a paint brush from its jar as he contemplated the blank canvas. He stroked his chin, cheek, upper lip with the brush's soft tip. He could detect a tang of turpentine in the hairs, and he swore irritably. He had always been extremely fastidious about his equipment, always rinsing brushes in warm water after soaking the pigment from them with solvent. He looked at the preliminary drawings. They seemed worse than ever.

What the hell's wrong with me?

He considered the possibilities. A virus? A slump in the ol' bio-rhythm?

Was Sheila actually getting to him?

Amused by the thought, he set the brush aside and looked over the top of the canvas, toward the fireplace. His gaze locked on the wax doll.

Did Sheila really put a whammy on me, little doll?

The doll eyelessly returned his stare.

"Well, screw you and her both."

Harry went to his bookcase in the den. He checked Bulfinch and *The Golden Bough, The Book of Imaginary Beings* and *The American Heritage Dictionary of the English Language*. No *sidhe*. Harry shrugged and gave up.

He showered and shaved, then spent a couple of minutes regarding his reflection in the bathroom mirror. He grinned experimentally, eyed his dimples critically, nodded with approval. Perhaps he did have the look of a predator. So what was wrong with that? He knew how and where to pick up women, and it went without saying that women who frequented those places expected to be picked up. That was how it was, whether Sheila liked it or not. It was a system that worked to most folks' satisfaction.

The Beasts of Love

Out of the domain of shadow. Into the world of men.

Harry met Virginia in a fashionable pub less than an hour after he had left his house. Within ten minutes of the meeting, he felt he had her all but eating out of his hand. She was a long, sleek woman with nice breasts, lustrous dark eyes, a mouth that virtually radiated carnality. She was a knock-out, Virginia was, and Harry knew that she was his from the word go.

He turned on the charm. He fed her the properly offhanded remarks which led her to ask what he did, and he made the words "magazine illustrator" sound as glamorous as any others in the language. He plied her with artlessly clever conversation and made a point of asking just the right number of intelligent questions when she told him that she had worked with an independent film-maker in California for several years. Harry worked his magic. He spun his web about her, savoring every moment, every twist and turn in the game of conquest, as he steered her, cleverly, subtly, so subtly, along the way toward his bed. Not all of Harry's talents were connected with commercial art.

When they reached his house, they did not immediately tumble into bed. There were, after all, rules governing this sort of thing. Virginia accepted a drink and asked to see his studio. "I've never met a *really* successful artist before," she said, and it was all Harry could do to keep from laughing out loud with delight. What a kitten this Virginia was!

He led her into the studio and let her wander about while he watched her, admiring the play of muscles beneath her sheer, clinging dress, occasionally answering questions about the mechanics of magazine illustration. Then, after several minutes, he moved to her side and slipped an arm about her waist. Virginia seemed to melt against him.

Harry felt her lips at his throat and shivered slightly, acutely aware of the pressure building up in his loins. One of his hands roved up her side to her breast. She moaned with pleasure as his finger massaged her nipple through the fabric. He considered having her right there in the studio.

Then the wax doll caught his eye, and he felt himself deflate. Virginia's hands played at the buttons of his shirt. He pulled away from her.

"Is something the matter?" she asked, looking startled.

"No. No." Harry fought to conceal his dismay. "Uh, let's try the bedroom. Much more comfortable there."

Virginia smiled wickedly and kissed him. Her tongue slid into his mouth.

Arm in arm, they walked to the door. Harry glanced about the room after switching off the lights. He fancied that he could see the doll in the darkness. There was something sinister about the angularity of his easel now. The gray rectangle of the untouched canvas seemed to mock him.

Tomorrow, he promised himself as they entered the bedroom. I'll be all right tomorrow.

Virginia walked over to the bed and came out of her dress with marvelous ease. His mouth went dry at the sight of her pale flesh. She hooked a thumb in the elastic band of her panties and slowly, teasingly, slid them down. As she stepped out of them, she said, "It's just occurred to me, Harry. I don't even know your last name. What if I should want you to autograph something later?"

Harry began disrobing. "Beckett. As in Saint Thomas."

Virginia giggled.

"What about you?" he said. "I don't know your last name, either."

"Dentata." She moved into his arms. "Anything else you'd like to know?"

"Sure." Harry grinned, enjoying this verbal foreplay. "What's a *sidhe*?"

"A malign spirit," Virginia replied, without a moment's hesitation.

Harry looked at her incredulously.

"It's a kind of succubus," she went on, "capable of assuming human form. But it's meaner."

Harry let his arms fall. "How ... I mean, *how* do you know about this? I couldn't find a *sidhe* in any of my books. How do you know what a *sidhe* is?"

"I told you, I worked in Hollywood for a few years. And one of the films I worked on was called 'Shriek of the Demon.' About a sorcerer who sends a *sidhe* to destroy his enemies."

"That's incredible. That's really incredible. I mean, I was joking when I asked you about it. I was just ... wow. That's really strange." Harry laughed nervously.

"The world is full of surprises," said Virginia, with a shrug. Her breasts jiggled invitingly. "I *also* worked on films like 'The Swinging Newlyweds' and 'The Flying Hookers.'"

Harry reached out to cup her breasts with his hands. She put her hands on his wrists and drew him toward the bed.

It was exquisite.

Harry had taken, by his own count, approximately one hundred women to bed in his time—good women and bad ones. Virginia was definitely the best. Seated astride him, she groaned, moaned, cried out, raked his chest with her polished nails, heaved and bucked and made animal noises as he rocked her with careful pelvic thrusts.

Then, just as he approached climax, she slipped off and rolled away from him.

He yelped, "Hey!"

"Relax," she gasped. "I'll have something special for you in a minute. Just let me catch my breath."

Something special? Harry's groin tightened in anticipation. He propped himself up on one elbow and regarded her. Her skin looked almost white, and the pale flesh of her hands and legs seemed to blend into the whiteness of the bedsheet. The rise and fall of her breathing caused all but imperceptible shiftings of shadow under her arms and in the hollow of her throat. Harry watched with an artist's interest for a moment, enthralled by the composition, then let his gaze travel to the magnificent breasts, the sensuous swell of the belly, the pubes, the thighs. Despite the furnace in his loins, he felt curiously at peace with everything all of a sudden. The day's frustrations had drained away. He might have to see more of this Virginia.

"You're really a gorgeous lady," he said sincerely.

"I'm glad you like me."

"I do. Now. About that something special."

Virginia laughed. He gasped as her hand closed around his throbbing member. "I aim to please, Harry. How would you like to be eaten?"

"Help yourself. Eat away!"

She smiled as he lay back, but it was a terrible smile. He saw that there was, suddenly, something not quite right about her teeth. He had just enough time for a quick, shrill scream before the *sidhe* shed its mask altogether and got down to the business of eating him.

And when it was finished, it went to the window to perch on the sill, a shape darker than the nighttime. There was a sweet, cooing voice on the wind.

"Wasn't that nice? Go now. Finish."

The *sidhe* looked out at the world of men and licked its lips in anticipation of the feast to come.

Losing Streak

I AM COMMITTED TO ASSASSINATING THE man who went to Mars, but it might not be such a bad idea to start by strangling my wife. I decide this without having to think about it for very long: the notion occurs to me precisely at midnight, just as the hall clock rings the first beat of the new day, and it has taken root by the twelfth chime. Yes, it might be best to kill my wife first, by way of declaring myself free of the losing streak. And it would be easy, a simple matter of rolling over onto her, straddling her, pinning her arms to the mattress with my knees, putting my hands on her neck. Pressing my thumbs against her throat, fracturing the little bone there. Easy. I have heard that death by strangulation is quick if the job is done right, and I have resolved to start doing things right for a change.

My wife sleeps at my side, snoring, dreaming angry dreams, no doubt. We argued after dinner, then made the mistake of trying to reconcile matters in bed. Another catastrophe. There is no silence like that between husband and wife in the aftermath of a failed coupling. Never mind, I tell myself, it's all part of the losing streak. Soon I will be done with it.

My wife is a disappointed and disappointing woman. Her marriage of eleven years, six months, and, ah, seven days has not lived up to the great expectations she had as a bride at the age of nineteen. She claims that I have not fulfilled her. I cannot make her understand that I have not fulfilled even myself.

Strangling her as she sleeps would be a proper beginning, an appropriate gesture of contempt for the past dozen years of my life. She is, after all, another part of the losing streak, and I am determined to change my life. I think about strangling her until the hall clock has announced the half-hour. Then I fall asleep and dream of the day ahead, when I shall shoot the man who went to Mars.

I am lying in bed, half-awake, half-listening to my wife as she busies herself in the kitchen. I am, I notice, tumescent; my groin throbs with an ache that is not really pleasurable but not quite painful, either. I raise the sheets and cluck my tongue reproachfully at my penis. Too late, I tell it, where were you last night, when I needed you? But my gonads insist that amends can be made. I think of my wife in the kitchen and experience a sunburst of desire, a vivid of image of her down on her hands and knees in the middle of the floor, flanked by the refrigerator and the pantry, her ratty dressing gown pushed up around her thickening waist, my hands separating the fleshy hemispheres of her ass …. I can't remember the last time one or the other of us made any sexual overtures on the spur of the moment. No more recently, probably, than the sixth or seventh month of our marriage. The thought of my creeping out of bed and attacking her while her attention is fixed on a balky can of quickie biscuits seems less and less appealing by the second. My sunburst fades. I wilt.

It's just as well, I assure myself. It is enough that I have spared her life, without making love to her on the grimy linoleum tile.

A sharp odor of burning wafts into the bedroom. Yes, just as well. Now she can't use me as an excuse for having ruined the bacon again. I get up and check the time. I still have six hours to wait out before I play my part in the ceremonies to be held in honor of the man who went to Mars.

My brother Ed, two and one-half years my senior, called me last night.

I am always happy to hear from him. We have always been close, remarkably close, even as children. Since going our separate ways in the world—up in his case, down in mine—we have exchanged brief but affectionate letters at an average rate of four times per annum, and we always get together when we can. My failures and his successes notwithstanding, we continue to relate to each other.

Bigger than me, smarter, more durable, Ed has been my ideal for a long time, my ideal, my hero. I have never resented the fact that he is on top of the world; there is, I firmly believe, such a thing as a law governing the conservation of good fortune; I accept its dictates. Ed has always sincerely cared about me, helped me out when he had to, had sense enough to let me extricate myself, however painfully, from bad situations when I could manage it without his help. I appreciate that. The bond between us, forged in childhood, remains unsundered. "If there's *anything* you ever need from me, take it": the pact we made years ago.

Ed and I talked last night. I had the telephone clamped between my cheek and shoulder. My hands were busy with the rifle, cleaning it, oiling it.

"I wish I could drop by," Ed said, "and see you and the wife. But they keep me very busy. You know how it is. Maybe I'll be able to get away sometime tomorrow."

"Of course, Ed. I understand." I did understand, I still do, I always have. Ed is a busy man, always rushing about, doing things. His schedule is incredible. Lesser persons than my brother would crumble under the strain. "Maybe tomorrow."

"If I can get away. Promise." I heard him suck in a long breath and realized then that he was wearier than he had been letting on. "Are you going to attend the ceremonies tomorrow afternoon?"

"Wouldn't miss them for the world. Yes, I'll be there. I'll certainly be there." They have gone back to ceremonies now, all these years since the first manned spaceflights. Enough time has passed since then for the public to again be amazed by and appreciative of space exploration. Astronauts must once more be accorded the honors of old. Parades, speeches, television interviews. I will not miss the ceremonies, no.

"Well," Ed said. "How goes it with you these days?"

"Oh, much, much better." I wanted to tell him how I had made up my mind to break out of my pattern of failure, how I believed that the law governing the conservation of good fortune could be affected by outside phenomena, but I couldn't concentrate on an explanation, not while my hands were busy with the rifle, not while my wife sat at the far corner of the room, glowering, waiting for me to ring off so that she could launch into her usual tirade, the gist of which being Why Can't You Be At Least A *Little* Like Your Brother Ed? My eyes locked with hers for a second, and I wanted to tell her, too, that I would, I would be, I had decided that I would be more like my brother Ed in the future, that I was off the losing streak for good.

But my deeds will speak louder than words.

It always makes my wife nervous and irritable when I have the rifle out of its case indoors.

The rifle is the one real luxury I have allowed myself in the past five years. I like guns, the feel and smell of them, the *essence* of them. I am a pretty decent shot, and I expect to make a clean job of the man who went to Mars, one bullet through the head, fired at half the maximum effective range. He must die instantly, painlessly. I don't want to hurt him. After all, he has braved the dangers of outer space, traveled forty million miles to walk upon the Red Planet, forty million miles back to Earth, and he is entitled to some consideration.

I dropped out of college after three and one-half extremely unsatisfying semesters. My parents and my brother pretended resignation, though they all believed that *nobody* could Get Ahead, Amount To Something, without a full college education. I supported that belief. In quick succession, I had jobs as a bakery clerk, a carpenter, a laundry clerk, a delivery-van driver, a plastics cutter in an advertising-sign factory, an auto-parts salesperson, a shoe salesperson, a hydraulic-press operator. When I was twenty-one, I met, fell in love with, and married the woman who, probably through sheer inertia on both our parts, is still my wife. Because we anticipated having a first baby within twelve months of our wedding, I managed to hold on to the hydraulic-press job for a while. No first baby has ever come. I have since been a vinyl-extruder operator, a used-car salesperson (for two days), another laundry clerk, a letter carrier, an assembly-line worker in a toy factory. My wife has worked off and on as a file clerk in various insurance offices. It is just as well that we have never had children, because we can barely keep ourselves afloat as is. At the age of thirty-three, I am a tired, terrified man who goes to work at seven o'clock every weekday morning and operates at minimum efficiency until four-thirty in the afternoon. I am tired because the work is monotonous. I am terrified because of Simpson and Roark, two old men who stand on either side of me all day long, Simpson to my left, Roark to my right. They have, they tell me, worked on assembly lines all of their adult lives. They know of little else, they will never know more than they do now. They are each nearing the mandatory retirement age; when they reach it, they will go home to pursue their few avowed interests as best they may. They will die. They will be forgotten. They are already forgotten, these two disintegrating men whose dreams encompass nothing grander than dime-an-hour raises every eight months, next Sunday's televised football game, and, at the wildest extreme, a piece of Vicki Foxe, the receptionist in the front office. And I, too, am already forgotten. I, who have dreamed of Mars.

When Ed and I were children, we occasionally went to Mars and found it to be rather like the empty lot adjoining our parents' house. There were Martians, of course: they were malevolent but stationary beings that looked like elm trees.

"I am going to be an astronaut," I told Ed, quite sincerely. "I am going to be the first man to go to Mars." He smiled.

I have, of course, seen the telecasts from Mars. The planet's iron-oxide deserts are as bleak as the Moon's unrelieved gray wasteland. As was the Moon, Mars has been a let-down for some people. They secretly harbored the hope that Life As We Know It would turn up, that the astronaut who stepped from the landing module would be greeted by John Carter and Dejah Thoris and invited home to Greater Helium for dinner. I do not share that foolish sense of disappointment. I am proud, and, I feel, justly so. What matters is not that I wasn't to go to Mars but that *someone* (not just *any*one: someone; the right person) was and did and has returned.

I am looking down the barrel of my rifle, through the telescopic sight, at the man who went to Mars. He stands among the dignitaries on the review stand, and he looks healthy, bright, reasonably confident of his ability to say something meaningful to the crowd that has come to pay homage to him, a true, an authentic hero. Like the heroes of that earlier Space Age, like the Wright brothers and Christopher Columbus, he has earned immortality for himself; he can go to his grave assured of the fact that he will never be forgotten, for his name has been inscribed indelibly in the Book of Human Progress. Immortality for the man who went to Mars.

And for the other man, the one who assassinated him. Afterward, they will swarm up to my rooftop perch and bring me down. I will have lain my weapon aside by the time they reach me. I have no wish to be gunned down. I will fire the one shot necessary to kill the astronaut, and then I will surrender without a fight. Whatever happens after that will happen; my end is achieved as soon as I have fired. The losing streak that has kept me down for the past dozen years will be destroyed along with the flesh (but, ah, not the memory) of the man who went to Mars.

I am looking down the barrel of my rifle, through the telescopic sight, the crosshairs centered on the astronaut's tanned face, the past falling from me like scales, the endless succession of horrible jobs, the incessant verbal knife-fights with my wife, the condition of semi-poverty, impotence, numbing terror of spending my entire life in total obscurity, going to my grave unnoticed, unnoticed, and I know, I *know*, in the instant before I squeeze the trigger, that he, this astronaut, this man who went to Mars, would understand if he knew what is about to happen, what I am about to do. Understand and approve. It would make him proud to know that I am finally about to make something of myself. We have a pact, Ed and I.

Night Life

PRIOR TO COMING TO AMERICA, ERICH had heard a lot about the muggers. Getting himself into the country and installed in what he considered suitable quarters was an energy-draining and at times harrowing business. Erich felt that he owed himself some amusement. He entered Central Park shortly before midnight and wandered about for hours in the hope that he would get to meet a mugger.

The sky had begun to lighten in the east when Erich finally gave up. Disappointed and hungry, he went home and slept through the day.

The following night, however, he returned to the park. Less than half an hour passed before a dark, hulking shape stepped out from behind a tree, waved a stiletto in his face, and demanded money. Erich laughed with delight, a reaction that obviously upset the already nervous mugger, for he gave a soft whimpering cry and lunged with the knife.

It took Erich by surprise. He gasped as the blade slid into his chest, just below and slightly to the right of his sternum, but he managed to seize the man's wrist and squeeze. The mugger screamed. The scream was punctuated by the sound of bones snapping. The mugger fainted.

Erich looked about, straining his eyes and ears in the darkness for a sign that somebody might be coming to investigate the scream. He knew, though, that this was unlikely. Before coming to America, he had heard a lot about apathy.

He turned his attention to the knife and slowly, carefully, eased it out of his flesh. Blood seeped through the fabric of his shirt. He looked around again, looked down at the stranger, knelt beside the body.

Afterward, when he had taken what he needed, he made deep, deliberate cuts across the man's throat. Wiping the blade clean and putting it into his coat pocket, he rose, made a mocking half-salute, and left. Satisfied. Sated.

Prior to coming to America, Erich had heard a lot about the hookers. The night after his Central Park adventure, he went out on the streets in the hope that he would get to meet a hooker.

New York City was dirty and noisy and crowded. It was full of people being driven inexorably crazy. The crime rate was staggering. The air was thick with stenches and felt gritty between his teeth. New York City was a vision of perdition, and, as he walked its streets, letting himself be carried on the tides of unfriendly throngs, Erich decided that he was beginning to fall in love with it. There was nothing like New York City where he had come from. New York City, in the land of opportunity! New York City, the realm of bright lights and deep shadows ….

On the streets, Erich saw any number of women whom he thought must be hookers, but, each time he found himself on the verge of addressing one of them, he held back.

A fine time to come all over shy, he told himself. A fine time to succumb to self-doubt! Yet it occurred to him that this one, or that one, or the one over there, might *not* be a hooker after all, but an undercover policewoman—and, if so, he would be running the risk of calling unwelcome attention to himself were he to make any advances. Attention was the last thing he wanted. Erich pondered this problem on the sidewalk, near a particular woman who stood beneath a theatre marquee and appeared to be fascinated by a movie poster. Let them, he finally told himself, come to you.

He sought out a quiet bar, sat down in a booth and ordered a drink which he did not taste … and waited.

Soon, because he was not unhandsome, because he dressed well and looked as though he had money, a woman came gliding through the smoky blue haze filling the room and asked if she might join him.

Because his English was touched with just enough of an Old World accent, interest flickered for an instant behind the woman's set smile and unnaturally bright eyes when he said, "Yes, please do."

"My name is Joyce," she said. Her voice was husky.

"I am so pleased to meet you, Joyce. My name is Erich. Would you care for something to drink?"

She nodded and gave him her order, which he passed along to the bored hostess. Business was slow. Joyce's drink was on the table inside of two minutes. Erich and Joyce toasted each other. Joyce sipped. Erich did not.

"Y'know," Joyce said, "I really like your accent. Where'd you pick it up?"

Erich smiled. "I am the end-product of a very old German family. But I have lived in France, Switzerland, Spain, Italy, the British Isles. I am, or I used to be, what you may call a citizen of Europe in general."

"That's fascinating." Joyce said it as though she were sincerely impressed. She took another sip of her drink and regarded him appraisingly over the rim of her glass. "So what're you doing *here*?"

"I live here now. I have become an American. I have been here in New York City for only three nights, but already I love it."

"You *love* New York City?" This she said as though she sincerely disbelieved him. "Erich, you're sweet ... but I think you're trying to put me on. I'd give *any*thing to be able to get out."

"Oh, no, no. This is a very interesting city. I heard so much about it before coming to America. I expect to get by very well here."

"Getting by is what life in this city's all about. And you have to be real careful all the time."

"I'm careful all the time, Joyce."

Joyce nodded. Erich stared at the blood-red enamel on her fingernails. There was little sound in the smoke-filled bar.

"Well," Joyce said at length, brightening her smile, "would you like to go someplace more private, Erich?"

"It would be my greatest pleasure."

Fifteen minutes later, they were alone in a small and shabby room two doors away from the bar. Joyce named her price. Erich paid her. She put the money away and undressed with professional speed.

Her body, Erich noted as she came into his arms, was extremely pale. It was the paleness of one more accustomed to life in half-shadow and under harsh artificial light than in sunlight. It was the paleness of the complete city-dweller. It was, Erich thought, beautiful.

And, as he held her close, as his teeth slid into her neck, as she opened her mouth and sucked in air for a scream that—because his venom was quick—came out a moan, Erich felt a stab of kinship.

The part he did not like was covering his tracks afterward. Joyce was still alive when he finished with her, though unconscious and even paler than before. He knew he could not give her a chance to recover.

Erich took the stiletto from his coat pocket and destroyed her throat, taking particular pains to obliterate the marks he made there. It was better that the police should have merely another unsolved murder in their files than evidence of his true nature.

Erich went to the window and forced it open. Below, the street still teemed with the city's night life, people who walked with their hands thrust deep into their pockets, people whose eyes smouldered in their sockets, all the people he had heard about before coming to America. They were muggers, hookers, pimps, pushers, rip-off artists, two-bit con artists, low-priced killers-for-hire. In the nights to follow, he would come to know them all better.

He climbed through the window, unfurled his glossy black bat's wings, and let the warm, fetid winds of the city bear him away to his shadows and imported grave mold. And there he slept the sleep of the dead, through all the days that followed.

My Wife

THE SEA WAS A VERY CLEAR BLUE, AND Windom, standing by the water's edge with cold foam sometimes between his toes and sometimes about his ankles, could see the woman's shadow moving beneath the waves.

She broke the surface twenty yards offshore and swam smoothly, rolled with deliberate grace onto her side, onto her back, pulled her knees up, went down under again. After a moment, he belatedly began to count, one thousand and one, one thousand and two, one thousand and three. He counted, marveling, all the way to one thousand and eighty-eight before she surfaced again.

The woman stood up in knee-deep water and began wading shoreward. She was small, trim, and as dark as stained wood. Her face and shoulders and breasts seemed to incandesce as beadlets of water on her skin caught and reflected the light. It took her until midnight to wade ashore. The sun descended in a smooth arc across the western half of the sky, his shadow stretched, the sky reddened and then purpled away to blue-black. Silvery crescents rolled in from the horizon to lap at luminescent white sand. A blood-red moon appeared low over the Gulf of Mexico. It was the Gulf, of that much he was now certain. And this was his beach on his barrier island, and a house a hundred yards to his left was his beach house on that island. And the woman wading in his Gulf of Mexico was his wife, and the sight of her first filled him with rapture and then made his heart feel like a hot stone in his chest.

I never knew you could hurt me, he thought. I never knew you, of all damn people in the world, could hurt me so bad. Or make me so mad.

The temperature had dropped. Windom realized that he was dressed in a white or light-colored robe and had another folded neatly over his arm.

He tossed it to her and said, Too chilly to be running around naked.

She snatched it out of the air, then looked at it warily.

It's just a robe, he said. You look like I just tossed you a badger.

Who's ever sure with you, Win?

Put it on, he said as the stone rose in his chest, searing, strangling, before you catch your death of cold.

She shook the robe open and draped it about her shoulders, then hunkered down on the sand about ten feet from him and began drying her hair with a sleeve.

Sweet clarinet music drifted from the house.

Old music, his wife said, smiling at last.

Encouraged by the smile, he moved closer and offered her his hand. She took it gravely and let him draw her to her feet. Feel more kindly all of a sudden, he said, or just cold?

Music hath charms, she said.

Love conquers all.

A stitch in time. A fool and his money. Early to bed. She gave his hand a quick squeeze. Nice dreamy tune, Win. "Smoke Rings."

You probably own it. In among all those old music catalogs I got you for our paper anniversary.

Owning it's not the same as just listening to it and liking it.

Well, I knew how much you like that old stuff.

"Smoke Rings" faded into something else. She hummed along with it for a moment, sang softly, "It must have been moonglow that brought you to me," and cut herself off with a laugh. Or is it "brought me to you"?

Whichever. Makes about equal sense either way.

She stepped closer, slid her hands and arms under his robe, embraced him tightly. She was hot against his skin. He felt her breasts flatten against him, and there was a tickle of lust down below that unaccountably dismayed him.

What's wrong? she said as he tried to pull away. I thought you wanted me.

Yes. No. No. This isn't what I had in mind.

She reached down and touched him. "*This* this?" Her touch became a grip. Don't know whether to use it or ignore it? Her fingernails began to dig into him. He tried to push her away, but she seemed fused to him and rooted to the earth. I thought you wanted me, Win. Isn't that why you said you'd never let me go?

I loved you.

No, Win.

You're the only thing I ever loved.

No, and she tightened her grip.

The only thing.

That's the trouble. I wasn't a thing.

You're my wife.

No, Win. Was. Was.

Windom screamed as her fingernails sheared through his flesh.

Then she spun away, the moon spun away, sky, sea, and beach spun away. Everything turned itself inside out and atomized into fine gray mist. The scream had come out as a moan loud enough to wake him up. He lay at the damp center of his bed, hating, as always, the brief but real disorientation, the being out of touch and out of control, the sheer helplessness, that followed awakening. This awakening was worse than usual. There was a batholith of sorrow and anger slowly cooling within his breast, and when he remembered that today was the day, he felt not exhilaration but an utterly unWindomish self-doubt.

Call it off, Win.

Let her go.

Let nature take its course.

Old dream's only in your head, he told himself after many seconds had passed. What's that quote on Kawanishi's wall? Something some other Jap said, or maybe a Korean, with a not-entirely Oriental-sounding name. Younghill Kane. Kang? Khan? Well, whoever the hell, it's something, anyway, about nature and sin and the mind of the West, though, God knows, Kawanishi's only got the mind of the West on his mama's side of the family.

Having given him sufficient time in which to turn over and go back to sleep, the clock quietly spoke. "The time is five twelve a.m., sir. Do you wish to rise now?"

"No," he murmured.

"Do you wish the staff awakened?"

"No."

"Do you wish the light turned up?"

"No. Shut the hell up."

"Very good, sir."

"Jerk."

He had it, finally, Kawanishi's quote, or its gist, at least: To lose control of nature is, in the mind of the West, sin.

Damn straight, Windom thought.

Quietly, with as much dignity as power, the Rolls-Royce followed its dark escort through the gate and into the street. Like a lion coming out of its lair, Windom reflected with profound satisfaction. Yeah. With a black panther walking point. He let himself settle by degrees into the upholstery, heaved a sigh of pleasure, stole a glance at the man who sat beside him. The sigh had been lost on Max; the man's expression was one of exasperation commingled with resignation.

The helicopter, Windom thought, it's still the goddamn helicopter, and murmured, "Rule number one, Max."

Max leaned slightly toward him. "Beg your pardon, Mr. Windom?"

"Rule number one. Never let anybody see you're impatient as hell. Not about anything." Max blinked bemusedly and seemed to catch himself just short of shaking his head. Windom had to smile. He reached over and gave the man a friendly pat on the arm. "Oh, sit back and stop fretting. Enjoy the ride. You've got to learn to relax."

Max sat back. He did not appear to stop fretting or to enjoy the ride.

Oh, Max, my man, Windom thought, you're never going to be more than a high-priced flunky. A taker of someone else's dictation, a runner of someone else's errands. Damn, you aren't even a good ass-kisser. No grace. No style. You frown too much, and you've got no talent for putting forward a good idea in such a way I think it's my idea. And sometimes you forget who you are and who I am. Really, now. *Insisting* that I use the helicopter. Get us there faster, sir. Bad road traffic today, sir. No class, Max. A Rolls-Royce is one of the very good things in life, always has been but now more than ever, what with everybody else putting around in those damn plastic three-wheelie things. I wanted a Rolls-Royce all my life, and now I've got a whole goddamn fleet of the things, including the last one they ever made, the very last one. And I'm damn good and well going to ride in them.

Anyway, helicopters are ugly, and they make my head hurt. Upset my stomach, too. Can't think with all that damn chup-whuck racket.

Goddamn, Max, give me break today....

Bit peevish, eh. Win? Bit on edge? Got up on the wrong side of the bed, did you? Little things conspiring to take all the fun out of this day of days?

Settle down, Win. Enjoy. Celebrate. And give some credit where it's due. Max always keeps his head. No class, no grace, but a memory like a trap and goddamn good reflexes. You can nettle Max, but you can't make him flinch under fire. He found her, didn't he? Found her in time for Kawanishi to go to work on her while you stood around looking like you'd just got drop-kicked in the gonads. Which is about true, in a manner of speaking. I made you, Max, and I'll keep you. You're the most loyal and trustworthy son of a bitch I've got. You're the only son of a bitch I've got who I like. You'll always be my flunky.

He heard the buzz of the car telephone and heard Max answer it but did not move until the other man said, "It's Pete Clements, sir."

Windom pinned the speaker under his chin. "Go ahead, Pete."

"It's trouble with Fisackerly, sir." The silence of embarrassment filled the receiver. Windom, staring at the pulsating red scramble indicator set among the telephone buttons, decided that Pete was probably chewing his moustache.

Slowly, icily, Windom said, "He threatening to stall the Brazil thing if he doesn't get his way?"

"He's sure making some noises to that effect, yes, sir."

"Now, Pete, it's your job to keep him from making noises."

"I realize that, sir. But he's very stubborn. He says he'll only talk to you."

"Well, damn it, Pete, you go *un*stubborn him." Windom frowned at his own tone of voice and felt Max's gaze on him. Rule number one, he cautioned himself. "I can't–I don't want to talk to him right now, so you just put him off for the rest of the day. How is up to you. Just keep the greedy little bastard busy so he can't flush two years' work down the crapper. Sit on him, if you have to. Brazil'll keep for the afternoon." Till I tend to little missy, he said to himself. With the thought came a small, quick stab of pain in his chest. He winced and repressed a gasp and hoped that Max hadn't seen, that Pete hadn't heard. Not my heart, boys. Just my *heart.*

"Look, you keep Fisackerly occupied. I don't care how you do it. Look in his file. Under the sex stuff. Find something he likes and give it to him. Or blackmail him with it, I don't care which. For crissake, Pete, just handle this."

"Yes, sir, Mr. Windom."

Windom handed the telephone back to Max and exhaled sharply. The muscles in his neck and shoulders ached with tension. He felt as though he were trying to balance on one foot atop a large ball. Motion in any direction was an invitation to disaster.

This Brazil thing's gonna kill me, he thought. I'm getting too old for this kind of crap. He ground his teeth in annoyance. No, no. Think that way, you old fart, and you may as well crawl on into your grave and not bother sending Kawanishi a forwarding address. Been working on this deal for two years, and someone'll collect your balls if it gets loused up now. You're too old to go to prison. Now *that'll* kill you. Yeah, well, but first I'd collect some balls of my own. Fisackerly's, Pete Clements', don't care whose. Sooner or later, I'm going to cut that bastard Fisackerly's throat anyway. Corollary to rule number one: the impatient, the hasty, the indiscriminately ruthless, the, ah, the desperate can always be had. It's just like in judo. Keep 'em off balance, and you can do anything you want to 'em. Fool 'em, buy 'em, whatever. Erect an overpass on their face, if you have to.

He looked out through the one-way window glass, at the glorious sprawl of Houston. That's how I got you, toots. All those oil boys and developers, all the rest of those dick-heads, they just crapped all over themselves when you started to go under back in the eighties. And I got you away from them, just a little piece here, a little piece there, then whole big chunks, I got you and everything and everyone in you, and I made you the goddamnedest greatest city in the world. And you're all mine, babe. The jewel in my crown. To have and to hold.

And you've always been loyal to me, good to me. You never broke my heart.

His eyes were stinging. Everything beyond the window blurred.

He kept his head turned away from Max and waited until his eyes cleared, and when they had, there, comfortingly, was his city again. And what I've done here, he thought savagely, I can do anywhere on the planet. Have and hold. Forever. Been to every continent on Earth. Been to the

Moon, too. Own pieces of them and it. Own about a zillion square miles of continental shelf. Man who doesn't 's got no business owning Rolls-Royces. Own some of everything worth owning. Presidents've called me Win. One of 'em wanted me in his cabinet. Owed me. Owned him. Not too bad for a kid from a trailer park in an armpit town like Garland, Texas. Not too bad at all, and more's better, more's always better, so here's to the Brazil thing.

But, sweet Jesus Christ, just leave me the hell alone about it for right now. Right now, I got to see a man about a zombie.

Kawanishi looked tired this morning and lacked his usual ebullience. Under different circumstances, Windom would have been grateful: the doctor's sunny good nature had always given him a royal pain in the ass. The day was rapidly, irrevocably souring in Windom's mouth, however. At first it had seemed that the prize was in sight, almost within reach. Then Kawanishi had begun to drone on, on, and on about glycerol and the limbic system and other arcana, proceeding with a deliberation that made Windom want to grab him by the lapels and scream, Get to the *point*, for crissake, until he realized that Kawanishi gradually was getting to the point: only Windom's most realistic expectations, and not his most cordial hopes, had been fulfilled.

Barnes was present, too, and that just made things worse.

Barnes had always got on Windom's nerves. She was in her early fifties, tanned, fit, with brilliant silver hair. He could imagine her jogging, playing tennis, swimming laps. It was that damned sympathetic expression of hers that he disliked; she had, he felt, worked so long and so hard at perfecting it that it was permanent; looking at it made the muscles in his own face tired. She wore a simple gold wedding band. He could imagine her lying beneath or sitting astride Mr. Barnes, looking sympathetic.

To avoid having to see her, to get as far away from Kawanishi's soporific droning as possible, Windom stood fuming before the tiers of monitors set into the far wall of the room. They did not offer much in the way of distraction. A ruler-straight yellow line crossed the lower row of screens, seeming to leap the gaps between display terminals. Approximately every five minutes, a muted but cheerful beep would sound as a minute peak ran across the section of yellow line appearing on the rightmost screen. Mounted above were television monitors. One offered a view of the cryogenics chamber, another, a close-up of the chrome cocoon that was the chamber's main feature. He could not see the sleeper in the cocoon, but he knew that she lay in it, dreaming no dreams, more patient than a stone. Now, as before, Windom found it somehow disconcerting that any room so cold should not look cold. It seemed to him that there ought to be a thin sugar-crust of frost on the cocoon and on the walls of the chamber, and that, despite their pressurized thermal suits, the two technicians hovering about the cocoon ought to exhale steam. That there was not and that they did not added an edge of irrational irritation to an already sharp disappointment.

Finally, he could bear Kawanishi's monolog no more and snapped, "You said she'd be alive!"

"Yes. Of course she is alive."

"She's still frozen. She's hard as rock."

Kawanishi seemed genuinely surprised by the complaint. He glanced at Barnes, who looked sympathetic. "I've been explaining. Only the brain is functioning. The other organs are still being by-passed, and peripheral circulation is still shut down. We're simulating cardiac action to keep the brain—"

"Alive, Kawanishi, you said she'd be *alive*."

"I-I thought you understood, Mr. Windom."

"I thought *you* understood. I said I want her to live. That means walking and talking, not goddamn 'only the brain is functioning.' I came here hoping for more than charts and lines on screens. I didn't come for a goddamn lecture course in cryogenics!"

"We explained all of this to you at the beginning, Mr. Windom. We aren't just raising and reanimating a corpse. The tissues were outraged. Brain, heart, lungs, liver, spleen. Lymph glands. All of it, everything. The entire complicated machine broke down. Some of it suffered irreparable damage. We haven't just rudely kicked it back into operation." Kawanishi gestured at the monitors, which acknowledged the gesture with a beep. "We had to repair everything. We saved what we could, transplanted what we had to, did our best to encourage a high percentage of function transfer. We can do only so much with cultures. We aren't just salvaging her. We have to rewire her."

"You sound like building contractors I know. Always need more time, more people. Always more money."

Kawanishi stiffened. An angry red spot glowed on each sallow cheek. "The money is quite sufficient. And my team is quite adequate."

"So how long's it all going to take?"

Off to the side, Barnes said, "Well, our original estimate—" A thought seemed to percolate behind the sympathetic expression. "How long is which part of it going to take, Mr. Windom?"

"From right this instant till the moment when she can look at me and see me and know who I am."

"The original estimate hasn't been changed," said Kawanishi. He sat back in his chair, laced his long, slender fingers together, and seemed to press them very hard against his abdomen for a moment. A knuckle popped softly.

"As long as it took with any of the other human subjects. Anything up to a year just to get her body to start taking over from life-support systems. As for getting her back on her feet, so to speak, getting her to talk—"

"Another year?" said Barnes. "Two? Six to eight months at the very, very least. Bear in mind what the poor woman will have to adjust to."

Windom swallowed hard and let himself collapse into a chair. "Try for the very least."

Barnes shook her head. "I can't guarantee it."

"You guaranteed everything before."

"Not in the way I think you mean."

"She's alive, right? The process works?"

"Better than voodoo."

Windom glared at her. "What?"

"Voodoo. The old way of raising the dead. With chicken blood and candles."

"Damn straight, Barnes!" His vehemence made her flinch. "Not voodoo! We're supposed to be talking highly advanced scientific research here. We're supposed to be talking new frontiers of science and medicine here, and some of the most brilliant minds of our age."

"We guaranteed that she'll be able to look at you and see you. We didn't guarantee that she'd know you. You may wait a year or considerably longer than a year, spend more than just several million dollars, and still end up with a—"

"A vegetable?" Windom said. "No. I'm paying for success. I want my wife back. And she's got to be my wife."

Barnes cleared her throat softly and said, "And what if she *is* your wife, Mr. Windom?"

"Well, that's sort of the point to all this, isn't it?"

"For us, yes. We've restored life to a dead human being. But put yourself in her place." She studied her immaculate fingernails for a moment. Windom remembered his dream and, in spite of himself, shifted uncomfortably in his chair. "To have been a suicide, and then to be suddenly returned to life—"

Windom felt heat and color rise in his cheeks. "My wife had no reason to take her own life!"

Barnes started to reply, but he silenced her with an angry wave and an inarticulate sort of bark. She and Kawanishi exchanged startled looks. The monitors punctuated the silence with a beep.

"I've financed this project," Windom said. "Let us all understand, I've bought it, and you, and everything you do. Now I need you to do this thing for me. You think you can just go somewhere else and offer yourself to someone else? Kawanishi'd still be keeping dead dogs in deep freezers out in California. And you, Barnes—"

"We must be frank," Barnes said, gently. "I realize that this must be extremely painful for you, Mr. Windom, but—"

"Shut up!"

Goddamn it, control yourself! Windom dug his fingers into the upholstery of his chair. Rule number one, Win. Not now. Not yet. Later. By and by. A year and a half from now, two, however long it's got to be, just put up with these people as long as you have to and keep your lid on and wait and think about then.

Rule number two: (a) reward loyalty; (b) punish ingratitude, incompetence, insolence.

Corollary to (b): take your time about it.

"I want a return on my investment, doctors. A particular return from each of you. My wife restored in body, Kawanishi. My wife restored in mind, Barnes. Nothing else, you understand? Not frankness. Not warnings. You'll get your money, and you'll probably even get your goddamn Nobels eventually." If I don't have you sent to prison for life. If I don't have you wrapped in cellophane. "Meantime, you just attend to my wife. You'll bring her back to me, alive and whole."

Kawanishi compressed his lips into a tight sphincter for a second, then said, "As you wish," and hesitated, and added, "sir." Barnes' face was blank, set, and yet somehow still sympathetic.

No. Not sympathetic. Pitying.

The cellophane, Windom decided. Definitely the cellophane.

They rose from their seats, and Kawanishi moved to open the door for Windom, who gave him a thin smile and murmured a dry "Thank you, my man." My man, you slant-eye son of a bitch, and you'll do what I ask, you and Barnes both, you'll give me back my wife, and then....

He paused just inside the door and took a last look at the monitors. One of them beeped, and his smile broadened. And then, little missy, he thought. Just you wait, you ungrateful bitch.

Die Rache

THERE IS NO PAIN AT FIRST, NOTHING THAT can be fixed in mind as being distinctly unpleasant, only a vague sense of tissues having been squeezed and stretched and pulled in all the wrong directions. There is something familiar about these sensations, something that frightens him. He tries to remember what is supposed to happen next.

Something *is* supposed to happen next, of this much he is certain. The harder he tries to remember, however, the more confused he becomes. Vivid but fragmentary impressions overwhelm him: the image of himself as a young child, eating black bread and cabbage soup in his mother's kitchen; the smell of wet shoes drying near the stove; the image of himself as an even younger child, nervously reciting his first lessons in numbers to his father, *eins, zwei, drei, vier, fünf*; faces like masks of stone, and his own voice, pleading. He tries to stop the rush of images, tries and fails and is borne by them to the old places, the old times.

There is a girl named Hilda who parts her great pale thighs and draws him into herself. There is a vast and unexpected sadness afterward.

There is the taste of ashes in the air, and he is clawing through the rubble, pulling out the pulped bodies, cursing the deadly efficiency of the enemy bombardiers, the ineffectual Luftwaffe, the shattered bricks and stones as they shred his gloves and tear his hands. *How many more times must I endure this?* he demands. *Haven't I suffered enough?* "Not nearly enough," someone murmurs.

A stone seems to sit in the pit of his stomach: now he is pushing bodies into the trench; the stench of putrefying flesh cuts through his cloth mask, forcing him to breathe as shallowly and as infrequently as possible. *God in Heaven*, he cries, *how many more times? When is this going to stop?* "When

227

the scales are balanced," comes the reply.

The pain and horror suddenly swirl away. A great happiness settles upon him. All is right with the world now. He stands at attention, proud in the black uniform of the *Schutzstaffel*, his gaze fastened upon the dully gleaming coal-bucket helmet of the man in front of him. The very air shakes with a sound like the laughter of God as, on cue, he and all the others give joyous utterance to a shared sense of mission, of destiny, *sieg Heil! sieg Heil! sieg HEIL!* And then the laughter of God becomes mocking, becomes the yowling of sirens, the muffled reports of distant anti-aircraft batteries, and the maddening drone of the bombers as they pass above the city and methodically punch it into the earth. He huddles with the others in darkness deep under the city, softly moaning to himself, wincing as the shrill whine of falling bombs is first punctuated and then drowned out by explosions. The bombs are landing close now, too close, all around, seemingly right on top of him. Dust and flecks of stone drift down from the ceiling. Then the bombers move on, the explosions keeping pace.

"Do you know where you are?" someone says.

"Yes." He is in the bunker, waiting for the all-clear signal to be given. The taste and feel of dust is in his mouth, up his nose, on his face and hands. The man sitting beside him coughs. Someone else sighs and makes a lame joke, and there is nervous laughter. It is good to be alive, he thinks, it is so very good to be alive. The hours pass slowly, however, and relief becomes restlessness. Somebody asks for and is angrily denied permission to smoke a cigarette. At last the Oberleutnant gives the order to go up. They ascend through pitch darkness and emerge into Hell. His own incredulous horror is reflected in the faces of his comrades as they survey the destruction. Awe and fear are in the Oberleutnant's muttered curse. There is the taste of ashes in the air. The ashes of the razed city. The ashes from the crematorium.

... the crematorium. He frowns. The images begin to warp. Perspective becomes distorted. But the crematorium was later, he thinks in panic. Much later and nowhere near the city, and again someone asks, "Do you know where you are?"

And then, so suddenly that he gives a wordless cry of alarm, his scrambled sensory perceptions sort themselves out. He is cold, and there are dull, throbbing aches in his marrow bones, the feel of needles under his skin. He can focus his eyes, and, hovering between him and the ceiling, there are faces like masks of stone. He can hear, and one of the faces speaks his name like a curse, spits it at him as though it tastes foul and brown on the tongue. He knows where he is and what this is: *die Rache*; the revenge. He begins to plead with the faces in a hoarse voice, "No more, please, no more …."

"You know the charges," one of them says in flawless German. "You have been judged guilty. The sentence must be carried out."

He groans and lies panting in the cold room, enduring the touch of their hands as they attend to his physical needs. There are no hesitations upon their part, nor is there urgency. Their precision and their imperturbability are machine-like. He says, "Monsters," and the word comes out a sob.

"But of course. We—" the speaker indicates herself and her three or four associates with a casual flick of her hand "—are indeed monstrous human beings. Not just anybody would be able to accommodate you in the manner you so richly deserve. Not just anybody would have the stomach for this. We are fiends in flesh, even as you."

"Even as *I*? This … this is *inhuman*."

"This is necessary." The speaker's voice is cool and neutral. "By now you surely understand how it is. We are performing a long-overdue exorcism, driving out an old and terrible demon. We are laying ghosts to rest here. And you are absolutely necessary. You're the last one, the only one left in the entire world as far as we've been able to determine. The others, great and small, have been dead for many years now. This makes you extremely precious to us. Fortunately, with the technology at our disposal, you're also endlessly recyclable."

"I won't let you do this to me any more!"

"The sentence must be carried out. We have our mission. You have your destiny."

"Mission. Destiny." He remembers how the very air shook with a sound like the laughter of God. "How long is this nightmare going to last?"

"Until it's over and done with."

"It's been over and done with for more than three quarters of a century!"

"Nevertheless—"

"What can it *mean* to you? What difference can it make? You weren't even born then. You're hardly more than children now, how can you possibly *care?* And I, I wasn't important then, I was only a common soldier. I gave none of the orders. I committed no murders. I drove a tractor!"

"You dug graves and put bodies into them. You were there. You were part of it. Others may have issued the orders, others may have been responsible for policy, but they're dead and out of our reach. Someone has to pay. Someone has to put the scales in balance, and you're the only person left who can do that."

"I have *paid,* damn you! Paid, paid, *paid!*" He looks from face to face to impassive face. Masks of stone. "What do you *want?* How many more times can you *do* this to me before you're *satisfied?*"

The speaker shrugs and says, "Something fewer than ten million times now," and then they put him back to death for another day.

Uncoiling

Lisa Tuttle and Steven Utley

MY DREAMS HAVE BEEN BOTHERING me for the past week. The details fade almost immediately, as soon as I wake up, but, for some reason, I spend the rest of the day feeling uneasy, trying to recall them, as though they were the most important things in the world to me. I don't know why I should be so disturbed about not being able to hang on to them, but I am. I'm always tired at work now.

Some impressions of last night's dreams. (They're becoming a little clearer each night, a little easier to remember, and I've started putting my journal under my pillow when I go to bed.) There was a dark, cold room, torches smoldering ineffectually, dim shapes moving in the background. A man in a black hood, only his eyes and mouth showing, thrust his face into mine, shouted, sprayed me with spittle. Rotten breath. "Confess!" he screamed. "Confess, confess," on and on, forever.
    Confess to what?

Dreams, I know, are the mind's safety valve. Dreams keep us, well, most of us, from going insane. But dreams are only dreams. Everybody dreams.
    Why, then, this constant dread, and why should I sometimes wake up in a rage and, other times, filled with longing, yearning, homesick for God knows what?

The dreams come in daytime now. Voices, half-glimpsed faces, sometimes moving, now revealed, now submerged, amid clouds of steamy fog. And the stench: I never thought that smells could be dreamed, so real they fill my nostrils, my throat, and I gag and choke to wakefulness.

At work today, I sat behind my desk and watched columns of familiar figures twist themselves into some strange lettering—like Arabic, I thought—which I could almost read. Something whispered behind me. Something else, in a drawer of the desk, chuckled.

My life, I suddenly thought, is no longer my own.

I left at noon, saying I was sick, and I was.

Here at the apartment, I found myself remembering a woman I had once come close to marrying. I hadn't thought of her in years, more years than I could count. We had been in love (I loved her; I thought she loved me, although we hadn't been intimate), and yet one day she came to me and told me that she had been called. She was going to go up the hill and ask the sisters at the convent to take her in. She hoped to become a nun, bride of God but never of mine.

"My life," she said, "is no longer my own. You don't understand that, do you, dearest? You've never known God."

"You're all I need or want to know of God," I had told her.

I sat on my narrow bed, feet thrust out before me to catch the weak rays of the sun as they sifted through the gauzy curtains, my head against the wall. Through that thin partition, I could hear the woman in the next apartment yelling at her children in Spanish. I listened to the names she called them, the crimes of which she accused them, and I had to smile at the outrageousness of both. I had seen the children. The oldest could have been no more than seven.

My sweetheart-become-nun, I realized lazily, had also spoken to me in Spanish, but hers had been a more precise, a purer and older Spanish than the neighbor woman's slurred, Americanized tongue.

Then I sat forward quickly, my head spinning with memories that couldn't have been mine. I could haven't walked with a Spanish senorita down the narrow, cobbled streets of Seville—a Seville of centuries past.

Not real, I decided, it was some movie or novel I was recalling. I rested my elbows on my knees and let my head fall forward into my hands. I was exhausted after too many nights torn by dreams of half-seen, half-apprehended things. Dreams from which I had begun to wake with screams (in what language?) lodged in my throat.

And now these memories of other lives and times (because this vision of Seville was not the first, there had been the man in the black hood), as clear and emotion-filled as if they were my own.

I lay back on the cot, closed my eyes, and grimly clamped my teeth against the chills that moved along my body. If I went to sleep in daylight, I reasoned, perhaps the dreams wouldn't come; I'd be rested and able to think clearly again.

But I was too frightened to sleep.

I'm still frightened, and it's very late now.

I don't speak any Spanish.

Late this morning, I awoke from the usual unrestful dream imagining that I was someone named Bruno Stahl. The telephone woke me up, somebody calling from the office to ask whether David Leonard felt better and planned to return to work. I almost didn't respond to that name. (Bruno Stahl?) I said no, I feel worse than ever.

Bruno Stahl, and now Gilbert Gibbons. I napped this afternoon. I am losing my name.

Early this evening, casting about for something to do that would put me in a normal frame of mind, I unearthed a piece of last week's mail, an application for a credit card, and filled it out. I've never had trouble with forms. The data pour from my pen. I hardly have to think about what I'm writing. Leonard, David D., 512-50-9001, 11-14-48, Fort Knox KY, M, 5′ 9″, 150 lbs., brown eyes and hair, all of the vital statistics, signed (with a slight flourish) and dated.

I could do it with my eyes closed.

Only, when I looked over the form I had just completed, my eyes fastened on the neatly printed capital letters in the first blank, LEONARD, DAVID D., and I wondered, *Who? Who is this person?*

I stared at the name, trying to remember David D. Leonard, trying to recall exactly what he had to do with me, how I had come to have his application form, where he might be at the moment. Trying and failing until, at length, I pushed my chair away from the table, rose, walked about the apartment, touching his posters (prints of Modigliani, Rousseau), the spines of the paperback books on his board-and-brick shelves (Pynchon, Nabokov, names).

Finding one of his shirts carelessly draped over the back of a chair and rubbing the material of its sleeve between my fingers. Holding the garment to my nose, inhaling slowly, thoughtfully.

Walking about the apartment, returning at last to the table, where I found a hardbound book of unruled white pages, his journal. Perplexedly reading his tight, careful script.

Taking up his pen.

Waiting for him to come back and tell me what to write here.

Yes, he is definitely slipping away from me now, beginning to fade like an old photograph.

Perhaps he is dying, if not as other people die, at least no less completely. I think he will soon be gone.

I found his shaving mirror and have it propped up on the table before me. I can look up from his journal and see the color going out of him. He has always been a dark person, brown hair and eyes, tanned brown skin, but he is lightening now, going from brown to a soft mocha color, like an old shirt bleaching in the sun, like old snakeskin. He has stopped going to work, stopped answering the telephone or the door bell. He will be gone soon.

My earliest memory (no, don't stop don't rationalize just let your mind go whirling or floating or flying until it lands — like a butterfly — on)

A weed, the tight, furled end looking like some kind of miniature caterpillar, a wing of grass across its back. The little butterfly (yellow and common) had been blown sideways by my approach, and I was left, bent over, with nothing to examine but the weed.

How clear it is, that memory. The sun was hot and tight against my back, like a shirt against my bare skin, but I wasn't sweating.

"You never sweat, Bruno," she said. I looked around at her (Bruno again?), at the space between her teeth. Her body was bathed with perspiration, and I was covered with it, too, but she was right: I didn't sweat; the wetness on my chest and belly and thighs was from her.

She gave a startled grunt as I dropped back onto her. I began kissing her, to distract her, kissing her and fondling her small, pale breasts. I didn't like it when such things about myself (that I didn't perspire; that I had no parents I could remember; that I couldn't, whether I wanted to or not, father children) were noticed, and I didn't even know *why* I didn't like it. I always acted, I never thought. She parted her legs, opened to receive me, and then I didn't have to think.

But I am thinking now, and (how easy it is, one thought giving birth to another; they emerge connected, like a strand of slippery beads from my insomnia-sharpened brain) I think I remember:

Standing, being made to stand, manacled to a dank stone wall, arms and legs spread, my unprotected body trembling with fear.

The room was gloomily illuminated by sputtering animal-fat torches and stank of excrement, blood, rancid bodies.

Three men in black hoods stood before me, some sort of tribunal putting questions to me.

This was not the time of pain, not yet. One of them thrust his face into mine and shrieked at me to confess confess confess to being a witch, a wizard, a consort of Satan. They wanted me to confess of my own free will before they put me to the torture. I had the witch's mark, they told me, the brand of Satan, confess. But I said nothing, because I knew that it would not matter what I confessed or held fast to, these men in the black hoods and long robes had their rituals to observe. In the end, whether I broke or was broken, it was all the same to them.

So they tried to destroy me on the rack, and they used the probes and the presses, and they applied the boot and the knotted ropes and the thumbscrew.

At some point, in the red-eyed center of that eternal and endlessly varied pain, they began to murmur among themselves that perhaps no human woman had given birth to me, perhaps I was worse than a witch, some unnatural creature, a demon, some monstrous child of the devil.

They tried to banish me, drive me from my body, with spells and incantations.

Then I did leave my body, though it was the pain and not their magic which was responsible. I learned (or remembered, or intuited, or imagined) that I wasn't human and that these men couldn't kill me. I would suffer torment forever, the torment of the truly damned, for this was truly Hell.

And I heard laughter.

There was a shock, a wrenching sensation. For just a moment, I was lifted truly apart from my body. The pain receded. I looked around and saw, suspended in the ether about me, the hideous countenances of the creatures who had borne me and among whom I properly belonged. For if I had been merely human, the sight of them would surely have driven me mad.

Perhaps it did.

They were soft mountains trembling in a strange light, moist jellyfish as big as buildings, fluttering their ribbed wings, caressing me with their sticky tentacles. When they touched me, I knew their homesickness, for this was not their rightful place. I felt their pride and faith in me. They spoke, their voices as harsh as the sound of old metal hinges, and they commanded me

abide

endure

await

....

Somehow, I knew that there was more. The command was incomplete. I sensed that there was, there had to be a fourth, unspoken part.

Take me with you, I begged them, and they laughed again (the time is not yet right but soon soon) and sent me back into my pain-wracked human body. For a moment, I was able to bear the pain. The men who were trying to torture the demon out of me were at once right and very, very wrong. They feared Satan, and Satan, I knew now, was totally insignificant.

Then I forgot it all, just as they, those monsters dwelling somewhere beyond the stars, somewhere in exile, had intended.

Soon. Soon?

How, I wonder, did I escape?

Who ever *escaped* from the dungeons of the Inquisition?

I decided to answer the door bell. David D. Leonard has (had) a girl friend, a pretty, soft-spoken young woman with very fair skin. Her name (I remember) is Robyn. She has come and gone. When she was here, we sat together on the sofa, silent, paying not very much attention to the television, until, after a while, she leaned toward me, put her hand on my forearm, and said, Dave?

Yes? (Thinking: my name is David not Bruno David not Gilbert Juan Glen Lyndon James my name is David D. Leonard David D.)

What is it? she wanted to know. Have I (a pause here, she was very nervous, her hand withdrew from my arm to her lap to writhe with its mate, the white fingers twisted like dying serpents; she had always been a terribly insecure woman shy easily bruised uncommonly modest) have I done something to make you (another pause, briefer than the first) angry with me?

Why no not at all what gave you that idea?

You're well I don't know you haven't called me in days you're so distant and cold you're making me feel like I should go home and (the words starting to come out of her in a rush now, she will be crying by the time she does leave) and and

And I almost said (somewhere deep inside me David D. Leonard unexpectedly stirred and rose up, weak, dying, almost dead but determined to make one last effort in spite of everything, and almost said) you don't understand my life is no longer my own (I don't understand my life is no longer

My life, my sweetheart-become-nun said, is no longer my own. You don't understand that, do you, dearest?

Not then, but, yes, I see it now. My life, too, is no longer my own, has never been my own. Bruno, Gilbert, Juan, David, all of the names just names and no more, the masks of the sleeper, to be adopted and discarded in turn over the years until finally I understand, until the time is right for their return and the last part of their command to be given *emerge set us free bring us home restore to us what was ours* and somewhere within I feel tentacles uncoiling.

Little Whalers

by Louisa May Alcott and Herman Melville

Chapter 13. A Clash of Temperaments

"HAUL!" CRIED AHAB, TURNING HIS blazing eye upon those at the oars as he took up his harpoon. "Haul, thou daughters of the devil, for it is great Moby-Dick himself! crusher of boats! chewer of men! I see thee, damned behemoth! O haul, thou worthless things!"

"Please, Captain, there are young ladies present," said Jo with fire in her own eye, "and I must ask you either to apologize or else to let us out of this boat at once!"

"I do not feel well," Beth confessed, and Meg and Amy sat closer to her to rub her hands, pat her forehead, and provide the other sisterly comforts which mean so much.

"Poor Beth," Amy said, "you have been weakened by grief ever since fever felled that poor tattooed gentleman."

"Yes," murmured Beth, "and after I did so try to help him give up his funny little idols, and prayed that he might find his way to salvation. But perhaps I succeeded better than I know, and will find him awaiting me in the heavenly throng, which I feel I am soon to join."

"I'll see thee delivered down to Lucifer if thou doth not haul!" Ahab shouted from the bow. "O, curse the day that I signed on such as thee!"

As the white whale bore down upon the insubstantial boat, Ahab turned his back on the weary March sisters, causing spirited Jo to stamp her foot against the deck in an irrepressible fit of irritation.

But Ahab did not see it, for he was taking aim with his veteran steel. "Come, devil," he shrieked, "come all-devouring but unconquering Leviathan! I face thee, I meet thee head to head! From Hell I spit at thee! *Thus* I strike thee!"

"What a distressing man!" Meg said, giving vent to a most un-Meg-like exasperation, for she was by nature a dear, patient, sweet-tempered girl who tried very hard to live up to the example which Mrs. March had set for her four daughters.

"I am afraid this is all my fault," Jo confessed bleakly, "for it *was* my idea that by taking some sort of work we might help Marmee while our papa is away."

The Beasts of Love

HE LAY FACE UP ON HIS SIDE OF THE bed and stared at the dark expanse of ceiling. The hall clock chimed the hour. Two o'clock, he thought, and all is … well ….

The final chime faded. He found himself listening as the house talked to itself, murmuring deep in its throat. Wood creaked and groaned, and somewhere far down in the house the thermostat clicked with a sound not so much actually heard as sensed. The house seemed to throb in time with the air conditioner's rumblings. After an eternity, the rumblings ceased. The machinery settled down. He heard soft whirs and purrings and tried separating them, identifying them, willing each in its turn to stop and let him go back to sleep. He became aware of the rustle of breath through nostrils.

Bitch, he thought.

There was a flutter of movement near his side.

Goddamn bitch.

The flutter stopped.

Thank you, bitch.

God, he hated her. He did not have to turn his eyes her way to see her. He had seen her on too many occasions, and it would be now as it had been always: the bitch would have kicked the light coverlet down around her calves, would have got her gown twisted up around her breasts, would be sprawled belly up in the semidarkness with her legs bent and spread and looking for all the world like some monstrous pale frog awaiting the point of the dissecting knife.

God, he hated her.

It was not just a matter of many minor annoyances and a number of major ones endured over the years. It had become, early on, much too early

241

on, a matter of retaining them, of collecting them and categorizing them and nurturing each small seed of irritation, disappointment, resentment, until it flowered into disgust and loathing. Someday, he knew, or some night, something would finally snap, and he would erupt like Krakatoa, she would turn to ice, and they would shatter the world as they destroyed each other.

It would come to that.

It could only come to that.

So why don't you get rid of her?

He blinked. He had not intended to think it as baldly as that. He repeated the question in his mind several times and experimented with it, shifting emphasis from the *why* to the *don't* and then to the *rid*. He tried revising the question: *So why don't you kick her out?*

The question revised itself: *So why don't you kick her off?*

Murder.

The word almost slipped out of his mouth.

Murder ....

The sweet, the smooth, the velvet persuasiveness of the word.

But ... *murder?*

But *freedom.* But no more listening to her as she sprawls there burbling and wheezing. No more watching her waddle about and wondering why, how, you could have married her of all people in the world. No more watching her eat and drink herself to the point of torpor. No more *her*, and no more *this*, but freedom and the chance to start all over again, to do it better next time, the way it should be done, to begin afresh ....

His face itched with sweat. He wanted to laugh. He wanted to moan. Murder. Freedom. My God. Murder. He closed his eyes and sighed softly. The how of it. The when, the where. It had to be done right the first time, the only time. It couldn't be hurried. It had to look good. Murder. Freedom. So why ... He was vaguely amazed to find himself drifting off. So why don't ... He heard the hall clock chime the quarter-hour. So why don't *you* get rid of *her?*

Let us pause for a moment. Let us have a brief intermission and a word, as it were, from the sponsor. Let us get something straight.

I am in control here. I will set the stage and adjust the lighting and conduct the incidental music as I pull the strings and make the voices, perhaps a low growl for him, a sharp high squeak for her. We shall see. I will be in charge of the special effects. I will move the drama along, not according to the dictates of any script, but as I see fit from moment to moment. Scripts are for those who are afraid or unable to take chances with their leading characters; I choose spontaneity, improvisation, and who is to say that I am wrong to do so? Who presumes to tell me my craft? I will make the choices. I will direct thoughts and deeds. My puppets will suffer the consequences.

So. Consider. We have before us a man, a husband, and are shortly to have a woman, his wife. They have been married for eleven years. They are unable to explain why they are still together after all those years, though the wife, who is actually the more sensitive if not the more articulate of the two, might (at my prompting, of course) shrug and say to someone whom she implicitly trusts, "Sheer inertia." There is, however, nobody whom she trusts; I have seen to that. There must be no relief for either of them, no relief of any kind until I will it. We have, then, a hugely unsuccessful marriage of two people who have gone (or, rather, because I *am* in control here, have been taken) from loving each other to what would seem to be the point of loving hating each other. I know what I am about.

The alarm clock rattled tinnily on the nightstand. With a groan, she rolled onto her belly and buried her face in the pillow. Mattress springs protested. The clock kept ringing. She muttered an obscenity into the pillow, pushed herself up on one elbow, and with her free hand turned off the alarm. She looked around at the man beside her. A smear of drool glistened at the corner of his mouth.

Yuck, she thought.

She got up and padded into the bathroom and relieved herself. The door of the medicine cabinet above the basin had once again swung open of its own accord. She scanned the untidy rows of prescription bottles and aerosol cans of shaving cream, deodorant, hair remover. The aspirin. The vitamin capsules. The sleeping tablets. The tranquilizers. The diet pills. The pep pills. Jesus, what a clutter.

She flushed the commode and washed her hands. As she brushed her teeth, she took one of the small brown prescription bottles from the cabinet, weighed it in her palm, gave it a gentle shake. It sounded half-full. She thoughtfully replaced the bottle, rinsed her mouth, and paused for a moment, listening, before stepping into the shower. Now he's snoring, she thought in revulsion. Jesus. Shake the house down, bastard. *Jesus*, listen to him!

She showered. She dried herself. She sprayed her armpits with deodorant. She took the same brown bottle from the medicine cabinet, twisted off the safety cap, poured the contents into the palm of her hand. Counted them. Returned them to the bottle and the bottle to the cabinet. Thought, Oh God. Oh *God*. You can't know what it's like. You can't know how it *is* with him. You just can't know.

Oh, but I can, I do, I know all about it.

Listen: think of me as a spider sitting in one strategic corner of a vast yet fine web that covers the entire city. So fine is this web that no one can move or speak or even think without the vibrations thereof being instantly transmitted to me. And, like a spider, I am discriminating. A leaf caught in my web will not rouse me. But let something with juice in it come my way, and I will suck it dry and … ah, well, you get the idea; it will hardly do to press too hard on my little puppeteer-cum-spider metaphor. I might just as well speak of driving dumb beasts before me.

What matters is that I know all about it. All about all of it. Nothing escapes my attention. I absorb everything, and I know, for instance, that everybody (and I do not mean to exclude myself; in *this* respect, at least, I am just like everyone else) is hungry for something. Power, immortality, love. Revenge. A combination, sometimes, of all four and more besides. I spread my web over the city, and back to me come all the great and small hungers, and all the knowledge of the various and sundry ways by which attempts are made to appease those appetites. There is the bottle, and the needle, and violence. There is sex. There are the selfish acts and the selfless ones. There is applause. There is death. In my case, there is the peerless ability to influence the thoughts and actions of two particular people whom I have methodically and with considerable cunning and precision manipulated into an earthly hell.

Fair is fair. I must be attended day and night, which is, after all, why I have been consigned to this place. Another earthly hell. I cannot feed myself: my fingers have one joint apiece and are webbed besides; my thumbs are stubs, mere hard bumps protruding from the sides of what pass for my hands. I cannot move myself: my legs are badly mismatched; my feet are only boneless swellings, with an odd number of randomly placed nails in the general area of where toes ought to be, at the bottoms of what pass for my calves—I have no ankles. Nor do I have much control over my stomach, my salivary glands, my bladder and bowels. My body is squashed-looking, shoulderless, chestless, all gut and buttocks. My head is equipped with the correct number of sensory organs, but they are erratically positioned, and only half of them function. I cannot talk. I cannot hear, though, with my web, I miss nothing. It has been thought of me that I belong with the other gargoyles atop Notre Dame Cathedral. It has been thought of me that I should have died the moment I entered the world. I will never know the love of another human being.

But.

They did not speak to each other at the breakfast table. They avoided eye contact. He did not give her even the usual perfunctory kiss when he left the house. She made herself another cup of coffee and sipped it slowly and thought about the brown bottle in the medicine cabinet. Abruptly, she began to cry.

At noon, he passed up lunch to drink instead. He imagined his wife lying broken and still at the bottom of the basement steps. He imagined himself standing at the top of the steps, looking down at her. He put his face into his hands and said, "Oh, my God," and trembled violently.

But I am in control.

So I draw them back from the brink of the abyss, not so far, of course, that they will not suffer great anguish for having actually, seriously contemplated murdering each other, but far enough so that they will attempt, once again, to regain that which I long ago took from them. The love. The real and shining and glorious love. The love that made me. The love that was to have sustained them when they saw how poorly they had made me. The love that they could not extend to me, and that has been no match at all for what I have here inside my grotesque nine-year-old head.

And now Mommy and Daddy are at home again. And now they *try* to kiss and make up.

The Goods

IT WAS STRAIGHT-UP NOON WHEN Beck parked his car on the road above the McElwain house. He turned on the hazard lights and hung the camera around his neck, then got out and opened the hood. That would satisfy anyone who happened by. He went to the guard rail and unenthusiastically surveyed the wooded slope below. Through the interstices of the trees he could see just a little of the house. The slope was steep and offered endless opportunities for major collisions with trees. Unwilling to risk having a Nikon driven through his sternum, he let the camera hang between his shoulder blades, took a breath, and eased himself over the rail.

He descended mainly by sliding and skidding from tree trunk to tree trunk, and had not gone far before he was panting, sweat-drenched, and smeared with dirt. Halfway down, a blue jay gave him a severe scolding as he paused beneath its branch to catch his breath.

"Same to you," he muttered, and moved on.

He found a place where he could prop himself against a tree and see the back of the house and Mrs. Carona's car sitting in the driveway. He took a picture, to loosen up, he told himself. He knew the shot would never rate as evidence with his client. Mr. Carona wanted the goods on his wife, the goods, pictures of the two-backed beast itself, if possible. A car in a driveway could be explained away. Beck was as yet unsure of how to go about getting the goods. He was reduced to playing hunches at the moment. There had been no way to get a picture of Mrs. Carona going into the house or so much as a glimpse of whomever had let her in. There was no cover opposite the front of the house, only a guard rail and a nearly vertical drop to the river. The best Beck had been able to do as he drove past was to note the name on the mail box, McElwain, and the position of the house relative to the loop of road on the terrace above.

247

In the back yard was a white metal table with a big metal umbrella growing out of it. A patio door slid open, and Mrs. Carona and a man Beck took to be Mr. McElwain emerged from the dark, cool-looking interior. She was carrying a tray loaded with tableware, glasses, napkins, a pitcher. He had a tray with plates and food. Beck examined them through the view-finder and concluded that they did not have the disheveled look of two people who had got together for a nooner. But it's only been ten, fifteen minutes since she got here. Beck thought, and maybe lunch is part of the foreplay. Eating can be sexy.

They were seated now, helping themselves from the trays. They appeared to have only lunch on their minds. Beck heaved a sigh of impatience. As if to oblige him, Mrs. Carona extended one leg under the table and rubbed her calf against McElwain's. It was not much, but Beck got a shot of it just the same. So far, it was all he had got. They were doing nothing much more illicit than eating pasta salad. Mr. Carona could make something of the fact that they were doing it here, together, but, still, it was not proof-dammit.

"I want proof, dammit!" Mr. Carona had said, hitting Beck's desktop with a fist like a small ham. That had come midway through as unnerving an interview as Beck had ever had with a client. Frank Carona was a physical type.

Beck kept Mrs. Carona and McElwain framed in the view-finder. They were about the same age, mid-thirtyish. McElwain was rather nondescript at first glance and balding and slightly overweight at second, but he became more appealing the longer Beck looked at him.

He seemed warm, relaxed, friendly. He had a good smile. He looked like the sort of man a man like Frank Carona might enjoy cracking open like a peanut. Gwen Carona looked better than she had since Beck had started watching her the week before. Gravity had eased up on her. She no longer sagged on her bones or moved as though there were ten-pound weights fastened to her. She seemed suppler, younger. She looked happy.

Beck found himself aching with envy. He glowered through the view-finder, snapped a shot just to be doing something, thought, Eat your damn lunch and get on with it, folks!

Gwen Carona glanced at her wristwatch and started, and then both she and McElwain rose and went inside. Beck snapped them going inside.

Moments later, they reappeared at the side of the house, in the driveway. Beck tensed and aimed the camera. Come *on*, folks, he thought, give me something. They touched hands. Snap. They faced each other. Snap. Come on, come on, get steamy.

They embraced, kissed lingeringly. The man slipped one hand down her back and tenderly cupped a buttock. Snap, snap, snap. Much obliged, folks. Explain that away. They separated reluctantly, McElwain stepped back, and Mrs. Carona got into her car and drove away.

You're such a busy, busy lady, Beck thought as he replaced the lens cap. No time for real hanky-panky this week, I guess. Or maybe the relationship's past the point where all you two want to do is buck and grunt. Still. That was a serious kiss. And thank *you*, Mr. McElwain, for copping that feel. Nice touch. And now off to the next event on your social calendar, Mrs. Carona, and then home to the Cobra King himself. Drive safely.

Ascending the slope was even harder than descending it had been. Beck sweated so profusely that the dirt on his hands and arms was a film of slime by the time he hauled himself over the guard rail. The car's air conditioner was shot. He broiled all the way down the mountain and all the way back to his office.

His secretary looked up from that week's list of bad-check writers as he came in. She said, solicitously, "You fall in a ditch somewhere, Mister Beck?"

"That's just the kind of two-fisted work this is, Rosa. Let me see your telephone directory for a second."

She handed it over. He flipped to MCEACHERN-MCGEHEE and found six names and addresses stacked under MCELWAIN near the bottom of the first column on the page. The name he was after was in the middle of the stack, James L.

"This detective-ing is a snap," he said as he handed the book back to Rosa. He picked up the camera. "I'll be in the back, developing. Please call Frank Carona and ask him if he can come by tomorrow morning, say, ten o'clock."

As ever, Jane Austen waited for him just inside the kitchen door. Beck heard her whimpers of anticipation as he slid his key into the lock. She went into propeller-tail mode as soon as she saw him, and he knelt in the doorway to pat her flank and scratch her behind her ears and under her jaw. He had got her from the animal shelter when she was twelve weeks old. She was some sort of poodle mix. As a puppy, she had been coal-black; at thirteen years, she was more gray than anything else, but she still had an amazing lot of puppy in her.

"Rough day, ol' woolly bug," he told her. "How'd it go for you?"

He closed the door behind himself, set the envelope containing the photographs of Gwen Carona and James L. McElwain on the kitchen counter, and waited there, listening, for just a moment. He had stopped expecting to hear Janet call out to him, but he had not stopped hoping. He got a beer out of the refrigerator, walked into the dining room with the dog trotting happily alongside, nails clicking on the hardwood floor, and shoved a compact disc into the CD player. Music filled the room. You've changed, sang Billie Holiday, the sparkle in your eye is gone. Oh, yeah, Billie, he thought, hurt me.

"Ready to go outside now?" he said to the dog. She wagged her tail and went purposefully through the living room to the front door. Beck unlocked it and stepped back out into the dry heat.

Jane Austen brushed past him and flew down the steps of the high front porch. At the bottom, she veered sharply to the right and disappeared among the post oaks at the side of the house, where she could stoop and poop in private.

Beck walked straight to a lone post oak beside the brick walkway and sat down on the ground. The prickly sun-burnt grass scratched him lightly through the fabric of his slacks. He pulled off his shoes and socks, rubbed one bare, pale foot with the other, wiggled his toes in the grass. I am so tired, he thought. The elation he had felt at getting the goods on Mrs. Carona and her boy friend was gone. He opened the beer and took a long drink. Someone's turned up the gravity on me.

The dog ploughed to a halt in front of him. She had a ratty tennis ball in her mouth. She let it fall to the ground between his feet, looked at it, looked at him.

"Oh, good," Beck said as he gingerly picked up the ball, "you got it all slobbered-up first. J. A., this thing is really nasty. How can you stand to have it in your mouth?" He hefted it. Her eyes never left it. "Okay, but let's not get overheated here. You're an old hound," and he slung the ball in the general direction of the downtown skyline, four miles away.

The dog darted off, kicking up a cloud of dust and yellowed bits of grass stem. She was spry for her age. She scooped up the ball while it was still rolling and trotted triumphantly toward him. He tossed it again and took another sip of beer as she charged off in ecstatic pursuit. He thought that it must be wonderful to be as happy as Jane Austen was now. He thought that it must be wonderful to be as happy as Gwen Carona and James L. McElwain had been at lunch.

He tossed the dog's ball for her one more time, then took her into the house. She went to her water dish and drank deeply and with enormous gusto. Then, having made sure that he was not about to do anything interesting, she vanished into the back of the house. He heard her bump about under the bed, heard a last, satisfied-sounding thump as she found her favorite sleeping place.

A boy, he thought, always has his dog. He opened a frozen Mexican dinner and put it into the microwave oven. Then he went into the bathroom, stripped off his clothes, and stood under the shower for ten minutes, pretending that the water would sluice away the day and Janet and everything.

At last he had to go into the bedroom. The dog was snoring under the bed. He peered about the room and into the maw of Janet's closet. A few more of her things were gone. He angrily jerked open the drawers of his bureau, snatched out socks, shorts, jeans, a tee-shirt, and thrust himself into them as though he intended to rip them apart.

Sometime after he had eaten his microwaved enchiladas and drunk a second and a third beer, he found himself sitting on the sofa and looking around bleakly. Another evening to get through.

He had finished reading the new García Márquez over the weekend and was still digesting it; he felt no urge to plunge into something else. He glanced over the television schedule. It was sitcom night on the networks; the cable channels offered last year's glob of Hollywood product, a computer-colorized Errol Flynn movie, talking heads, a documentary about monkeys. He tossed the schedule aside in disgust and began pawing through his box of compact discs.

He lingered over Cab Calloway. Back when they had been dating and

Janet had just learned of his love for old swing music—back when, he thought, we still kept our music on vinyl, the way God intended—she had remarked that it was impossible to listen to Calloway and be in a bad mood. He crammed the cassette into the machine and listened to a few hi-de-hoes. After a minute, he thought, Fat lot you know, Janet. But he let the music play on.

He got a fourth or fifth beer—he could not remember how many this one made—and took it and the envelope containing the photographs back to the sofa. He upended the envelope and filled his lap with eight-by-tens.

He could not say why he had brought the pictures home, unless it was that the camera liked Gwen Carona. She was prettier in black and white than she had been in his view-finder. She looked not just happy but radiantly happy. James L. McElwain looked happy, too. Frank Carona would probably look happy when he saw how happy they looked together. He had not struck Beck as a man who would be truly unhappy to discover that his wife was seeing someone else. He had struck Beck as a man who already had his mind made upon that account, and as the sort of man who was happy when he was making someone else unhappy and happiest when he felt he had a good excuse not to exercise much self-restraint. What Beck had seen in Carona's face during their interview was not jealousy, but gleeful malice. Beck looked at one of the pictures of Gwen Carona kissing James L. McElwain and thought, Enjoy it while you can, lady. Then anger, regret, and loneliness welled up in him, and he believed for a few seconds that he was actually going to cry.

Damn it, Janet, what do you *want*?

But he knew. She had told him, and he knew.

It was not the process-serving he sometimes did that got to her, or the credit checks he ran for local businesses and landlords, or even the occasional nights he hired out as a security guard or floorwalker. It was the divorce work that repelled her.

"It's one thing," she would say, "to trick people into accepting a summons, or find out who's a good credit risk or isn't. Or nail shoplifters. Those things really have to be done. But it's another thing entirely to go peeking into people's bedroom windows. What people do in bed is private in a way their finances aren't."

"I've never actually peeked into anyone's bedroom window," he would say. "Not since I was ten, and this teenage girl who lived next door —"

"I'm serious. Some women's husbands sell cars or real estate. Mine finds out what people do in bed."

"I don't care what people do in bed. I'm paid to find out who they do it with."

"Why can't you stay out of it? Don't they have enough problems? People commit adultery because they're unhappy in their marriages."

"Janet," he would say, in the soothing, patient voice that always made her growl with irritation, "sometimes they do it just because they're sleaze-weasels."

"Whatever they are," she would growl, "if people're running around on their wives and husbands, why not just leave them to it?"

"Because those wives and husbands care." He would look at her very seriously. "Wouldn't you care, if I was running around on you?"

"Aiee. Suddenly I feel like we're on the wrong sides of this argument."

"Janet. I'm just the person whose legs and eyeballs and camera they rent. It's no different from someone down at the courthouse hiring me to serve papers. Mr. Sleaze-Weasel's fooling around with some bimbo, and Mrs. Sleaze-Weasel wants to know."

"I hate that word *bimbo!*"

"Don't change the subject."

"I'm not changing the subject. Your use of the word bimbo is a perfect example of what I'm talking about. Bimbo's a nasty, sexist word."

"The world is a nasty, sexist place, and there are real live bimbos in it."

"Divorce work is doing things to you. You're getting cynical and nasty. There's so much unhappiness involved, and you're just cashing in on it."

"I'm not cash —"

"Oh, stop! You make a living off it! I wish you'd take that job managing one of your dad's book stores. You'd be doing something you enjoyed and something it wouldn't turn my stomach to think about."

Beck and his wife had played variations on this argument for three of the four years of their marriage. The more variations they had played, the better they had got at having the argument. Their best recital had been three weeks before and had ended with her storming out of the house to go stay with a friend. Now she was looking for a place of her own. She and Beck had as yet said nothing about legally splitting the sheets. They had as yet said nothing about getting back together. Janet Beck was every bit as proud, contentious, and mule-stubborn as her husband.

Beck drank his beer and one or two more after it. By and by, he decided that it was time for bed. He wobbled into the bathroom, brushed his teeth, rinsed, spat, regarded his reflection above the sink. He thought that James L. McElwain could never be as unhappy as the man in the mirror.

Beck was asleep within two minutes of collapsing into bed. When he awoke at eight-fifteen the following morning, he remembered dreaming no dreams, but while he had slept, decisions must have been reached, for he found that his mind was made up about several things. He hummed "Minnie the Moocher" in the car all the way to his office.

Beck put the envelope containing the photographs into the middle drawer of his desk and closed it just before Rosa showed in Frank Carona. Carona was a former high-school all-star long fallen into beefy, brick-complected ruin. He owned a construction company in town and still spent a lot of time at building sites, if his tan was any indication. He had the look of a man used to getting his way with those whom he regarded as subordinates. Now, as he sat down across from Beck, he had another look as well. For a moment, Beck was at a loss for words that did it justice. It went beyond the merely expectant. Then he had it. Once before he had thought that the man's stare was as flat and hard as a cobra's; now he thought it was the look of a snake waiting for its keeper to hand over a live mouse. Carona already had some kind of punishment picked out for his errant wife and her lover. Beck could not believe that a divorce suit would be the limit of it. Whatever it was, the man had rehearsed in his mind, knew exactly what he would do, how it should go. All he needed was proof-dammit.

Beck met the stare and said, "As far as I've been able to determine after a week, your wife absolutely is not having an affair with anybody."

The Cobra King's cheek twitched. He was sitting with his hands in his lap; they began to curl into fists. He said, almost snarling, "You have proof she isn't?"

"In the absence of proof that she is, you do sort of have to presume that she isn't."

"I know she's having an affair with somebody."

"For the past week," Beck said, "I've followed her from home to ladies' luncheons to the mall to clothing stores to an art gallery to restaurants and home again. Your wife's too busy to have an affair."

Mr. Carona smacked a fist into a palm and evidently liked the sound and feel of his knuckles against flesh, because he did it again, twice. He seemed not to know what else to do. He had the baffled, angry expression of a predator whose quarry has escaped. Beck knew, though, that he would start hunting again before too long.

"Go home. Mister Carona," he said, in his most soothing and patient voice, the one that drove Janet crazy because she knew it was his most insincere voice. He had his friendliest and most understanding expression on his face, too. "Go home and kiss your wife hello," and thought, if she'll let you, "and tell her how much you love her," if you don't think it'll make her run shrieking from the room. "It helps marriages to talk things out. Oh, but don't under any circumstances tell her you put a private detective on her trail. Just, you know, be sweet. Maybe you could even take her some flowers."

Mr. Carona looked about wildly, as if searching for something to bite.

"And now," Beck said, getting to his feet, "I won't keep you any longer." He smiled pleasantly down at his client, adding to his confusion and discomfort. Mr. Carona lurched gracelessly to his feet so that Beck could not tower over him, but he had been punctured, his morale had collapsed. "We'll bill you later, Mister Carona," and Beck made a mental note to sidetrack that bill the instant Rosa had it prepared. There was no way he would or could take the man's money now.

Mr. Carona let himself be guided to the door. He was barely capable of muttering a goodbye as Beck turned him over to Rosa.

Beck went back to his desk and sat down. He wondered how much time he was really buying for Mrs. Carona. He wondered if the book store job his father had offered him was still open.

The clock on his desk told him that it was 11:28 a.m. He would be unable to talk to Janet until after five. He took the envelope containing the photographs from his desk and copied James L. McElwain's address onto it, making the letters as characterless as he could, all straight lines and right angles. Then he tucked the envelope under his arm and went into the front office.

"Rosa," he said, "let me take you out to lunch right now."

She looked startled, then suspicious. Boss-employee relations in the office had been somewhat strained lately; Beck had sometimes brought his anger at his wife to work.

"I brought lunch today," she said. As though she thought he would not believe her, she fumbled open a desk drawer and held up a brown bag. "And besides, it's not lunchtime."

"I don't care. Rosa, dear heart, I can't wait any longer. I want to take you to lunch. I have to take you to lunch. It's my treat."

"Uh, Secretary's Day isn't for another week. Besides, Mister Beck, if this is, um, I'm, ah ...." She gestured to call attention to her engagement ring.

"I know, I know," he said, "you're going to be married. Happily married, I trust. I've been happily married, too, and intend to be again. You're perfectly safe with me. We're perfectly safe with each other." He opened his jacket and turned to display his pot-belly. "Is this the body of a vile seducer?"

"Oh! I didn't mean, I mean, you know," and then, in spite of herself, she had to laugh. "Uh, no offense, but, no, it is not the body of what you said."

"Then let me take you to lunch. My life's just turned a corner. I have to celebrate immediately or explode."

She reached for her purse. "Where to?"

"The oyster bar? The chili parlor? The beer garden?"

"The chili parlor. I can have the triple-x chili."

"Make you burst into flames."

"Not this muchacha."

They were shown to a table at the back in the chili parlor. Beck let out a long sigh and absorbed air-conditioned coolth for a moment. Then he said, "After lunch, I've got some errands to run. Why don't you close up the office and take the rest of the day off?"

She looked at him almost warily.

"My treat, Rosa."

"You're full of treats today." She glanced at the envelope on the table. "Want me to mail that for you."

"Thanks, no. It's a special delivery."

The goods would put a real scare into them. There was nothing quite like learning that private moments had been spied on to put a chill on romance. Those eight-by-tens might even scare them right out of their relationship. If so, then maybe it wasn't much of a relationship. If not, at least a maiming might be averted, maybe even a murder or two. From now on, they would always look over their shoulders. If they had only suspected before, now they would know. If they hadn't even suspected before—Beck wondered how that could be possible, how anyone but especially Frank Carona's own wife could meet his serpent stare, hear the smack of his fist against his palm, and not see the violence and venom in him—now they would realize. They would probably never be as happy again as they were in those pictures. Beck regretted the damage the prints would do, but he knew he would have more keenly regretted the damage Frank Carona could do with his hamlike fists. He only hoped that by enclosing the negatives in the package Gwen Carona and James L. McElwain would understand that they were being warned of danger, not threatened with blackmail.

He knew that they would never understand that they were being repaid for a debt.

Drinks arrived. Beck proposed a toast. "To happiness," he said, raising his beer mug.

"To happiness," Rosa said as she carefully tapped the rim of her wine glass against the heavy mug.

Beck drank deeply and with enormous gusto.

Once More, With Feeling

WANDA CALLED TO SAY, "LET'S GO to Mars for lunch." Jack made a puzzled sound into the telephone. Wanda said, "Lunch with Eldean. His birthday. Remember?"

"Of course I remember. But I thought we were going to—"

"Mars is his new favorite place. It's closer, so you won't have to take your car."

Jack, who did not like disruptions or deviations, looked down at the paper he had been grading and satisfied himself that the tip of his red pencil still marked his place. He said, "What've they got?"

"Eldean says he's partial to the skirt steak with garlic mashed potatoes."

"Sounds heavy."

"He says they've got all kinds of lunch specials. Gyros. Fish wrapped in rice paper. All kinds of Mediterranean, Indian, and Sino-Japanese things. They've got grilled Pacific salmon." Wanda waited. Then: "It's just *lunch*, dear."

"Sorry." Jack made a check mark next to a mistake on the paper and set his pencil aside. He said, "I hate leaps into the unknown."

Wanda laughed. "Don't I know. You two come on, I'll meet you there.

It was a September day, humid but cool, and Jack paused on the steps of the mathematics department to don his jacket. He automatically looked to make sure his Subaru still occupied its reserved parking space across the street. Then he set off down the long hill. His brother-in-law Eldean met him in front of the English department. They crossed the commons at the bottom of the hill, with Eldean, small and bird-quick, setting a brisk pace. When a student called out, "Great class today!" Eldean accepted the compliment as his due and said to Jack, "Today in Tragedies of Shakespeare, I taught *Titus*

Andronicus as if it were one of those godawful psycho-splatter movies."

"Did it work?"

"Well, it obviously did for at least one person. I may try it in Nineteenth-Century British Authors next."

They walked two blocks and entered an oak-shaded street lined with well-kept Victorian houses now occupied by law firms and other businesses. When Jack saw the Mars logo adorning one facade, he said, "This used to be—"

"Yes," said Eldean, "and before that—everything's changing faster than I can keep up with it. The city's growing out of control.

"When I was a student, the population here was a hundred thousand people or so." Jack shook his head disbelievingly. "Now they say, in another twenty-five years, it'll be a round million."

Wanda was waiting inside Mars, where the walls were painted a vivid pink and embellished with gold stars, crescent moons, and comets. The decor somehow avoided garishness. Jack and Wanda quickly exchanged kisses. He asked about her day so far, and she said, "The usual." He did not press for details. She was a psychologist at the county jail, specializing in juvenile offenders. While he spent his days with young people who did not know how to work the most obvious problems in geometry, she dealt with young people who did not know how to live their lives. The hostess showed Jack, Wanda, and Eldean to a corner table and handed out menus. "Your waitperson will be right with you."

They scanned the menus. "Everything sounds so good," Wanda said, "I don't know what to order."

Eldean put his menu down and slapped his hands against his own narrow torso. "I haven't been disappointed with anything I've had here."

Jack glared at him. "Not all of us are blessed with efficient metabolisms. Wanda makes me walk miles every day to keep the weight off."

The waitress arrived, and Jack, still studying the menu, heard her ask what they would care to drink. Her voice was a warm Southern purr.

"Iced tea, please," said Wanda.

"Make it two," said Eldean.

Jack looked up. The waitress was in her early twenties, trimly built, with honey-colored hair, light skin, and an abundance of freckles. She had alert brown eyes and a good smile. "Same here," Jack croaked, and she thanked them and glided away.

Jack felt heat creep up his neck and across his cheeks. He was helpless to stop it. He forced himself to look down at the tabletop directly before him.

"Now," Wanda said, "it's time to attend to business—Happy Birthday, Eldean'" and she handed him a birthday card and Jack, after some confusion involving the pockets of his jacket, handed over a flat, rectangular gift wrapped in shiny foil.

Eldean laughed and gave his sister a hug. Then he read the message on the card and unwrapped the gift—a double-disc collection of old jazz standards sung by Anita O'Day. He excitedly turned it in his hands and looked at Jack. "Tunes from the tone-deaf?"

"Wanda said you like her."

"I do. I guess I owe one of you an extra hug."

The waitress returned with their beverages and asked to take their orders. Jack tried to stare at her without seeming to stare at her. There was just a hint of reproach in her expression when he admitted that he still had no idea what to order. He fumbled with the menu, ordered the first thing that caught his eye. The waitress seemed to regard him with amused tolerance for a moment before she turned and left.

Wanda aimed a finger and a mildly reproachful look across the table toward Jack. "Close your mouth, dear."

"What?"

"You're gaping."

"I—what? No. I'm not."

"Yes, you are. Bulging eyes, slack mouth—in my book, that's gaping. Or are you just window-shopping?"

"What?"

She inclined her head in the general direction taken by the waitress. "I have to admit, she is pretty."

"No. Of course I'm not—"

"Oh, leave him alone, sis," Eldean said, "you know he's your thrall." He leaned low over the table with an exaggerated air of confidentiality. "Before he took you to wife, the only figures Jack looked at for forty years were in math books."

"Don't listen to anything he tells you about me," Jack said.

Wanda said to Eldean, "I like a man who can balance a check book."

Jack had always enjoyed Wanda and Eldean's banter when it was not directed at him. He said, "If you're through discussing me — discuss Eldean instead."

"Let's," said Eldean. "I have the soul of a poet, not an adding machine. Yet all I've ended up with is ex-wives."

"Maybe," Wanda told him, "you shouldn't have waited until you were married not to have sex."

He laughed loudly enough to draw glances from the far end of the room.

Jack saw, over Eldean's shoulder, the waitress returning with their food. He looked away hurriedly, too hurriedly, he felt, but Wanda appeared not to notice. He kept his eyes on the table as the waitress placed his order before him. He ate mechanically, hardly tasting the food, and had no idea what it was. When the waitress paused at their table again to ask if everything was okay, he made some comment, slightly off the beat of the conversation and instantly forgotten. When Eldean suddenly spoke directly to him, he started.

"What?"

"I said, Mars to Jack, come in, Jack. Enjoy your flight?"

As they were leaving Mars, Wanda said, "This was good. We'll have to meet here again sometime,"

"If it's still here," Eldean said. "Restaurants come and go in this town faster than anything."

Wanda offered to drop them off on campus. They got into her Nissan and had traveled a block when she said, "Jack, there's that noise again."

"I hear it," he said distractedly. "Better give Jimmy at Apex another call."

In front of the English department, Jack and Wanda again wished Eldean a happy birthday, and he thanked them again and went inside. The car ascended the hill, dodging jaywalking students and still making the noise. The mathematics department occupied a red-brick building located near the crest. Below, in descending order, were the buildings that housed the music, English, and art departments. On the crest above the mathematics department was the science and engineering complex. The order of ascent, the rightness of it, had always appealed strongly to Jack's sense of orderliness; now it soothed and reassured him. Art *belonged* at the bottom: any nitwit could slop paint on canvas and call it art. English was only relatively more orderly, and music meant nothing to him. But mathematics—in mathematics you were right or you were wrong. There was no dissembling in mathematics. And in life as on campus, to get to science and engineering, you had to pass mathematics.

"I'll see you later," said Wanda as she pulled the Nissan toward the curb in front of the mathematics building." He started to get out, but her thoughtful expression made him wait. She said, "Tell me now, what's bothering you?"

"Nothing's bothering me."

"I can tell something's bothering you." The thoughtful expression yielded to a smile. "It's oh-kay. I'm a trained expert. And your wife. You can tell me things."

"You're going to think I'm being ridiculous."

"You are the last man in the world who's capable of being ridiculous. Now what is it?"

"That waitress." He barely managed to get the word out. Something had come up out of his heart and lodged itself in his throat. He was mortified and blushing as uncontrollably as he had in the restaurant.

"A cutie, for sure," Wanda said evenly, "but young enough to be your daughter."

"That's just it. She *is* young enough to be my daughter. She could be—she's the image of my first girl friend. I mean, my first serious girl friend. My freshman year of college. The waitress looks just like her. It's uncanny Same hair, eyes, face, everything. Even the freckles."

"Why didn't you ask her about her mom when she came back to the table?"

"I—I haven't seen her—the girl friend—or heard from or about her in almost thirty years. I haven't even—" He let that sentence go, he had been at the point of saying that he had scarcely thought about her during all those years. "But I remember exactly how she looked."

"Well, that girl at Mars was nowhere close to thirty. Eighteen or nineteen is more like it. She's someone else's daughter. I know we promised never to ask questions like this, but since you've brought it up—what was her name? The girl friend."

"Jonesy. Catherine Jones."

"Jonesy," Wanda said, "not Cathy. Interesting. So what happened between you and—" she hesitated for a fraction of a second, long enough for Jack to feel, first, the beginnings of embarrassment, then, a flicker of resentment at being made to feel embarrassment "—Jonesy?"

She was watching him closely. Jack nodded past her, past the faculty parking lot. Trees grew thickly on the far side, where the hill sloped away, and visible above their tops were the upper levels of a parking garage. He said, "The math and music buildings weren't there back then, and that hillside was all wooded. It was a real thicket, and it grew all the way down on the other side to a blacktopped parking lot. The garage wasn't there, either."

Wanda considered the hillside. Then she said, uncertainly, as though she knew she was expected to respond but did not know exactly what that response ought to be, "Well, that's progress," and looked as though she knew that she had somewhat missed the mark .

Jack said, "In the evenings, before we had to be back in our dorms, Jonesy and I used to, you know, do it on that hillside."

"What? You are kidding."

"No. Down the opposite slope, among the trees. We discovered a tree house someone'd built. We never found out who or why. Maybe bird watchers, maybe someone from the engineering department. It was a good solid tree house. When I came back here to teach and saw the trees'd been cut down on the other side and the hillside bulldozed—" Jack thumped his breast with the side of his fist, "And now, all day every day—" he jerked his head toward the mathematics building "—I can look at what's left from my window." He studied her expressions. "I can't believe I just told you that. You look absolutely amazed."

"Actually, I am amazed. The thought of you, of all people, getting it on in the great outdoors—"

"Well, it was the Sixties. Later, we got a place together, in an old house that'd been cut up into apartments. It's gone, too. Torn down to make room for condos. Progress, eh?"

Wanda looked at her watch. "Jack, this is fascinating, but I've got to get back to the jail."

"Sure. Thanks."

"For what?"

"Listening to me babble like an idiot."

He kissed her, got out of the car, and watched as she drove away.

Jack's afternoon classes went unsatisfyingly. He finally conceded to himself that he was off his stride and dismissed his last class as early as he felt he decently could. He cloistered himself in his office and tried to do other work until it was time to change clothes and go meet Wanda.

She had changed at work, too, and was waiting for him at the entrance to the hike-and-bike trail. "I called Apex," she said after a kiss, "and they said to bring the Nissan in first thing tomorrow. They said they'd try, repeat, try and have it fixed by five tomorrow. So you have to follow me to Apex and take me to work in the morning and pick me up and take me to Apex in the evening." She widened her eyes, widened her smile. "And how was your day, dear?"

Traffic on the trail was as heavy in its own way as that on the street. Jack let Wanda set the pace and managed to stay abreast of her, though she ran more often than she walked and he hated running. They did not talk. He was grateful for that, his attention fixed on something within himself, and when at one point he abruptly became aware of his surroundings it struck him that he must have completed the first two miles on autopilot. At the halfway mark, he followed her to one side of the trail and watched as she knelt to adjust her shoe. His eye followed the line of her body from her hand up her arm, over her shoulder and along her flank, around the curve of her hip, down along her smooth strong leg, back to her hand. It was as though he were seeing her for the first time. She is so, he thought—and then he could not think of a single word or any group of words that might do her justice, but, looking down at her, he did experience a rush of feeling for her so intense that his throat slightly constricted and his eyes stung.

At home, when he emerged from the shower, he found her brushing out her hair at her vanity table. Jack stepped close behind her and gently began to massage her shoulders, near the base of her neck. She said, "Ah," and let her head loll forward. "Can't tell you," she said after half a minute, "how good that feels."

"Lie down on the bed. I'll give you the full treatment,"

"Don't have to ask me twice." She slipped out of her robe and lay prone on the bed. He sat on the edge and went to work on her.

After a while, she told him, "You missed your calling. You could do this for a living."

"The secret of giving a good back rub is just to listen. Whatever you do that elicits grunts of pleasure, do more of it."

"Whatever. Mm." After several more minutes, he stopped massaging her but lightly stroked her lower back with one hand, and she said "Mm" again, and then, "Thanks." He ran his hand over her buttock. "Buns of steel," she murmured into the crook of her arm. "Just another way of saying I'm a hard-ass."

Wanda rolled suddenly under his hand, onto her back, and drew a corner of the robe over her pubic area. He found her modesty endearing. She lay looking up at him with one arm across her breasts and the other arm cradling her head. His hand rested on her smooth firm stomach. She moved a hand down, placed it upon his, squeezed gently. He saw after a moment that she was trying to keep a straight face. She grinned suddenly and said, "Making love in a tree house!" and laughed. She rolled her head from side to side and said, "I'm sorry'" and laughed again.

He wanted to laugh with her; he managed a grin. He bent forward and kissed her shoulder. "Didn't think I had it in me?"

Wanda put her hand upon his forearm; her expression was mock-solemn again. "I've always thought you're a good egg, but I've never quite figured you out."

"You promised to love, honor, and not try to analyze me."

"Well, sometimes I regret that third part."

He kissed her again, softly, on the cheek, leaned closer, slid his arms around and under her, held her. Her arms pulled him tight against her. "Ah, Jack," she murmured. They lay quietly holding each other for at least two full minutes.

Then he pulled back slightly and said, "Are you hungry?"

"Starving."

"Me, too. Want to go out? My treat."

"Back to Mars? Not twice in one day. I'm just too tired."

She kissed him. "Check out cute young waitresses on your own time." Jack felt guilty and relieved at the same time. "Maybe we can do something this weekend," she went on, "if there ever is a weekend," and groaned elaborately. "Meanwhile, I'm still starving."

"Why don't you lie here and relax while I fix dinner? If you can relax, knowing I'm fixing dinner."

"That was a joke!"

"Not much of one."

"True." She put her arm around his neck, drew him to her again, pressed her cheek to his, nuzzled his ear. "But enough of one."

"I'll call you when dinner's ready. Dinner or a reasonable facsimile thereof."

"Don't try to be funny twice in one night."

He kissed her and went and made a respectable dinner. The effort relaxed him. Afterward, they briefly watched television, then made respectable love.

The following afternoon, after dismissing his last class, he called Wanda at her office. She sounded tired and unhappy as she told him that the Nissan would be spending the night at the repair shop. He suggested the hike-and-bike trail. She said, "I don't think I'm up for it today. Just pick me up and take me home, okay?"

"Sure. I'll see you soon."

He left the mathematics building swinging the tote bag containing his sweatshirt, shorts, and walking shoes. He stepped off the curb to cross to the faculty parking lot and immediately jumped back at the sound of a car horn. A black Volkswagen Beetle muttered by. Affixed to its rear bumper were two stickers. One was a circle containing a peace symbol. The other read,

VIETNAM: LOVE IT OR LEAVE IT

He stared after the Volkswagen, thought of an imprecation but did not unleash it, then got into his Subaru and went down the hill, straight into rush-hour traffic. It took him an eternity to drive the ten blocks to the county courthouse. Wanda stood waiting on the steps; she looked as she had sounded over the telephone. She accepted his kiss, however, and gave him a wan smile. The corners of her mouth turned up slightly, but the muscles in her forehead remained contracted. "Bad day," he said; he was not asking a question

"Tell you later. Maybe." She exhaled harshly, then tried another smile, but still the effect was not reassuring. "You?"

"The usual," he said.

He drove, and she sat with her head tilted back and her eyes closed.

Finally, she said, "I lost my temper today and yelled at somebody from the sheriff's office."

"Bad day. "

"The worst. The kind of day that makes me think seriously I'm not cut out for the work. The kind that's hard on my professional objectivity. That makes me think I'm not dealing with disturbed people, but plain old stupid ones, stupid and evil ones, and some who're just purely evil. I may have met one of the purely evil ones today. Ah, Jack." She looked sadder than he had ever seen her. "I'm preparing a psychological profile of a sixteen-year-old monster at the jail. He stabbed another kid last week, then hid out until his own grandmother turned him in. He already had a history of—but, anyway -- today, while he was being processed, some idiot put another boy, a fourteen-year-old, into the cell with him and left them unattended. The sixteen-year-old talked the fourteen-year-old into hanging himself. Later, when I asked the sixteen-year-old about it—why he'd done it—he said because he'd always known he could do it, and he'd waited long enough. The devil in him was ready to show itself."

Her eyes glistened, she smeared at them with her hands, clutched her head between her forearms, and exhaled a heartbroken and heartbreaking sound. The thought darted through Jack's mind that this could not be his own reassuringly calm and collected wife sitting next to him, looking tireder than tired, looking exhausted, used-up, fighting back tears, speaking nonsense. Her talk of monsters and devils disturbed him—he thought that he could not have been much more disturbed if she had spouted obscenities—and yet, as he had on the trail the day before, he experienced a rush of feeling for her that was almost painful in its intensity.

"I'm sorry." He did not know what else to say. He let go of the gearshift knob and touched her arm. He did not know what else to do.

"No, I'm sorry," she said in an occluded voice, "I promised I'd never take my work home with me. And listen to me. I'm talking about devils and monsters."

"It's okay. If you want to talk about it, who else are you going to talk about it with?"

After a few seconds, she said, "Would that sentence stand Eldean's scrutiny?" and essayed a fresh smile, more or less successfully, and he touched her arm again. Then she said, "Do you mind if we stop somewhere for a drink?'

"Anywhere special?"

"Somewhere with wine and ferns and no local news on the tee-vee."

Soon, Wanda sat lost in her own thoughts and nursing a glass of white wine. Jack sipped from his own glass and waited patiently. He started when he noticed the black Volkswagen parked across the street; even as he jarred the table and wine slopped from his glass, he saw a young woman with honey-blonde hair walk around the car from the curbside and unlock the door on the driver side.

"Jack," Wanda said, like a harried mother, as she grabbed a napkin.

"See that girl across the street?"

Wanda, occupied with sopping up wine, scarcely bothered to look. "Not without my glasses."

"Put them on! Quickly! I want you to see her. The one in the—the Sixties clothes—getting into the VW—"

As Wanda dug through her purse for her glasses, she said, "Jack, Sixties fashions have been back for some time now. Retro-retro-retro, and I may even be leaving out a retro. Don't you pay attention to what your students are wearing?"

"*Look at her.*"

As she fumbled her glasses into position, the Volkswagen pulled into traffic and was gone.

"It was—" He could not bring himself to finish the sentence. Instead, he said, "Just as I was leaving the math department to come get you—I almost stepped out in front of that same car."

Wanda wagged a finger at him. "Always look both ways before you cross the street."

"It was her."

"Who?"

"The waitress from Mars," he said. Jonesy, he thought.

Wanda leaned back in her chair. She said, "Tell me what finally happened between you and your college girl friend."

Jack meant to say, We broke up, or simply, I don't know. Instead, he said, "I treated her very badly."

"Ah. Remorse. You are just full of surprises." She took a careful sip of wine. "Remorse can be a bad thing or a good thing. Hell is truth seen too late. Then, again, remorse comes out of remembrance and may lead to redemption."

"I hardly remembered her at all until I saw that waitress. Could I almost've forgotten someone if she really ever meant anything to me?"

"It depends on what you mean by *meant anything*. How badly, exactly, did you treat her?"

"I don't—can we change the subject?"

"You brought it up. So, tell me—"

"I don't feel like being analyzed right now."

"I m not trying to analyze you, I just want to find out—"

"Wanda, I'm not one of your juvenile offenders!"

Wanda set her wine glass down with a sharp click. "No, you're not. Let's get the hell out of here."

They went home and ate dinner in excruciating silence and did not speak to each other for the rest of the evening. Jack could not occupy himself with homework papers or television, and the house itself seemed to contract around him. Then, at bedtime, as he sat in his pajamas on the edge of the bed, he looked around at Wanda, who lay on her side with her back to him. He stretched out beside her. He said, "I'm sorry," and touched her shoulder "I'm so sorry. I never want us to be mad at each other. I'm sorry."

He could feel her hesitate. Then she reached back with her hand and patted his arm. "I'm sorry, too. Sorrier. I'm the psychologist."

"Bad day."

"Yes. Bad day."

"Wanda."

The moment seemed to stretch to infinity. Jack did not want to talk any more, did not want to speak the things he thought, and Wanda, evidently sensing this, said, "We don't have to talk about anything," but it was as though a hole had suddenly been punched in him and words came pouring out.

"She said she wanted to be with me always. I wanted to be with her, too—but it wasn't safe. So our pattern for the year we were together was start up, stop, start over. I kept cutting her off. Whenever I'd cut her off, she'd call me up in tears, send me anguished notes by mail. *What's wrong, what have I done, what can I do?*"

Wanda turned toward him, propped her head up on one hand, and let the other rest on his sternum. "It was always you who cut her off? And she was always the one who wanted to get back together with you?"

"Yes. She — it was almost masochistic."

"In those days, girls were raised to be masochists."

"Maybe it was something worse. Maybe, the more vulnerable she became, the crueler I became."

"Why, Jack?"

He started to say, I have no idea, for he had suddenly recognized the greater extent of the minefield that lay ahead. He had not let himself tread upon that ground for many years, he did not want to do so now. He also knew that he had no choice but to go on. He said, "I knew if I let myself feel something for Jonesy, I'd have to feel other things as well."

"All of this happened around the time your mother died, didn't it?"

Jack took a long slow breath. "She'd died in the spring — while I was still a senior in high school. When she was diagnosed with cancer — I didn't really realize until near the end how serious her illness was. She and my father didn't prepare me for what was going to happen. I think it was because they never stopped believing that their prayers would save her, even after the doctors couldn't. When my mother went into the hospital for the last time, I wasn't all that worried. She'd been in the hospital before — I thought she'd be coming home again. She always had before. When she died, it shattered my father. Just shattered him. That shook me as badly as her death. Worse, really. What her death made me feel was shame and horror because I — I didn't feel anything else. Just cold and empty."

"You were in shock," Wanda said gently.

"*I* didn't *know* that. Nobody told me I was in shock. And I saw my father, who'd always been the strong, silent type, reduced to — till then, I'd always believed that adults were *in control* of their lives and their feelings. That they took things in stride. I saw how my father fell apart, and I thought, Well, maybe being all cold and numb inside isn't such a bad thing after all. Maybe I'm better off never feeling anything. So I stayed in shock. That fall, when I left for college, I didn't just leave for college, I — left. *Left.*"

"And met Jonesy."

"We started dating soon after I started college. She was a year older than me, a sophomore. It was casual at first, but we finally did the deed. Deflowered each other. After that, it was like she was determined to make things work on almost any terms. I think she tried so hard because she just couldn't believe she'd made a horrible mistake."

"Losing one's virginity means more to girls than it does to boys. In those days, a girl was still strongly encouraged to save herself for one special person."

"Then Jonesy's one special person was supposed to be me. And I wouldn't cooperate. I'd cut her off, I'd relent, we'd get back together for a while. I guess even that finally paled, because, finally, I betrayed her. With other girls. She moved out, and I never saw her again. That was near the end of my freshman year. She wasn't at school that fall."

"What about those other girls?"

"I betrayed them, too. I got better at betrayal as I went along. Finally, all that—crying and—it started to sicken me. I stopped bothering. I found more worthwhile interests. And then I finally met you. And—and it was like—like when Beauty transforms the Beast and redeems him."

Wanda lay her head on his breast. She said, with such tenderness that his eyes watered, "Why, Jack!"

Jack stroked her hair. "I've spent too much time around your brother."

"He does go on."

He looked at the clock on the nightstand. "It's late. We really should go to sleep."

They kissed lingeringly, turned out the light, and settled beside each other, holding hands.

In the darkness, Wanda cleared her throat softly and said, "If you could see Jonesy now—what would you do?"

"I don't know. Yes, I do."

"What?"

"Ask her forgiveness. Tell her—tell her how sorry I am. Tell her how much I wanted to—return her—feelings. Back then, I mean."

Wanda squeezed his hand. "Jack," she said, "would it kill you to ever say the word *love*?"

A long time after he knew she was asleep, the black Volkswagen passed fleetingly through his mind, trailing a montage of images, incredibly condensed and yet incredible in their vividness, of another time and almost another place. He suddenly became aware of his own moist heavy breathing, and of his own skin, bare and hot, and of the touch of even hotter, burning-hot, fingertips. He raised his head slightly and looked, and now he saw and felt the girl, the waitress, kissing his belly just below the navel, tracing designs with her tongue and moving her head in a lazy back-and-forth motion so that her cheek repeatedly brushed against the swollen head of his penis. But how—

She turned her face toward him and whispered, Ssh, and turned her face away and made him groan, half in ecstasy, half in complaint, *it feels so good, don't make me wait.* But—

—how—

He could not remember how she had managed to come to him, how things had got this far. On finding oneself in bed with a woman, he thought, one ought to remember how one got there. After all, it was supposed to be such a momentous thing. Who had kissed whom, this time or the first time or any time? And how had the kissing gone beyond lip contact to tongues, and what then? And from that to fumbling with buttons and zippers, running the whole obstacle course of feminine underthings—?

He suddenly wondered, Why am I naked, where are my pajamas?

He awoke with a start and a cry. Wanda slept beside him, breathing quietly. At some point after falling asleep he had released her hand. He turned away from her, onto his side, stared at the dimly moonlit rectangles of the bedroom windows. He lay clutching the edge of the mattress until he saw gray light through the windows.

He was groggy throughout the morning, and his nine- and ten-o'clock classes and his undergraduate-advisor session were unmitigated disasters. Helpless to stop himself, Jack left his office early and returned alone to Mars. He asked for, and was shown to, the table he and Wanda and Eldean had shared. His waitress had pale skin, reddish blonde hair, and heavy eye makeup. He asked what had become of the waitress who had served him before. "Could you please tell me her name? I may have known her mother, years ago."

The waitress regarded him frankly, appraisingly. "This is my table," she said, "and I'm the only blonde."

"Are you sure?"

She made an effort to humor him; there was only the merest edge of impatience in her voice. "Look around."

This is crazy, Jack told himself. He tried to maintain his composure, to will himself not to blush. He had a horror of scenes.

"Now," she said after waiting several seconds more, "may I get you something to drink?"

He left without ordering, strode back to campus with arms swinging and fists clenched, feeling foolish and humiliated and vowing to himself never to return to Mars. On the steps of the mathematics building, he hesitated, turned, looked across the parking lot. A student said hello as he went by, and Jack muttered a reply but did not see who it was. He stood with his hands thrust into his trousers pockets and his head pulled down between his shoulders, as though against a cold wind, and he watched the trees. At last, he crossed the street and walked past his Subaru sitting in its reserved parking space and entered the trees. The woods closed around him, swallowed him. He knew that he should at least have been able to glimpse the rear wall of the parking garage through the trees ahead, but he could not, and when he looked back he could not see the parking lot or the mathematics building. The woods seemed to stretch away forever in every direction. Day had somehow become night, yet he saw perfectly well, as though the air itself were suffused with light. He saw the tree house and said or thought *No!* and looked up through a gap in the leaf canopy and imagined for an instant that he saw not the familiar and dependable moon and stars but a jagged rent in the sky, beyond which was true engulfing darkness. He felt the ground tilt and crack beneath his feet, and he lurched toward the tree house with outstretched arras. The tree house was substantial. The tree house was real. It consisted of a wooden platform with low sides and a partial roof. A ladder afforded access. He put his foot on the first rung. After a moment, he heard a sound from within the tree house, perhaps a voice, perhaps calling to him.

He fled blindly. The ground turned treacherous underfoot,

He slipped, fell, rolled against the base of a medium-sized tree. He lay there breathing heavily with earth-smells in his nostrils and the taste of dirt and blood on his tongue. He wondered if he would ever get back to where he belonged, but the matter no longer seemed particularly urgent. This is good, where I am.

From somewhere close by came the sound of approaching footsteps.

Get up, he told himself. Get up. Run.

He got his feet beneath him and used the tree to pull himself erect. He glimpsed movement among the trees close by and ran clumsily in the opposite direction. Something whipped his cheek. His toe connected solidly with an exposed root, and he went sprawling, cried out, clawed at the ground. When he pushed himself up on his forearms, he found himself at the edge of the trees, looking across the faculty parking lot at the mathematics building. The sun was farther down the sky than seemed right.

Jack got up, pulled a twig from his hair, tried to brush the dirt and bits of plant detritus from his clothes. He discovered a welt on his left cheek. He limped halfway across the parking lot and then looked back over his shoulder. The parking garage loomed above the trees.

He turned away from the mathematics building and made his way down to the English department. The door to Eldean's office was ajar. Jack knocked on the door frame and leaned into the room. Eldean looked up from behind his untidy desk. His mouth fell open, and his eyebrows rose.

"Jack! My God! What happened? Did you get mugged?"

Eldean had started to rise from his seat, but Jack motioned him back down onto it.

"I fell down."

"Fe—? After you blew off two classes in a row, your office practically put out an APB on you. They called Wanda, she called me. Where've you been all afternoon?"

Jack looked first at the electric clock on Eldean's wall, then at his wristwatch. There was discrepancy of almost three hours. Jack closed the door and sagged into a chair across from Eldean. "I'm not sure where I've been," he said. "In the woods." Eldean picked up the telephone and dialed. "Who're you calling?"

"Who else?" Eldean spoke into the mouthpiece. "Sis, Jack's here in my office." He held the telephone out to Jack.

"I don't know what to say her."

"Try *hello*."

Jack accepted the telephone. "Wanda ...."

"Jack! Are you all right? Where've you been?"

"I'm fine. I'm okay."

"What's going on?"

He did not answer immediately. Then: "I think I'm being haunted."

"Haunted." Her voice was inflectionless. Two seconds ticked by. "By whom or what?"

"Jonesy."

"Ah, God! Jonesy! Listen to me. Jack, you stay right there with Eldean. I'll be there as soon as I can get a cab."

Jack handed the telephone back to Eldean, who said, "Don't you want to call your office?"

"No. I'm going to stay right here with you till Wanda gets here."

"Oh. Well." Eldean looked concerned. "Can I get you anything?"

"Professional help." Jack grinned as Eldean blinked at him over the tops of wire-rimmed glasses. "That's a joke. Or maybe it isn't. Either I need professional help, or I'm—look, you know me well enough. You know I'm not the type to dwell on the past and not the type to have panic attacks. But it's like I've been brushing up against moments from my own past. From my first love affair."

"People forget years," Eldean murmured, "and remember moments. I forget who said that. Somebody—"

"I wandered into the trees at the top of the hill. Suddenly, it was night, and everything was the way it used to be, thirty years ago—the same but different. The sky became different, everything was different. I think I heard Jonesy—my old girl friend, the one who looked like the waitress at Mars. The tree house was there, just like it used to be, and she was waiting for me there."

"The waitress?"

"No! Jonesy! But I got scared. I ran and fell and found myself—back here. Back now." Jack considered the expression on his brother-in-law's face. Neither of them spoke for several seconds. Finally, Jack said, "So you tell me, do I need professional help?"

"Well, if you do, surely, Wanda can help you get it."

"I don't want professional help! I want a reasonable, rational, real explanation for this!"

"Does, um, that mean you want this thing to be real?"

"I don't want it to be a hallucination. I don't want it to be me. I know it isn't."

The concern in Eldean's expression had transformed itself gradually into some keener type of interest; now he brushed his palms together and sat forward in his chair. "But if this thing is real, Jack—by which I mean, if it isn't a hallucination — then what've you got?"

"I don't know. What have I got?"

"Ghosts?"

"Eldean, I don't believe in ghosts."

Eldean looked exasperated in his own right. "So then what've you got? Time travel? If we must rule out the unreasonable and irrational possibility that you're imagining weird stuff, it follows that it's got to be one of those other things. Now which one sounds most reasonable and rational to you?" and he counted them off on his fingers "Ghosts, time travel, *or* you need professional help?" Jack said nothing, only glowered at him. Eldean held up his hands with his right index finger hooked on his left middle finger. "Right — number three!"

"No! I'm going to solve this. If Jonesy's back — "

"How hard can it be find out if she's back? One call, and Wanda can have one of her buddies in the sheriff's office run a driver's-license check for you. Or you can start conducting an investigation yourself, right here, right now." Eldean pulled out his city telephone directory. "What's her name?"

"Catherine Jones."

"Jones." Eldean thumbed through the directory, then handed the opened book to Jack.

There were three and a half pages of Joneses, but only six C Joneses and no Catherines or Cathys.

"What should I do?" Jack asked bitterly. "Call? Ask each one of them, Are you the girl I used to meet in a tree house, thirty years ago? What're the odds she's married and changed her name and moved away?"

"You're the mathematician."

Jack threw the book to the floor and sat with his head in his hands. Ghosts, he thought glumly. Time travel. Madness.

Wanda entered without knocking. She uttered a little cry of alarm when she saw Jack, bent over him, took his face in her hands. "What *happened* to you?" She scarcely blinked while he repeated the story he had told Eldean. She lowered herself onto her calves in front of him and put her face close to his.

He said, "I'm not drunk."

She said, "Let's get you home."

"I'm not nuts, either."

"I know you're not nuts. No one says you're nuts."

"You never say anybody's nuts. They're always disturbed. I'm not disturbed, Wanda. My mind is working perfectly. It's trying to figure this thing out. I want a rational explanation!"

"Okay. Okay." Wanda rose and leaned against the edge of Eldean's desk. She held up a hand, palm out, fingers spread, and moved it back and forth as though she were testing the resiliency of some invisible membrane. She said, "Try tearing this whole thing apart, Jack, starting from the top. The girl at Mars reminded you of your old flame. But she wasn't your old flame."

"And she wasn't at Mars today. I checked."

"Oh, you did, did you?"

"If I took you there now, you'd see she's not the same girl. And that in itself means something. You saw her, too—you both did. I didn't imagine her."

"We saw a girl. Maybe she just looked different when you went back. Maybe, in the interim, she had a complete makeover."

"No. I can't have been mistaken."

"No, not you," Eldean muttered from behind his desk.

Jack said, "What about the old VW?"

Wanda started to answer, hesitated, looked at a loss. Eldean came to her rescue. "You saw an old black VW," he said to Jack. "How could you tell it was old? The whole time they built those things, they never looked any different from one year to the next. I don't remember when they stopped building them, but I'm sure those things are classics new. Maybe they're making a comeback. Maybe they've started building them again, too. I don't know about cars. Maybe all you saw was a new one."

"With the same bumper stickers my girl friend put on her car thirty years ago? Wanda, what about the hillside and the tree house?"

Wanda lowered her head and shook it wearily. "I don't know, I don't know, I don't know."

"Eldean says ghosts, or time travel." He looked sharply at his brother-in-law. "What do we know about ghosts, Eldean?"

"Ghosts are the spirits of the dead. Sometimes, they appear to the living for the purpose of delivering warnings or other messages, or they come bent on making trouble for their killers."

"Eldean," Wanda said, "you're not helping matters."

"Well," Jack said, "after all this time, she could be dead, but even if she is — why would her ghost be appearing to me now?" Before either of them could reply, he remembered, with an unpleasant shiver, Wanda's words the day before ... *he'd always known he could do it, and he'd waited long enough. The devil in him was ready to show itself.* He rallied by reminding himself, I do not believe in ghosts. Even if I did, I couldn't believe they wait tables or drive Volkswagens. Or engage in foreplay.

He said, "Even if I believed in ghosts, what could this ghost be trying to tell me?"

"Maybe," Wanda said, "it's not trying to tell you anything. Maybe you're trying to tell yourself something."

"Like, maybe I'm trying to tell myself I need professional help? Funny how it keeps coming back to that." He slumped on his chair. "I don't even want to think about time travel."

"Jack, let me take you home."

"I should call the department."

"We'll do it when we get you home. Where's the car?"

"Parked in front of the math building."

"I'll go get it. You stay here, and, Eldean, don't you encourage him."

She left. Jack and Eldean regarded each other across the desktop. At length, Eldean said, "Are you sure you don't actually want this thing to be a mystery? Because if you do, watch out. Mysteries force a man to think and so injure his health. Poe said that, and look how his life turned out."

"I intend to solve this mystery."

"You solve puzzles. Puzzles are sterile, they're safe. A mystery's something you have to fathom—stick your hand in up to the elbow. Sometimes you have to dive in headfirst. You can drown in a mystery."

Jack stood up. "I don't give a damn about Poe."

They spoke no more. Wanda returned for Jack, and when they walked outside together he saw the Subaru illegally parked in front of the English building.

"Let me drive," he said, producing his own keys.

"Better let me."

"I haven't been declared incompetent yet."

"Will you stop?" She threw up her hands in resignation as he slid into the driver seat. Through a series of abrupt, angry motions, she got in on the other side, closed the door, and buckled her safety belt.

As Jack pulled the car away from the curb, he spotted the black Volkswagen at the bottom of the hill. He started to speed up, then had to step on the brake as two students jaywalked in front of the Subaru. Wanda yelped a warning. Jack snapped, "I see them." As the Subaru entered traffic and turned after the Volkswagen, a minivan abruptly moved in from the left-hand lane to fill the gap between the two vehicles. Jack found himself boxed in by another vehicle in the left-hand lane; he could see around the minivan but could not get around it. The Volkswagen, the minivan, and the Subaru turned at the intersection as though threaded together on a string.

Wanda said, "Jack, where we going?"

"See it? The black VW?"

"Ja—"

"Do you *see* it?"

"Yes!"

Jack gripped the steering wheel so tightly that his knuckle bones looked and felt as though they were about pop through the skin. "She's in that car! She wants me to follow her!"

"Who?"

"Jonesy! She's come back!"

"Jack, this is crazy!"

He laughed wildly when the minivan turned right, then cursed when he saw that the Volkswagen had managed somehow to put another vehicle between itself and the Subaru. The Volkswagen turned onto a narrow street leading into a neighborhood full of big old houses and huge old trees. At the far end of the block, the Volkswagen turned onto a gravel driveway. Jack turned after it and found it sitting parked and empty in the shade of a tallow tree that grew next to a peeling Victorian house. There were no other cars and no one in sight.

He pulled the Subaru in so close behind the Volkswagen that he could no longer see its brand-new-looking ancient bumper stickers. He turned off the motor and sat back in his seat; it almost hurt when he unwrapped his fingers from the steering wheel. Wanda looked around perplexedly. He heard her ask, "Where are we?" but he did not answer her. He gazed up at the house. It been built sometime before the First World War and cut up into apartments sometime after the Second. A venerable oak shaded it. The apartments were cheap and reasonably easy to keep clean and had private entrances. A brass letter C adorned the door on this side of the house, and paisley-print bed linen had been pressed into service as curtains for the two windows. What luxury, Jack thought, after that tree house ....

He listened to the sound of the cooling engine and of his own excited breathing and marveled that he was not astonished to find the house intact, though he knew that it had not survived a building boom during the 1980s.

"Jack," Wanda said.

"What do you see?"

"Jack --"

"Tell me what you see!"

"That car. An old house." She clutched his arm as he opened his door. "What are you going to do?"

"Find out.

"Find out *what?*"

"*I don't know,*" he said. "But I hate enigmas. And if this is what I think it is—whatever it is I think it is—after all this time, I have to seek forgiveness."

"What if her reason for coming back isn't to forgive you?"

He hesitated, with the door half-opened and his left foot on the ground, and after a long moment had passed, he thought, I also hate leaps into the unknown. He got out of the car and walked up to the door of apartment C. He inclined his head toward it, listened, felt a chill between his shoulder blades when he heard movement within. He looked back at the Subaru. It was still parked behind the Volkswagen, but it suddenly seemed a lot farther away than it ought to have been. The street was a million miles away. The sky was all roiling incandescence, illuminating Wanda's face as she peered through the Subaru's windshield. Jack saw, across that great distance, that she appeared distressed, appeared to be calling to him, but she was too far away for him to see or hear her very clearly. He made a fist and knocked on the door and thought he heard another, different sound, a voice, perhaps, saying, perhaps, *I'm coming.*

About the Author

In response to a request for personal data, Mr. Utley replied only that he is "an internationally unknown author." The publishers have resorted to a simple name-search on the internet to glean the following information: Mr. Utley was born on March 28, 1736, and is also a professional golfer, a former NFL Pro lineman, a jazz musician, and a corporate executive. Married since 1894, he currently teaches middle-schoolers and died at the age of 62.

Acknowledgements

"Abaddon" and "Creatures of Habit" copyright © 1979, 1985 by Flight Unlimited.

"And for Ourselves, False Powers" (original title: "The Thirteenth Labor") copyright © 1977 by Random House, Inc.

"Ants" (original title: "The Queen and I") copyright © 1973 by Ace Books, Inc.

"Ember-Eyes" and "The Man at the Bottom of the Sea" copyright © 1974, 1976 by UPD Publishing Corporation.

"Flies by Night" and "Tom Sawyer's Sub-Orbital Escapade" copyright © 1975, 1977 by Lisa Tuttle and Steven Utley.

"In Brightest Day, In Blackest Night" (original mistitle: "In Brightest Day, In Darkest Night"), "Leaves," "The Mouse Ran Up the Clock," and "Uncoiling" copyright © 1976, 1977, 1978, 1979 by Ultimate Publishing Company.

"Mysterious Ways" (original title: "The Reason Why") copyright © 1973 by Mankind Publishing Company.

"Never Mind Now" copyright © 1976 by Looking Glass Publications, Inc.

"Night Life" copyright © 1977 by Michel Parry.

"Outlaw Glory," "Pan-Galactic Swingers," "Pretty Meat," and "Someone is Watching" (original title: "The Voyeur") copyright © 1975, 1976 by Knight Publishing Company.

"Sidhe" copyright © 1977 by Linda Lovecraft and Michel Parry.

This book collects stories originally published, in more or less their present form, in the following magazines and anthologies: Adam, Amazing Science Fiction, Bewildering Stories, The Daily Texan: Images, Fantastic Stories, Galaxy, Isaac Asimov's Science Fiction Magazine, The Magazine of Fantasy and Science Fiction, Mystery Monthly, P.I. Magazine, Perry Rhodan, Pulphouse: A Fiction Magazine, Shayol, The Trinitonian, Vertex, and the following anthologies: Ascents of Wonder (edited by David Gerrold); Dying for It: More Erotic Tales of Unearthly Love (edited by Gardner Dozois); More Devil's Kisses (edited by Linda Lovecraft); The Rivals of Dracula: A Century of Vampire Fiction (edited by Michel Parry); Stellar Science-Fiction Stories # 3 (edited by Judy-Lynn Del Rey).

Polyphony 1
Edited by Deborah Layne and Jay Lake
First volume in the critically acclaimed slipstream/cross-genre series with stories from Maureen McHugh, Andy Duncan, Carol Emshwiller, Lucius Shepard and others.

All-Star Zeppelin Adventure Stories
Edited by David Moles and Jay Lake
Original zeppelin stories by David Brin, Jim Van Pelt, Leslie What, and others; featuring a reprint of the zeppelin classic, *"You Could Go Home Again"* by Howard Waldrop.

American Sorrows:
Stories by Jay Lake
Four longer works by the 2004 John W. Campbell Award winner; includes his Hugo nominated novelette, "Into the Gardens of Sweet Night."

Greetings From Lake Wu
Jay Lake and Frank Wu
Collection of stories by Jay Lake with original illustrations by Frank Wu.

Paradise Passed: A Novel by Jerry Oltion
The crew of a colony ship must choose between a ready-made paradise and one they create themselves.

Twenty Questions
Jerry Oltion
Twenty brilliant works by the Nebula Award-winning author of "Abandon in Place."

Dream Factories and Radio Pictures
Howard Waldrop
Waldrop's stories about early film and television reprinted in one volume.

Thirteen Ways to Water
Bruce Holland Rogers
This collection by the Nebula and World Fantasy Award winning author spans a period of ten years and brings together several award winning stories.

Order on the web at:
http://www.wheatlandpress.com